I0825165
HOLBORN HILL
SKINNER ST.
NEWGATE ST.
FLEET STREET
LUDGATE ST.
ST. PAULS CHURCH
CATHEDL.
CHEAPSIDE
CANNON ST. WEST
CANNON ST.
POULTRY
BANK
CORNHILL
LEADENHALL ST.
ALDGATE HIGH ST.
FENCHURCH ST.
GRACECH. ST.
BISHOPSGATE
MOORGATE ST.
ALDERSGATE ST.
FARRINGDON S.
N. BRIDGE ST.
BLACKFRIARS B.
BLACKFRIARS PIER
PAULS WH. PIER
SOUTHWK. BR.
LONDON BR.
LONDON BR. PIER
CITY PIER
CUSTOM HOUSE
BILLINGSGATE MARKET
TOWER OF LONDON
SURREY ST. PIER
BLACKFRIARS ROAD
BOROUGH ROAD
WESTMINSTER RD.
LONDON RD.
ST. GEORGES RD.
BETHLEHEM HOSPITAL
SOUTHWARK BRIDGE ROAD
BOROUGH HIGH ST.
BLACKMAN ST.
GT. DOVER STREET
NEW KENT ROAD
OLD KENT ROAD
NEWINGTON BUTTS
NEWINGTON
KENNINGTON RD.
KENNINGTON ROAD
WALWORTH ROAD
WALWORTH
SURREY GARDENS
GOODS DEPOT
UNION ST.
EWER STREET
GREAT GUILDFORD ST.
SNOWS FIELDS
BERMONDSEY
GRANGE RD.
ABBEY ST.
BRICKLAYERS ARMS
E.C.

An Artful Dodge

An Artful Dodge

Karen Odden

SOHO CRIME

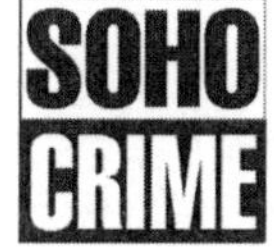

Published by Soho Press
Soho Press, Inc.
227 W 17th Street
New York, NY 10011
www.sohopress.com

Library of Congress Cataloging-in-Publication Data
Names: Odden, Karen author
Title: An artful dodge / Karen Odden.
Description: New York, NY : Soho Crime, 2026.
Identifiers: LCCN 2025051374

ISBN 978-1-64129-762-2
eISBN 978-1-64129-763-9

Subjects: LCGFT: Fiction | Novels
Classification: LCC PS3615.D4 A88 2026
LC record available at https://lccn.loc.gov/2025051374

Interior design by Janine Agro
Interior map by Loren Ward

Printed in the United States of America

10 9 8 7 6 5 4 3 2 1

To George, Julia, and Kyle, always

"Change places; and, handy-dandy,
which is the justice, which is the thief?"
—William Shakespeare, *King Lear*

An Artful Dodge

Character List

Kit Jimeson, twenty, an adept needlewoman and thief

Sarah Jimeson, Kit's younger sister, a scullery maid in Mayfair

Patrick Jimeson, Kit and Sarah's father, who left shortly after Sarah was born, when Kit was seven

Annie Avery Jimeson, Kit's mother, who died when Kit was fourteen

James Kinnon, twenty-three, Kit's friend, former smuggler and ex-convict, now employed at the Custom House

Emma Kinnon, James's older sister, who owns a dressmaker shop where Kit works occasionally

Seamus Ardle, who owns a pawnshop/fence in Marshall Street, where Kit works occasionally

Amelia Lyle, thirty-eight, head of the thieving ring, niece to Patty Wirth, who gave Amelia leadership on her deathbed in 1865

Mary Pratt, Kit's closest friend and her partner (a.k.a. her "jenny") on most thieving expeditions

Rose Pratt, Mary's mother, a thief in the ring, who was murdered several months ago

Other thieves in the ring:

Nell Simmons, one of the older thieves, cousin and close friend of the late Rose Pratt

Josie Elwes, bawdy, a bit reckless

Bea Peters, an astute thief and Josie's jenny for most dodges

Fanny Mills, Caleb's sister

Cathy Quincy, Fanny's roommate and close companion

Harriet McHugh

Charlotte Dobbs

Patty Wirth, leader of the thieves before Amelia, died in 1865 of cholera

Maggie Wirth O'Connell, forty-one, daughter to Patty Wirth, convicted thief, recently returned from Swan River, a penal colony in Australia, after twenty years

Silas Pike, head of a network of fences in Vine Street, runs extortion, gambling, and gaming in Southwark, with connections across London, and an old friend of Maggie's

Pat Hollings, barkeep at the Elephant and Castle Inn

The Willits Family, Sarah's employers; children Clara, John, Philip

Gordon Stiles, Scotland Yard detective inspector

Ed Fuller, newspaperman for the *Mirror*, a London daily

Sid Pratt, Mary's young nephew, assists in thefts, runs a dice game

Members of the Elephant and Castle gang

- **Billy Winston**
- **Tommy Finch**
- **Nick Tolbey**
- **Jake Dilts**
- **Robbie McKenna,** who fancies Kit
- **Caleb Mills,** Fanny's brother; also a card sharp

The Fairleighs, a wealthy family whose two servants are murdered

Roger Simonson, sixty-five, jeweler in Hatton Garden

Roger Simonson, Jr., his son, who caught Maggie stealing twenty years ago

The Most Honorable Lord Alfred Carroll, Marquess Hargrave, owner of an heirloom necklace

LONDON 1879

Chapter 1

The Society for the Suppression of Vice would have you believe crime doesn't pay.

It does, of course. Thieving especially.

One glance into our second-story practice room would convince anyone. Heaps of stolen finery from pocket watches and jeweled earrings to kid gloves and lace handkerchiefs littered a long wooden table. Around it, fourteen of us rehearsed our dodges upon each other.

"I felt that, Kit," Mary said, and my fingers stilled on the necklace I was trying to lift.

"You didn't," I said, pulling back.

"I did," she insisted, touching her nape below the chignon of fair hair. "Your fingers, here."

"Try again," Amelia said, looking over from instructing Bea on nicking a pocket watch one-handed. "Use the side of your thumb."

Her tone was sharpish, without its usual good humor.

"What's wrong with Amelia?" Mary kept her face toward the window and her voice low. "You don't think it's because I'm going back out today, do you?"

I felt her anxiousness, pin-sharp inside my own ribs.

"I doubt it," I replied. "She's riled over something. But likely it's Harriet and Elsie."

They'd both nearly been caught by constables the previous week, which is why the air in the room was subdued, and our practice more intent than usual. While we thieves shoved our fears down far enough to step over them, we also took a warning from anyone else's narrow escape. This was later in summer than we usually changed over to doving, but we always shifted to the theaters and music halls during election season, when city officials needed the support of the West End shopkeepers and pushed the police to reallocate uniformed constables to Mayfair and Marylebone. After the votes were tallied and the officials safely in their seats, the coppers would slink back to their usual boroughs, and we'd return to the shops.

"Why don't you have a go," I said to Mary, over her shoulder. "Nicking a necklace is harder than pockets."

"It's because your hands are cold," Mary said.

Because this whole room *is cold*, I thought. The bustling taproom on the ground floor of the Elephant and Castle Inn was warm, but the practice room was two full stories up, and the heat didn't rise through the thick old plank floors. A coal fire burned in the potbellied black corner stove, and the room held the heat of us thieves, but the unseasonable chill this August afternoon shoved in around the leaded windowpanes.

I rubbed my palms together and blew on my fingertips.

From behind one of the reproductions of wood-and-glass store cabinets, Josie called out, a sly laugh edging her voice. "Robbie downstairs'll warm 'em up for you, Kit!"

"Robbie downstairs is an eejit," I replied in the same singsong, curling and straightening my fingers. "It's not fair," I said to Mary, as I jostled her elbow lightly and undid the clasp, taking care to drop the loose end on top of her collar instead of on bare skin. "You know I'm coming."

"I'm playing fair, I promise," she protested. "See? I'm looking out the window, letting myself be distracted like a lady watching a show. There's Sophie, going into the bakery . . . and Mr. Ardle heading toward his shop."

I showed her the necklace. "There."

Her blue eyes widened in approval. "Oh, that was bloody good."

I grinned. "Your turn now." I clasped the necklace around my own neck and turned to face the room.

Our chief concern today was with necklaces, bracelets, pocket watches, handkerchiefs, earrings, reticules, brooches, rings, cuff links, cameos, and pins—all objects easily nicked from the theater crowd and passed to the fences of Vine Street. We were in pairs, each working with our usual jenny, taking turns at playing the mark, as Amelia walked among us, showing us new ways to distract, directing our hands, reshaping the positions of our fingers. Fanny was showing her new jenny how to tuck a bracelet inside her hat brim. Another new girl watched carefully as Charlotte demonstrated how to palm an earring and slip it into her hairnet. They say there's no honor among our sort, but there's a certain thickness to us thieves.

On the other side of the room, in front of a large printed wall map of London with Amelia's pins in it, Josie swung a silver-headed walking stick she'd nicked the day before. "Look at me, like one of the music hall toffs, singing about how the ladies love my big stick." She swung her hips back and forth, drawling the words long, and her jenny, Bea, burst out laughing.

The necklace slid along my neck. "Felt that," I said.

"Argh," Mary said. "Are *my* fingers cold?"

"No. The chain moved." I tapped my collarbone. "Here."

"Ah, right."

Here we are again, I thought, recalling the first week we practiced our tooling in this room, slipping our hands into each other's pockets, when I was fresh to all of it and Mary only a few months along. The difference now was we knew each other, down to a darted side-eye toward a plainclothesman, a long breath to sketch a warning, a shilling-thin shoulder lift when the dodge was done. It takes time to earn that sort of knowledge. We'd been each other's regular jennies for almost four years, and I counted myself lucky Amelia had paired us early on. I wouldn't have done so well with any of the others. Not that they weren't good thieves, just not the sort I'd ever truly trust, the sort who'd play every card she had to be sure I got away.

"There," Mary said, dangling the necklace between her thumb and forefinger. "Did you truly not feel it?"

"Not a thing," I said honestly. "You're better at touch work."

At the center of the room, Amelia clapped her hands crisply. "That's enough for today, yeah?" We all broke off, and amid the chatter that burst out after several hours of intense concentration, we emptied our pockets, reticules, and hairnets of practice objects. Amelia took up four empty trays and began filling them with goods. We all started toward the stairs that led down to the first story, which consisted of the goods room, where we unloaded our poke each day, and the costumes room, where we stored our thieving clothes. Josie gave one last twirl of the walking stick before she vanished through the door.

"Kit," Amelia said as I reached the threshold.

I stepped back. Mary shot me a meaningful look that I

returned—*Don't worry*—and Mary departed with the rest, shutting the heavy door behind her.

The afternoon sun coming through the window caught the silver threads in Amelia's dark hair, the fine lines around her mouth. She laid the last of the bracelets on the third tray and tucked it into the hidden wall safe before she met my gaze. Her blue-gray eyes were steady. "Well? Is Mary ready?"

"Aye," I said. "It's been four months, and she says she'll go stark raving if she's kept out much longer. She's used to working."

"I know." Amelia transferred the fourth tray, handkerchiefs and reticules, into the safe, spun the lock, and shut the wooden panel. "But it won't do her or you any good, if her nerves aren't steady."

The thought of Mary's mother knifed twice under the ribs and left to die in an alley still unsteadied *my* nerves, if I let myself think on it.

"You can skip today, if you want," Amelia said. "Given the constables."

"We're fine," I said. Even if Mary wasn't quite ready, she was a skilled thief, and I wanted to let her return in the shops, where we'd succeeded a hundred times. Besides, I'd be the lead today; Mary was the decoy. Even if she was caught, they'd find nothing on her.

"I don't want you covering for her, Kit," Amelia added. "And they've just stationed a plainclothes at Bradley's, so take Pickford's instead, yeah?"

Amelia had a source at the Yard.

"When will we begin doving?" I asked.

"Soon," she said. "After tomorrow, I'm pulling you all out of the West End."

Recalling her sharp tone during our practice, I asked, "Is something the matter? Besides the extra constables?"

A flicker in her eyes came and went. "No." She tucked a dark lock of hair back into her hairnet. "Just being cautious. Elsie had to run for it, and Harriet would've been caught if not for Gus."

That hair tuck was Amelia's tell. But the set of her jaw told me I'd get nothing more, so I said only, "That's what I heard. Gus set his dog on the constable." Harriet had told the story for a laugh in the pub room, but her voice had held a shrill note.

"Aye." Amelia glanced up at the clock, and I followed her gaze. Half past one. Three hours before people headed home for tea, the crowds thinned, and thieving was harder. "All right, then," she said.

I took it as a dismissal and started for the door.

"Wait, Kit. How's Sarah? Is she doing better?"

I turned back, feeling a warm glow of gratitude at her concern. Amelia knew my younger sister had just taken a position as a scullery maid, where the work was hard. "I think so, but—well, she hasn't sent her usual letter, though she's home tomorrow."

Amelia saw my worry. "No doubt she's busy working," she said reassuringly. "And knowing her, she's likely making friends with any time left over."

I smiled. "Thanks, Amelia."

"*Ádh mór ort*," she replied with a wave of her fingers.

The ring's founder, Patty Wirth, had been Irish, and though she'd been dead these fourteen years, this phrase was still how we wished each other luck.

Downstairs in the taproom, I found Mary sitting at a

corner table with Josie and Bea, who were drinking pots of golden ale with a thin layer of froth, drawn fresh from the taps. Mary was not; we never drank before a dodge, not even ale. As I approached, Mary rose and stepped away from the table.

"She asked about me?" Mary murmured.

"She did, but there's something else troubling her," I replied, my voice low. "She wouldn't say."

"Hm. Well." Mary turned to beckon to her nephew Sid, her palm up, her quick fingers folding in twice. He slouched away from the table where he sat with other boys.

"What?" he asked.

She rumpled his hair, and he ducked away.

"Pickford's at half past three," I said. "Don't be late."

"Yah." He sniffed and turned away and went back to his friends.

Mary turned to me, rolling her eyes, half annoyed, half amused. "Let's get ready." We went upstairs to the costume room, where racks held dresses with thieving pockets that reached to the bottom of the crinolines, coats lined with fisherman's netting that easily caught jewelry, trousers with adjustable turnups, two-sided cloaks, paste jewelry good enough to pass for genuine, hats, spectacles, paste-on moles, and such. Mary carefully braided my brown hair tight to my scalp to fit under the wheat-colored wig. We each chose a cloak, a reticule, gloves, and a hat, then set out for the West End.

Chapter 2

From the far street corner, I eyed our mark for the day.

The roofline of Pickford's rose against low, scudding clouds. Like every other building on this street, the department store had a white façade interrupted by arched windows, like high-and-mighty eyebrows. If our borough of Southwark was the pickpocket of London, Kensington was the bride, regal and fair.

Ahead of me, Mary reached the door and vanished inside at twenty past three. I dallied on the pavement, holding my cloak closed against the breeze, watching the horses, omnibuses, and cabs pass, and counting out three full minutes so no clerk would think, even looking back, that we'd entered together. Approaching Pickford's, I cast one final look for a uniformed constable before I crossed the street. Usually I smiled at sweeps, even offered a coin, but this boy I ignored, to prevent him from taking notice of me, and upon reaching the opposite curb, laid my hand on the shining brass doorknob, stepped in, and drew in a breath. People say that dry goods are pretty to look at, but I liked the smell of these brightly lit shops, with the leather, silk, linen, felt, feathers, and ribbons, and the waxy linseed oil used to polish the wooden cabinets.

We timed the dodge for midafternoon, so the shop would be busy. There were five—no, six—men and nine women, some with their maids in attendance, making selections at the various counters. Mary was one of three looking at men's neckwear, and the clerk had taken out half a dozen cravats, laying them on the wooden counter to be examined. Mary was very pretty, taller than I, with a creamy complexion, fair hair, and blue eyes; I was plainer, with brown eyes, which I dimmed behind spectacles, and though we always traded off as decoy—Mary wanting to divide the risk fairly—the role fell more naturally to her. I worked my way along the counter on the opposite side of the store, gazing at the women's hats for three minutes, and then halting by the gloves case. The clerk obligingly pulled several pairs from behind the counter, along with different silk ribbons to match. The tall case clock in the corner chimed once for half past three.

We have rules for thieving, and one of them is to never, ever look at one's jenny. So I kept my attention focused on the gloves, hiding my annoyance that Sid was now late. The longer Mary and I stayed, the more risk we'd be recognized later. Ideally, this dodge took less than a quarter of an hour. The clerk's mouth twitched with impatience as I peered through my spectacles and tried on this pair of gloves, then that one, fidgeting with my gold band—the mark of a husband's ability to purchase—all the while.

From across the room, Mary's anxiety came like heat on my own back. When I saw Sid tonight, I was going to smack the bloody little bugger. Another minute or two, and we'd have to call it off. It had been years since I'd given in to those early lurches between fear and frustration, but wanting this to go well for Mary, I felt them now.

Damn it, where is he?

The front door swung open and closed. I had positioned

myself so I could see the entrance in the looking glass behind the clerk, and my nerves eased. With his cap pulled low, Sid appeared and vanished out of its gilded frame. His dark-coated figure would be strolling toward Mary—ten seconds, then five—and then came Mary's scream.

Like everyone else, I spun to see her hands up—"My reticule! It's been stolen!" she cried, whirling about and peering around the shop desperately before she put her hand to her side, shrieked "Oh," as if in sudden pain, and slumped to the ground in a spectacular fashion.

It was exactly the way she'd always done it, and relief rolled over me.

The gloves clerk edged around the counter and pushed past me, rustling my skirts. Together with other clerks, he crouched down, bending over Mary's limp form as the customers gathered around.

"A glass of water! Smelling salts!" cried the cravat clerk. "And catch that rascal! He went out there!" The gloves clerk leapt up from Mary's side and headed for the side door to give chase.

With all eyes on Mary, no one paid me a whit of attention. My hands were already slipping gloves and wooden spools of ribbon into my thieving pockets, the bulky shapes vanishing into my crinoline.

I was stashing the fourth pair of gloves when a man in a brown suit stepped out from behind a pillar. His eyes weren't on Mary; they darted around the shop. Even as I noted his features—medium height, a bit thick around the middle, dark wavy hair, clean-shaven, a rounded chin, forty years of age or thereabouts—I clasped my empty hands before me and peered worriedly at Mary, like everyone else.

A few moments later, the gloves clerk burst back into the shop, breathless. I wasn't worried he'd catch Sid, who would have already handed Mary's purse to Harry, who would stash it inside his waistcoat and stroll on. Even if Sid was nabbed—which was unlikely, as he'd have stuffed his cap into a pocket and slowed to an amble immediately after fleeing the shop—he wouldn't have the reticule. No evidence, no arrest.

I longed to snatch one more look at the brown-suited man, to determine whether he was a Yard plainclothes detective or a shop-hired privy. But I wouldn't have risked meeting his eyes for the world. As I kept my gaze on Mary and the cravat clerk, her would-be rescuer—who was running his hand over her breast, pretending to feel for her heartbeat, the filthy git—a woman who had been trying on hats approached me. Her jowly chin shook with indignation. "It's dreadful! London's full of devils these days, vicious wretches who will steal *anything*!"

"Devils and wretches," I murmured in agreement.

I was, after all, one of them.

Chapter 3

Outside, I rounded the corner, flipping my cloak from blue silk to black for good measure. It had been a narrower escape than I liked. My heart beat out of time until the next street, where I forced it back into order.

I strolled south and east, the weight in my thieving pocket lying heavy along the crinoline. We were all used to being off-kilter, accustomed to hiding the limp it gave us. Better to have a limp from the pocket than to be a man and limp between the pockets, as Josie would say.

I reached the west end of the Charing Cross rail footbridge and started across the Thames, knowing Mary would have taken the Waterloo. I paused, resting my hands on the parapet, and looked east, for it was one of the rare afternoons when the sun slipped the clouds, laid the bridge's shadow across the river, and dusted gold across the boats' chop. From below rose the rank smells of rotting fish and tangy brine, of filthy old stone and molding green muck crawling up the pillars.

From behind me came the distant blare of a locomotive whistle followed by a screech of brakes as a train drew into the London and South Western station. The sound was lost in the grind of a motor as a tugboat avoided ramming a lighter not fifty yards from me. I shaded my eyes to watch as a coal carrier plowed its way along, its flaring blast overwhelming the sound of the tug. That's the way London was, one sound drowning another. I walked on and waited for Mary at our usual corner on Waterloo Road. As she appeared, I was gratified to see lightness in her step and a quietly confident smile on her face.

I felt a moment of misgiving at the thought of deflating her spirits by telling her about the brown-suited man who'd escaped her notice. But Mary and I told each other the truth.

"That was neat," I said as she looped her hand through my elbow.

"Except for Sid, the little wretch. Another few minutes and I was going to call it off."

"We'll box his ears tonight," I said.

She let out a groan. "It's the bloody dice, Kit. He's running a game on Water Street. He probably lost track of time."

My steps slowed. "What? He's running a game? *Here*?"

Southwark was Silas Pike's patch, not just for gaming but for gambling, extortion, and receiving stolen goods. For Silas Pike, Sid running a game meant he was old enough to be punished for it, no matter if he was only twelve.

"I've tried warning him, believe me," Mary said.

"How much is he bringing in?"

Her eyebrows rose. "Two or three pounds a week. Now he won't leave off it, and with my ma gone, he doesn't mind me."

It gladdened me to catch Mary slipping in the mention of her ma. She'd done it several times lately, as if testing her ability to say that syllable without her voice breaking. The first month after her mother died, Mary had folded in on herself with grief, sobbing so hard in my arms that I begged her to breathe. Eventually, her grief had softened, along with her need to know why her mother was killed. A murdered woman from this part of London didn't hold the attention of detectives for long.

Not like us thieves.

I drew Mary into the alcove doorway of an abandoned shop with the glass panes broken, the empty window frames covered by splintered wooden planks. "Mary, there was a detective in Pickford's."

Her jaw sagged in dismay. "What? I didn't see—"

"There's no way you could've," I interrupted. "He was in plainclothes and out of sight until you fell."

Her eyes darted as she retraced the shop in her head. "The wide pillar in the back corner, by the table linens."

I nodded.

"Damn." She bit her lower lip white. "How did *you* see him?"

"He stepped in front of the pillar. He wasn't watching you. He was looking for me."

Mary drew a breath. "You're sure he didn't make you?"

"I was staring at you by the time he turned in my direction."

"Bloody hell," she whispered, and her gaze drifted across the muddy rutted road toward the Three Boars pub, with its crooked shutters and a two-bit boardinghouse on the upper floor. I kept silent until she nodded, slowly at first then more firmly. Her eyes returned to mine. "You didn't keep it from me."

"You said you were ready. That means I tell you, like we always do."

Her look of gratitude pinched at my heart.

"I am *not*, however, telling Amelia," I added. "There was no harm done, and I don't want her wondering if you should've seen him."

"Thanks for that." She looped her hand through my arm, and we walked on to the corner. We paused, waiting for two carriages to pass, and she gave a little shake of her head, as if to put the detective out of her mind. "Sarah's home tomorrow night, isn't she?"

The sudden shriek of a railway engine made us press our hands to our ears.

As the noise subsided, Mary spoke over it. "We could have tea together before she goes back, with Sid." Sid and Sarah had grown up together, and they got on. He never mocked her for the wine-colored birthmark by her temple like other boys did. "I could make a cake for us, special," she added as we paused at the corner of Granby Street. "Mrs. Jonas has me baking pound—"

The screech of railway brakes drowned the rest of her sentence. Again, we covered our ears, I nodded agreement, and we hurried south to leave the noise of the station behind. To St. George's Circus and onto London Road; past Marshall Street, with Seamus Ardle's pawn shop where I worked, and the Trunk Lodging House in York Street, where Mary and I roomed together since Sarah went out in service two months ago.

At the end of London Road sprawled the cobblestoned quadrangle where six old stagecoach roads coming from as far as Dover and Canterbury met in front of the Elephant and Castle. Together Mary and I approached the square front of the inn with the famous motif above the door: a left-facing elephant with the crenellated tower on its back.

Dusk had fallen, and the light from the windows feathered onto the cobbles. To the side of the inn lurked a few Castle men—Billy, Tommy, Jake, and Nick—in a rough scrum, talking in low voices. If the Castle men were dogs, always scavenging for more, these were the four most dangerous, the sort who would maul a mark half to death if he fought back. Some of the younger ones, standing slightly apart, were friendlier with us, more like pups, all horseplay and boasting talk. Although even pups could cause trouble, as any woman knows.

Fanny's brother Caleb, a card sharp who ran a spieler of *vingt-et-un* in rooms nearby, called out to Mary, "Good take today?"

"Aye," she called back noncommittally. To the Castle men, anything more might sound smug.

Still, Jake's eyes had latched on to us, his face sour, his mouth twisted. Two years ago, our ring was clearing three times what the men were from dead lurking and dragging luggage off cabs, and Amelia had taken the inn's upper stories for our own. Jake had been the one who'd resented it most, throwing a brick through our goods room window one night when he was in his cups. Amelia had a word with Silas Pike, who ran the Vine Street fences that received most of our take, and from then on Jake only growled; he didn't bite.

I pulled open the door. As we stepped inside, the warmth of the room and the tang of ale from the taps came at us in a wave.

I started up the stairs to the goods room, while Mary, with nothing in her pockets, stayed below to have a pint. I pushed open the door to find Amelia seated at the desk, recording the day's take in her neat hand, with the bottle of ink and an open ledger before her. Nell was loading boxes of goods into the dumbwaiter, which would be lowered to the ground floor, where the goods would be retrieved by one of Pike's henchmen. For secrecy, this occurred on different nights each week.

Before the drawn curtains stood other thieves—Josie and Bea, Fanny and her new jenny, Cathy—in various states of undress, having doffed their thieving garb. Here in this room, the danger that kept us keenly watching our backs dropped away. Wordlessly, I turned so Nell could undo the buttons at my nape.

"How are you?" I murmured over my shoulder.

Nell's fingers paused, and I felt a stab of regret. I was never sure if I should ask, in case I recalled her grief at a moment when she wasn't thinking on it. Mary's mother, Rose, had been Nell's cousin and dear friend, and Rose's murder had hit her hard.

Nell's fingers restarted on my buttons. "Some days I can't stop thinking about her."

The cool air chilled my shoulder blades. "Sorry."

"Mary all right?"

"Perfect."

Nell's hands continued down my back as I watched Cathy roll the long stem of a silver hatpin between her thumb and forefinger, her eyes fixed on its sparkle in the lamplight. My mouth twitched in sympathy. We'd all felt longings like that when we started, some fancying the pretty trinkets, others hoping someday to be the sort of woman who could wear one in public without anyone wondering if she'd stolen it.

Well, we all want things, I thought.

I'd never longed to keep the items I stole, even the pretty ones. They were just fripperies that turned into money for necessities—the extra rent so Sarah could stay in my room without having to work for Amelia, food, tea, a full scuttle of coal, warm clothes, boots because Sarah's feet grew a size every six months, a rag rug for warmth, a new feather pillow. Between my take from thieving and wages I'd earned, I had some money put by, a collection of coins in a small pouch under a floorboard in my room, a decoy for a larger pouch hidden in yet another compartment beneath the first. But no matter how heavy those pouches, my fears were heavier. Sarah depended on me, and we had no one else. What would happen if I got sick for a spell? If, God forbid, I was caught? Or if she needed a doctor for weeks on end, like when she had whooping cough? When Ma lay dying, our money had dwindled until we'd scrounged for halfpennies. I took to visiting the butcher at day's end for scraps, and Sarah fixed her eyes on the pavement to avoid seeing the bread loaves in the bakery windows. I never wanted to return to that. No, I wanted enough money that I needn't worry ever again, though I wasn't sure if there was such an amount.

Nell's hands finished unbuttoning and shifted the fabric over my shoulders, and I shimmied out of the dress.

"Cor, look at the filigree work," Josie said, eyeing the hatpin Cathy held. "That bit o' peridot is gorgeous, ain't it?"

"Aye," Cathy agreed, setting it on the table with reluctant fingers.

Amelia paused in her writing and her mouth tightened; some of the girls tried her patience. Her gaze shifted to me. "Ready?"

"Yes." I laid the dress on the table, like a corpse in a casket, and Bea's hands slid below the hand-sized false pocket into the large thieving one.

"Four sets of gloves, fine kid," she said as she withdrew them, and Amelia noted it. "Satin ribbons, six. And . . ."

Bea's eyebrows rose as she examined the coins. "And two pounds, ten?"

"The clerk's pocket." I grinned and laid the back of my hand theatrically to my forehead. "He was overcome with distress over Mary. Easy mark as he pushed by me."

Bea laughed.

"Hmm," Josie said, leaning over with a sly look. "Anything else worth grabbin' in his pocket?"

"Ach," I replied with a shrug. "'Twas too small, couldn't find it."

Josie threw back her head, giving her bright laugh, and continued chuckling as she headed downstairs. Fanny and Cathy grinned as they followed, but Bea's face was pinched as she left the room. Clear as day, there was something amiss between Josie and Bea. I looked to see if Amelia had caught it, but she was writing down my poke. Well, it wasn't for me to say anything. Amelia turned up the wick on the lamp and slid the ledger toward me so I could put my initials beside each item for tallying at month's end. I handed back the pen, wondering how many times I'd scribbled *KJ* on these pages in the last few years.

I stepped into my own dress, and Nell buttoned me and slipped away as I sat to put on my boots. Knowing Amelia would ask about my afternoon, I took my time fastening them.

Amelia was giving one final look over the goods book. The corners of her mouth were tucked in concentration; her left forefinger slid down the side of the page as her right hand made quick notations in the margins.

Fourteen years ago, when I was six and Sarah wasn't even born, Patty Wirth, on her deathbed, had passed the ring to

Amelia Lyle, her niece, who had only improved it. She made sure her thieves knew how to read and do simple ciphering, how to add grace to their walks, soften their expressions, and tuck their vowels up their noses when the occasion required. Now, over a dozen of us lived in rooms near the inn, paid for by the ring. Amelia was a good mistress, practical and unexcitable, who gave us a fair cut, so even after paying for our board and other necessities, most of us earned a nice amount each month.

Amelia blotted her last few handwritten lines, closed the ledger, and stowed it on the shelf, then gestured for me to take the chair across the large wooden desk. From a cupboard concealed in the wall's panels, she took out a bottle of wine, poured a crimson inch into two glasses, and set one in front of me.

Her hands moved with their usual steadiness. Still, her expression made me ask, "What's the matter?"

"Mary was good?"

"She was fine," I said. "A fainting spell worthy of Drury Lane."

Amelia sipped her wine. "Anything unusual at the shop?"

I studied her. Her tone told me that this second question was why she'd held me back.

I drank the wine—bitter to my tongue—and thumbed the corners of my mouth to remove any purplish stain. Mary and I would deal with Sid, so there was no need to mention him being late. And if I told Amelia about the detective, Amelia might wonder if Mary was fit to work. "No," I lied.

"Did you see more constables than usual?"

I answered, honestly, "We didn't see any."

"Good." Amelia's face relaxed into a smile. In silence, we

finished our wine, and she corked the wine bottle, putting it back inside the cupboard along with our glasses after wiping them with a towel. It was supper hour, and the jolly rowdiness rose through the floorboards. Amelia flapped her hand toward the door. "Get on with you, now. Have some fun, yeah?"

I made my way downstairs, pausing at the landing to observe the pub room below. A bright fire threw light fitfully, forming and dissipating shadows upon the beamed ceiling, the tattered chairs closest to the hearth, and the three long wooden tables that crossed the room, where men, women, and children crowded the benches. Card players sat at the square tables along the far wall. We thieves gathered by the fireplace. Sid watched worshipfully as Caleb drew a grand arc in the air with his glass of ale, telling a story that brought shouts of laughter. Mary watched him from the bar, her expression amused. He caught her eye and winked. Caleb flirted relentlessly with Mary, who was friendly with everyone, but she saw him for what he was—a fine-looking bloke, but shiftless, like most of the Castle men.

I started toward Mary and the bar, where people stood two deep. The barkeep, Pat Hollings, passed glasses of ale across the high wooden plank to open hands, the tattoos on his forearms rippling as he worked the taps, his thick fingers quick but not sloppy. While I waited my turn, I surveyed the room. It wasn't family, but it was familiar to me.

Except at one of the tables sat a striking woman, new to the inn. She was about forty years of age, decently dressed in blue wool, her thick dark hair threaded with gray but still lustrous. Her countenance was lined around the mouth and at the brow, as if her life had been hard, but even so it was evident she'd once been a beauty, with large dark eyes under well-shaped brows, high cheekbones, a firm chin, and a full mouth. It was an arresting face, handsome rather than merely pretty. I might not recall people's names, but I have a peculiar memory for faces, and I'd seen hers once before. Not here, and only briefly, some months ago, somewhere dim, as if I'd passed her on a bridge in the late afternoon or observed her in a market.

She sat at the end of a long table with a group of four women who gathered there daily, joining the conversation, laughing at their remarks, leaning in with her chin in her palm, as if she'd done it every Friday night since forever.

Her pretense of belonging made me wary.

I'm not one to ignore that feeling. I attend to it, for more than once it has kept me from choosing a poor mark or showing too much of my hand. Having the mother I did, I'm quick to detect when folks are acting a part or passing lies.

Perhaps the woman felt my stare, for suddenly she returned it. Her gaze sharpened, held, shifted away for a moment, then settled back on me, hardened, as if she recognized me somehow, or at least knew a good bit about me.

It set a chill like a cold finger at my neck.

Then she gave a bland, indifferent smile and turned back to her new friends, making me wonder if I'd imagined it.

Beside me, Mary nudged my arm. "What's the matter?"

I started. "Ah, nothing." I looked pointedly at Mary's half-empty pot. "None for me?" I teased.

"I didn't know how long Amelia would keep you. She asked about me?"

"Of course," I said. "But she was more concerned about constables."

"Constables?" She drew back. "I didn't see any."

"I didn't, either. That's what I told her."

"Ah." She raised her pot with a smile. "Well, get yours and come on."

"I will." I turned toward the bar. Like a tide, people shifted forward and back to make room for others, and I nudged in between old Connors, who raised a sloshy pint and belched his greeting, and Mrs. Wiggins, whose upper lip with its dark hairs held droplets of ale. Connors flung an arm around me, but I was ready and slithered away before he could squeeze my arse. Pat winked at me with his one good eye—the other having been put out years before in a ship's brawl—and passed me a glass of ale, hoppy and bitter at once, which I drank down thirstily until it was half gone. Mrs. Wiggins stepped away and James Kinnon materialized beside me, his hazel eyes bright with laughter. "Hullo, Kit."

"Hullo," I replied. "Haven't seen you in weeks."

"I've been working extra." He set his empty glass on the bar. "Took the afternoon off to help Emma fetch a shipment from the wharf." He leaned in close with a show of sharing a confidence, though he had to speak up to make himself heard over the clamor. "Josie says you're sticking your hands in men's pockets now. It has Robbie all excited." One side of his mouth curved up, and his voice was sly with teasing.

I rolled my eyes. "You can tell Robbie I won't be sticking my hand in his pocket. I'm sure I'd be disappointed."

He laughed and set his elbows beside mine, avoiding the spots sticky with spills. "How've you been? How's Sarah?" He'd always had a soft spot for my sister. "Is she getting along?"

"From what I can tell, the work is hard, but she doesn't complain. I think she's afraid I might make her quit."

"She probably likes earning a wage," James replied. "Makes

her feel like she's grown, and she's helping you, after all you've done."

"I haven't done much," I said dismissively.

He left that alone, caught Pat's eye, and pointed at his glass. "Another?" he asked me, and I nodded.

As our full glasses appeared, Pat leaned over the bar toward James, raising his voice to be heard. "You're staying with Emma tonight? I've some chairs that need mending."

"Aye, I'll come by in the morning," James replied and put down coins for our glasses. Pat made to wave them off, the drinks part of an easy exchange of favors, but James shook his head and shoved them toward the till.

We backed away from the bar to make space for others, and James gave me an inquiring look and raised his glass toward a small round table in the corner. I nodded and followed in his wake as he threaded his way between tables, greeting people he knew. James was one of the few Castle men who'd left and found legitimate work—at the Custom House, in his case, after being in prison for smuggling. I asked Emma once how he'd wrangled that, and she'd shrugged and said she had no idea. Rumor was he'd ratted out other smugglers, but I never believed it. James might be a rogue, but he was no copper's nark.

Though he lived north of the river now, James came around to the inn most Fridays, joining the group of us by the fire. I wondered why he was pulling me aside. As I sat in one slatted wooden chair, James turned his sideways so he could rest his forearm along the top rail. "Emma says you've been helping her a good deal."

"Well, someone had to. She had two trousseaus to finish last week," I replied. "Needed by some West Ender in a hurry, as usual."

One eyebrow rose. "She told me about some woman who changed her train three times."

I snorted. "It wasn't just her train—she couldn't decide if she wanted her flounces gathered, box pleated, or fluted. She drove Emma half distracted." I sipped my ale. "How is the Custom House?"

"Good," he said. "Busy."

"You miss smuggling? The dodges?"

He spun his glass on the table. "Nae. Clerking's easier."

I eyed his hand. The thick calluses along his thumb and forefinger weren't from clerking.

"I thought you were on weights and measures," I said.

"Started there, but I'm on records now," he said. "Most days it's like trying to catch a runaway train. We work till after dark—and there's still ships lined up to be unloaded and counted the next morning, with the captains cussing at the delay. But they come from all over, Kit. The East Indies, Egypt, Spain, France." He reached into his pocket. "Look here." He chose a coin from the half dozen in his palm and held it out. "It's from Greece."

I took it, peering at the circle of silver with a young, straight-nosed man in profile on one side and on the other wheat sheaves encircling a word. "*AERTON*," I puzzled out. "What is it?"

"One lepton," he said. "Their letters are close but not the same."

"Does it make you want to go places?" To my surprise, a note of envy crept into my voice.

"Sure," he said. "Though some of the stories they tell of pirates make me happy to be right here." I made to give the coin back, and he waved it back toward me. "Keep it. It's a curiosity. Can't spend it." He drained his glass and smiled at me. "What would you say to a proper night out? We could go to a music hall, see a show."

I drew back. "With you?"

"Aye, why not?" he asked, unperturbed. "We've been friends a good while."

I was silent.

James raked his dark curls back from his forehead. "Stop it, Kit. You're looking at me like I'm running a confidence game."

I laughed. "Do you know how to do anything else?"

He gave me a mock-wounded look and laid a hand across his chest as if I'd stabbed him. "Humor me. What's the harm in a night at Wilton's?"

"There was a man murdered there last year," I reminded him. It had been in all the papers. A violinist had leapt into the crowd, fists flying, and landed a blow that sent the spectator down, his head smacking the floor, with blood everywhere, and the performer had been tried and thrown in prison.

He laughed. "You're right. Tell you what," he said, drawing a pack of cards from his pocket. "We'll play. If I win, you have dinner with me."

I rolled my eyes. "Everything is a game with you."

He shrugged and dealt the cards.

Five hands later, I laid down rummy with two left over.

He laid down his cards, played the eight of spades on my run and had only an ace left over. His eyes brightened with triumph. "Saturday night, then."

"I can't. Sarah's here."

"Sunday?"

"I walk Sarah back to work."

"What time?"

"Around five o'clock."

"So, we could have dinner on the north shore."

Still, I hesitated. He was a Castle man, born and raised, who'd been in prison. If those calluses on his hands were to be believed, he was still rowing at least a few nights a week, which meant he was back to smuggling.

He leaned forward, his dark eyebrows raised. "It's just dinner, Kit."

"All right. I'll meet you around seven," I said.

He opened his mouth to protest, then shrugged. "As you like." He rose from his chair and pulled on his coat. "The Silver Plover." He gave me the address and took up his empty glass to return it to the bar. "I've something to do for Emma. See you Sunday."

He gave a cheerful grin, and I watched him leave, the burly shoulders under his rough brown coat, the dark hair that curled over the collar. He paused at a table, where a cluster of men urged him to stay for another drink. With a mix of familiarity and deference, he rested a hand on old Dick Yellen's shoulder, one of the men who had known him since he was "Jimmy" and "boy."

I couldn't help but think of the last badger scheme we'd pulled together, the week before Amelia invited me into the ring.

The mark that night was married, which I knew not just because of the ring he wore, a gold band I could fence easily at Mr. Ardle's. I'd seen him at the inn before with his wife on his arm. This time he was alone and blinked rapidly when I asked if he wanted company. I could tell he was a safe mark; there were some who were flat-out dangerous, the ones who stared bold as brass, smirking as if they expected your attentions all along. This bloke was about thirty or so, with weepy mustaches and a shy, uncertain manner. He finished his supper hastily, and I brought him to Mrs. Donnelly's lodging house next door, up the stairs to the room James and I rented for a shilling for the hour we needed it.

I eased the mark out of his coat—a bit worn, four shillings—and undid his cravat—another two—and came close, letting him peck me a bit as I shook out my hair. Like most men, he took it as an invitation to run his fingers into it, kissing my neck. I flinched and pulled back.

"What's wrong?" he asked.

"Oh, no matter," I said. "Just your ring caught my hair. Here, let's put it in your pocket, and you can play with my hair all you like."

He hurriedly slid the ring off and tucked it away, and we went back to kissing, which gave me ample time to transfer the items in his pocket into my own. His hands ran over my back and down to my arse—

"Take off your trousers," I whispered. "Let me sit on your lap a bit."

He was out of them faster than a greyhound coursing a rabbit, dropping them in a heap on the carpet.

Trousers nice, almost new, a neat label inside. Six shillings.

I sat down on his lap, put my arms around his neck, held my breath against the scent of Macassar oil in his hair, and kissed him again.

Suddenly there were heavy footsteps in the hallway outside—the knob turned—and James flung open the door, slamming it into the wall behind.

"Who the devil are you?" James bellowed, his eyes blazing, his cheeks red. "And what are you doing with my wife?"

The man leapt up, dumping me unceremoniously onto the floor. James took a step toward me, his hands reaching, leaving the path to the door clear. This mark had the presence of mind to snatch up his trousers and boots before he raced off, his bare feet pounding down the hall.

Damn it, I thought. There went six shillings and four more for the boots.

James closed the door, grinning. "That was an easy one."

I put out a hand for him to pull me up, rubbing my hip where I'd landed. "Easy for you," I grumbled.

"What'd you get?"

I drew the poke from my pocket—the gold ring, six pounds and a few shillings in coins and notes, and a silver pocket watch. I examined it closely. There was a monogram, *SRB*, but that could be churched. Plate, not real silver, but Mr. Ardle would take it.

James picked up the gold ring. "I can't believe these fools fall for you saying it gets tangled in your hair."

"They're not thinking with their brains," I reminded him. "A few kisses and you're all fools."

He had thrown back his head and laughed. "You're right, we are."

It was the same laugh James was giving now, with Dick Yellen and the other men. Unreserved and buoyant and easy. Nearly everyone liked James, perhaps because he genuinely liked most people. He had more faith in them than I did. Then again, he didn't grow up with a ma who made a fussy show of locking the door carefully at night, as if she wouldn't open it later for Jack McShane. Who topped up the gin bottle with water, to make it appear she hadn't been drinking all afternoon. Who looked shocked at coins missing from the tin cup, as if she hadn't filched my meager wages for herself.

One last loud guffaw from the men and James turned away and pulled open the door. Unexpectedly, he turned and caught me looking. A roguish grin creased the skin at the corners of his eyes. With a quick lift of his chin in farewell, he closed the door behind him, leaving me rolling my eyes. He might work away from the Castle now, but he was the same as ever.

Chapter 4

The weather turned warm and humid overnight, and the next morning I woke sweaty under the bedclothes. Mary snored softly in her bed against the other wall. Trunk Lodging House could be stiflingly hot in the summer, but our coal stove kept us warm in the winter. Of the two torments, cold was the one you could die from.

I dressed quietly, carrying my boots into the stairwell, and on the way to Seamus Ardle's shop, I stopped by the inn for tea and toast.

At eight o'clock, half the people in the taproom were like me, starting their day; the other half were still snoring off the previous one. I counted nine men asleep, with an arm flung across the table for a pillow—or face down on the wood. Some dark impulse made me kick one of the benches as I walked by, just to see the man lift his head, his eyes red and bleary, his cheek crosshatched with the wood grain and a knothole. He grunted and plunked his head back down, the other cheek on the boards this time. Well, he'd look balanced when he finally woke.

I headed to a table that held some of yesterday's newspapers, glad to see *Reynolds's* on top. My father—the son of a schoolmaster—had taught me to read from its illustrated pages, and together we laughed at how they mocked the police, with a regular cartoon about Constable Jack Anapes spinning haplessly as thieves made off with pouches of loot. The *Dover Chronicle*'s headline was TRAGIC MARITIME DISASTER! about a small French ship that had run into the shoals and capsized the previous day. The front page of the *Canterbury Journal* featured an orphanage that had burned to the ground, and the article made an impassioned plea for donations to rebuild. I refolded the pages, pleased at a newspaper doing some good in the world.

Under the last paper was a dog-eared penny dreadful, which I took for Sarah—though I had to be careful with what I brought her. A few months before, I had found her in our room weeping as fiercely as when Ma died. Panic stricken, I'd taken her by the shoulders. "Sarah! What's the matter?" She held up a tattered yellowback, a cheap version sold in railway stations. The front showed the title: *The Old Curiosity Shop*. I'd never read it myself. "Little Nell *died*, Kit!" Sarah wailed. "How could he *do* that?" I'd released her and slumped against the wall, silently cursing Dickens and letting my heart settle back into its usual place.

"More?" Pat's wife, Jane, asked, the pot ready to pour, and I nodded.

I sipped my tea—blessedly hot, though murky, from the bottom of the pot—and munched my toast, which Jane put before me with an extra pat of butter. When finished, I handed Jane my coin, and together we observed the snorers. "You think their wives miss them?" I asked.

"Nae, not at all," she grunted. "Best they're here, let their poor wives sleep of a Saturday morning."

I laughed, thanked her, and headed out into the street, pausing on the pavement to let a costermonger cart pass, the wooden wheels clunking across the uneven cobbles, jouncing the crates of parsnips and potatoes inside. As Mrs. Dobbs, the cat's meat woman, sang out "Meat! Meat!" from across the way, Mrs. Jonas's tabby nearly tripped me up in his dash. I crossed the cobbles to Mr. Ardle's shop, with its green-striped awning flapping against itself in the morning breeze, the wooden door carved with the letter *A*.

Ardle's was one of three shops on the short street, occupying a building between a chandler and draper, and a role between a lawful pawn shop and an unlawful fence. The plate glass window was crammed with goods—lamps, dishes, gloves, hats, bottles, boxes, porcelain shepherds, maps, mourning bands, frayed books, bits of ivory, clothes, and an aspidistra that drooped in a pot shaped like an angel's head—a tumble of items that would have been laid out neatly in a West End department shop. The shelves of Ardle's were poorly lit, which gave an extra measure of delight when people stumbled across a treasure. Often, it was as surprising to Mr. Ardle as to themselves. He wasn't a shrewd proprietor like his father. However, the Ardles had served Elephant and Castle for over thirty years, since before Silas Pike, and had earned Amelia's loyalty, so his stock was constantly renewed by goods we brought him.

I knocked at the back door at half past nine and waited. Mr. Ardle was a solemn giant of about forty-five, stoop shouldered and ponderous, with a shock of brown hair turning gray, sad pale blue eyes, a horsey face, and a reclusive demeanor at odds with that of most of the Castle men. Unmarried and with no remaining family, he lived above his shop. Even with his spectacles, he couldn't see well enough to do the fine handwork jewelry and watches required, so at Amelia's suggestion, he'd hired me. Each Saturday, a wooden tray held rings with twisted prongs, bracelets with loose stones, watches that no longer kept time, ceramics that needed gluing. Some items I repaired were legitimately pawned, but most were poke, and I'd change out the stone from opal to garnet, say, or cleave a gold necklace into three bracelets, so it no longer matched the police's descriptions of stolen goods.

At a rumble of thunder, I knocked again, louder. For God's sake, where was he? I didn't want to get drenched. At last, the lock clicked and Mr. Ardle opened the door. The emanating odor was the same as always—vinegar and linseed oil—but Mr. Ardle's appearance most certainly wasn't. He'd had his hair cut, and his overgrown beard and mustaches had been trimmed neatly by a barber. Instead of one of his old shirts, yellowed at the collar, he wore a crisp white new one and a jacket taken from the rack of finer clothes in the shop.

"Mr. Ardle," I managed.

He gave me a nod.

With any other man in Elephant and Castle, I might have teased him about sprucing up for a woman. But I'd never seen Mr. Ardle with one. The last time I'd seen him neatly barbered, he'd inherited fifty pounds from an uncle.

"You look . . . well," I said.

A tentative smile stretched his mouth, revealing his front teeth. "I've had a bit of news."

"Oh?" Another unexpected inheritance?

He didn't elaborate, however, and after an awkward moment, I patted his arm. "Well, whatever it is, I'm pleased for you."

I took my usual spot at the workbench in the back

room, turned up the two lamps, and drew the tray of work toward me.

"The hands on that silver repeater ain't turning proper," Mr. Ardle said. "The rest, you'll see the problem easy enough."

"All right," I said, and he moved away, leaving me to it.

I slid out the drawer that held my tools. It had taken me months to find ones that suited my hands, smaller than Mr. Ardle's great paws: pliers of different sizes, some with flat edges and others curved, tiny screwdrivers, a ring clamp, a holder, a sliding gauge, a prong lifter. A wooden box held spare springs and miniscule parts, false gems made of paste, glue, buttons, and thread.

Mr. Ardle's shop didn't open until eleven o'clock, so all was silent as settled dust. I bent over my work, my hands mending fine objects and my mind mulling problems that, for the most part, I couldn't fix.

The rain spat on my umbrella on the way back to the inn. I flapped the black folds and pitched the wet mess into the dented tin bucket by the door. Mary sat at our usual table. The new thief, Cathy, sat with her, and in front of them stood a squat green teapot, three cups, a wooden board with cheese, and half a loaf of bread. I took the third chair and shifted out of my cloak as Mary poured my tea.

"How are you getting on, Cathy?" Mary asked as I tore off a piece of bread.

"Aye, all right, I think," Cathy replied. "Fanny's a fine jenny. I'm looking forward to working the theaters, though, rather than the shops. It's where I come from—"

The front door swung open, hard, and we all turned. Bea entered the inn, alone, and headed straight up the stairs.

Mary set down the teapot with a thunk. "Where's Josie?"

"Did you see her face?" Cathy asked, her voice tight. "Something's the matter."

I was already standing up from the bench.

The three of us hurried after Bea to the goods room, pushing open the door that stood ajar.

"What happened?" I asked.

Amelia looked over, her face emotionless. "Shut the door, Mary. Josie was caught. Bea's just telling me now, yeah?"

"We were at Whiteley's," Bea said. "I was looking at brooches, and the clerk took three of them out, putting them on velvet. They were only silver plate; and when I started to leave, the clerk added more of silver. I went to the looking glass, and that's when I saw a man near a pillar, standing too still."

"A privy or a Yard man?" Amelia asked.

"I'd say a Yard man," Bea replied.

"What did he look like?" I asked, my heartbeat uneven. By keeping silent about Pickford's, had I put Josie in danger?

Bea considered. "Around forty, tall, thin, egg-shaped head, pale hair."

Not the brown-suited man, I thought with some relief. He'd had dark hair, which could have been a wig, but he couldn't change his height and weight.

"I gave a yawn and three pats." Bea mimed the action, covering her mouth. "But Josie didn't notice. She kept slipping brooches into her sleeve, and I yawned louder, and she *still* didn't notice." Bea's voice was fretful.

Into my mind came the image of Josie in the practice room the day before, swinging the walking stick. Her boldness and bright spirits stood her in good stead most of the time, but sometimes she verged on reckless, which is why, after one outing, I'd refused to be her jenny.

"Go on," Amelia said to Bea. "What happened next?"

"I dropped my parcel, and this time she noticed, but she could hardly put the brooches back. I stood at the counter for another few minutes, raising a fuss to give her time to get away, but the Yard man went straight after her, and he and a constable dragged her back to the store. I left, turned my cloak, threw my parcels in a bin, and came straight here." Bea's face was tight with worry. "She never looked at me, not once," she added softly.

Amelia paced to the window, her habitual serenity slipping. "Damn," she whispered under her breath.

If the police found the brooches, Josie would be tried within days; if convicted, she could serve up to four years. Amelia could produce eyewitnesses who would swear to Josie's character, insist it was her first time thieving, call into question the veracity of the plainclothesman or constable, and even suggest the goods had been planted on her. But paying witnesses carried its own risks, and two police testimonies were harder to refute than one.

"Did she have time to shift the brooches?" Mary asked. The police might know about the thieving pocket, but no matter how avid a copper was, even he wouldn't grope a woman's skirts in a West End shop. He'd likely take Josie to the station or the Yard, and on the way, Josie might have a chance to tear the bottom of the long pocket to ditch the poke. If they didn't find it, they couldn't convict.

"I don't know." Bea looked at Amelia. "What do we do?"

"I'll do what I can," Amelia said evenly as she retrieved her reticule from a drawer.

We all knew Amelia kept a mental ledger of allies and spies across London—some inherited from Patty Wirth, others gathered over the past fifteen years: politicians, theater managers, judges, barristers, doormen at gentlemen's clubs, heads of gambling rings, gaolers at Newgate, clerks at the Old Bailey, even costermongers and sweeps. She kept a special fund for the rare instance when one of us was nabbed. In Josie's case, I assumed Amelia would distribute bribes to the necessary officials, though none of us knew their names, or the cost, or any of it. It certainly wasn't written down.

Amelia left, and the four of us soberly filed down the stairs after her. Cathy said something about it being rotten luck, and Mary assured Bea that Amelia would manage it; she always did.

My thoughts, however, had leapt to my own narrow escape. What were the chances of two of us thieves being caught, or nearly caught, in two days, by plainclothes? Unease ran like heat down my spine. Something had changed, and it wasn't just the number of constables.

That evening, in the thieves' corner of the taproom, the air was thick with resentment against the police, dour predictions for Josie, and, in Bea's absence, muttered questions about her loyalty and adeptness, which brought sharp words from her brother John. Night fell, the rain persisted, and Amelia still hadn't returned.

Sarah knew to find me here, for we usually had supper together when she arrived. I left the group to sit at the bar and sip my ale. What was I to tell Sarah about Josie? *Should* I tell her? Keeping it from her forever was impossible. But by the time my sister learned of it, Amelia might already have got

Josie off. The arrest would only worry Sarah about me, and what was the point of that?

Sarah usually arrived before eight, and by half past, my nerves were bunched like badly carded yarn. The rain slapping at the windows made me fret at Sarah walking alone from Mayfair. I wished for the hundredth time she wasn't working, that I'd stood firm in refusing her.

When Sarah told me she wanted to go out in service, "to make a wage, so I can help," I'd imagined her slender form bent over huge copper pots or hauling iron scuttles up and down narrow stairs and said no straightaway. But her brown eyes were so earnest, and her pointed chin rose as she'd reminded me that plenty of girls went out in service even younger than she was. Did I forget that I'd worked for a seamstress at age ten? In the end, I told her she could try, but if it was too tiring or dangerous, she'd quit. After her first month, she handed me her wages proudly, insisting it was going well. She didn't even want me to come to Grosvenor Street to fetch her anymore. "I'm old enough to walk home by myself," she'd said stoutly. "Or I can take an omnibus." She'd rolled her eyes. "And yes, I know about the nips and knuckles on the buses."

I looked out the window. With this rain, the omnibuses would all be packed tonight. She'd be walking.

When the clock struck half past nine, Pat offered, "She might've waited, hoping the rain would stop."

I slid off the stool. "I'm going to meet her."

"Take my umbrella." Pat thumbed toward the corner where it leaned. "And wear a warm coat."

Upstairs in the costumes room, I pushed aside the fancy silk cloaks and found a plain woolen one. I took a sturdy black umbrella as well as a lantern, the loop of the metal handle cold against my fingers, and headed out. I'd made Sarah promise that she'd always take the same roads home, so I walked the reverse, reaching Waterloo Bridge where the lights on the far bank blurred and bobbed in the rain. As I reached the middle, I spotted her at the end. She carried no umbrella, and her head and shoulders were hunched forward, her face buried in her bonnet.

I hurried toward her. "Sarah!"

She looked up, her face startled, and as I reached her, she threw her arms around me. She was more demonstrative than I, but this was rather more than her usual display. I couldn't return her embrace, as my hands were full.

"Is something the matter?" I asked, holding the umbrella over her.

In the light from the lantern, her eyes were wide, her face shiny with rain, despite her bonnet. She shook her head and gave a shiver. "Just cold. Thanks for meeting me."

"All right," I said, relieved it was nothing more. "Here, take the lantern."

With my right arm around her, and my left holding the umbrella, we matched our steps back across the bridge and toward the inn. I pushed open the door for her, shook out the umbrella, and stepped inside as she removed her sodden bonnet. She was trembling with cold, and her lips were blue. "Take off your cloak, it's drenched," I said. With shaking fingers, she did as I said, but her dress was damp too.

"I'll be fine by the fire," she chattered, and we made our way toward it. As she put her hands out, I looked at her sideways. My sister was nearly as tall as I was, and there was less of the childish softness in her cheeks than there had once been. She was thinner, and something in her manner made me uneasy. Still, my first thought was to get her fed.

"Are you hungry?" I asked, and she nodded. I caught Pat's eye, and as we sat at a table, his wife, Jane, brought us steaming bowls of soup with bread and butter and glasses of ale.

Sarah finished every drop of her soup, and I pushed my half-finished bowl toward her. "You're sure?" she asked, and I nodded.

But as Sarah ate, I had the growing sense that something besides cold and hunger troubled her. She kept her eyes on her meal, which wasn't like her. Curiosity and fear sprawled like an itch over my skin. Time was, she would have blurted out any worry the moment she saw me. What was she keeping from me?

"Did something happen?" I asked quietly, studying her face. "You didn't write to me these two weeks, and you usually do."

She looked up, contrite. "I'm sorry, Kit. I've just been tired by day's end. Honest."

"All right," I said dubiously.

She finished the last spoonful, and we left the inn and went to our lodging house. As we climbed the stairs, my stomach knotted, for I knew what could happen to young maids in wealthy houses with sons, and the Willits family had two, Philip and John, in addition to a daughter, Clara. My fear was Sarah wouldn't tell me if something happened because I'd never let her go back.

As we reached the landing, light from under the door cast a glow onto the stairs. Mary was still awake. With a hand on her arm, I pulled Sarah to a stop.

"What happened?" I said, keeping my voice low. "Did someone hurt you? Was it one of the sons? Or the father? Did he come at you?"

She drew back, her astonishment genuine. "*No*, Kit. *Nothing* like that. I hardly ever see the gentlemen, and if I do, they walk past as if I'm not there—which is exactly as it should be."

Some of the tension along my neck and shoulders eased. "Then what?"

She slid her arm away and set her back against the wall. "I wasn't sure I should come home tonight."

"Why?"

Her face was solemn. "Because I don't want to get a chill and be ill again." I grimaced, remembering Sarah's whooping cough, the weeks of her fighting for breath, the hot poultices. I still couldn't bear the smell of mustard or boiled onion. "The last scullery maid was always begging off sick, though she was perfectly well, so Betty had to do *her* chores on top of her own, and finally the housekeeper dismissed her without a character." Sarah's gaze was appealing. "I don't want to get sick and have them think I'm a shirker, too."

"But it wasn't raining so hard earlier," I said. "Why were you late?"

"We had the chimney sweeps, so I couldn't polish the candlesticks and service from the dining room till after they left. I stayed late so's I wouldn't have to do it on Monday, when we'll all be busy for Miss Clara's engagement party the next night." She folded her arms across her chest. "I like it there, Kit. Mrs. Rice said I'm 'wonderfully meticulous.' Everyone's been kind, and I don't want to disappoint them."

Her eyes were entreating, and the last of my tension ebbed. This sounded like my sister; she tried to please, and she was making friends. "Of course not." I touched her arm.

"I'm proud of you for doing so well. And that's kind of the housekeeper to notice. From what I've heard, most only shout when you've done something wrong."

Gratefully, she threw her arms around me.

When she pulled back, her face had resumed its usual brightness. "That's another thing I like. No one shouts. Not even Mrs. Rice, no matter how displeased she is. She just sighs, like this"—she heaved dramatically—"and looks sorry." I laughed, like she wanted me to. "But if it *is* terrible weather, I don't want you to fret if I don't—"

"It's all right," I interrupted. "From now on, if it's terrible weather, don't come, and I'll know why."

She gave a smile full of sweetness. "And if something frightens me at the Willitses' house, I'll tell you. I promise."

Relieved that the truth was so harmless, I pulled her close, shutting my eyes, laying my cheek against her hair, still damp from the rain and smelling of cleaning lye and coal dust. It was all I could do sometimes not to clutch Sarah tight, until she squealed, like she did as a child. But I let her go and followed her to the room we had once shared.

When we entered, I gave Mary a look so she wouldn't mention Josie, and we talked of other things for an hour. Finally, with Sarah yawning so widely her jaw popped, she and I curled up together in my bed.

Sarah was asleep within minutes, her breath slowing, a small wheeze through her nose. I turned onto my side to face the wall, my eyes open, thinking of Josie's boldness and bawdy sense of humor, and my mind leapt to Mina Simmons, who had been hanged last year.

Mina had been a pretty girl, with rich coils of straw-colored hair and large brown eyes, and if she had a fault, it was that she longed for people to look at her. Men, mostly. She dimpled at clerks and sashayed out of stores, her skirts swaying over her hips. She wanted to be a proper anonymous thief, but she wanted to be admired, too. The two roles fit badly together, for when she was finally caught, clerks from four different shops remembered her.

The memory of the night the constables came for Mina made my muscles tense, rustling the feathers and horsehair inside the cotton ticking. Truncheons pounding on the door of her lodging house, visible from our window. Mina dragged away, screaming, the silhouette of her writhing between the two constables as they vanished around the corner. It was the last we saw of her, for hangings now happened behind closed doors.

But I could well imagine Mina's hanging because I'd witnessed one. I'd been seven, and I remembered it as pictures, perhaps because I had no words to describe it properly. It was one of my last memories of my father, likely another reason the memory was sharp.

Everyone had left their homes and shops empty to watch. (Years later, I realized a public hanging was a fine opportunity for thieves.) There had been hundreds, perhaps thousands, of people in the square in front of the prison, and my father had boosted me onto his shoulders and bought me a tuppence's worth of roasted chestnuts. I clutched the small smoky sack without eating them, wanting to keep them because gifts were rare, and Da had given them to me. Perhaps even then I sensed he was preparing to leave us. Later that day, I hid the chestnuts under my bed, where they eventually rotted, and Ma shouted at me for my stupidity. I didn't bother trying to explain.

The condemned was a woman who had murdered her husband and child.

Until that day, it hadn't occurred to me a woman could do such a thing. But shortly afterward, when Da vanished, I feared Ma had murdered him and Sarah and I might be next. Ma's rages since he'd left made this less unlikely than one would imagine.

The murderess wore a gingham dress with a filthy apron, and her hands were tied behind her back. As she mounted the steps, people shouted words I didn't know and pelted her with rotten apples and potatoes. A priest approached, made signs, and spoke, his words drowned by the crowd. At last, the hangman slipped the black hood over her head, followed by a pale rope knotted in a loop. The trapdoor snapped open, and as she fell through, a triumphant cry went up, the weight of her bounced, and the rope jerked straight. Her feet flailed for a moment, and then the body went limp as a handkerchief with black boots sticking out of the bottom. I must have snatched my father's hair, for he let out a yelp of pain and grabbed my hand. I loosened it immediately, and bent over his ear to shout: "When will they let her down, Da?" Surely a few seconds of punishment was enough, I thought, for her neck must be hurting terribly.

Fool that I was.

There was danger for us thieves, always. Now that no one was transported to Australia anymore, women thieves were sentenced to years in prison if the judge was feeling charitable and were hanged if the judge was not. And with what seemed to be a newly zealous police force? The thought of leaving Sarah unprotected in London turned my bones to water. I believed Amelia and Mary would watch out for her and keep her safe, but in prison or dead, I'd have no way of knowing if my sister was all right day to day.

This was perhaps the hundredth time I'd considered this possibility, and it always churned my insides to the same sharp pinch. I lay awake, listening as Sarah and Mary breathed in a mistimed rhythm—Sarah slower, Mary faster—while shouts and scurries from the street pierced my window, and panic spread like spilled ink through every inch of me, black and thick enough to drown in.

Chapter 5

By the morning, the rain had stopped, though gray clouds hung like dirty bedsheets, unmoving over the city. Sarah and I bought her favorite cinnamon rolls from Mrs. Jonas's bakery—Mary waved to us from the kitchen—and cheese from Bender's shop and went for a long, pleasant walk across the bridge to St. James's, where we found a bench and enjoyed our makeshift picnic, stopping to feed the swans and ducks with the scraps.

On our way back to my room, we paused on Waterloo Bridge. The rain had washed away the bird droppings for a day, and we settled our forearms on the metal railing. Under the low-hanging clouds, the Thames was daubed in grays with black and white flecks. The river was at flood tide, high, half an hour from turning. Four hours from now the mud larks would be on the south bank with their buckets, scrounging for bits of metal and wood by the light of handheld lamps. The next bridge to the east was Blackfriars, where the great underground River Fleet emerged on the north bank, flowing into the Thames through a large semicircular opening. As a child, looking at the papers over my father's shoulder, I'd seen a cartoon of Old Man Fleet, shaking his fist in rage at us Londoners for burying him beneath roads and railway lines. The thought of a powerful spirit dwelling silently underground had frightened me.

"You don't have to walk me back," Sarah said. "Unless you want to."

"Oh, I don't mind," I said, my eyes on a barge headed straight for a rowboat, whose two oarsmen were paddling furiously to get out of the way. "I'm meeting James for dinner over the river anyway."

"*What?*" At the shock in her voice, I turned. A smile bloomed across her face. "Kit! That's wonderful!"

"Why is it wonderful?" I asked, genuinely puzzled.

"Because . . ." She studied my face. "Don't you want to go?"

I didn't answer at first. Did I? Didn't I?

"Well, *I'm* glad you're going," Sarah said.

"Why?" I asked again.

"Because." The river breeze blew strands of her fair hair into her face, and she tucked it behind her ears. "I want you to have some fun. You deserve to."

"I suppose," I said dubiously.

A slow smile dimpled her cheek, and she gave a sly sideways look. "I'm going to fix your hair. Come on." She nipped her hand through my elbow and tugged. I groaned and made a show of rolling my eyes but let her drag me back to our room.

Mary wasn't there, and Sarah pushed me into our one chair, then rustled through the drawers and took out a comb and brush, pins, and Mary's hand mirror. She brushed my hair until the knots from the wind were gone and the curls fell almost straight, then set to work, tugging and pinning. I tried not to wince.

When she finished, she handed me the mirror. "See? It's pretty."

I turned my head to one side and then the other to see the brown braids and coils. "It is," I said. "Who taught you?"

"Betty. She's Miss Clara's maid, so she practices on me."

"Well." I handed the mirror back. "It doesn't quite look like me, but I like it."

"*I* like that it's James."

"You do, do you?" I returned.

"He's handsome."

"I suppose so."

"And he's kind."

Something in her voice made me swivel to look at her, wondering if Sarah fancied him herself. "What makes you say so?"

She hesitated. "Don't scowl when I tell you this."

"Well, that's never a good beginning."

Sarah sat on Mary's empty bed to face me. "One night, when you were gone somewhere, I was coming home from the market. There were three boys at the corner by Sawyer's shop. They were teasing me, calling me ugly and a toad."

"Little buggers." I knew the corner, could imagine the three of them surrounding her, not letting her pass. "Who were they?"

She shrugged. "Ben Tucker and two of his friends. I don't remember. But James was nearby, and he grabbed Ben by his coat and pushed him against the wall. Not overly hard, mind you, like he was showing off being older and bigger, but enough to put the wind out of Ben, making him gasp and cough. James didn't yell, just said if he ever caught them bothering me again, in any way, he'd flay them alive. They left me alone after that."

"You never told me." My voice held a note of accusation.

"Because I knew you'd scowl over it, like you're doing now."

I smoothed my expression. "When was this?"

She considered. "Around four years ago. Before he went to prison."

"That was kind of him," I admitted.

Sarah looked at me with perplexity. "I thought you liked him."

"Well, we've always been . . . friends, but he's still a Castle man," I replied, thinking of the calluses on his hands. "God only knows what he's still mixed up in."

The stuffing inside the cotton mattress ticking rustled as Sarah rose and put the comb, brush, extra pins, and mirror back in the drawer with a small sigh.

"We should go," I said. "Mary and Sid'll be waiting."

It being a Sunday afternoon, the taproom was subdued. Mary was already at a table, with a pot of tea and a basket of rolls. Sid detached himself from a group of boys scrapping over a card game and joined us.

Mary knew not to mention Josie, but Sid had no such restraint.

"Did you hear? Josie's trial's likely this week." His brown eyes were wide as he chewed a roll. "Ow!" He stared at Mary, who had kicked him under the table.

Mary glowered. "Do you even think before you open your gob?"

Sarah swiveled toward me. "Josie was arrested?"

"Cor, don't you know nothing?" Sid asked. "Happened yesterday."

Sarah's mouth tightened but she said nothing as Jane set a plate of cheese in front of us.

"Amelia says she's taking care of it," I said as Jane left.

"I heard she couldn't," said the irrepressible Sid. "Bribe didn't work. Too much in her pockets." He turned to Mary. "And don't kick me again, neither. She's going to hear from somebody. She ain't a baby."

Mary leaned across the table toward Sarah, her blue eyes sympathetic. "I'm not one to talk ill of people, but Josie wasn't being careful. She ignored all Bea's warnings."

I shot her a grateful look for trying, but Sarah's pursed mouth told me what she thought of me keeping the arrest from her. Mary took a bakery box from beside her on the bench, opening it to reveal an iced pound cake. She cut the slices and put them on plates. Delicious as it was, it didn't sweeten anyone's temper. Sarah remained stubbornly subdued, Sid sulked, and after a few attempts at conversation, even Mary gave up. Afterward, we all slid out from the benches, relieved. Sarah started for the front door, and I rolled my eyes at Mary. Her look wished me luck.

We weren't five steps across the cobbles before Sarah burst out, "Why didn't you tell me? For God's sake, Kit!"

"To what end?" I asked. "You'll just worry."

"Of course I will! How did it happen?"

I told her everything Bea had said, concluding, "Josie was my jenny once, and Mary's right. She's careless. I'm sorry she was caught, but Bea warned her." I shoved my hands into my pockets against the river's evening damp. "And you know how I am. One whiff of danger and I leave off."

"I *know*," she said. "But still, Kit."

We walked to the back of Willits House in silence. At the black wrought iron gate atop the steps to the servants' entrance, she said softly, "I wish you'd just *stop*."

I'd known it was coming. It wasn't the first time.

"I think there's part of you that *likes* the trickery of—"

"Believe me, I don't."

She drew back at the harsh note in my voice.

"Are you . . . afraid?" she asked, as if it had occurred to her for the first time.

My hands curled into fists inside my coat pockets. Sarah had no idea the cost of rent if the ring wasn't paying, not to mention food, clothing, shoes, sundries, doctors and medicines—

"Of course I am," I said quietly. Her face lit with hope. "But I can't stop, Sarah. Not yet. I only work for Mr. Ardle once a week and at the dress shop when Emma needs me. It isn't enough."

She looked crestfallen. "Not even with my wages?"

I shook my head. "I've told you I'm not against stopping. When I've enough to keep us for—say—a year, we'll talk about it."

She looked as if she didn't believe me.

"I promise."

Her shoulders slumped with a despondency that wrung my heart. But there was nothing more I could say; I wouldn't lie to her. I hugged her goodbye and watched her descend the brick steps and knock. A metal bolt scraped, and the door swung inward. She gave one final look and vanished, the door shutting with a solid *thunk*.

I fastened the latch on the black iron gate, then started for the Silver Plover, my spirits an unpleasant tangle of worry and regret, making it impossible to enjoy the walk down Fleet Street in the cool August air. The rain had settled the dust and smoke, and the lamps glowed like golden orbs, gilding the cobblestones. At the corner, a costermonger rattled a pan of chestnuts over the coals, the rich nutty scent briefly overcoming the bitterness of burning coal. The churches hadn't yet struck seven when I spotted the pub's painted sign hanging aloft, but James was there standing underneath it, his hands in his coat pockets, surveying the street with a pleased air as if the carriages and cabs, the people with their parcels, and the gasman lighting the lamps with his long stick weren't things he'd seen hundreds of times before. With some effort, I put aside my unsettled feelings as I reached him.

"Everything all right?" he asked.

I gave him a smile, and he put a hand on the doorknob and paused. "Your hair looks different. It's pretty."

I'd already forgotten. I touched the braids. "Sarah did it. She insisted."

He pulled the door open, and we stepped inside.

The room was warm from the fire at the hearth. A young woman greeted James by name and directed us to two seats at the end of a long, lively table. As I unbuttoned my coat, I looked about and felt unexpectedly shy.

This was nicer than anywhere I'd ever eaten. It was still what people called a public house, but it had a more prosperous air than the taproom at Elephant and Castle, with a gilt-framed mirror over the fireplace, turned silver candlesticks that would've fetched at least a pound each at Mr. Ardle's, and two oval oil portraits over a broad sideboard. The tables were wood but shiny with veneer and polish rather than rough planks. Along the wall nearby stood a wooden slatted rack draped with the *Times*, the *Falcon*, the *Examiner*, tidily folded. At the hearth stood armchairs draped with antimacassars, and the orange flames sprang properly upward instead of smoking. Sconces and lamps cast a steady light over the smooth plank floor swept clean. Several people called to James, and the barkeep waved from across the room.

"My lodging house is around the corner," James explained as he took my coat and hung it on a rack beside us. "So I'm here quite a lot."

"The food looks delicious." I observed the filled plates of the other diners. Fish in a creamy sauce, potatoes with herbs, and some sort of long green vegetable I didn't recognize.

"It is," James said as he took his seat across from me. "There's only two dishes each night, but Augustine is French, so they're all good."

"Oh," I said uncertainly. So far as I knew, I'd never eaten French food.

Glasses of wine appeared before us, along with a handwritten card listing the day's offerings.

He picked up his glass and raised it toward me. "I brought you here because there's something special on Saturday and Sunday nights." His eyes were warm and sparkling in the light from the lamps.

"What?"

A piano chord struck up, and I turned to the corner of the room. There sat a young man of perhaps fourteen or fifteen, gangly, with large hands and wire-rimmed spectacles that rode halfway down his thin nose. His eyes were on the keys, and he played without music.

"It's Augustine's son," James murmured. "He's a student at the Royal Academy in Tenterden Street. He's why they moved to London."

A series of chords rolled out, and then the boy began a melody that I'd never heard, something haunting and slow, something that roiled my heart. I listened, mesmerized, until the end. There was polite applause, and he began another.

I turned back to see James pleased at having surprised me. "I thought you'd like it," he said. "I remember you sitting on the stoop at Three Boars when Mack used to play."

"That's right." I dragged up the memory from years before, when Ma was still alive. "They wouldn't let me in."

His dark eyebrows rose. "Because back then it was a brothel upstairs."

I laughed. "That's right, it was."

"*Bonsoir*," came a woman's voice, musical. Beside us stood a slender woman of about forty, with dark hair and eyes, a narrow nose. She wiped her thin hands on her apron.

"*Bonsoir*, Augustine." James stood and kissed her on both cheeks. "This is my friend Kit Jimeson."

"Enchanted," she said, and I smiled back.

"Would you like the beef or the fish tonight?" she asked. Her accent was like lace, making our English words prettier.

I hesitated.

"We could have one of each, so you can taste both," James offered, and I nodded.

Augustine said something approving in French and took the card from the table before she whisked away.

I turned my attention back to the pianist. He was so young his cheeks were pale and smooth as a girl's. What would it be like, to be so talented at making something beautiful?

The song ended, and he rose, gave an awkward little bow, and pushed his spectacles back up his nose.

"I heard about Josie," James said. "It's a rotten thing." His expression altered. "Though I heard from Benny she was in her cups."

"I hadn't heard that," I said uneasily. "I heard she ignored Bea's warnings."

"Might be that, too," he said. "I'm sure Amelia's doing what she can."

As I sipped my wine, I spotted the evening edition of the *Review* newly placed on the rack. The pages were slightly askew, but on the front page below the masthead was the bold headline, clearly visible: MAYFAIR MURDERS!

"James, could you hand me that paper?" I pointed.

He fetched it off the wooden rack and handed it to me. I read the first sentence—*There has been yet another housebreak in the West End with tragic consequences, resulting in the death of two servants*—and tore through the paragraphs below with increasing unease.

"What's the matter?" James asked.

I looked up. "A housebreak in Mayfair. The family was away—but they'd left two servants behind, and the burglar stabbed the housekeeper to death in the parlor and then went upstairs and killed the maid in her bed."

James grimaced. "That's awful. Does it say where in Mayfair?"

"No, just the family's name. Fairleigh." I bit my lip. "But Mayfair's small."

Understanding flickered in his eyes, and genuine sympathy lit James's face. I half expected it. Sarah brought out the sweetness and sincerity in people. "You think it might be near where Sarah works."

I nodded, but I was thinking more than that. Did Sarah know something about this? Was that why she'd been so secretive? I scanned the first paragraph again. The burglary had happened last night. So she couldn't have known about it before she'd come home.

And yet—

"Kit? Can I see it?" James asked. I handed the shuffled pages to him, and he refolded them to read the article. His frown deepened as he read through the list of the goods that had been stolen, a reminder of the Yard's recent failures, a description of the crowds of hundreds gathering in front of the Fairleigh house to gawk, and the final line, which to my mind was absurd: "Anyone with information is asked to contact Inspector Stiles of the Yard forthwith."

Who would have information? And who would talk to the Yard?

"Hmph," James said.

"What?" I asked.

"The list of things stolen," James said, and read aloud: "Diamond-and-ruby earrings, three strings of pearls, several unique rings, silver spoons and candlesticks, and small pieces of art, including an oil painting by Rembrandt. Police are canvassing known fences in the area in search of the stolen items."

"Beg pardon."

We looked up. A young woman stood beside our table, patiently waiting so she could put down our plates. Hastily, James folded the newspaper away from the table and returned it to the rack.

The server had placed the fish before me, and though the flavor reached my nose, my stomach revolted at the idea of eating it.

Servants murdered in Mayfair. Sarah's peculiar reticence last night. The fear in her face when I encountered her on the bridge. A chill ran over my bones as the gossamer thread of suspicion thickened and took shape. Had *she* been threatened somehow? And had she concealed it from me, for fear I'd make her leave her position?

James had picked up his knife and fork, though he had yet to begin. His eyes met mine, questioning. "It's a terrible thing, to be sure, but there's no danger to Sarah. In fact, now the constables will be all over Mayfair. It'll be safer than ever." As I remained silent, he began to cut into his steak. "It says the family was away. Does Sarah's family leave London often?"

"I don't know. They're here now. Sarah mentioned a party for the daughter this week." I shook my head. "It's just so . . . brazen."

"Less brazen if they think the family's away."

He glanced at my fish, which was getting cold.

Obligingly, I cut into it and put a bite in my mouth. It dissolved on my tongue, tender, buttery, flavored with spices I didn't recognize. I took two more bites before I set down my fork. "It's delicious." For it was. But my mind was fixed on what James had just said. "How would the thieves know that the family was away?"

"Announcements in the papers," he said, "about house parties outside of London. Sometimes they print the guest lists, especially if titles are attending."

"Why would they do that?"

He shrugged. "To make people who aren't invited feel low, I expect. Thieves check the lists to know when families will be traveling. Or they keep their eyes peeled for a pantechnicon van removing paintings and furniture. It's a dead giveaway the family's leaving for their country house or the Continent."

Something about the way he said it made me blurt, "Are you caught up in this?"

James stopped chewing for a moment, then swallowed. His

face showed a mix of surprise, indignation, and disappointment that I'd even ask. He leaned in and lowered his voice. "I told you I'm done with dodges. But I hear things."

Of course he would. James still had plenty of friends in Elephant and Castle.

"Are Castle men doing this? Hitting homes in the West End?"

His fork and knife paused over the plate as he gave me a look. It wasn't a yes, but it wasn't a no.

It called to mind the evasive look on Sarah's face the previous night, and trying to sift the truth, I retraced the steps of our conversation: her insistence that the Willits sons had done nothing wrong, which I believed; her explanation about the chimney sweep and the silver polishing, which felt true but shuffling, as if she was buying time before she had to lie to me; and her assurance that she'd tell me if something frightened her at the Willitses' house, which now struck me as a carefully narrow promise.

She didn't say she would tell me if something frightened her nearby.

"Damn," escaped under my breath.

James's brow furrowed. "What's the matter?"

"Sarah was odd last night. She was late, so I went to meet her, and when I found her on the bridge she seemed . . . upset. And when I asked why, she said she hadn't wanted to walk home in the rain because she was afraid of getting sick and losing her position." I bit my lip.

"You think she was lying to you?" He looked dubious.

"Well, no. I think it was true." I hated the thought of Sarah lying outright. "But it may also have been a shell for something else."

He rested his fork and knife on the edge of the plate. "Do you think she might know something about this? Could she have seen something as she walked past the Fairleigh house? Or someone?"

The way he'd arrived so easily at a similar conclusion meant I wasn't over-worrying. I was likely worrying just enough. "It's possible, isn't it?"

He put up two hands to caution me that it wasn't the only explanation. "Whatever she was hiding from you—if she *was* hiding anything—it might have nothing to do with this."

I snicked my tongue in frustration. "If the article had given the address, I'd at least know if it was on her way home."

James's silence made my gaze return to him. His hazel eyes were on mine, watchful. "Almost seems that if Sarah *did* see someone, it would have to be someone she knew, wouldn't it?"

"For her to bother taking notice of him?"

"For her to bother hiding it from you," he corrected me.

A spike of fear ran down my spine. "You mean she might've seen someone she recognized. A Castle man in Mayfair. And she'd know he didn't belong."

"Can you ask her outright?" he asked. "If she did see someone, it's likely eating at her. She'd probably be relieved to tell you."

I looked at the mantel clock. "Not tonight. It's too late. But I could try tomorrow. Though if I cause trouble for her by going to the house, she'll be furious."

We were silent for a long minute. At last, he pointed his chin toward my supper. "Are you not hungry?"

I looked down at my plate.

James folded his napkin and set it aside. "Then I'll take you home."

The very absence of resentment threw a wave of regret over me. He'd spent his hard-earned money to bring me to a nice restaurant, with music and a fine meal. It should have been a lovely time. But I couldn't think of what to say about it. I couldn't apologize for my fears.

He held my coat so I could slide my arms in, donned his own, bid his friends good night, and followed me out into the street. At the corner, he raised his hand for a cab, helped me in, and got in afterward.

I sat staring out the window, desperate to see Sarah for just thirty seconds, long enough to ask one question, though logically it made no difference if I saw her tonight or early tomorrow. She was safe in her bed in a West End house with other people and a servants' door with a metal bolt.

James let me be as we rolled toward Elephant and Castle. Perhaps he sensed the wave of anger rising inside me, anger toward myself for having let Sarah convince me nothing was wrong. A groan escaped me. Every time I loosened my grip on the reins of my worry, something bad happened.

"What?" he asked.

"I wish I had enough money she didn't have to go to work," I muttered.

"Wouldn't keep her safe."

I glared at him. "That's a bloody awful thing to say."

"Is it?" he asked, his voice subdued. The cab was dark, his face shadowed, his expression invisible. "I hate the thought of losing people I love, Kit. It scares me more than dying. But I don't care how much money we have. We can't always keep the people we love safe." His voice fell, as if the weight of the thought dragged his spirits low. "I'd like to think so, but it's just an artful dodge I'm playing on myself."

The rawness in his voice melted my anger and put a burn into the back of my throat that I couldn't swallow down.

We reached the far side of the bridge.

"How could she not tell me?" I asked, my voice cracking over the words. "She's never lied to me outright before. She knows I can't bear a lie. Not from someone I love."

He didn't reply.

The hansom jolted over a pitted patch in the macadam, and my hand came up to the leather loop strap. The edges were frayed and sticky from other palms, but I didn't let go.

The more I considered, the more my imagined version of the previous evening seemed plausible: Sarah coming from Mayfair—the streets well lit—and by one gas lamp's light, seeing a Castle man, perhaps on the corner or coming toward her on the pavement.

I shivered.

Would she have known not to speak to him? To turn away? Or God forbid, would she have greeted him? Had they come face-to-face?

If it was a Castle man, he likely never intended to commit murder; it was the surest way to draw police attention. It had started as a robbery—but once the servants had seen him—well, he'd have no choice. But the murders would be discovered, an investigation mounted, and if he'd seen Sarah, he knew she'd suspect him.

He'd kill Sarah to keep her quiet.

My left hand clawed the edge of the seat, and James put his on top of it. The warmth of his showed me how cold mine were.

"Wait till you talk to her before you go too far down that road," he said.

I managed a nod, and he removed his hand from mine. He remained quiet all the way to the inn, where we dismounted and he paid the driver. I looked at him uncertainly. Wasn't he going back to Fleet Street?

"I'm staying with Emma. She's expecting me." He rested a hand on my shoulder. "Good night, Kit. Try not to worry. Sarah's a sensible girl." With that, he turned away, vanishing into the shadows.

But Emma's was in the other direction.

Full of misgiving, I picked up my skirts and followed. As I rounded the corner, a strong hand came out and grasped my arm.

I yanked back—until I saw it was James.

"Where are you going?" I hissed. "You can't ask about Sarah—"

"Jaysus, Kit!" He rolled his eyes skyward as if I was being ridiculous. "What do you take me for?"

My voice hardened. "This is *serious*, James. I need you to *promise* you won't—"

Every bit of humor vanished from his face. "When have I *ever* betrayed you, or been unfair? When did I ever fail you? Or arrive too late?"

The fierceness of it startled me, and I stepped backward for space to sift my memories of our badger dodges. Foremost of my recollections was laughing with him afterward. But he wasn't wrong. He had never let the mark get beyond a kiss or two, and he'd always made me take more than half the poke. "You're doing most of the work," he'd say. "It's only fair."

The way he looked now, his eyes deadly serious and fixed on mine, gave me a peculiar feeling, like the pivoting of a small screw, a gear of a watch slipping a quarter turn under my fingers. Was it possible I'd been wrong about him—or had he changed from what I once knew, and I was just noticing? Was this what Sarah had been trying to tell me?

"Didn't I?" he asked. "Keep you safe?"

"Yes." It came out barely above a whisper.

His expression eased. "Then trust me now. I'm not going to *ask* anything, and I won't mention Sarah. I'm just going to listen."

I swallowed. "Listen where?"

"Caleb's game," he said. "Half the Castle men will be there. If I hear anything, I'll send you word."

"All right."

"Go home," he said. "Sarah's safe for tonight."

As he dropped his hand from my arm, I nodded again. "I'm going." I took a few steps, but as I heard his footsteps fade, I returned to the shadows to watch. Across the street, he swung open the door to the staircase that led up to the rooms where Caleb ran his spieler. There James paused. By the light in the stairwell, I saw him in profile, and his right arm down, he spread his hand, all five fingers wide. It had been our signal, during our badger days, that the dodge was on, that I needn't worry.

But the very fact that James could walk into that game, without a second thought to wonder if they'd welcome him, meant he was still a Castle man.

Chapter 6

The next morning early, keeping a keen eye out for a tail, I took an omnibus to Grosvenor Street and walked a circuitous route past a noisy crowd peering up at what must be the Fairleigh house. Reaching the Willitses', I hurried down to the servants' area and knocked. The door was jerked open by a harried-looking maid.

"I'm Sarah's sister. Can I see her?" I asked. "It's important. And I can wait until she has a free minute."

"There ain't no free minutes," snapped the maid. "We've the young missus's engagement party tomorrow and we're already behind."

"Please." I pressed a half crown into her hand. "I only need a minute."

Her eyes wide, she snapped her fingers shut over the coin, disappearing it into a pocket. "I'll send her when she's finished with the pots."

I sat on the cold stone steps for over an hour. Finally, the door opened and Sarah stepped out, wiping her hands on her apron. "Kit, what are you doing here?"

"You heard about the murders," I said.

She nodded. "O' course. The whole house is in an uproar."

I took her arm, drawing her away from the door. "Do you

know something about it? Is that what you wouldn't tell me Saturday night?"

She tried to pull away, her eyes on my hand clutching her elbow.

I gave her arm a shake. "Sarah, for God's sake!"

Her face screwed up like she was about to cry. "Kit, don't yell at me! Why do you always get so angry? You're just like Ma."

The accusation stung, and I dropped her arm. "I'm not angry."

"Well, you look it." Tears glistened in her eyes. "You should see your face."

I drew a breath. "I'm just worried. Because you're not telling me the truth."

"You didn't tell me about Josie," she said defensively.

"That's different," I said.

"How?"

"I don't love her," I replied. "Sarah, please. Did you see someone you knew? A Castle man?"

Her eyes widened. It was as good as a confession, and her face collapsed into relief and remorse. "Two of them, on the far side of the street." She wrapped her arms over the soft part below her ribs, as if the memory made her queasy.

"How hard was it raining?"

"Not so hard I couldn't see." Her voice was a murmur. "Billy Winston and Tommy Finch, dressed like proper gentlemen. I saw them plain under a lamp."

I stiffened. Tommy drifted in and out of trouble, but Billy was ruthless and ran straight toward it. "Do you think they meant to hit the house?"

She gave me an incredulous look. "What else could they be meaning, dressed like that here?"

With effort, I kept my voice soft. "Did they see you?"

Her palms curved over her elbows as her gaze skittered away. "No-o-o."

"Sarah, please. I'm not going to yell."

With a sigh she looked at me. "They might've."

My heart plummeted.

I swallowed down the first hasty words that came to my lips. "That's dangerous for you."

Her brown eyes were wide, wounded. "You think I don't know? I'm nearly fifteen, Kit. God sakes, you were running a badger scheme when you were my age. Do you think I'm a fool?"

"No, of course not." My hands formed fists inside my pockets. "Can you . . . tell me exactly what happened, one moment at a time?"

"I *told* you. I saw them across the street, under a lamp. I recognized Billy's walk and heard Tommy's voice—you know its high pitch. I stopped, stepped out of the light, and turned my head. I stayed in the shadows until they were well past." Her eyes were sober, earnest. "I swear, Kit."

"When you stopped—was it a sudden movement?"

Her face fell. "I don't know. Likely it was. I was surprised."

I drew a breath. "Why didn't you tell me straightaway?"

"Because I knew you'd be like this!" She spread her hands. "You might even try to get me to quit, and I like it here," she said pleadingly, her chin tilting up. "And they like me."

"I *should* make you quit, Sarah." Although she might be safer here than at home, where Billy and Tommy lived. If they had seen her, they might assume she worked in Mayfair, but they wouldn't know which house—*unless* Sarah had mentioned the Willits name to someone at Elephant and Castle.

I longed to ask, but Sarah's face told me she felt guilty and frightened enough already.

I scrubbed my palm against my forehead and let my hand drop. "You can't tell anyone. Just because Billy and Tommy know you doesn't mean they wouldn't hurt you to keep you quiet. And a secret like this could be hard for someone else to keep."

"I know what those men are," Sarah said softly. "No one will know but us."

Except that James had already guessed she'd seen someone, though he didn't know who.

A cart clattered to the top of the stairs, drawing her gaze. She looked at me miserably. "It's another delivery for the party." Her face was pinched with worry, but she stepped away. "I have to get back."

"Be careful about going out until I know they didn't see you."

She nodded her promise and slipped back inside.

As two delivery men carrying wooden boxes of food came down the steps, I put my back against the wall to let them pass. The door opened and the housekeeper—her silver chatelaine at her waist—shooed the delivery men inside.

How difficult would it be for Billy or Tommy—or any thief dressed as a delivery man or a remover—to enter the house? Not very. Certainly not during the days before or after a party.

This house was as much a target as the Fairleighs'—indeed, more so, with all those engagement gifts stacked in piles and ready for the taking. No doubt the engagement, if not the party, had been announced in the papers.

I turned away, my stomach in knots.

As for her accusation that I was acting like Ma? That was a shot that stung and burrowed deep. But I could bear that, so long as Sarah was on her guard.

Dreading the thought of seeing Billy and Tommy at the inn, I spent the day away from Elephant and Castle, so it was dark by the time I reached my lodging house and made my way upstairs. A light came from under the door, and I composed my face, conscious of all I couldn't tell Mary. I opened the door to find her in her wrapper, with her brown day dress in her lap, squinting as she sought to thread a needle. The curtains were drawn, and the lamp cast a dull yellow glow. "Ach," she said with a look of relief, holding them out to me. "Could you? The eye's tiny."

With the ease that came of long practice, I slid the thread through the eye and passed it back to her. "I'll do it for you, if you like. Just let me get out of my things."

"Thanks. I've fixed one rip, but this one's tricky. It's not along a seam."

I hung my coat on its nail and removed my boots, placing them under the bed.

"Are you all right?" she asked.

"Just tired." I took the dress, casting a quick eye over the long stitches that puckered the fabric. Mary's hands were thieving clever, but she was no seamstress. I rustled around my drawer for my small scissors, slipped a point under the threads, and began to snip. In the corner, the coal hissed inside the stove.

"Any news of Josie?" I asked.

"Not yet," Mary said. "Trial will likely be tomorrow or the next day." A pause. "Bea's in a state."

"I hope she knows it wasn't her fault. I heard Josie'd been drinking."

Mary nodded. "She still feels rotten, though."

We all knew what a guilty verdict meant. Amelia had influence, but it only went so far.

I pieced the edges of the first rip together. "Turn up the lamp, would you?"

Mary spun the key to brighten the flame, and I made a series of tiny, regular stitches, holding the fabric taut to prevent puckering. I sewed in silence until Mary broke it: "Bea was talking tonight about what she'd do if she wasn't thieving. She wants to work in a shop."

I looked up to meet her gaze. "Did you tell her your plan?" Mary wanted to open her own bakery someday.

Mary shook her head deprecatingly. "No. It's years off. I need at least another two hundred pounds to open anywhere decent." She paused. "Sorry about Sid blurting out about Josie. Did Sarah ask you to quit again?"

My eyes on my stitches, I replied, "Mm-hmm."

"I figured she would." The horsehair and straw crinkled as Mary shifted on the bed. "Brings the danger close, doesn't it?"

A flare of cold prickled at the back of my neck. "We're more careful than Josie."

"But shops are getting sharper."

"So are we," I retorted, looking up. "Why are you being like this, when you know neither of us can afford to stop?"

"Kit." Her blue eyes looked hurt.

"There's no bloody point in talking about it." Bending back over the dress, I jabbed the needle into the cloth and sewed until the second rip was mended, knotted the thread, and bit it off, close. "There." I handed it back without meeting her gaze.

"Thanks." She hung the dress on one of the nails, then climbed into bed. "Should I turn down the lamp?"

"I'll do it." I changed into my nightdress, hung my dress, and twisted the lamp key before turning on my side.

"Good night, Kit." Her voice was kinder than I deserved.

She understood I was angry, but not at her.

"I'd quit if I could," I said, my voice a rasp.

"I know."

"Good night, Mary."

The church bells struck the hour, the toll lingering in the curdled air of the foggy night.

Chapter 7

The taproom was busier than usual for a Tuesday afternoon, and I sat at one of the triangular corner tables with a sloppy stack of newspapers, a serving of piping hot shepherd's pie, and a pot of ale for my tea. Both the *Times* and the Kent *Advertiser* carried reports of the Fairleigh investigation, railing against the Yard for making no progress at all. Not for the first time, it occurred to me that an anonymous tip-off to the Yard could put Billy and Tommy away—but Sarah would have to testify for a charge to stick, and even if the Yard tried to keep it anonymous, word might leak out. The Castle men might scrap among themselves, but they closed ranks when needs must and took their revenge.

My one shred of hope was that I hadn't heard from James. I took it to mean Sarah hadn't been mentioned, although it could simply mean Billy and Tommy were keeping silent for now.

As I scavenged the pile for another paper, a dark-haired woman rose from one of the tables on the other side of the room. Her back was to me, but I noticed her fashionable woolen paletot with a neat turned down collar and lapels, the sort of coat not often seen here. She approached Pat, put her empty glass on the wooden bar, and laid down a coin. Pat didn't give his usual amiable smile—didn't even nod—merely continued scrubbing at a brown whiskey bottle like he'd caught it stealing from the till.

That sent my curiosity high as the rafters.

Then, to my amazement, she stepped around the end of the bar and started up the steps to the private rooms above, and Pat didn't say a word to stop her. Now that I saw her profile, I realized it was the handsome woman I'd seen here a few nights ago, who had given me that peculiar, sharp look. She must know Amelia, and if I had to guess, she'd climbed these stairs before, more than once. The staircase was steep, and from the first step she plucked her skirts high the way we thieves did. My eyes went to her fingers, pale against her dark skirts. The skin on her near hand was shiny, as if it had been badly burnt, and two of her fingers—the index and the second finger—were twisted from being broken and not reset properly.

Pat's usually cheerful face was sober and slack, as if a heavy weight pulled upon it. My nerves tightening, I watched the woman's short-trained dress vanish up the stairs and heard the goods room door squeak open and closed. The newspapers forgotten, I sopped the last of the gravy with my bread and brought the bowl to the bar.

"Who was that?" I asked Pat.

He looked up from wiping the bottle. Before he could say he didn't know or joke my question away, I added, "I saw how you looked at her. And you let her go upstairs."

"She's an old 'quaintance of Amelia's."

"You don't like her," I said.

He frowned and kept his eyes on the bottle, which was already plenty clean.

I set my palms on the bar.

"Don't bother me about it," he snapped. "I expect you'll find out soon enough."

I drew back in surprise and returned to my corner table to wait until I could see Amelia myself, for Pat's manner made me want to know sooner than soon enough.

Well over an hour later, the woman descended the stairs, her face placid. She left quietly out the door, using her good left hand to turn the knob. Amelia did not appear.

The room was busier now, the bar two men deep, the tables filling. Avoiding Pat's eye, I went upstairs to find the door to the goods room ajar, the way it never was. I entered and closed it behind me. Amelia stood at the window, her back to me, her tall figure straight and still as an iron lamppost, her dark hair tidy in its usual net.

"Amelia?" I crossed the room.

Her gaze remained on the street outside. "Hullo, Kit."

"What's happened with Josie?"

The skin around her eyes tightened. "Half a year, down from four."

I studied her profile. "How?"

Amelia continued to study the street below. "The judge has a mistress, a French actress." She drew a long breath and huffed it out. "Josie'll be all right."

I nodded. Six months would be awful but survivable, and Amelia could make sure Josie got decent food and a cell in one of the better blocks. "Who was that woman?"

Amelia gave a sidelong glance and a snort. "Might've known you'd be the one to come asking, faster than a railway minute." Her mouth pressed into a wry line. "Well, you've a right to know, more than most."

Opening the secret panel, she removed the whiskey rather

than wine and poured herself an inch of the amber liquid without offering me any. I pulled out a chair from the desk and sat, though she returned to the window, her left hand holding the glass. Her gaze tracked something down on the street, perhaps the woman who had just left.

"Her name is Maggie Wirth O'Connell," she answered. When I didn't reply, she added, "Her mother was Patty Wirth."

Astonished, I asked, "Where's she been all this time?"

"A penal colony in Australia," she replied. "Twenty years ago, there were ten men for every woman. The coppers were snatching up and transporting any woman they could, no matter how small the crime, so men would have something to do in the evenings other than trouble the bloody sheep." Whatever she was watching had vanished, for she turned toward me. "She wrote letters the first year, but then there were two bouts of cholera in Swan River. We all assumed she died in one of them."

"And you're certain it's her?" I asked.

One dark eyebrow rose. "You've seen her face. How likely is it I'd mistake her for somebody else?"

"True," I admitted. Her beauty was memorable. "What does she want?"

"The ring, o' course." Her forefinger came away from the whiskey glass, as if to halt my protests. "Her ma gave it to me on her deathbed, but only because she thought Maggie was never coming back."

Her tone of practical acceptance made me stare. "My God, Amelia. You'd turn it over to her? Without a fight?" I hated the idea of the ring changing. And instinctively I didn't trust this woman.

"It's hers, by birthright, Kit. There's no question of *that*.

And o' course I'd quit someday." She raised her glass toward me. "Only I thought I'd be leaving it to you, in a year or two."

I blinked in surprise. I'd suspected, but this was the first time she'd said it straight-out. "Not Nell?" She was the only other one of Patty's thieves still in the ring.

"She doesn't want it."

"Oh."

My thoughts must have shown on my face, for her expression softened and she drew out the chair behind the desk and sat across from me. "I'll miss all of you, but I won't be far. I've family in Whitechapel. Like as not, I'll go there."

But once people left, they built lives elsewhere, found new friends, different pastimes.

"We don't even know her," I protested. "Can we trust her? What if she starts changing things?"

"Why would she?" Amelia tilted the whiskey to her mouth. The amber liquid caught the pale sunlight. "I'll stay on for a bit to show her the ropes, though she knows a good deal about the ring already." She replaced the glass on the table. "She's experienced and practical . . . and very clever, Kit. Bear that in mind."

"She was caught twenty years ago," I said pointedly. "Is she any good?"

Amelia looked at me from under her brows. "Maggie's one of the best there ever was—and she didn't even begin as a thief."

I settled back in my chair, the turned wooden rail rigid against my spine. "What was she?"

"A magician's assistant, in one of the music halls, at first," she replied.

"A good chance to learn sleight of hand."

From outside the window came the clatter of wheels. "Carrots and turnips! 'Tatoes and peas! Fresh and full weight! No false bott'ms in these!" The costermonger's bellowing song had been scraped down to a rough shout, for he was nearing the end of his day. Amelia waited for him to pass before she replied. "Maggie was sixteen and very beautiful. She was always a favorite."

"I can imagine," I said. "I noticed her the other night, sitting at one of the tables. She acted like she belonged."

Amelia heard the edge in my voice and shrugged. "Likely she feels she *does* belong. She spent her first twenty years in Southwark and still has friends here. 'Tisn't surprising she made her way back."

"So . . . she went from magician's assistant to thief."

"Well, between those, she was an actress and a chanteuse."

"A what?"

"A singer," she said patiently. "The papers called her 'the peerless contralto.'" Her eyes took on a musing look. "She was a sensation, yeah? Men were bloody mad for her—everyone from MPs to gang leaders. The morning papers would report who she threw her kisses to the night before. She had a second dressing room just for flowers and presents they brought. She was a legend."

I felt a jolt of surprise mixed with awe. "What ended it?"

"The manager threw her out for running doves in his theater."

"*Was* she?" I asked. "Would she risk all she had to do that?"

"I doubt Maggie would've risked it. But her mother might've."

Patty Wirth would compromise her daughter, for the sake of profits? I shivered, feeling grateful that Amelia never would.

Amelia turned her glass on the desk with nearly invisible movements of her fingers. "Naturally, Maggie was blacklisted across every theater. It was hard on her, but she joined the ring after that."

I could well imagine Maggie's resentment, if her mother had caused such a thing. "Famous as she was, didn't she have trouble thieving?"

Amelia shook her head in reluctant admiration. "She changed once for the stage; she simply changed again. A drab wig, some spectacles, a limp, and a shy, lisping manner. It was remarkable, honestly." Amelia's fingers stilled. "She only thieved for a few years, but she knows enough to take it on."

"But you've changed our dodges," I said. "Does she even know about the new privies and constables? And the new stores and shops?"

"No, but it won't take long to explain it." From the railway station came a train's blaring whistle, thinned by distance. Amelia paused with the glass on her lips, letting the sound fade before downing the last sip of whiskey. "Besides, she's been here a few weeks already, watching you all."

That pulled me up short and told me plenty. Maggie was shrewd and observant, someone who didn't rush in without looking about herself first.

"What about your ledger?" I asked. "Will you be giving her that, too?"

Amelia's mouth twitched wryly. "Oh, she has her own. And Silas Pike was her lover before he became my fence."

"Oh," I said, again taken by surprise.

She settled the empty glass between her palms. "I've had a good run, and it's not a bad time for me to step aside. She offered me a fair sum."

I fell silent. It seemed to me Amelia should be resentful, but that wasn't her way. She was practical, the least excitable person I knew, and as she often said, she didn't cry over what was already broken.

"What if we don't want to thieve for her?" I asked.

Amelia frowned in disapproval. "I'm counting on you to help the others get used to the idea. If you do it, they'll follow."

"What about Nell?"

"She stays on as bookkeeper. Nothing else will change." Amelia reached inside the desk drawer for a cloth to wipe out the glass. "I appreciate your loyalty, Kit, but I've made my choice." The tightness about her lips told me she wasn't happy with my pressing, so I stopped.

"When will you tell everyone?"

"Soon. Likely early next week." She replaced the cloth, sliding the drawer silently closed. "Keep it in your pocket till then, yeah?"

Her announcement would release a swarm of rumors like summer gnats. I'd seen it happen before, suspicions and outright lies clabbering the air, murky as a miasma.

But as unshakable as Amelia was, this wasn't the sort of change she would adjust to within an hour.

"Today wasn't the first she came to see you," I said slowly.

"No."

"When was it?"

"Three weeks ago. Soon after her ship landed in Liverpool."

Three weeks? Amelia had hidden all signs of it. Or I had been too preoccupied to notice.

Amelia replaced the glass in the cupboard. "You know, Kit, she didn't even know that her mother died. I had to tell her how and when. It was a shock, to be sure, and her brother gone, too. Not to mention how London's changed. It can't be easy coming back."

"Then why did she?" I asked. "Surely she had some sort of life in Australia, after twenty years. Her name changed, so she had a husband."

"But we've no idea what sort of man he was. In her mind, she was twenty years a prisoner," Amelia reminded me.

"Twenty years," I echoed. "Thieving's usually only seven."

"'Twas doubled to fourteen," Amelia said. "I don't know why."

We all knew the usual reasons—carrying a knife or other weapon, teaching another woman to thieve during the dodge, fighting back against the constable at the arrest, showing no remorse, being suspected of a previous theft. Or a judge was simply in a foul humor.

"I don't know why Maggie stayed the extra six," Amelia added. "She might've been caught thieving again." Dusk had fallen, and she lit the lamp on the desk. With the burst of yellow flame came the oily smell of kerosene. She turned the key to raise the wick. "The day she was caught, your mother was her jenny at the shop—"

"*My mother?*"

"Yes. Why?" Her expression was curious.

I swallowed down the sudden thickness in my throat. "Ma never told me one of her jennies had been caught."

"Well, I imagine she hated thinking on it, yeah?"

A chill ran down my nerves as I recalled the way Maggie's gaze had fixed on me. Had she known who I was? I resembled my mother, to be sure. Did Maggie blame Ma for her arrest? I could easily imagine my mother turning on her jenny if it served her.

"My mother got away," I said, my voice wary.

"O' course." Amelia turned up a palm. "Maggie would've made sure of that. Annie ran all the way here to tell Patty, who raced off in a cab, but it was too late. Maggie was already in gaol, and she was tried before Patty could do anything to change the verdict. Back then, they put women thieves on a prison ship quick as they could." With the oil warmed, the lamplight flared up the glass chimney, and Amelia lowered the wick. "The important thing is, she's back and I want you to get on with her. It'll be for the best. All right?"

I swallowed. "It won't be the same without you."

"No. And you don't like change."

It felt like an accusation, and I crossed my arms over my chest. "No one does."

"You more than most."

"Because in my experience, when things change, they get worse." It came out snappish.

Pain flickered in her eyes. "Well, this will be a change for all of us."

Her most of all.

Ashamed of my own whining, I reached across the desk by way of apology. "We're all loyal to you. Let us know where you are. We can visit."

"I know." Amelia touched her fingertips briefly to the back of my hand. "Remember, Kit, not a word to the others. Not even Mary or Sarah, yeah? I want to tell everyone at once, myself."

"I promise."

Slowly I started downstairs, considering. Parts of Amelia's explanation rang true. It was Maggie's mother's ring. She had every right to return and claim it. Still, there was something in Amelia's demeanor that was at odds with her words. The edges didn't align neatly. They puckered as I tried to fit them together.

I couldn't help worrying that Maggie's arrival would cause trouble, and not just for the ring. Amelia didn't seem to suspect my mother of betraying Maggie, but she didn't know Ma the way I did. Ma might've felt jealous of Maggie, or wanted to save herself, or perhaps she'd seen something to be gained. If Maggie had discovered my mother tagged her in the shop or turned Queen's evidence, wouldn't Maggie take it out on me?

That was one trouble. The other was I would miss Amelia terribly. The thought of her leaving trenched up an old sadness that billowed like a stretch of fabric thrown wide. I paused on the landing to fold it back down into something small enough to cram in a pocket as I left the inn and made my way into the busy street.

Chapter 8

The following day, Wednesday, wasn't my day for thieving, and I went to Emma's shop. As I entered, she handed me a folded note. "From James."

My heart hammering, I opened it. *No mention*.

I crossed the room to the stove and put the note in to burn, feeling a small softening of my hard fear. Still, how could I find comfort in the absence of a sign?

Emma's eyes were bright with curiosity, but she said not a word except, "Start with the napkins, would you? Then the shirts," and I took my usual chair and began the delicate task of embroidering *L*s on the linen. Emma stood before a mannequin, fitting the white satin bodice of a wedding gown, pulling pins from the felt wrapper on her arm.

Not for the first time, I wondered why Emma had never married. She was pretty, with a wry, pleasant humor. Her eyes were the same warm hazel as James's, her jaw a more delicate version of his angular one, and her hair a rich chestnut brown, scraped into a tight coil to keep it out of the stitches.

The napkins finished, I began on the gentleman's shirts, whipping the thread over the raw buttonhole edges, double at the ends. Meanwhile, Emma had moved to the sewing machine. She pumped the treadle, working the needle at a reckless pace and bringing to mind what James had said about the Custom House being like a runaway train.

At last, the machine paused. Emma snipped the threads with tiny silver scissors, shook out the bodice, and laid it on the worktable. "There, all ready for Miss Parker tomorrow."

"Did you leave extra at the seams?" I asked, remembering that Miss Parker's waistline sometimes expanded with the state of her appetite—"delicate, very delicate," she insisted—and once Emma had to recut a bodice at her own expense.

Emma grinned. "O' course."

The bells of the tabernacle clanged six as she turned the sign on the door to CLOSED and clicked the bolt on the door. "Thanks, Kit. I'd never have managed if you hadn't helped. Will you stay for tea? I know it's late, but I made stew."

It was the first time she'd invited me to eat with her, and it would have been rude to refuse. Even as I thanked her, my stomach rumbled, reminding me I hadn't eaten since breakfast. Her face betrayed nothing, but I sensed she wanted to discuss something; I hoped it wasn't James or the note he'd left me. I followed Emma back to the small kitchen, a whitewashed galley, neat as her thread box, the corner stove squat and well blacked, the single brass tap dripless, the sturdy wooden table no wider than three planks but polished and clean. I wondered if James had built it for her. She donned an apron, wrapping the ties around her slender waist to knot them in front. I sat at the table with a cup of tea while she stirred the simmering copper pot on the stove. My mouth watered as the flavor carried, and she served me a generous bowl before filling her own and sitting diagonal from me. She cut a piece of bread from the loaf and pushed the plate to me so I could do the same.

I put the first spoonful in my mouth and didn't want to

swallow it was so good. Real lamb, potatoes, and some spice that gave it sweetness.

"Fresh lamb from the butcher," she said.

"It's lovely," I said. "I'm trying not to gobble it."

She let out a small laugh and let me eat. My bowl was mostly empty when she pushed away hers, and I felt the air shift and looked up. In the lamplight, I saw the skin around her eyes crease, the double furrow between her brows.

My pulse quickened. Here it was.

"I wanted to talk to you 'bout Amelia," Emma said.

I swallowed the last bite of bread and set down my own spoon. I shouldn't have been surprised. Despite the difference in their ages, Emma and Amelia had been friends for years.

Emma touched her apron to her mouth's corners. "I know she told you she was letting go o' the ring."

"She told you why?"

"About Maggie? Aye." Emma rested her sleeved forearms on the table. "I know you're loyal to Amelia, but the best way you can show that now is to make it easy for Maggie. Don't fight it."

I squirmed inwardly at the thought of them talking about me as if I were a stubborn child, digging in my heels against the change. "I told her I wouldn't. And Amelia seems not to mind much, so I suppose I shouldn't, either."

Emma blinked, and the corners of her mouth tucked in like a bodice dart.

"Does she mind more than she's showing?" I asked.

"God's sake, Kit. What d'you think?" She rose from the table with an impatient movement, taking our bowls to the sink.

I felt ashamed that I'd asked. My mother's feelings had

always burst out of her, but Amelia muted hers. It soothed my own unhappy feelings some to know Amelia shared them, at least in part.

Emma turned back toward me, setting her hips against the sink, her arms crossed. "The others'll have questions. 'Twould help if you could answer them."

"I'm sure Amelia will explain herself."

"She will, but you know how rumors start. People will make guesses about what she *doesn't* say. After she's gone, just stick to Amelia's story, a' right?"

That caught me up.

"*Is* it a story?" I asked. "Because if there's—"

"I'm asking you not to ask," she said, her voice rising over mine. "If you care about Amelia like you say, don't fuss."

I sat back. "If you're trying to make me less curious, it's not working."

Her hands dropped to her sides and curled over the chipped white enamel at the sink's edge. "God's sake, Kit! Can you just trust me that Amelia's doing the best she can for everyone, including you? I know you have questions. But keep 'em to yourself and . . . eventually Amelia may be able to tell you everything."

"Do *you* know everything?"

"I know enough," she said soberly.

The look on her face ran a shiver down me. "Is she safe?"

"She'll be fine."

I wasn't wholly reassured.

"Believe me, I don't want her to go, either," Emma added.

You're losing a friend, I thought.

"You can tell her I'll do what I can to help smooth things along," I said.

Emma's eyebrows rose in warning. "She doesn't know I'm talking to you."

"And I won't tell her you did," I said. "But if she asks."

"Thanks." She reached for the brass tap, twisting it until water burst forth then slowed.

I stood and came to her side. "Is there anything else?"

She met my gaze and held it. There *was* more, but she only said, "No, no. That's all."

I nodded. "Thanks for tea."

"Wait." She dried her hands on her apron, went to the wooden box where she kept money, and counted out fourteen shillings for two days' work.

For the first time, I felt uncomfortable accepting it. When she saw my hesitation, she took my hand and folded my fingers over the coins and spoke with the forthrightness I liked about her. "Whether you're keeping company with James, and if I share my tea once in a while, it doesn't change anything. I'm still paying you for your work. And come on Monday 'nless you hear from me. I'm expecting cloth at the warehouse."

I bid her goodnight, dropped the coins into my pocket, fetched my coat from the cupboard in the shop, and headed toward my room. As I crossed the cobbled square, my mind dwelled on what Emma had said and what I hadn't thought to ask. Emma had never thieved, but their mother, Adelaide, had been a thief with my mother, Amelia, and Maggie. Had Adelaide ever told Emma about Maggie? Did Emma know about the day Maggie was caught?

One thing was clear: It mattered to Maggie that we thieves didn't cause difficulties. What might she do, if we did?

Chapter 9

The next evening, Amelia gathered all of us thieves—minus Josie—together in the goods room. From the taproom below came the sounds of evening supper and the beginnings of card games. Some of us perched on the long table where we laid our dresses for emptying, others sat on the benches where we relaced our boots, and I leaned between Fanny and Mary against the wall near the costume alcove. But we all faced Amelia, who stood beside her desk, her fingertips brushing its wood surface. Did I imagine it, or did she long to keep them there, to touch her desk, until the very last possible moment? The thought twisted at something inside my chest, pinched my breath.

I surveyed the room. Most faces wore an expression of wariness, for no one but us thieves ever came in here, and half a step to Amelia's right stood Maggie, with that air—again—of belonging. She was dressed in a gown that was fashionably cut but of a medium blue that wouldn't stand out in a crowd, her dark hair in a neat chignon, her hands quiet at her sides.

Amelia began, "I know this will come as a surprise to all of you."

She did not even cast a glance in my direction, but I heard the reminder to guard my expression.

"As most o' you know, I've always meant to step down

eventually. And now is the right time." Amid some shallow gasps, she gestured to her right. "This is Maggie Wirth O'Connell, Patty Wirth's daughter. After twenty years away, she's come home. The ring is hers by birthright, so she'll be leading you now." She turned her head slowly, meeting our eyes, one by one. "I'm asking you all to do your best for her."

A quick glance around the room confirmed that I was the only one who knew of this announcement beforehand. Every face showed shock and dismay verging on rudeness toward Maggie.

Maggie took it in but seemed undisturbed. Amelia opened her mouth to continue, but Maggie stepped forward, clasping her hands at her waist, the injured one wrapped around the other.

"O' course you're surprised," she said.

It was her voice I noticed first, low and musical, and I recalled she'd sung on stage. But it was Maggie's intonation that caught my ear. The raspy Southwark consonants, the vowels throaty.

She took one more step forward, one that made her skirts sway gracefully. "And why should you trust me, a stranger steppin' in for Amelia. Like as not, I wouldn't, either." Maggie's frankness was disarming, and a few muttered in agreement. A smile tugged at her mouth, and her entire expression and demeanor altered. "But while I can't replace Amelia in your hearts, I hope I'll prove to you over the next weeks that I can lead this ring."

We all gaped, for now her consonants were clear and clipped, her vowels pure. Even the way Maggie held her shoulders and hands and the very tilt of her chin were no longer those of a woman from Southwark; they belonged to a lady from the West End.

Maggie hadn't only been a chanteuse, I reminded myself. She'd been an actress too, a mimic. This was her small performance for us, a transformation to show us her abilities. Amelia's face showed no surprise, and it occurred to me that whatever Amelia had taught me about speaking like a proper lady had come from Maggie first.

Maggie relapsed into her natural manner. "No doubt you're wonderin' where I've been these twenty years. I got copped for thieving and sent to Swan River. I was lucky to escape with only this," she said, raising her injured hand. "When they finally cut me loose, I came back. I haven't much left here, to be sure. My ma's dead, and my brother's run off, and some of the best friends I had are gone. But this is my home, and . . . if you do right by me, I'll do right by you." She scanned the room, letting her eyes move from face to face. "I'm not planning on changing much. No reason to, with the ring doin' so well."

The tension was already beginning to ease from people's faces, replaced by curiosity.

Maggie continued to speak about how she would be spending the next fortnight jennying for each of us, learning about the shops and our methods, though she'd been going over the books with Amelia, and she was acquainting herself with our dodges and takes. She spoke well, pleasantly even, and people attended her words, their faces telling me that they were each working out what this change meant for them.

My eyes slid to Amelia. Her blank expression sent worry knifing through me. I'd have been more reassured by resentment or concern or acceptance.

Her eyes caught mine and narrowed, flicking to Maggie and back to me. Telling me to pay attention, or at least make a show of doing it. I shifted my gaze to Maggie and kept it there, but I longed for one last quiet minute with Amelia to ask her—Maggie's charm notwithstanding—what was really happening here.

Maggie asked us all to give our names, with surnames, and we went from one side of the room to the other. When it was my turn, I said mine. She studied me for a moment before moving on to Fanny, to my right, and I wondered if Maggie had worked out who my mother was, and what that meant to her.

When there was nothing more to be said, Maggie let Amelia dismiss us, but she stood by the door saying goodbye to each of us by name. It was a clever trick; I couldn't have done it myself, as names never fixed themselves in my head the way faces did. I had hoped that Maggie might leave so I could speak to Amelia, but clearly Maggie intended to forestall that. I was the last to go, and she touched my arm to stop me. "Kit Jimeson, you said?"

I nodded.

"You look like someone I knew. Annie Avery. You aren't by chance related?"

"She was my mother."

"Ah." Her face brightened with the satisfaction of a correct guess. "How is she?"

"I'm afraid she died several years ago, ma'am."

"Oh." Her face fell. "A shame. She was kind."

My ma? Kind?

"Is it only you then?" she asked. "No siblings?"

"I have a younger sister, Sarah. She's out in service."

"Ah." She laid her good hand on my arm, briefly. "Well, I'm sure it was a comfort to your ma to have you both."

True about Sarah perhaps, but hardly so for me, I thought, but I merely nodded and said goodbye.

The door to the goods room closed behind me, and I paused on the step. I could have sworn Maggie waited by the door to hear my footsteps on the stairs, so I left, planning to see Amelia privately as soon as I could.

Perhaps I was being too suspicious, perceiving Maggie's frankness as a ploy to earn our trust; her story about Swan River and her injured hand as tactics to soften us toward her; her regret over my mother's death and interest in Sarah as attempts to get round me. Then again, Amelia was right; I didn't like change, and I didn't trust strangers who brought it.

Chapter 10

In the following days, Amelia continued to be present in the goods room as Maggie took each thief out to watch her work. This had tugged at the nerves of some, and two of the younger ones, Cathy and Ann, had returned with a subdued air. When I asked Cathy about it, she admitted she'd been bolder than usual to impress Maggie, who had taken her to task for carelessness. I was determined to thieve as I always did and not allow her to rattle me.

My nerves were being rattled badly enough by learning that Billy and Tommy had left Elephant and Castle. Were they lying low somewhere? Was this ordinary caution, or did they believe there was a heightened risk because Sarah had seen them? Or—God forbid—were they in Mayfair, looking to intercept Sarah as she ran an errand?

I was scheduled to go out with Maggie on Wednesday afternoon, Amelia's last day. Mr. Ardle had asked me to come extra, as he had a good deal of work, so I spent the morning fixing loose prongs in two necklaces and a ring and repairing the hinges and handles on two jewelry boxes. Afterward, I went to the costume room, changed into a thieving dress, and found Maggie in the goods room. "Ready?" she asked, and I followed her downstairs.

When we reached the street, she said, "Let's not walk." I

assumed we'd take one of the omnibuses that crossed the river, but she led me to the railway station, where the cab stand was lined with hansoms. She approached, spoke to the driver, and climbed in; I followed, taking a seat beside her as the driver climbed onto his box, above and behind us. The closeness of the space, the way our skirts couldn't help but meet, suggested an intimacy at odds with how I was feeling, but I did my best to arrange my face and hands into an attitude that was amiable.

"I find it's easier to talk in a cab, where we won't be overheard," she said. "I've been enjoying meeting all the girls."

"I appreciate riding," I said.

"Good." She smiled and settled her skirts. "When did you start with Amelia?" she asked with a warm interest.

So she wanted my history. *Well, all's fair*, I thought. I was certainly curious about hers. For now, I wouldn't tell her that I knew my mother had been her jenny the day she was caught. I wanted to hear that story from her, without her knowing that I knew, and this was my opportunity to build some trust. I'd lose nothing by telling her how I came to thieving.

"You said you knew my mother," I began.

She nodded. "I did."

"She died when I wasn't yet fifteen."

"Leaving you with Sarah to support," she said.

Maggie had a good memory.

I nodded. "Ma had apprenticed me to a seamstress when I was ten, but that didn't bring in near enough, and I was too young to start thieving. I didn't look old enough to go to the shops. But Amelia suggested I could run a badger scheme, so my friend James and I did that for a while."

"James Kinnon," she said.

I nodded, increasingly aware that she knew a good deal

about me, and—moreover—she wanted me to know she did. *Clever*, I thought. It was a good way to caution me not to try to keep secrets from her.

"James was working for smugglers on the river, and one night he was caught and put in prison, which put an end to that. But by this time, I was old enough to thieve, and Amelia trained me up herself. I was her jenny for a few weeks and then I was ready to try."

"What was your first shop?"

"A dry goods store in Bond Street," I said. I couldn't recall the name, but the storefront appeared like a picture in my mind. "It had a large plate glass window, a wood-framed door to the left with a diamond-shaped mottled glass pane, two locks, no bell above the door. Inside, on three sides of the room, there were tall wooden cabinets with glass fronts and shelves. I took seven yards of lace and a pair of gloves." My mouth curved at the memory. "And the clerk's pocket watch."

Maggie's eyebrows rose, and her lips twitched in amusement.

"You know how men can be," I said. "He was rubbing up against me, touching my arm. That watch was begging to be nicked." I still remembered the sight of it, the chain within inches of my fingers as he leaned in to murmur in my ear how pretty I was. His breath had smelled of onions. "When Amelia and I met on the bridge on the way home, I showed it to her. She scolded me for the risk but couldn't help laughing. She said it earned me extra, but I should consider myself lucky and not to do it again. The extra from that watch bought Sarah and me new shoes and the first meat we'd had in months."

"You said Sarah was out in service. What does she do?"

"She works as a scullery maid up this way." I cast my eyes in the direction we were traveling.

"She won't thieve?"

"She has a birthmark, here," I said, touching my forefinger to my temple. "Makes her too noticeable. Besides, I don't want her to."

"Ah." Maggie seemed to put that together with another thought. "A birthmark *would* make it difficult." She raised her right hand, turning it over in midair, as if she were inspecting it as well as inviting me to. It almost gave me the feeling she'd steered the conversation toward Sarah so she could broach this. "I can't thieve anymore with this. Too noticeable, but also, my fingers don't work as well."

She was begging the question, so I gave it to her. "What happened?"

"What do you know of Swan River?"

"Nothing, other than it's a penal colony in Australia. Seems a strange name for the place. Makes me think of the swans in St. James's."

She snorted. "It's not St. James's."

"I can imagine."

"No, you can't," she replied, but not as sharply as she could have.

"No, I suppose not," I acknowledged. "Although when I was a child, I saw the hulks in the Thames once. I watched prisoners being loaded on. Only men, though."

"They don't mix us together, thank the lord, or every woman in the ship would have been up the pole by the time we landed," she said drily, her hand sketching a bump over her belly. "As it was, half a dozen were, thanks to the crew."

"Was it very dreadful?"

"Hellish, from the first day of the journey," she replied. "Imagine a hundred of us in a dark hold, drinking fetid water and surviving on stale bread and moldy cheese, pissing in a bucket that turned over when the seas were rough." She drew a breath as if grateful for this air, fresh by comparison. "When we finally got off the ship, we could barely walk. All of us, filthy and stumbling into each other, trying to find our land legs. We were taken to the market square and displayed. I can't imagine we were much to look at, but still the men picked and quarreled over us. I was one of the prettier ones, so I was picked early, by a man whose wife had died the previous year. He'd murdered her when he found her trying to run off. I didn't know that then, of course. That was actually his second wife. His first wife had died in childbirth. His name was Turner, and he was a drunk and cruel, and I worked from sunrise to sundown, washing, cooking, cleaning, and minding his children." Her voice was curiously flat.

The cab jolted over a rut in the cobbles.

"You survived," I said.

"Nearly not. Have you ever been buried alive?" she asked, almost idly.

I started. "No."

"One day, when Turner was in the barn, I had a knife with me, brought from the kitchen. I took it out, thinking to stab him in the neck. The man knew somehow, and he was quick as a snake. He grabbed it from me and flung it away." Her eyes flicked to me. "That's all he did at first, it being daytime, but that night, he dragged me out of my bed by the hair and pulled me out of doors. I struggled, which is when he broke my fingers. Then he threw me in a ditch at the edge of one of his fields and covered me with dirt and rocks."

My throat scratched with sudden dryness.

"The next morning, he dug me up. I'd stayed alive by clawing away enough dirt to breathe, but I couldn't shift the stones. He said that if I had died, he'd have left me there, in that grave. Then he dragged me to his house and put my hand on the stove. He did it because my broken fingers would mend, and he wanted me to always have a reminder that he held the upper hand."

Maggie's voice slowed over the last words, and she turned to look out the window. I wondered if she'd told this same horrifying story to the others, while traveling to their mark for the day. But I had been listening carefully, and I would swear the pain in her voice was genuine. Then again, perhaps she could tell that story a hundred times and the pain would still carve as deep.

I shivered at the thought of being buried alive, of leaving Sarah utterly alone, not knowing what had become of me, or having to identify my body when it was eventually found—

"I wouldn't trade that night, though," Maggie said, turning back to me. "Because I touched death, and I learned something important. The dead can truly see what happens here on earth after they're gone, like a play on a stage."

I stared. That was an odd fancy, to be sure.

"You don't have to believe me," she said, "but some of what I envisioned that night has come true already. It's as if I'd lived a full life instead of only a third of one, and was given all the wisdom of it, in that instant."

The cab drew to a halt, and there was no opportunity for me to probe what wisdom she'd been given—not, perhaps, that I wished to, for there was a darkness to her life that made me draw back from any truth she'd discovered. As the driver slowed the horses, I found myself of two minds. My initial wariness hadn't vanished, certainly; but though Maggie may have taken the ring unfairly from Amelia, if this story was true, she was a victim as well.

It wasn't until I was climbing out of the cab that it occurred to me to wonder how Maggie had escaped from this man.

We walked down Burnham Street, and Maggie paused in front of an apothecary. "Not this shop," she said quietly. "The one across the street."

I used the apothecary's plate glass storefront as a mirror to observe it. A sundry shop, with a large front window, a paneled front door, a shining brass bell above. "May I go in first?"

"If you like."

"Give me two full minutes before you enter. When I come out, I'll follow this street west and turn south at the corner to meet you. I'll turn my cloak if I'm being followed."

She laid her hand on the apothecary's doorknob. "Very well. I'll stop in here."

I waited until two carriages and two gentlemen on horseback had passed, then picked up my skirts and walked across the street to stand in front of the chandler's window to the right of the shop. I fingered the reticule I'd brought, as if I anticipated making a purchase of candles, all the while surveying the shop immediately to the left. It took less than ninety seconds to glean what I needed.

I entered the busy shop, followed shortly after by Maggie, and after achieving my aim, I left, turned west and then south, slowing my step on that street. I hadn't bothered turning my cloak. Maggie caught up with me a few minutes afterward, greeting me with an approving smile and looping her hand through my elbow as if we were old acquaintances. "You're even better than I was told. I watched you in the mirror across from the glove cabinet, and I didn't see it."

"Most of what I took wasn't from the cabinet," I said.

That surprised her.

"It was an easy mark," I said.

"Have you been to that shop before?"

"No."

"Then tell me why."

It was a test of sorts, I understood that. "There's a large front window, with a full display that must be taken down and put back up each day, or the star-glazers would steal everything at night. To save time, the shop owners don't pin everything down but merely set it in place on the stands and shelves, with the lace folded or in coils, the ribbons hung from hooks. There's a shiny bell over the door that rings when a customer enters. I slipped in when a customer left, so it didn't ring for me; but *you* rang it when you entered, and the clerk's eyes went to the door just for a moment while I slipped my hand inside the front window case." We halted at the corner to let two carriages pass. "Then, while you went to the cabinet on the other side, I went over to the cabinet to look at gloves because there was a second customer there. Between the two of us, the clerk pulled out six sets, one of which is now in my pocket."

She laughed. "I watched your face the entire time. You look bored, even dim-witted. Do you not feel your nerves?"

"Of course I do. But Amelia taught me early on to spend time in front of a looking glass, to see how emotion flickers across. She taught me to keep the sparkle out of my eyes, and the triumph off my mouth, until we reached the goods room. Then we could gloat a bit."

"Remarkable," she said. "Like an actress in a play, earning money by arranging your face."

I felt the pull of her hint, strong as an outright question.

Suddenly I understood. She'd never believe I hadn't heard of her stage career; if I didn't say something now, she'd know I was deceiving her. And in that split second, I chose. "Amelia told me you were an actress once. That you sing beautifully."

"Aye." A flicker of warmth lit her eyes, and the faint tension I'd felt in the hand resting on my arm eased.

I'd said the right thing, and I felt relieved enough to make a joke. "Well, a shop is like a proper stage, I suppose. Only we steal the props."

She chuckled at that. "Well, I may have a special dodge I'll be putting together. I'll certainly keep you in mind."

That prickled the back of my neck, but I thanked her, and the moment seemed right to ask: "How were you caught thieving?"

She gave a sideways look and stepped around a pile of horse shite on the cobbles. "Not much to tell. I was nicking a bracelet at a jewelry shop in Clerkenwell. They called the constable and I was taken away, tried, and put on the ship within two days. The sentencing judge doubled the usual sentence for me having 'dangerously clever hands.' Those were his very words."

She made no mention of my mother being her jenny.

The distrust that had abated over the afternoon returned.

I might have probed further, but she said, "I understand you work at Mr. Ardle's shop sometimes."

We stepped onto the pavement at Fleet Street. "Yes."

"He's one of the friends I was glad to find still here."

They were friends? That surprised me. The more I saw of Maggie, the more I could imagine her as a girl—bright-eyed, quick-witted, with a ready laugh. I imagined she wouldn't have given him the time of day.

Suddenly I suspected why Mr. Ardle looked sprightlier a few days ago.

"Did he admire you?" I asked.

"Oh." She gave a deprecating shrug. "For a time."

Likely he worshipped you, I thought.

"Have you stopped by his shop?" I asked. "Let him know you've returned?"

She stepped over a crack in the pavement, wide enough to catch a heel. "Last week," she said. "He's the same as he ever was." There was a note of satisfaction in her voice.

A woman like Maggie knew her own power to draw a man in. Indeed, Maggie had made efforts to charm me this afternoon—confiding about her past, showing an interest in mine, chuckling at my quips, praising my abilities. I could readily imagine how Mr. Ardle would feel, seeing the sparkle of delight in Maggie's eyes at their meeting, hearing her laugh at a jest he attempted, absorbing the pleasant interest in her voice. She would know how to wrap him around her finger as easily as thread around a spool. But to what purpose? I'd be sorry to think she stirred his hopes, only to take advantage of him.

As for myself, I wondered the same. What was Maggie's intention toward me? Did she merely want to secure my continued presence in the ring? Or to draw me into her special dodge? And had Maggie's story of the horrors in Swan River been true? Every instinct I had told me it was genuine, but it had also seemed deployed with a purpose.

We neared Elephant and Castle, and I found myself thinking that Maggie's intentions were rather like my money stash—the small purse a decoy for the larger one. Part of me admired her for surviving, but she wanted something more than ordinary thieving from me. I could feel it.

Chapter 11

When Maggie and I arrived in the goods room, none of the others had yet returned. Nell helped me change into my usual clothes, I emptied the thieving pockets, and Amelia recorded my poke, keeping her eyes on the ledger as I leaned over and initialed the margins. Today was Amelia's last day here. I longed to ask her where she would go and what her plans were, but there was no chance. Leaving the three women together, I headed downstairs to the taproom. I made my way through the crowd to the bar, where I asked Pat for a glass of ale.

For this past week I had kept my qualms about Maggie to myself, for it seemed I was the only one who felt them. In the taproom and in our rooms, where we could have quiet conversations among ourselves, it seemed people were relieved, as Cathy said, that Maggie wasn't changing the ring a whit. Bea reported that Maggie was full of praise and admiration for our cleverness, and with one week gone, it seemed all would be well.

I might have believed the chatter myself except that I hadn't been able to have a minute alone with Amelia. At first, I thought it was simply because she was busy helping Maggie settle into her new role. But as the week passed, I sensed Amelia was avoiding me—and my questions—which told me something was amiss. With this her last night, I vowed to corner her, and I planted myself by the bar until Amelia appeared and asked for an ale. I maneuvered around old Connors to reach her.

"You're leaving tomorrow, and we haven't had a chance to talk," I said.

She sipped from her pot, one hand on the metal handle, the other cupping the bottom. "I've been busy, Kit, and so have you."

"Have you found a place to live?"

"Not yet. I'll stay with a friend for a time while I look about for rooms."

"Will you send me your address?" I persisted.

"When I know it, of course."

"And what will you do?"

"I haven't decided," she said with a show of patience.

"Amelia." I lowered my voice and rested my hand on her arm. "You're not easy with this. I can tell. Why?"

Her expression softened with affection and something like regret. "It's naught that concerns you, Kit." She drank down her ale, set the pot on the bar. "Take care of yourself and Sarah—and Mary, too." She put her hand to my cheek—her fingers were cold from the ale—then, to my surprise, stepped forward to kiss my forehead, swift and feather light. She murmured, "I'll write soon," and was gone before I could reply.

I might have stood there swallowing ale and my sudden loneliness except that James appeared at my side, curving his arm around my waist with a wide grin, and I felt a stab of surprise and disappointment. Had he forgotten my worry about Sarah? Did he not know about Amelia leaving? I gave him a look that told him I wasn't in the mood for teasing.

"Oh, come on, Kitten," he wheedled. He leaned over, his voice a murmuring singsong close to my ear that would have looked like flirting to anyone looking. "Have a drink with me."

I caught my breath. "Kitten" was our old warning, a signal that the badger scheme was going awry, a sign to retreat. Or that someone was watching, and we needed to slip into character. Mindful that he might have news about Sarah, I fell in with it.

I rolled my eyes in laughing protest. "Aye, fine. Then you're buying."

He grinned in triumph. "Aye, then." He picked up two glasses of ale and lifted one toward an empty table near the loudest group of card players, and I led the way to it. Clearly, he'd chosen this table for cover. I took the chair that put my back to the wall and my face toward the room, so he could speak without anyone seeing his lips.

"So you're only pretending to flirt with me now?" I said, dimpling and looking amused for the benefit of anyone watching.

He plunked the two glasses on the table, sat in the chair opposite, and raised an eyebrow. "I'll flirt with you in earnest as much as you like."

I felt myself flush but held on to my smile. "What is it?"

"Let's play." He drew out a pack of cards and began dealing for rummy. I set a coin on the table, and he matched it. Under cover of the noise from the next table over, he asked, "How's Sarah? What did she say?" He picked from the deck and laid down a seven.

I picked it up, mistrust and trust dragging at me like two warring tides. I made my voice noncommittal. "She's all right."

"*Kit*." His tone made me look up. His eyes were searching, every bit of humor gone. "Do you not trust me for this?"

I wanted to, and it seemed he was trying to be kind.

"I know you wouldn't hurt me or Sarah on purpose," I said. "But you're still tight with the Castle men." I laid down a queen. "And—I know you're still mixed up in something."

He drew back, his expression baffled. "Why would you say that?"

I didn't answer, and he settled a forearm on the table and leaned in. "Why would you say that?"

My eyes darted to his hand where it rested, a loose fist, on the table. "Because you don't get calluses like those from recordkeeping at the Custom House." I reached to pick another card, and he laid his hand on top of mine, wrapping his fingers around.

"It's my turn to draw," he said quietly. "And yes, I do get calluses like this from work. There aren't enough docks at the Custom House, so the ships moor three or four deep in the river, which means I have to row out to count the casks and crates before they offload." Gently, he removed my hand from the deck, picked, and laid down the card. "Jaysus, Kit." His voice was subdued. "Why didn't you ask me? I'd've told you the truth." The bruised look in his eyes was like a hook in my heart.

"I'm sorry," I said, my voice breaking on the words. "But—it's Sarah."

"Yeah, it's *Sarah*," he said pointedly. "You're not the only one who looks out for her, you know."

Remorseful, I said, "She told me you have."

The lines around his mouth softened. "You're not the only one looking out for *you*, either, Kit."

My surprise at the notion held me utterly silent, and after

a moment, he gave a small shake of his head and his gaze dropped to the cards. "It's your turn."

I picked from the pile, holding the card long enough to consider my words before I played it and said under my breath, "She says there were two Castle men in Mayfair that night, and the moment she saw them she ducked out of the light and hid her face."

"I heard it was Billy and Tommy, but still no one's mentioned her," he said.

The hard rock of worry inside me softened.

"Is that who she saw?" he asked.

I nodded.

"They're lying low in Bermondsey."

Relieved at the thought of them far from Mayfair, I grinned for the benefit of whoever was watching. Still, I'd join the group around the fire before I left, to see if any of the Castle men acted strange around me.

"There's something else." James leaned both elbows onto the table, holding the cards in a fan before him to half cover his mouth. "What do you know about Maggie?"

My nerves twanged. "She was sent to Swan River for stealing a bracelet twenty years back, was married to a monster, and came back quick as she could. She's shrewd and clever, and a good actress. I don't much trust her. Why?"

"Don't show surprise." He laid down a seven.

I gave him a look. "You know I'm collecting sevens. You're helping me win."

"Yeah, I'm bloody trying, Kit." The look he gave me was half humorous exasperation and half such kindness it tipped my heart sideways. I wasn't used to having someone trying to take some of the worry off me.

"Thanks," I said quietly. I took up the seven and laid down a nine.

"Emma's wondering if Maggie's here for more than just taking over the ring." He picked up the nine and played a knave. "She might be here to even scores."

A sudden coldness slid along my veins at the thought of Maggie, artful, resourceful, and clever, coming back here for that. "What sort of scores?"

"Emma said she heard there was bad blood between Maggie and her jenny," he said, "over a man they both liked."

Despite myself, my hand halted on the way to the deck, sudden as if someone had grabbed my wrist.

"We're just playing cards," James reminded me softly.

I picked.

But I couldn't even read the card in my hand while the pieces were fitting together in my head.

The idea that my ma had betrayed Maggie to steal a man's attentions was easy to believe. What if Maggie came back bent on revenge against my mother? Would she now take it out on me?

My voice shook as I tucked the card into my hand. "My ma was Maggie's jenny the day she was caught. Amelia told me."

"Jaysus, Kit." James's voice rasped, and he reached a hand to his glass, taking it up for a sip.

"The very first time I saw Maggie here," I said, "she stared like she recognized me."

"Because you look like your ma."

I nodded. "And ever since then, she's made a point to be friendly. Asking about Sarah, praising me for being clever, even saying my ma was kind to her."

James had known my mother, so he understood how unlikely that was. "You think she's trying to get round you."

"Of course. The day Maggie took me out thieving, I asked her about being caught. She told me the bare facts—but she never mentioned my mother was her jenny. It would be a natural thing to tell me, wouldn't it?"

"Sounds like she was hiding it." He took up the three and discarded a king. "But your ma's beyond her reach, and she can't blame you for what she did."

I picked a card from the pile. "Maggie believes the dead can see what happens on earth. What if she thinks my ma can see her hurting me?"

James's eyebrows rose. "She said that? That the dead can see things?"

"Yes." I laid down a six, my blood running cold again as I recalled how earnest Maggie had looked. And now I had a good idea why she'd said it to me.

Shouts of laughter from the group by the fire made us both look over. Caleb was juggling three raw potatoes, with Sid standing nearby, ready to pitch him two more.

James scanned his cards. "If she's as clever as you say, Maggie'll keep how she feels about your ma and you separate." He paused. "You're also the best thief she has. My guess is she knows it."

"I hope so." I didn't mention the special dodge Maggie said she might have for me. I didn't need James to warn me against it; I was doubly wary now, plenty for both of us.

James laid a card face down. "Three." He laid down his melds and set the three of clubs to the side with his usual grin, reminding me to keep up the pretense of our game.

"Two," I said, laying down my own cards and sitting back with a satisfied look.

"Ach, Kit, how do you do that?" he grumbled in protest,

his head bowed over the table as he swept up the cards. His voice was low. "God's sake, just be careful. I don't want you or Sarah hurt."

When he looked up, I raised my glass toward him. "Thanks."

He pushed the deck across the table. "Your deal."

Before I left the taproom that night, I edged into the circle of thieves by the hearth, the fire crackling and spitting with the damp descending the chimney. Cathy stepped back to include me, and I joined the general laughter, listening to Caleb's story about having stolen a horse from a gentleman's carriage house for a ride. Jake and Nick—Billy and Tommy's best mates—were there, and my every nerve was attuned to their responses to me, to stories, to everything. As usual, they paid me absolutely no attention at all, but I couldn't measure if they were avoiding my gaze or careless of my presence. After half an hour, sipping my ale slowly so it wouldn't soften my mind, I left the circle, unable to reassure myself that Sarah was safe.

James, standing at the bar, caught my eye. He read my look and gave the barest nod—not even the usual small lift of his chin, more just his eyes lowering and returning to mine. He'd keep an ear to the ground.

That night, awake in my room with Mary asleep nearby, her breath barely audible, I stared into the darkness, picturing the day Maggie was caught.

Ma tagging Maggie, somehow drawing attention to her so the jeweler knew to summon the constable. Knowing if Maggie was caught and sentenced, she'd have at least seven years to get her hooks into whatever man stood between them.

This was all supposition, but knowing what I did of my ma, I could see it.

My feelings toward Ma were so tangled, they were like knots on badly done embroidery. Try to take them out, and you'd rip the cloth for good. My mother had told me many times how selfish I was, that I'd driven her to drink, and toward the end, that the silver lining in her dying was she'd never have to see me again.

Afterward, I told myself that Ma didn't wholly mean it, that she was ill, her heart rotten with gin. She drank to submerge the fear we both lived and breathed and slept and for Sarah's sake tried to pretend wasn't there, that we'd lose our two small rooms, that we'd starve on the street. It tore at my ma the same way it tore at me. In this we were the same.

But it gave me little pleasure to think of my mother, as most of my memories were not happy ones. Entering our rooms to find her snoring by the stove, a half-empty bottle standing upright on the floor, for even drunk, she'd be careful not to spill it. Waking to the scrape of our door to hear her giggling, taking a man to her bed, just on the other side of a hung curtain. Turning over in our bed to see Sarah's eyes open, shining in the light coming between the broken shutters. "I don't like it," Sarah would whimper. I'd hush her, and she'd roll toward me, her hands covering her ears, one side of her face pressed against the bed, while I covered her other hand with my own.

My mother didn't have friends the way other women did. The first time I went over to my friend Livvy's house, her ma and her friends were laughing together over their cups at their corner table. The sight made me stare, and when Livvy asked what was the matter, I made no reply. But that afternoon altered the way I saw my family, trenching my heart with an uncomfortable sense of difference. Later, I realized that Ma didn't trust other women, though she never said why. Now, I suspected that if she'd done this terrible thing to Maggie, she might imagine every woman capable of the same.

Restless, I turned from one side to the other, yanking the quilt.

As for James, his recent seriousness and kindness surprised me not a little. At the Silver Plover and again tonight, his manner had revealed genuine concern, even real affection. He said he didn't want to see Sarah or me hurt, and I believed him, for what other reason could he have for warning me about Maggie?

I thought of how James had taken every precaution against anyone in the taproom knowing what we were saying. Likely he'd become more cautious and less trusting because of his time in prison. I could understand how that would change someone.

But James had served less than a year. Maggie had served many times that amount, in brutal and cruel conditions.

God only knew how it had changed her.

Chapter 12

For the next few days, with James's warning fresh in my mind, I studied Maggie to see if she treated me any differently than the others, but I saw no sign of rancor. She seemed to be unfailingly agreeable. She looked approvingly over Nell's shoulder at the record book; she continued jennying with different thieves; and she seemed to have no favorites, which would have been a certain way of instilling ill will. But it was early days yet.

On Saturday morning, with Sarah due that night, I wondered if she would come home—if she would be afraid to, for fear of seeing Billy or Tommy. I'd written a discreet note to tell her they were no longer here, but perhaps she worried they might have returned. As I worked at Mr. Ardle's shop that morning, fixing and mending, my mind turned over what I knew, what I surmised, and the worst I could possibly imagine. It was not an exercise conducive to soothing my nerves. Still, I emptied the tray of jewelry and watches before I headed to the inn.

Maggie was taking Mary out, so she'd paired Fanny and me for the afternoon dodge, assigning us Hunt and Roskell on Mortimer, away from the West End.

Fanny and I started out, but a few blocks from Elephant

and Castle, she looped her hand through my arm to slow my steps and halted us on the bridge. "I've been wanting to talk to you," Fanny said. Her round face, usually cheerful, was anxious. I understood why she'd stopped here, despite the wind and the chipped green railing covered in bird droppings. The noise from the passing boats and ships meant no passersby would hear us.

Her light blue coat flapped open, and a spiral of Fanny's red hair came loose from its pin.

"Here, let me fix it," I said, and fastened the curl back in place. "What's the matter?"

The sudden blare of a ship drew Fanny's brown eyes to the river. "I went to see my mum last Sunday."

"She's still living in Erith?" I asked. Fanny's mother, June, had been a thief under Patty Wirth and now spent her days in this small town well east of London, famous for its marshes and as a place where the steamships docked to let the shilling trippers off to picnic.

Fanny turned toward me. "I wanted to ask her about Maggie."

My heart gave a thump. "Why?"

She sniffed and folded her arms across her plump chest. "I know *you* don't believe in the tarot, but I laid out cards the day I went thieving with Maggie, and there were all sorts of bad signs. The Devil and the Tower, both."

"Did the dodge go badly?"

"Oh, it went fine," she said, her brown eyes wide. "But the cards told me it was Maggie being deceptive and dangerous, in ways we don't know yet."

In this case, the cards likely aren't wrong, I thought.

"Maggie asked if my mother was still here," Fanny said,

"and I didn't want her to know, so I pretended I thought she meant London proper and said no."

"You don't trust her."

"Do you? No matter what Amelia says, I don't think she'd have let the ring go unless Maggie snaked it from her somehow. If Amelia told anybody, I thought it would be you."

"She didn't." Fanny's face fell with disappointment at my answer, and I asked, "What did your mother say?"

Fanny turned to put the breeze to her back, and it pulled the same corkscrew of red hair loose, blowing it around her face. "Mum said the police knew something that doubled her sentence. About a snooze Maggie did at a fancy hotel, going into the rooms. It was one of the biggest pokes of the year. Might be the police were only looking for someone to pin it on, but 'twas likely her jenny that told them."

I went cold, thinking of my mother doing this. "Did she say who the jenny was?"

"Oh, it warn't my mum," Fanny said hastily. "But she couldn't recall. Her memory isn't what it was." As Fanny dug into her reticule, my shoulders eased with relief that at least her mother hadn't named mine. "Look at this," she said, handing me a photograph. "It's my mum and Maggie. The date on the back is 1858, about a year afore Maggie was caught. Don't let it blow away. I had to beg Ma to lend it."

I took it with both hands. There were four people in the photograph, all unsmiling, as they'd no doubt been instructed, although Maggie, in the center, somehow managed to convey that she was repressing a laugh. Her large dark eyes, made more dramatic with stage makeup, sparkled; her shining black hair was piled high and dropping ringlets on her shoulder;

her chin was lowered coquettishly; her full lips were slightly parted, as if about to whisper a secret.

Consciously or not, the three others had all leaned in toward Maggie. To her right was Fanny's mother, June, with fair hair and a pretty face. Her hand was looped loosely through Maggie's bent elbow. Standing behind June was a gawky dark-haired boy of about thirteen, who rested his pale fingers on Maggie's right shoulder. He looked uncertain, even shy, in what might have been his best clothes. Beside him stood a fair-haired young man of about twenty-five. In the style of previous decades, he was clean-shaven except for his small mustaches. Was this the man who had stirred up trouble between my mother and Maggie? He was handsome enough, certainly.

There was something familiar about the boy. "Who are they?" I pointed to him and the man.

"Mum couldn't remember their names," Fanny said. "The boy looks almost sweet, don't he? He was a cousin of Maggie's—she took him in after he left home or was thrown out or some such—and the other was one of Maggie's beaus. Mum said there were plenty of 'em. Maggie was an actress for a bit—a proper one at a theater, and famous even. Did you know?"

"I'd heard something about it."

"That's why this was taken. The photographer came backstage one day and asked to take a picture for the program. She said yes, but she wanted this photograph taken, too." Fanny looked at it critically. "She's pretty, ain't she?"

"Very," I said.

I handed the photograph back, making sure Fanny had it securely in her fingers before I let go. "Did she say anything else?"

She slipped it into her reticule. "She said Maggie was the brightest, liveliest girl, with a lovely singing voice and slender hands. Men would come to her dressing room, beggin' to take her out for supper after. She used to bring bouquets of flowers to the lodging house."

"Until she became a thief."

"She did it to please her mum," Fanny said. "Patty wanted Maggie to take the ring."

That wasn't what Amelia said, and my mind jumped again to Maggie's belief about the dead knowing what happens to the living. "I wonder if Maggie's mother is pleased with her, at last."

Fanny looked at me oddly. "What do *you* think o' Maggie?"

"She's not changing much, leastwise not yet," I said. "But I think she's treading carefully."

"I've heard now that Amelia's gone, she's going to trim the ring," Fanny said.

"What?" My heart skipped a beat. "Who's she cutting? We all pull our weight."

"Nell, for sure, and possibly Mary." Her eyes were regretful. "I know Mary's your friend. I wanted to warn you."

I felt a spike of anger. "Who told you this?"

"She told Nell that she wants to keep the books herself—and that Nell won't be the only one to go." Fanny shrugged. "The only one who hasn't worked much is Mary."

"Because her mother died!" I retorted. "She's fine now. I should know."

Fanny raised a hand in protest. "Don't yell at *me*. I'm just telling you what I heard."

"Besides, Mary's earned plenty for the ring over the years."

Fanny rolled her eyes. "I know."

I wonder if Maggie had spoken to Mary yet. "Damn," I swore. "Doesn't she know what loyalty is? And what's Mary supposed to bloody do?"

Fanny shook her head, not as if she didn't care but as if she had no good answer, and the wind, damp and chill, flapped our coats open.

I would have to tell Mary tonight. It was only Fanny's guess, but I'd put her on her guard.

We turned and headed across the bridge.

Fanny and I reached Hunt and Roskell, one of the few jewelers who hadn't moved to Hatton Garden. I'd passed this shop before, as had Fanny, on a casing trip not long ago. Two large windows up front, a glass-paned door, multiple cabinets, locks on the left after two thefts some years ago. The shop was busy, and Fanny waited patiently, admiring the necklaces in a case. Meanwhile, I edged closer to a woman examining some gold bracelets. She had a distracted air, asking the clerk to take three out—no, four—and I stilled my face. I was supposed to be merely Fanny's jenny, but this woman was making it almost too easy.

Or was she a bouncer herself?

It was a simple matter to find out.

I dropped my reticule and stooped to retrieve it, meanwhile putting a bit of snuff into my glove. I sniffed and as I stood, I began to sneeze, violently, in a manner that could not be feigned. I had a handkerchief in my reticule, but instead of taking it out, I pressed my fingers against my nose. Instantly, the clerk offered me his linen square. "I beg your pardon," I managed between sneezes. "This London air. Sometimes this comes over me."

"Goodness! How dreadful!" the woman said. But there were still four bracelets on the black velvet.

Not a thief, then.

I set my reticule on the counter, close to the black velvet board upon which the bracelets lay, and dabbed at my nose. The woman picked the bracelets up one by one, trying them on, and as she asked for two more, one of them slid under my reticule and vanished. Slowly, I moved away and out of the shop and headed for home, south and west as usual, and soon Fanny caught up. Her right hand slipped a necklace into my left, under cover of her coat flapping.

"See you home," she said and walked on.

The necklace went into my thieving pocket.

The bracelet remained in the palm of my glove. I wasn't sure what I could do with it—I couldn't use one of our usual fences; and a fence who didn't know me wouldn't trust me. I couldn't give it to James or Mary or Sarah for safekeeping. Amelia had vanished without giving me her address.

But I wasn't sorry I had it. The future felt damned uncertain.

Chapter 13

Breaking one of Amelia's rules, I stopped in my room on the way to the inn.

I knew better than to hide the bracelet anywhere here; our rooms had no locks, and because the ring paid for our rooms, if Maggie suspected me of hoarding, she could search every drawer, every inch of mattress, every stitch of clothing down to the hems. Amelia had done it once, catching a girl named Leonora with a pair of cufflinks worth twenty pounds, easily four months' rent in a decent boardinghouse. I held the two chains in my left palm, the little heap of gold, one yellower than the other, but both shining. The bracelet was probably fifteen carat, with thick curb links, probably worth twelve pounds. Fanny's necklace was more delicate but longer, with bits of turquoise inlaid and finer workmanship; likely fifteen. If I had to bet, that jeweler would not let another day go by without hiring a private detective for his shop. I wrapped the bracelet in black paper and tucked it into my pile of hair, clipping it with pins inside my hairnet. I used the mirror to check; it was invisible.

After dropping off Fanny's necklace in the goods room and changing clothes, I started for Mayfair to walk Sarah home. She might not like me coming for her, but I wanted to talk privately.

The church bells struck six as I reached the northern end of Waterloo Bridge. I'd reach Mayfair long before Sarah could leave, and I decided to take a roundabout route toward Willits House.

What would it be like to live in this world? I wondered as I looked about me. Aside from the gilt-wheeled carriages and shining new hansom cabs on the street, the traffic on the pavement had a wholly different quality than in Southwark. It was a decorous parade of bell-shaped skirts and parasols, well-heeled boots and silk hats that would be ruined if it rained. There seemed to be no urgency, for no one hurried; indeed, there seemed to be a purposeful languor, a slowness with these people. Their days weren't measured by the time it took to get from their rooms to their place of business, to the baker before it closed, to Mayfair to collect their sisters. Human activity meandered in the open streets rather than hurrying down alleys that provided shortcuts.

My own roaming eventually brought me to the corner of Brook Street, where the Fairleigh house stood, the white front of Willits House visible in the distance. The gas lamps were already ablaze farther down the street, and I watched as the lamplighter made his way toward me and then passed by, though it wasn't anywhere near dark yet. Trust West Enders to have light when it wasn't even needed, I thought. Gazing at the Fairleigh house and the crowd of spectators across the street, I paused under a plane tree whose branches extended beyond the gated park behind me.

The daily crowd of spectators had diminished, but it was curious how people behaved a fortnight later. Some pedestrians took pains to cross the street, hurrying along with their eyes averted out of decency or perhaps fear that the violence might infect them, like one of the Thames miasmas. Others slowed their steps to look, while others stood boldly at the gate, their hands, gloved or bare, curling around the wrought iron bars, and stared at the house as if it might reveal some truth about what happened there.

"Strange, isn't it?" said a man's voice.

I turned to find a man to my right. I'd missed him in the shadow of the plane tree.

He was a head taller and a few years older. Wheat-colored hair, a pleasant face, clean-shaven, brown eyes, an air of calm steadiness. A good overcoat, tailored to fit his shoulders; neat turnups without frays on his trousers; well-heeled leather boots, though dusty, as if he'd spent the day walking; an ordinary black umbrella, without an ivory or silver handle, resting with its metal point on the stones. Despite everything, I felt my mouth twitch. If he'd appeared at Elephant and Castle as a traveler, he would have been led to the fire, settled in a comfortable chair, fed wine laced with laudanum, and woken the next morning wearing nothing but his shirt and underthings.

However, we were here, he was no traveler, and the way he stood and surveyed the house sent a warning heat down my nerves.

If I had to guess, this was a Yard man.

"What's strange?" I asked.

"People's fascination with death," he replied. When I said nothing, he added, "Do you know what happened in that house?"

"Anyone who's seen a newspaper knows what happened in that house—and they haven't caught him yet."

His jaw sagged. "I know," he said heavily.

I felt unexpectedly sorry for him, but this confirmed my guess about his profession.

Two carriages rolled past, temporarily blocking our view, and by the time they passed, a young newspaper boy had appeared. "Latest news on the murders!" he croaked, and the crowd pivoted toward him as one.

The Yard man's eyes narrowed, and he went still the way Amelia did when she was angry. As pleasant as his countenance was, I would not want to be on the wrong side of him. Together we watched the boy distribute his papers, pocketing his coins cheerfully.

The man swung the tip of his umbrella toward the house. "Do you know them? The Fairleighs?"

"Not at all."

"Is it your first time seeing the house?" His manner was easy; he kept his curiosity about my presence friendly.

There was no harm in telling him. "My sister works here in Mayfair, and I've come to walk her home. She's only fourteen—although she doesn't like me treating her like a child."

A smile tugged at his mouth. "No, they don't, do they? I have a sister who's fourteen, too."

"Oh?"

"Cathy. She still lives outside London, on our farm." His eyes followed a carriage that slowed but then sped up and passed. "I imagine this has spooked your sister a bit."

"I imagine it's spooked everyone in the entire borough," I corrected him. "With decent folks murdered in their beds."

"Fair point." He paused. "Is she to meet you here? Your sister?"

"No. I'll meet her up the street."

He looked concerned. "Do you feel safe walking? I'd be happy to escort you."

I let a smile seep into my voice. "Kind of you, but it's not needed. Besides, if you walked me home, you'd cause me all sorts of trouble with my husband."

He chuckled. "What's your name?"

"Mary Lacy." It was a name I'd used before.

"And what do you do for work, Mrs. Lacy?"

"I'm a needlewoman," I said, patting my pocket as if I had my needles in it.

Out of the corner of my eye, I saw Sarah approaching. Her steps slowed as she saw me, and I twitched at my skirt with my left hand. She caught my signal and walked on, keeping her face toward the house.

"I should go find my sister," I said once Sarah was out of sight. "She'll be waiting."

"Ah. Well, have a good evening," he replied with a smile. "Home safely."

I turned left and then left again toward Blackfriars Bridge, where I found Sarah peering about. As I approached, her shoulders lifted with a sigh. "I told you, you don't have to come fetch me."

"I wanted a chance to talk before you got home."

Her face sobered. "Why? Are Billy and Tommy back?"

"No, they're still gone," I said. "James says they're in Bermondsey."

"So they're not up here," she said, visibly relieved. "And what's happened to Josie?"

"She got six months."

"Oh." She wrapped her hand around my elbow, and we started for home.

"There's something else I need to tell you," I said. "Amelia has left the ring."

Sarah's fingers tightened. "And she's asked you to head it."

"No, no, no." I couldn't get it out fast enough.

She looked bewildered. "Who else would she ask?"

"Amelia didn't ask anyone. Maggie Wirth—Patty's daughter—came back from Australia and asked *her*."

As we walked, I explained all that had happened. At the end of my recital, she shook her head as if stunned.

"I never dreamed Amelia would leave," she said. "Where will she go? Do you think we'll see her again?"

"She said Whitechapel, and we can visit it, surely, but . . . well, you know how it is."

"People leave, and they don't come back," she said, her voice flat with certainty. "But Amelia's been good to us since Ma died."

"I know."

A gust of wind on the bridge drove the chill of the river into our bones and kept us from speaking again until we crossed. By the time we reached the other side, Sarah's shoulders drooped, and her mouth was pursed in a way I knew.

I laid a hand on her arm to draw her to a stop. "What's the matter?"

She turned toward me, her expression sober and resolute. "I don't want to quarrel, but you must stop thieving, Kit. Six months is long enough to die in prison."

I had no answer to that.

She crossed her arms over her chest. "Do you know why I wanted to go out in service?"

"To help," I said.

"So we'd have enough money that you could do something different, something away from Elephant and Castle."

"I've been thieving for years," I said slowly. "Why is this bothering you now?"

"Because I'm finally old enough to know how dangerous it is! And now that Amelia's gone? *Please*, Kit." Her eyes begged. In the wind coming off the river, fine strands of her fair hair escaped her pinned braid and blew about her face. "Those murders just made death seem so . . . close and so possible." Her face was pinched. "I am more afraid of you dying than of *anything* happening to me. Do you think I don't worry every day, knowing what you're doing at the shops, knowing you could be caught? Even hanged outright?"

"I told you, I'll quit when I can." My voice cracked over the words.

"I want you to *find* a way to quit, Kit."

"I will try. Truly, I will." I swallowed. "But you'd be all right. You're in service, you—"

Her jaw dropped and her eyes filled with tears, as if I'd slapped her. "How can you say that? You think just because I've gone into service that I don't *need* you?"

I didn't reply, for she'd laid her finger on the crack that her leaving had cut in my heart, though I'd done my best to pretend otherwise. I *did* fear it.

"Kit," she said, her voice breaking. She clutched both my hands in hers, her face earnest. "If anything, I know better how much I need you. It's *different* than when I was a child and couldn't fend for myself. But it's not less, Kit. *Never* less."

Tears burned at the corners of my eyes, and I blinked them back.

"I know I still have things to learn," Sarah said. "But . . ."

"You're not a child and you're not a fool," I finished. "I know. And I will try to find a way to stop. I promise."

It took a moment, but her expression eased. "Well, at least you've acknowledged I'm not a child."

"But you *were* one for fourteen years," I reminded her. "You've only been in service a few months. I need time to catch up."

Her laugh, brief and teary as it was, showed her dimples.

My sister was never one to drag a quarrel beyond its natural end. She'd said her piece, and I'd said mine, so she slid her hand around my elbow, and we talked of other things the rest of the way home.

When Sarah and I arrived upstairs, I found two items on my bed: a note from Mary saying she was visiting relations for a few days, so Sarah could use her bed, and a prettily wrapped box tied with a white satin ribbon.

Mary and I didn't usually buy each other presents.

I opened it to find a pair of beautiful gloves of fine, supple kid, the kind I'd steal first from a store shelf. "What's this?"

Sarah made a show of peering at them. "Well, I can't be sure, but I *think* they're what folks call gloves."

I gave her a look.

"There's a card. You dropped it." Sarah retrieved it from the floor and read it. "All it says is 'Kitten.'" Her eyebrows rose and her eyes brightened. "Who calls you that? Is it James?"

Heat rose to my cheeks, and a delighted grin curved her mouth. I took the card from her and saw that, indeed, it had only the one word. There was an elaborate monogrammed *W* on the card, the same *W* displayed above the door of Whiteley's department store.

Sarah took the card back and examined it once more with an air of satisfaction. "I told you, I've always liked him."

"Hmm."

I returned the gloves to the box, feeling as off-kilter as if I had rocks in only one thieving pocket. I perceived the significance of the fine paper wrapping, the shining ribbon, and the monogrammed card. James didn't want any misunderstanding about how he'd obtained them. My mind darted to the moment in the carriage when he'd put his warm hand over my cold one. It was a thoughtful gift, and an elegant one. My heart tripped, and warmth washed over me, a wave of more feelings than I could name.

"Those gloves probably cost two weeks' wages." Sarah unbuttoned her coat as she studied my expression. "Why do you look like that?"

"Lately, he's been . . . different. Trying to help me . . . and he's been keeping an ear out, to see if any of the Castle men mentioned you."

"You told him?" she asked, surprised.

"He was with me when I saw the newspaper article. He guessed as much as I did." I undid my coat and hung it on a nail by the door. "I figured there was no harm. He's looked out for you before."

"Not just me, Kit," she said.

I raised an eyebrow.

"He'd likely not want me telling you this." Sarah hung her coat beside mine. "But he asked Emma to hire you for piecework after Ma died. And the badger scheme was his idea, although he asked Amelia to propose it, so you'd say yes."

I blinked at yet more instances of his kindness. "How do you know all this?"

She shrugged. "My point is, he's been kind all along. You should give him a chance."

"Goodness, Sarah. You're puffing him like he's a railway share," I said, half joking. "Have you sold me to him as well?"

Her eyes slid away guiltily, and I felt a prick of suspicion. "Wait a moment. Did you say something to him? Is that why he's changed?"

She looked apologetic. "He's been sweet on you for ages," she said, her eyes pleading on his behalf, or for my forgiveness, or both. "I just hinted it might be time to try."

The blood fell from my face. "Sarah!" Mortified, I sank onto my bed. "What exactly did you say?"

She plumped down on Mary's bed. "I only told him that with me being gone, you might be lonely, and you'd be less occupied, seeing as you weren't taking care of me anymore." She had the air of making a clean sweep. "In fact—I, er—I said the same to Mary. She was grateful, Kit. She liked the idea of being needed, with her ma gone."

"Well," I managed. "Aren't you one for arranging things."

Sarah studied me warily. "You're not angry?"

"No, I'm not angry." My fingers pleated my skirt. "But I don't want James feeling obligated."

A chuckle burst from her. "*Obligated?* Trust me, he doesn't." She planted her hands behind her on the bed and leaned back, swinging her feet gently above the floorboards. "I never said a word to him about gloves, and I think it's lovely of him. You never buy yourself nice things."

"Because I don't need them," I retorted.

Sarah's mouth opened, but then she seemed to think better of her reply. "Don't be peevish, Kit. I just want to see you happy. You haven't had a fellow hanging about since Dan Wist, and he was *awful.*"

"You remember him?"

"Of course I do! He came around all the time, all leering and sly." She made a horrid face. "Besides, I saw him making up to Bea one night you weren't around. He was as harebrained and fickle as they come."

I was dumbfounded at all she'd noticed, and even more at how she'd been looking out for me, when I'd thought I was looking out for her.

"James isn't harebrained *or* fickle," Sarah said firmly.

But I wasn't thinking of James at that moment. I was looking at Sarah with a feeling of wonder and a dawning sense of gratitude.

When I didn't reply, Sarah rolled her eyes as if I was hopeless. "Suit yourself in a set of fool's clothes. I wash my hands of you."

Chapter 14

Monday morning at Emma's shop, I was bent over a man's shirt making buttonholes, one part of my mind counting twenty stitches for each side and the other combing back over the previous year with Sarah and wondering what other sorts of things she'd been thinking of. Dan Wist? For God's sake, I hadn't thought of him in years—in fact, I might have been hard-pressed to give his last name. What else did she recall that I'd let drop away, out of my thoughts?

"What d'you think o' Maggie?" Emma's voice was casual.

I looked up in surprise, pulling my thoughts back from where they'd wandered. Emma's eyes were on an organza ruffle that she was basting onto a skirt near the hem. The fabric shushed across the narrow sewing table as she kept the section she was working on under her hands.

My needle paused as I considered what I might say, for I wasn't about to share the alarming conclusions James and I had reached. "Honestly, I don't trust her. There's talk that she's pushing some of us out, which is rotten after she promised she wouldn't change anything. On the other hand, she's been pleasant enough to me. But she was an actress. There's no way to know if she means any of it."

"Or what her intention is, in being pleasing," Emma said.

"I 'magine twenty years in Swan River has toughened her, made her hard."

"I know." I bent over the buttonhole again. "Part of me feels sorry for her. That penal colony sounds like hell, with her marriage the worst part of it. He tried to kill her and burned her hand on the stove."

"Agh." She brought the cloth to her mouth to bite the thread. "The things folks do to each other."

"I know. But she shouldn't be ruthless to us because of it."

"No," Emma said. "There. Ruffle's done."

It seemed a good moment to ask the question that had been nagging at me, though even as I spoke, I wondered if I shouldn't. "Did James ask you to take me on here at the shop? After my mother died?" I wanted to see her face as she replied, so I paused in my work, keeping hold of the needle with one hand and my place on the buttonhole with the other.

Her eyes were clear, frank. "Aye. Why?"

Heat crept up my neck. The thought of people knowing how desperate we'd been made me squirm. "I didn't want charity."

"Oh, it wasn't charity," she replied. "He knew I could use the help." She eyed me for a moment, and when I didn't reply, a sharp note crept into her voice. "It's naught to be ashamed of. He was only looking out for you. Some folks might be grateful."

"Oh, I know. I mean, I am." I bent over my work to hide my shame at the thought of how that conversation had gone: James pitying me because Ma had died, telling his sister how we might be thrown out on the street. Emma sighing and saying she supposed she could pay me a wage of some sort—

"He's had your name stitched on his heart since the badger days," Emma said, more gently.

I felt a second wave of heat rising to my cheeks.

"I was the one who told him to wait," she said. "You were too young, both o' you. And you'd just lost your mum and had Sarah to take care of."

I dropped the sewing into my lap, surprised that she'd spent time thinking of me at all.

Emma's mouth twitched. "Honestly? You'd no idea?"

She had misinterpreted the reason for my surprise. But I answered the question she asked. "No. I didn't." Into my mind came recent moments, like photographs: James's hand resting on Mr. Yellen's shoulder, pushing coins into Pat's till. "He . . . he likes most everyone."

Her expression softened, and something like pride lit her face. "True."

I forced a smile and returned to my sewing, thinking she was satisfied. But I'd only made one stitch when she said, "I'm not saying you ought to care for him." Her voice had sharpened again. "But you should tell him if you don't, so he doesn't think otherwise."

I had the sensation of stumbling backward faster than my feet could manage. "No—that's not it. It's not that I don't like him. Of course I do. But for years, he never said anything, so I thought . . ." I was doing badly at this. "Everything's always been a laugh with him. Even the way he asked me to go to dinner. He did it by tricking me in a game." I drew a breath. "I didn't know he'd been looking out for me."

"I see," was all Emma said, but I could see I'd mollified her. "As for you being here on charity, put it out o' your head. Many a time, I've been glad it's you working here, not someone else." Her voice was as practical as Amelia's. "You come when you say you will, you don't shirk, and you don't pilfer ribbon or lace. You don't run a stitch long when it needs short ones, and you stay late if I'm needing the help." She darted her chin toward the garment in my lap. "And your buttonholes are better'n mine."

The last line, and her wry smile, softened my discomfort.

"I don't mind you and James keeping company, providing you can keep this"—she pointed toward the sewing in my lap—"separate from that."

"I think I can," I managed, the flush starting up my neck again.

"Good." She gathered up the organza remnant into a tidy pile, and went to her desk, pulling out a drawer. "I found something the other day. I kept it out for James, but you might like to see it."

Emma handed me a cardboard folder embossed with the name of a photographic studio. *Another picture*, I thought.

This one was yellowed at the edges, sepia toned, and again, all four people in the photograph were unsmiling, even grim. A man and woman, seated. To the left of the woman stood a girl of about ten, with her skirts still short, and a boy of about four sat on his mother's lap. His small plump hand was wrapped around his sister's index finger.

"This is you and James with your parents?" I asked. James's face was round and soft, with large dark eyes, feathery hair that lay flat against the top of his head, and a rosebud mouth. If I looked, I could see the beginnings of the handsomeness he had now.

"My father died about six months after this was taken," Emma said. "Mum was afraid for his health. She wanted a picture to remember him by, in case."

"Was it cholera?" It had swept through Southwark when I was too young to remember, but I'd heard about it plenty.

"Influenza," she replied. "He had black lung 'cause he worked in the mines up north as a child, so his lungs were too weak to fight it off. Or at least, that's what the doctor told us."

"I'm sorry," I said.

"Mum's heart was broken something fierce," she said. "I know marriages aren't always happy, but Mum and Da loved each other." Her voice dropped. "They were kind. She always said he was a good man."

I handed the photograph back. "It's a nice picture." I didn't have a photograph of my father. My ma certainly hadn't wanted something to remember him by; after he left, she found everything in the house that reminded her of him—down to the glass mug he used for his shaving soap—and took it to Mr. Ardle's shop. Not to mention we wouldn't have had the money for a photograph.

With the corners of her mouth buttoned down, Emma replaced the folder in the drawer. "Well, then."

It seemed we were finished talking. She resumed her place at the table. I finished the buttonhole, slipped the button through to check it, and moved on to the next, all the while wondering why she'd showed me that photograph. The best I could guess was that Emma wanted me to see that she and James were close from childhood, like Sarah and me. Or that she knew what my parents' marriage was like—Ma was more likely to scream "bloody eejit" out the window at Da than call him a good man—and she wanted me to know James would expect something different.

We worked in silence for another hour, until Emma snipped her thread, put away her needle, and draped the skirt over a table. "Some fabrics came in this morning. I'm goin' to fetch them." She took her coat down from its hook. "When you finish the buttonholes, can you baste Mr. Nichols's shirts? I'll be back in less than an hour. There are no appointments."

"Of course," I said. The door clinked closed behind her.

Three buttonholes left. My hands worked them of their own accord, my mind busy with my thoughts.

I wasn't sure I was ready to admit even to myself how the thought of James privately caring for me softened my heart. It wasn't the sort of secret I usually discovered, with the truth better than I imagined.

It took me two hours to baste the seams on Mr. Nichols's three shirts with red thread and long stitches that showed on both sides of the cloth. I'd barely finished when Emma returned, her eyes sparking with annoyance and her mouth tight.

"What's the matter?" I asked.

She unbuttoned her coat, her fingers quick with irritation. "Three bolts of cloth I ordered went missing. And I need them for Mrs. Tompkins's new dresses. She'll be fit to be tied."

"They didn't arrive?"

"No, they arrived. The duties were paid, and they were logged and shelved. At first, the clerk thought they were just mislaid."

"Not surprising." I'd been to the warehouse once with Emma, to help her carry some bundles of woolens and notions, and it was enormous, a cavern of shelves and boxes and narrow aisles, people bustling in and out, fetching and carrying all manner of goods. I'd nearly been knocked over by a man hurrying through with a wrought iron fireplace grate over his shoulder.

"But when we looked at the book, there was an *X* instead of my signature."

"Oh," I said, dismayed.

"We asked one of the clerks in that department—a brainless gob—and he couldn't recall anything, but a different clerk said he remembered a woman coming in to fetch them and givin' my name."

That was straight-up thieving.

I wasn't a fool; I knew the damage stealing caused, but I rarely saw it firsthand. I was always already gone by the time it was discovered. "Who knew you were picking them up?"

"No one but you."

I blinked.

"O' *course* I don't think you did this," she snapped. I didn't take offense; it was worry that made her sharp.

"What's going to happen?"

"Well, I filled out an inquiry, and they'll send for new ones."

"It was insured, wasn't it?"

"Aye. But it's going to take at least another month to get more—and they were dear—Brussels lace, silk, and chiffon. They took a good part o' my ready money. Not to mention that Mrs. Tompkins will take five pounds of stuffing out o' me when she hears."

"Well, it's not your fault," I protested. "Tell her she should go down to the warehouse, if she puts up a fuss. Perhaps they'd find it for her."

"There's a thought," she said, with a snort.

Chapter 15

The following morning, after breakfast, I returned to our room to find Mary, home from her visit, sitting up in bed reading a letter. Her jaw was set and her face was pale. The sight drew me to sit on the edge of her bed.

"What's happened?" I asked, dreading the answer.

"Maggie's pushing me out of the ring," she said, her voice low.

A curse slipped from my mouth.

"I don't understand it." Mary was never one for blazing fury, but her eyes flashed at the injustice of it. "I'm good at thieving. You and I bring in more money than most, and I'm ready to come back. But some doctor she knows thinks my grief makes me susceptible to nerves. Have you heard the like?"

I shook my head.

"She's giving me a fortnight to clear out."

"A fortnight!"

She swallowed. "I wouldn't mind so much if it was fair, but it isn't!"

"No, it's bloody not." I gestured to her lap. "What's that?"

"A letter from my aunt. I was afraid this might happen, from the way Maggie acted the day she took me out, so I wrote to see if I might stay with her, if I needed to."

Dismay sank my heart. "Your aunt Jane? In Reading?"

She flapped the page. "What with my cousin getting married and having a baby, they don't have room."

"Well, I'm not sorry. I don't want you to leave London," I said. She managed a smile, and I leaned to squeeze her hand. "We'll figure out something. And we've money put by. We can find you a place."

"It's good of you, but it doesn't solve the problem." Mary dropped her head back against the wall. "What am I going to do, Kit? All I know is thieving—and how to bake a decent loaf of bread."

"Perhaps Mrs. Jonas can use you more than a day or two a week."

"She can't," Mary replied. "I asked."

"Well, there are other bakeries," I said.

"I know." Her mouth twisted. "I don't want to fret you. I'll find something."

A knock sounded at the door, and Mary slid the letter under her skirts.

At her nod, I called, "Come in!"

The door was pushed open, and Bea's face appeared around the edge, her gaze shifting between Mary and me. "Maggie wants to see you."

Mary swung her legs off the bed.

"Not you," Bea said. "She wants Kit."

Worry pricked along my spine.

"I don't think it's bad," Bea said hastily.

"Now?"

Bea nodded. "In the goods room."

"Don't fight it, Kit," Mary said.

She meant she didn't want me to argue about Mary being

pushed out. There was no point in Maggie questioning my loyalty.

Trust Mary to think of me, even in the face of this.

As I left, Bea slid inside the room, asking, "Are you all right, Mary? You look peaked."

I closed the door and headed for the inn. The fireplace was aglow, half the tables occupied, and Pat lifted his chin in greeting as I passed. I climbed the stairs to the first story. The door was shut, so I knocked, and upon hearing her call to come in, I entered.

She had repositioned the desk closer to the window, where she sat with a cup of tea at her elbow. It was fresh, still steaming. "Ah, Kit. Please sit down."

I took the chair opposite, folding my hands in my lap, resolved to conceal all resentment at how she was treating Nell and Mary and to glean whatever I could, including what she didn't intend to show.

She sat back, eyeing me for a moment. "Well, this is one way you're different from your mother. You keep your face quiet."

"She showed enough for everyone," I said.

Maggie arched one eyebrow. "She was . . . spirited, to be sure. She knew what she wanted." My heart lurched, for I suspected what she alluded to. When I didn't reply, she added, "Your mother took drink to steady her nerves. I notice you don't."

"Amelia always said not to."

That raised her eyebrows, but she didn't remind me that she was the leader now. "A good rule," she said. "I daresay you're all better thieves than we were."

It was too sweeping a statement to sound sincere. Was she

trying to get round me with flattery? Or learn how cocksure I was?

"Amelia told me that you were the best," I replied.

Maggie ran her broken forefinger lightly along the edge of the desk, left and right, just once. "Amelia told me you're *her* best. After watching all of you, I agree. Your hands are quick and quiet. You notice everything and your memory is superb."

This flattery was leading up to an ask.

"I mentioned I have a special dodge I'd like to try," she said. "And I want you for it."

Perhaps someone else might have been gratified, even eager, at being singled out. I only felt my nerves tighten because I couldn't be sure how Maggie truly thought of me, given what my mother had likely done. I didn't bother to conceal the mix of curiosity and wariness I felt, for only a fool jumped into a dodge without knowing the particulars.

"You'd receive a higher percentage, of course," she added. "And believe me, it'll be worth your while."

"What is it you're thinking of?"

"How well do you know Hatton Garden?" she returned.

Hatton Garden?

The name was a misnomer for an area approximately one square mile in Camden, north of the river. There was no garden of flowers or herbs, only a tight weave of streets with nearly sixty shops, mostly jewelers and dealers in gold, silver, and the new Kimberley diamonds. Six months ago, there had been two thefts in broad daylight, and since then, the stores had doubled their precautions, including adding private detectives, Chubb safes, and Yale locks, and going so far as to create paste reproductions of the most expensive items, leaving the real jewelry in a locked safe to be brought out only for the most discerning of customers.

I arranged my thoughts before I answered. "Amelia never had us work it because there are privies during the day and constables patrolling at night."

"Let's look at it."

I expected we'd use Amelia's wall map, but instead Maggie slid open a desk drawer and withdrew a page that showed Hatton Garden, hand drawn. "Leather Lane to the west," she said. "Saffron Hill to the east, Holborn south and Hatton Wall north. What else can you tell me?"

At one time Amelia had thought we might work there, so we'd all walked it. "There are three churches and Wren House, the big redbrick building, about here." I pointed to the locations of each. "A railway station to the east, on the other side of Farringdon Street. A brewery on the northwest corner and a fruit and vegetable market to the southeast." I looked up to find her mouth curving in an approving smile.

"You know it well."

I let that pass. "What sort of dodge are you thinking?"

She shrugged. "I'm not sure yet. But I'd like you to visit some of the shops and give me your impressions."

"Do you have any in mind?"

"Not in particular. Any that might serve our purposes."

I had a feeling she did have one in mind, but I was being lured in slowly, softened up like a potato brought to boil in a pot.

"I'm not sure I'm interested in this dodge," I said cautiously. "With all the constables and new precautions, it won't be easy."

"All I'm asking is for you to look about, tell me what you

see." She studied me, her eyes looking a brighter green than usual. "There'd be no proper cut for doing this, but there might be something I could do for you in exchange."

Such as let Mary stay on more than two weeks, I thought. It was likely Maggie knew that mattered to me, but I wasn't going to show her that card. Not until I had something to trade.

"It might take a few days to visit all of the shops," I said.

"I can give you the week, take you off dodging until next Monday."

I didn't trust Maggie's intentions toward me. But for now, I was only taking a measure of part of the city. There was no risk in that. Also, staying close to Maggie, having some idea about her plans, might keep me safer than ignorance; and it wasn't much to do in exchange for Mary possibly being allowed to stay.

The following day, I donned the most elegant dress I could find in the costume room, put on the gloves James had sent, and took an omnibus across Blackfriars Bridge. At the far end, I walked north on New Bridge Street, crossing Fleet where the road became Farringdon. I passed St. Andrew's Church and cut west. Knowing shops had likely changed in the year since I'd been here, I planned to walk all the streets of Hatton Garden in a large *S*, drawing a provisional map of shops in my head, before dividing my task into Leather Lane, Hatton Garden, and Kirby Street and Saffron Hill, one each day.

I walked up and down, examining the buildings. On every street, the original buildings had been divided into two or three shops, for although each one had its own door on the ground floor, there was a continuity of rooflines and similarity in the brickwork or the size and shape of the windows, particularly on the upper floors. I observed three uniformed constables in constant motion. It wasn't surprising that of the eight thousand constables in London, several would patrol here. The two recent dodges, by thieves bolder than us, had netted one hundred watches, which were smuggled to the Holland market. It would have been a triumph, except that the four thieves were betrayed by one of their fences; two were in Newgate and two had taken to rowboats, attempting to evade arrest, and drowned in the Channel.

After my initial stroll, I entered the northernmost shop on the east side of Leather Lane. I approached the door, wood and glass, two locks, one a dead bolt. When I pushed it open, the bell above the door clinked softly. Everything about the place was soft—a light shade of sage on the walls; a thick, patterned Turkey carpet underneath my feet; sconces with shades that dispersed a pleasing golden glow; two long mirrors, each throwing light into dark corners, dispelling the shadows. I spotted three clerks and one man who stood slightly apart, with watchful eyes and hands that were rougher than the neat coat and trousers he wore. His shoes were dusty around the toes, which told me he walked rather than taking a carriage. A privy.

The clerk who approached me nodded, his voice silky, with proper vowels. "May I help you, mum?"

"I'd like to look at a new pocket watch for my husband," I said, in my own proper vowels.

"Of course," he said and gestured. "Please, come this way."

We stood before a glass case lined in black velvet, with trays holding pocket watches of gold and silver, some with elaborate carvings on the cases, others with tiny jewels. The faces were perfect ivory, the delicate hands moving silently forward each minute. Some numbers were ordinary and curving, but most were Roman, tall and stiff as soldiers.

I turned my head from side to side, as if surveying the many different watches, to examine the case. A solid polished wooden back; glass front and sides. In fact, glass of a double thickness, harder to smash. A single cam lock in the middle of the back panel.

I removed my gloves and pointed to one particularly handsome Swiss watch, a Breguet.

"Could I see that one, please," I asked.

The clerk tucked his hand inside his coat to reveal two chains: one gold, no doubt attached to the watch in his own pocket, the other silver, which held a key that he inserted into the lock in the middle of the cabinet. The lock would be difficult to reach from the sides and far enough down the back that I would have to sprawl stomach down on the glass top to reach it from where I stood.

An amusing thought, if not a useful one.

He removed the watch and opened the spring-hinged metal cover. "A Breguet, with a special mechanism called a tourbillon."

"Oh, what's that?" I asked.

"The watch escapement and the balance wheel are mounted in a rotating cage, to eliminate errors that might occur from movement." He lifted the chain, showing me the gold T-bar on the other end. "It also comes with a gold Albert chain for attaching to the waistcoat, to insure it cannot be dropped or stolen by a pickpocket."

I knew better. Indeed, I knew a good deal about these savonnette watches, having repaired some with a tourbillon mechanism in Mr. Ardle's shop. This was an older model, for the decorative gold cover hinged at the nine, and the stem, crown, and bow were at the three. The newer models tended to hinge at the six, with the winding stem up top.

"It's called a hunter-case watch," he said. "As opposed to an open case, like these others."

"Hunter case," I echoed, as if I'd never heard the term.

"It's named so because fox hunters wanted to be able to open the watch with one hand, while holding the reins with the other. It's also known as a 'savonnette' in France."

"What a pretty name." I closed the case and clicked it open again, enjoying the smoothness of the polished gold against my palm. If I opened the reverse, I'd see the inner workings, all the springs and notched wheels and gears.

"And what about that silver one?" I asked, wondering if I might be allowed to see two at once.

He held out his hand for the gold watch, and I gave it to him. He replaced the first and drew out the second. "Another fine piece, although it's American. The Waltham company. This one is graded for railway use." He placed it in my hand.

"Oh my. It's quite heavy, isn't it?"

"Heavier than the Breguet, yes."

"Thank you." I smiled and returned it to him. "Honestly, you have so many fine ones. I'll bring my husband to see them because I'd like him to pick for himself." I lingered by the cabinet of earrings, admiring a pair with emerald-cut diamonds surrounding cabochon sapphires.

One solid theft from here and I could knock off thieving for good, I thought.

But between the privy, the paired mirrors, the lack of dim corners, the three clerks, the locks on the individual cases, the double-thick glass, and the practice of taking out only one piece of jewelry at a time, I didn't see how a dodge here could be done easily, if at all.

I visited nine shops that day, and with few variations, most of them had the same precautions in place. The following day I visited the shops in Hatton Garden Street, and on the third day, I tackled Kirby and Saffron Hill, lingering as the shops were closing. Four different uniformed constables appeared around corners at random, with the streets quite empty; as dusk fell, three more took up fixed positions at the south ends of the major streets. It would be nearly impossible to walk down a street, much less reach the front door of a particular jeweler, without being seen by one of them. Evening fell, and as I walked south on Farringdon toward the river, I was approached by a man who took me for a streetwalker. Knowing I'd be staying late, I'd brought my knife, which I removed from my pocket. The glint of the open blade deterred him sufficiently. He backed away, his hands raised, and turned, muttering unflattering epithets under his breath.

I studied these shops not only for Maggie's benefit, but for my own. If I did work this dodge—or if I refused and she asked one of the others—any knowledge would be useful. I continued south, pausing at a street corner just below Holborn, where I looked to the west. Against the mottled dark rose of the sky, I could see the dome of St. Paul's, overlaid with copper that could have been melted down to feed and clothe any number of the people living hand-to-mouth below.

At busy Fleet Street, I waited as a queue of cabs and carriages rolled by. In their wake was a Black Maria, a police wagon with separate locked cubicles used to carry prisoners from gaol to court. The windows had thick, hammered iron bars, and from behind them, men stared out with expressions of resignation, resentment, hatred toward the world. One met my eyes and spat, and I thought of Josie and the danger of being caught.

I didn't blame him. Caged like an animal, I'd spit too.

The threat of arrest for a Hatton Garden dodge was very real, given the number of privies and constables. With everything I'd discovered, I could not imagine what Maggie was thinking of doing. What sort of dodge would work in a store with bells and locks all over the doors and cabinets? What sort of disturbance could a jenny create that would draw everyone's attention long enough for me to snatch something? And if Maggie intended for me to go in after dark, how was I to get in without a constable noticing?

Or was that the point, to get me arrested? I recalled what Maggie had said about the dead seeing what happened on earth. Did she intend me to be caught as some sort of twisted revenge upon my mother?

I dismissed that idea. If Maggie wanted me arrested, she could have done it with an anonymous tip to a shop that I'd be thieving on a particular day.

But that didn't mean she wouldn't mind risking me for something she wanted.

Compared to West End shops, Hatton Garden was as impregnable as London Tower's vaults. I would not be doing this dodge.

Chapter 16

I found Maggie alone in the goods room the next day standing before the large map of London that hung on the wall. All Amelia's pins had been removed, and it was bare.

"Well," Maggie said. She crossed to her desk and drew up her chair, motioning me into the one opposite. "What do you think?"

"I can tell you a good deal about Hatton Garden," I said, as I sat. "But you mentioned a favor I might ask."

She turned over a palm. "Go on."

"I've heard you're pushing Nell and Mary out of the ring. Is it true?"

"Nell has decided to move to Lambeth, to live with her sister," she said matter-of-factly. "And Mary shouldn't be thieving."

I swallowed down my argument that I'd seen with my own eyes that Mary was fine. Instead, I said, "I want you to let Mary stay in my room with me."

Her green eyes met mine coolly. "The ring pays for the rooms, and it isn't fair to the other girls if one isn't pulling her weight. It cuts down their take."

"Mary has earned the ring plenty over the years, and she needs time to find a new situation. I know the beds are for the ring, but I'll pay her share of rent. The only thing you'd be losing is her take."

"Which is not insubstantial. She brought in nearly fifty pounds a month back when she worked."

"All the more reason you should bend on this," I retorted.

"Very well." She tapped the first two fingers of her good hand lightly on the desk. "I'll give her three months. Is that sufficient?"

It was something. "Yes."

"Now, what did you find?"

"I think it's foolish to try Hatton Garden when there are so many other places," I said frankly. "I visited twenty-four shops, and most have more than one clerk. Nine have private detectives. Sixteen have at least one mirror for visibility around corners, and most have two. All have locks on the cases, most of them keyed. Most have Yale locks on the doors and, from what I saw, black Chubb safes in the offices and workrooms."

She appeared unperturbed. "That's all excellent, Kit."

"Of all the shops I went to, only five would take out more than two items at a time."

"Oh? Which ones?"

I named them.

"Ah." Her eyes glinted.

"But every one of those had clerks and mirrors."

She smiled. "But you have only thought to thieve during the day, when the shop is open."

"Actually, I considered what it would be like after dark, so I stayed late last night. Most stores have two or three locks on both doors, front and back. There are very few with windows in the back, none on the ground floor, and at closing, everything is removed from the plate glass windows in the front, which are so large that if they were broken, a constable would notice immediately. There are four uniformed constables that patrol and three more that are fixed—not to mention there might be plainclothesmen I didn't see."

"Hm." Maggie pulled open a desk drawer and drew out the map she'd shown me before. "It's easy enough to get in through the back alleys, here." She pointed.

"All of the alleys I saw had iron gates with padlocks," I said.

"There's a narrow wall to one side that wouldn't be difficult to get over, with a boost." She glanced at my dress. "If someone wore trousers."

"And the constables? There was one posted at the end of the alleys at dusk."

"He could be paid to look the other way," she said placidly.

A hefty bribe, no doubt.

"So you're thinking to hit a shop after dark, when it's closed."

"It's a better time," she agreed.

From inside an alley, one might pick the back door and enter the shop. But there was still the problem of entering the room with the safe, not to mention the safe itself.

"You said you were thinking of me for it, but I'm rubbish with picks, and I'm useless with a safe," I said.

She waved away the objections. "I have a cracksman."

That twanged at my nerves. Amelia never would have planned a dodge that required bringing in a man from the outside. I wondered who it was.

Maggie looked at me expectantly.

"I'm sorry. I'm not interested," I said. "I know you're clever, and you probably have it all planned. But this is too risky for me."

"Would the risks be worth it," she asked, "for a cut of two hundred pounds?"

That figure silenced me.

"You would certainly secure your place in the ring by it," Maggie added, her voice cream smooth. "Or you could leave with Mary."

Was that what she wanted? Me to leave?

It would please Sarah, no doubt.

Two hundred pounds.

"What do you have in mind?" I asked.

"I'm after a special piece of jewelry. You may have heard of it," Maggie said. "It's a family heirloom belonging to the Marquess Hargrave. The family has a full page in *Debrett's*." My ear caught the faint sneer about their listing in *Peerage and Baronetage*. "A necklace."

She unfolded a paper and slid it across the table. The paper was thick, of high quality, and shiny, which suggested it had been taken from a bound book or a catalog of some sort. It showed a tinted drawing of a choker-length necklace of gold, cabochon sapphires, and round diamonds, ascending in size as they approached an enormous ruby pendant dangling at the bottom.

I'd seen this, or something very like it, recently. In a shop window, somewhere in Hatton Garden.

The description, in elegant script, was below: *Designed by Pierre Couillard of Couillard and Sons, Place Vendôme, Paris, 1820, for the first Marquess Hargrave, given to his wife the marchioness upon the birth of his first son.*

My mouth twisted at "his first son." Did the son not belong to the marchioness as well? But perhaps not, in families such as this.

"How much is it worth?" I asked.

"The marquess would likely say it's an heirloom beyond price. But the gold is worth about five hundred quid and the sapphires and diamonds around fifteen hundred. The ruby is from India, a cabochon cut, very singular."

"If this is to scale," I said dubiously, "that ruby is the size of a guinea."

"It is," she said, a smile playing about her mouth. "I told you this would be worth your while."

Providing it in fact can be stolen, I thought. *Otherwise, it's not worth the paper this picture is printed on*.

"It's been deposited at Simonson's jewelry shop for cleaning," Maggie explained.

Simonson's. My mind flicked through the shops. It was near the south end of Hatton Garden Street.

"They had it on display in the window," I said. "They'd want to advertise that they had the piece—unless it's a paste copy." It was a common practice of late, given the thefts. "Either way, the real one will be locked in the safe every night. But your safecracker can bring it out. What do you need me for?"

Her eyebrows rose. "Do you really need to ask?"

I wanted to hear her answer. What would she admit?

"You've worked at Seamus's—Mr. Ardle's shop," she said. "You'll be able to tell if it's real jewels as opposed to paste. I don't want to go through all this just to have some worthless glass."

Did she think I was a fool? A few days with a jeweler's loupe and she could show anyone how to tell the difference. My guess was she didn't wholly trust her cracksman.

I passed the illustration back to her. "So you'd want me to verify it's real."

"Yes. That's all."

"You'd share the plan beforehand?" I asked.

"Of course."

Two hundred pounds, I thought. And if I knew the plan beforehand, I could minimize the risks. "I'll consider it."

"Good," she nodded. "Let me know what you think of Simonson's."

Knowing the jeweler, I could study the mark more particularly.

In a heavy disguise, including a flaxen wig that covered my ears so a jeweler wouldn't be able to detect that my earrings were paste, I retraced my steps to Hatton Garden. Simonson's shared a roofline with Willingham's to the north. They occupied one of the taller buildings, with several windows on the two floors above. The two shops had similar brickwork, and the doors were positioned at the far edges, away from each other, the large plate glass windows between them.

I visited Willingham's first, briefly, to examine the composition of the common wall, just to see if there might be a passage between, giving the possibility of going into one shop to reach the other. The wall was plaster, and a large vertical mirror that hung in the middle could potentially hide a door. The floor was wood planks, bare but nicely polished. I left and went into Simonson's, adopting a pronounced limp favoring my right leg.

I recalled the shop from my first visit; it had been one of the nicer ones, well lit, with four gas-lit chandeliers and half a dozen sconces on the walls. The cabinets were wood, with glass at the front and top. There were two locks to each, one at each back corner. A thick red Turkey carpet covered the center of the floor, which was made of wide wooden planks, clearly old but polished to a high gleam. The wall shared with

Willingham's had a long horizontal mirror, not a vertical one, behind the case of watches. Still, there could be an overlap of nearly three feet square between them.

Behind one counter was a man of about forty-five with blue eyes, dark hair, and a face that had likely been handsome once but was now heavy, the skin on his neck gone to jowls underneath his beard. The owner, perhaps? His coat was a fine serge, fitted, and his collar and cuffs pure white with no visible frays on the buttonholes. He'd be less agreeable than the young woman who stood between two display cabinets, and I turned toward her, adopting the guise of a wealthy watch-buying wife.

"It's my husband's birthday next month," I explained. "He has two watches already, but they're both silver. I thought I might buy him a gold one. Do you think he'd like it?"

I felt the man's gaze alight on me, but I kept my eyes on the young woman, and he left us alone.

She smiled. "I'm sure he would like anything you chose, mum."

I beamed and went to stand before the case of watches. A careful survey of the plaster wall behind her indicated not a single crack—nothing that suggested an opening, unless it was behind the mirror.

The bottom of the cabinet was lined in a cream-colored silk, with the watches laid out six inches apart. Some were closed, to reveal the elaborate carving of the covers. Others were open, to reveal the delicate hands.

Despite my true purpose, I found myself admiring them. Each showed the same time as the standing clock nearby.

Now I needed to discover if they did repairs in the shop or sent them elsewhere.

"Mum?"

"I was just admiring how perfectly they keep time," I said. "To the minute. It's remarkable."

She dimpled. "We pride ourselves on selling objects of beauty that work properly."

"But if it doesn't keep time?" I asked and added apologetically, "My husband is rather particular. He despises lateness in anyone." My tone suggested that I'd been on the receiving end of his ire, and sympathy flashed across her face.

"If the watch ever fails to keep time, we will fix it at no charge, if you buy it here."

The back of the shop consisted of three doors. One, set back farther than the others, clearly led to the alley behind; it had two shining dead bolt locks. The short hallway to it was between two other rooms that jutted into this main one, each of which had a closed door with a crystal handle and simple keyhole. One was likely an office and workroom, the other a set of stairs going up.

"Do you do all your work on the premises?" I asked. "You don't send the watches away, do you?"

She glanced toward the door behind me. "No, it's all done here by our jewelers."

"Lovely." I tapped the glass with a gloved finger. "Could I see this one, please?"

She brought it out. "This is a beautiful Breguet," she began. "Only a few of these were made . . ."

With half my mind, I listened to her describing the watch. With the other half, I took in the rest of the store.

Large gilt-framed mirrors hung on the walls, and two smaller mirrors hung at an angle from the ceiling. I hadn't seen ceiling mirrors in the other shops, but the value was obvious.

Next, I asked to see a Le Phare repeater, and as she withdrew it, the door to the right opened and a man of about seventy emerged. He stepped forward to converse in a low tone with the younger man, who resembled him enough that I'd guess he was his son, or a nephew, perhaps. The two men disappeared behind the door. The creak of the stairs as they climbed was audible.

"Was that the owner?" I asked. "He reminds me of my grandfather, with the stoop and the spectacles."

"Yes, that's Mr. Simonson. He began the shop in Clerkenwell and moved it here two years ago."

"Does the family live upstairs then?" I asked.

She gave me an odd look.

"I had a friend whose parents own a haberdashery," I said by way of explanation, "and they lived above it. We used to go upstairs for our tea. I imagine it was convenient, although sometimes I think her parents wished they could've lived away from it."

"I daresay they would," she murmured. "But the younger son is bedridden and needs help all day. He came back from the Crimea just a boy of sixteen with his leg blown off."

"Oh, that's awful," I said, feeling genuine dismay. "And he's been an invalid for twenty years? The poor man."

She nodded. "It was a terrible thing, and he's in a good deal of pain."

The door opened, revealing the son, whose face was dark with anger. I handed back the watch I held.

"Would you like to see another?"

"No, thank you. But I will bring my husband. I think he'd like this one best"—I pointed to the gold Breguet, the first I'd held—"but I'd like him to choose."

I stepped away, pausing by a case that held gold rings. In the mirror, I watched as the man approached the clerk, coming close enough that her body tensed and she leaned away, although she held her ground. His left hand clawed around her elbow, and she flinched. His jowls shook as he quietly berated her—for answering my questions? Not making the sale?

Abruptly he released her and turned away. She rubbed her elbow and caught my eye in the mirror. She flushed with embarrassment.

If the man hadn't been standing there, I'd have told her he was the one who should be ashamed. This was impossible, of course, so I did what I could. I turned back and said in my sweetest tone, "Thank you again. You've been so much more helpful than the clerks in other shops. I'll be back with my husband soon."

With that, I departed and started in the direction of the fenced alley that ran behind the shop.

Given that there were constables stationed by the alleys after dark, I had wondered if we might come in through an upstairs window or across the roof instead. The presence of the Simonson family in the quarters above made that unlikely. But at least I'd learned the necklace was on the premises, in the workroom to the left.

There was no constable at the alley's entrance; apparently, he didn't arrive at his post until later. When I could be sure I was unobserved, I approached the gate. A padlock hooked through a metal loop secured two iron bars as thick as my arm. With all vertical bars, the gate provided no convenient footholds, and the height was such that no one could easily be boosted over. It would require a rope ladder with grappling hooks. Good lord.

I walked around front again, strolling the pavement opposite Willingham's and Simonson's. It was then that something curious struck me. From left to right, the façade of the building consisted of a wooden-framed door, then a narrow bit of brick, a large plate glass window, then an expanse of brick, then another window, then Simonson's door. But recalling the main rooms of both stores, I thought the brick section in the middle seemed oddly large. Was it possible that the inside walls of the two jewelers didn't touch? It seemed there was a gap of a few feet between them. What could be the reason for that? Privacy from each other? Storage?

I left Hatton Garden considering these additional obstacles and possibilities. How I wished I knew where Amelia was, for she might have helped me. But she had left the night I saw her at the inn, and keeping herself to herself, she hadn't yet sent me her address.

As I crossed Leather Lane, I turned back to examine the row of plate glass windows glinting in the late-afternoon light, the cloth awnings fluttering in the breeze, the pedestrians on the pavement, the traffic thinned from earlier. I exited Hatton Garden and walked south, as I had before. At the corner, I observed a wine and spirits store across the way and a cheese shop beside it—both of which no doubt stocked commodities brought in from across the Channel.

I halted, thinking.

The shop clerk had said Simonson's had moved to Hatton Garden only two years ago from Clerkenwell, like many other jewelers. Before that, the area was home to a miscellaneous collection of shops, many of which received smuggled goods.

James knew this area, for it was here he'd made his nighttime escapades, transferring goods through secret passageways and back alleys. The shops were cheek by jowl; no doubt some of the passages remained. And perhaps he'd have an idea about why there seemed to be a space between the two jewelers.

If I was reading him right, he wouldn't mind me finding him to ask.

Chapter 17

I didn't know where James lived, but if a woman wants to find a man, there are ways.

I started for the Silver Plover, where James had taken me. When I entered, it was the same warm, cheerful room crowded with men and women and children. I scanned every table, to no avail. Bad luck, but by no means insurmountable. I made my way to the barkeep. "I'm looking for James Kinnon. Has he been in tonight?"

"Aye, come and gone, not ten minutes ago."

"I know he's in a lodging house nearby. Do you know which?"

His head cocked, and a knowing grin curved his mouth. "Aye." He drew out the syllable teasingly, but I refused to flush. He pointed with his thumb. "Out the door, take a left and then the second right. Look fer two side-by-side front doors, painted dark red."

I found it easily enough and entered the foyer, glad for the lighted lamp hanging on the wall. I climbed the wooden steps and knocked on the first door. There was no answer. At the second door, a young woman answered, and I asked if James Kinnon lived here.

"Never heard of him." She scowled suspiciously and turned her head. "Is this another of your sluts?"

My eyebrows flew up, but before I could retort, a masculine voice growled from the room beyond: "Don't be stupid." It rose in pitch to add, "He's next floor up. Room over this one."

I called a thank-you to the faceless voice and started up the next flight of stairs. There was no carpeting on the stairs, but the steps were swept clean, the walls decently painted, and the banister polished and in good repair. James was doing well working at the Custom House, I thought, feeling pleased for him. I reached his door and was relieved to see a light emanating underneath. I removed one glove and knocked, and after a second, bootsteps approached and the door was pulled open.

James stood in his trousers and a loose white shirt, open at the throat and rolled back from his wrists. A slow smile lit his face. "This is a good surprise for the end of a day."

"I hope you're not hiding from anyone," I said. "Because that barkeep at the Silver Plover will tell *anyone* where you live." He laughed. "Can I come in?"

He stepped back to allow it. The room was warm with the heat from the black stove in the corner, and I removed the other glove, holding them both in one hand and lifting them toward him.

"Thank you for these. They're lovely."

"You're welcome." He looked somewhat perplexed, as if he wasn't sure what to make of my visit.

Indeed, now that I was here, I wasn't sure what to make of it myself.

I stuffed the gloves in the pocket and undid my cloak. He hung it on a wooden rack by the door. I stood with my hands on the top rail of a wooden chair, my thumb tapping lightly, uncertain where to begin.

His hands were quiet at his sides. "Is something the matter?"

I thought of everything Sarah and Emma had told me about James, not least about how he'd had my name stitched on his heart for years. Now, studying his expression, I could see it: kindness, to be sure, even curiosity. And a faint smile, almost rueful.

"You're looking at me like that again," he said. "Like I'm running a con."

I allowed a laugh, feeling the heat rise to my cheeks, and drew a breath.

He'd asked me if I trusted him for the important things. Well, I would try, and I'd see where it took us.

"Do you remember the night you warned me to be careful about Maggie?" I asked.

"O' course."

"Well, she wants something from me."

He drew two chairs toward the stove, but I stood, my fingers pleating the gathers in my skirt, and so he remained standing as well, his fingertips on the top rail of the wooden chair.

"She has a dodge in mind," I said. "It's difficult, near impossible even, and likely dangerous, although my cut could make it worth doing. But I want to know what you think."

His brow furrowed. "Well, I'll help you if I can, but I can't do much without you giving me some particulars."

"I can tell you what I know," I said. "But you can't tell anyone. Not even Emma."

"I won't."

I remained silent a moment, considering where to begin.

"Not everything is a game with me, you know." His tone was subdued, tentative.

His words startled me out of my thoughts. "What?"

"You said that," he reminded me, "the night at the inn."

I winced, ashamed of myself. "I shouldn't have. It's not true. I know that."

There was a long silence.

He pointed to the chair he'd drawn for me. "Sit down, Kit. I need to tell you something."

As I came around to the front of the chair, he pulled the other chair to face me straight on and sat, his elbows on the chair arms, one hand on his thigh, one rubbing his chin. "What do you know about my time in prison?"

That wasn't what I expected.

"Well," I began slowly. "I heard you were caught by a Yard man and sentenced to a year for smuggling." I hesitated, but the glint in his eyes told me to go on. "You were let out early, and there was a rumor that you ratted on someone—not that I believed it."

The skin around his eyes tightened briefly, in a way that drew an old memory from whatever murky ditch it occupied in my brain. It was how he'd looked when he told me he couldn't run our badger scheme one night because his mother was sick.

It was a tell of the more unusual kind. One that pointed toward truth instead of a lie.

Still, I wasn't sure what his time in prison had to do with Maggie's dodge. But it seemed he wanted to tell me about it, so I asked, "How *were* you caught?"

James settled his left palm on the carved end of the chair arm. "I was on the river, moving whiskey and wine for a French merchant. It was pitch-dark, and they had dozens of us lightermen working by lamps hanging from the side of the ship. They'd anchor at night about a mile downstream"—he flicked his forefinger to the east—"completely overloaded with barrels. They had small ones for us, easier to handle. They offloaded the larger ones at the Custom House."

"Because otherwise, if the ship was spotted, Customs would wonder why it wasn't unloading anything," I guessed. "But wouldn't they notice the hold wasn't full?"

He gave a half laugh. "Of course you'd think of that. There are false walls running the length of the ship for the small barrels. Officers are too busy to be checking if the innards of a ship and the outer hull match."

"Ah." Like the short pockets that concealed our thieving ones—and possibly the walls between Simonson's and Willingham's.

"To avoid the river patrols, we had to row upriver to a hidden dock." His finger beat a quick tattoo. "But one night, as I pulled in, three bull's-eye lanterns all switched on for me and two other blokes about twenty yards behind. They both jumped and swam off, but two Yard men got hold of me, and another had a pistol pointed at my face."

My breath caught. "What did you do?"

"Do?" James gave a short chuckle. "What do you think? It was me against three of them and a pistol, so I went. Next afternoon, I was tried and thrown in gaol, and a few days later, this Yard man named Pickford paid me a visit. He pulled me into a private cell, wanting to know who the others were."

"You didn't tell him."

He gave me a look. "Course not. But he had to try."

I nodded.

"Next, he asked about the merchant. They had the barrels of wine, so there was no denying they were French, but the merchants don't put names on the barrels until they reach the warehouses. Pickford beat on me, but I wouldn't tell him anything about the merchant, either."

"Because they'd catch other lightermen by keeping watch for those ships."

He briefly turned over a palm. "Pickford said I'd get one year for certain and threatened to make it three or five by pinning more charges on me. When I still didn't talk, he changed his tune, said he could spring me, perhaps even find me work with a decent wage in exchange for information." A bitter smile pulled one corner of his mouth. "I told him for the last time, I wasn't a rat, and that's when he said, 'No, but if I find those other two men in the next few days and bring them in here, everyone will think you are. And I won't correct them.'"

"Oh." The word escaped with a gasp. James would be a dead man.

James raised an eyebrow. "Aye, he was a bugger. And that week, I stayed up every night, hoping to hell he wouldn't find my friends, not just for their sakes."

"Emma must have been terrified," I said.

"Oh, she was." His voice was emphatic.

"You saw her, then?"

"They let her visit the once."

I felt a prick of shame. "Sorry I didn't."

"I knew Sarah was sick, same as plenty of others. Emma told me." He was being kind.

"I could've come when she was well."

"They only allowed family."

"Stop," I said sharply. "They'll let anyone in for a coin, and I could have said I was your sister. We were friends. I should have come. Let me say I'm sorry."

"You've said it, then," he replied mildly. "But don't fret about it any longer. I got out."

"How?" I asked. "Pickford?"

"No, he never came back. My next visitor was named Fuller. I was dragged back into that foul room, and he walked in, and I thought, hell, must we do this yet again? Only he was different. Decent." He saw my doubtful look and his mouth twitched. "He wasn't a Yard man. He worked for a newspaper, and he wasn't interested in me ending up dead, it served no purpose. He'd help me if he could, but I had to give him something." He sniffed. "I started to say I wouldn't, and he interrupted, saying there were dozens of cases of smuggling going unsolved, and he was writing articles about them. People talked in prison, and if I learned something that might help him, he might help me find an honest day's work, especially seeing as I spoke French."

"How did he know that?"

James snorted. "When he came into the room, I said *merde*. Means 'shit.' I said it more than once."

"Oh."

James shifted in his chair. "I figured nothing would come of it. But a week later, there were two new men in my cell, and one of them was drunk and started bragging that he dragged two women out of a carriage, stole their jewelry and clothes, then killed them both and threw them into an old boathouse. He was laughing like a bloody Punch puppet."

"Oh, God." I shivered.

James stood and opened the square stove door, crouching to tong a few pieces of coal from the brass hod. "About a week later, Fuller comes back and pulls me into that room again. Only this time, I told him I had something to say."

"You told him about the dead women."

He shut the metal door with a clank and settled back in his chair. "It wouldn't help Fuller with his articles about smuggling, but I thought the families should know they didn't just vanish."

"They could bury the bodies properly," I said.

"Aye." Absently, he raked his hair from his temple. "He said he'd look into it. If the bodies were where I said, he'd be back. I started to say he couldn't spring me straightaway, it would kill me, seeing as everyone in prison has someone outside, and it would be clear who told about the murders. But as Fuller left, he played it proper, called me a bloody eejit, cussed me under his breath, saying I'd lost my chance. Made it clear I'd given him nothing and he was fed up with me, without overplaying it." His tone was one of grudging admiration.

"But you were right," I said.

"Two days later, two guards came to the cell, threw a black hood over my head, and dragged me out like I was done for."

His voice sobered as he spoke, and despite him sitting in front of me, alive, my heart skipped a beat as I imagined the terror of it. Into our silence came the evening's sounds from the street—carriage and cart wheels, men's laughter, the whinny of a horse, the slam of a door, the scrape of a shovel against the cobbles as the nightsoil men began their labors.

"So no one knew he'd sprung you," I said at last.

He shook his head. "They brought me to the Yard by carriage and took off my hood. An inspector named Stiles had ordered my release, though he was none too happy about Fuller stepping on his toes."

"Oh."

"Anyway, one murdered woman was a rich man's

daughter—the family'd paid to keep the case out of the papers—and the other was her maid. They'd been missing for three months." He shifted in the chair. "Stiles thanked me, and Fuller gave me a letter of introduction to a Custom House agent who owed him a favor. He made me swear I'd never tell a soul about what I'd done for the Yard or the paper, or what he'd done for me." His mouth twitched, curved into the grin I knew. "Stiles was waving his hands, like he didn't want to know anything about it. The agent at the House gave me a week's trial to prove myself, and I've been an honest man since."

"Lucky for you, you speak French."

"Aye." A wistful look. "One of my ma's blessings. I use it all the time."

He settled back in his chair with an expectant look.

My fingers twined themselves in my lap. "You've never told anyone about your deal with Fuller?"

"No. Not even Emma."

I held his gaze, considering, and he waited for my next question.

"Were you afraid," I said slowly, "when that Yard man said he'd let people think you were a rat?"

His entire body stilled, his very breath halted, but he answered. "I was afraid from the minute I entered the cell and heard the clang of the latch behind me."

The rawness took away my breath, and I sat for a long moment, silenced by the ache in my throat.

Now I understood. I could have asked him anything, and he'd have answered. His story had nothing to do with Maggie's dodge. This was an offering, with both hands turned up, as open and honest as he could make it, to show how much he was willing to trust me. To show me I could trust him.

The words came chokingly out of my mouth: "Maggie wants me to steal a necklace. A family heirloom worth several thousand pounds."

He leaned forward, dropping his elbows onto his knees, his hands clasped loosely between them. "Where is it?"

"She says it's at Simonson's in Hatton Garden, for cleaning."

He frowned. "So it's safe-kept, isn't it?"

His mind ran in the same direction as mine.

"If I were to take it during the day, it would have to be when it's out of the safe being cleaned or repaired," I replied. "I can't imagine how to do that, unless it's at knife-point. It's not as though they'll have the real thing displayed in a case, like a piece for sale." I bit my lip. "But I think Maggie intends to steal it at night, after the shop is closed. Only the constables are all over Hatton Garden. There's a swarm of them."

"Does she know about the constables?"

I spread my hands. "I told her. I might be able to scale the gate that blocks the alley, but I'm rubbish at picking locks beyond the usual ones, and I've certainly never cracked a safe. But she has a man who can manage that." I saw the look he gave. "I don't know who. She's only telling me bits and pieces."

"Hm." He sat back, resting an elbow on the chair arm, rubbing his mouth with his fingers. "What necklace?"

"It belongs to the Marquess Hargrave. French made, with a ruby the size of your thumb."

He let out a soft whistle. "No small prize."

"I know."

"Where exactly is this jeweler?"

"Do you have some paper and a pen?"

He fetched them for me out of a drawer, and I sketched Hatton Garden, the three main streets and the crosses.

"Here." I pointed to the southern corner of Hatton Garden Street, which ran down the middle of the rectangle. "Just below Charles. It's on the east side of the street, so the front door faces west."

He studied it a moment. "Is Simonson's part of one building, or its own?"

"It shares with Willingham's to the north."

"You probably know that whole area is a rabbit warren of vaults and doors and secret passageways among the buildings," he said.

My heart skipped. "That's what I was hoping. You don't think they've crumbled or been bricked up?"

He shrugged. "Some might be but I'm guessing most are still in use, one way or another. Maggie might've picked this jeweler because she knows about one that's still open."

I frowned, thinking back to what Maggie had said and how she'd said it. "I could be wrong, but I think she picked the necklace first. And I got an odd feeling about it. She sounded . . . bitter when she mentioned the marquess's family. Mocked them for being in *Debrett's*."

"Hm." He lowered his gaze to my scribbled map. "I imagine most jewelers have Yale locks on the doors, front and back?"

"Simonson's does. I checked. Two in the back, one in the front."

"Tell me more about the shop."

I gave him all the details I'd given Maggie, and I could see him building the shop in his own mind.

"Do you feel you have to do this for her?" he asked. "Or do you want to?"

"She offered me two hundred pounds as my take," I said.

His eyebrows shot up.

"I *know*." I hesitated. "I just don't know how much to trust her. I mean, I've told you why I'm leery—not least because she's tried to gain my trust, flattering me, telling me I'm the best thief she has, confiding in me about her time in Swan River, making me feel sorry for her." I rubbed my thumb along the end of the wooden arm. It was worn smooth from years of hands curving around it. "But now she's pushing Mary and Nell out of the ring."

"Oh." His face registered dismay.

"So I don't trust her to look out for me. I think she's putting together a dodge that ends up with me in prison."

"All right, then," he said. "Let's think on this."

We were silent for a long minute, and then his face changed.

"What?" I asked.

"Well, I'm just wondering if there's a reason the marquess is having it cleaned now."

I should have wondered that myself. "You think his wife will wear it to a special event? I could steal it there instead?"

It would likely be easier to steal the necklace from the Marchioness Hargrave's neck than from the shop. But it was curious that Maggie hadn't considered this. She, who used to take necklaces from women's necks. Perhaps she doubted I could do it.

James shrugged. "We could find out."

"How?" I asked.

He rose from his chair. "You stay here, make us some tea, and I'll be back."

"Where are you going?"

"I've a friend who keeps newspapers."

James put on his coat and left, and I poured water from the jug into the kettle, stoked the fire, rummaged in the cupboard for a pot, cups, and a tin of tea. I opened it and sniffed. Bergamot.

But a kettle takes time to boil, and my eyes wandered around his room. There wasn't much to it—a bed, made, covered with a beautifully quilted counterpane that I guessed was Emma's handiwork; a large table with wide wooden planks and four chairs; a smaller table for a lamp; some books; a wardrobe for clothes. I wanted to play fair; he'd left me here, trusting me not to snoop, but by my reckoning, that gave me license to look at anything out in the open. I approached his shelves and examined his books. There were only eight, and three were in French. I opened one to find a signature—his mother's—*Adelaide*.

His step sounded on the stairs. I replaced the book in its space and returned to the stove, where the water was close to boiling. He entered bearing a sheaf of papers under his arm, the cold dampness of the night entering with him.

"Why does your friend keep papers?" I asked.

He dropped them on the table and rehung his coat on a nail by the door. "My guess is he keeps them for the obituaries, but I don't ask."

My mind darted to possible occupations for his friend: a solicitor, an art gallery owner, an estate auctioneer, a thief, a funeral parlor owner, a resurrectionist, or a medical student. Any of them might want to know when someone died. Death was an opportunity for the vultures.

"I bought copies of today's papers, too." James tossed them onto the table.

SCOTLAND YARD FLAILING! trumpeted the *Times*.

MURDERS THWART THE DETECTIVES announced the *Standard*.

"The police are taking a beating," James said. "I assume you'd have said, but have Billy and Tommy come back?"

"Not that I've seen," I said.

James split the pile of newspapers in half, setting the stacks on either side of the table.

"What should we look for?" I spooned tea leaves into the pot and poured hot water from the kettle.

"Something fancy. An opera or a theater opening." James grinned. "I don't know the schedule offhand."

I snorted.

"A party would be best," he said. "People drinking spirits or champagne, and they're talking or dancing."

My mind leapt to the day I'd taken the necklace from Mary while she talked.

"Another possibility would be to take it from the marquess's house," he said. "Do you know where they live?"

"Somewhere in the West End, I assume."

"Hm." He poured out hot tea for us into two mismatched cups, clinked the kettle back on the stove, and brought two more lamps over, lighting them with deft hands.

He paused, and I looked up. He'd caught me staring.

Feeling warmth creeping along my neck, I picked up my cup and bent my head over the first page of the newspaper.

Two hours went by, broken briefly when one of us would find an interesting news item—the ridiculous, the startling, or the peculiar. Someone had broken into a butcher shop in Bethnal Green, taken several shanks of meat, and left behind an old boot. A mud lark had found a battered shield that appeared centuries old, but it turned out to be a "Billy and Charley," one of the fake medieval objects metal-cast by two confidence men in the 1850s. There had been an outbreak of cholera at the King's Bench, the notorious debtor's prison, not far from Elephant and Castle.

Then my eye caught a notice about a ball to be held at Lord Charleton's house in St. James. In the third paragraph was a list of half a dozen titled people, including two of Queen Victoria's daughters, Princess Alice and Princess Helena, with their respective husbands. I scanned the remainder of the article for other names but found none.

"James, look." I turned the paper toward him. "What about this?"

He looked to where I pointed. "Aye, that's likely. Let's see if there's a list of other people invited. Hand me some of the next few days, will you?"

We were silent, turning pages, seeking only news items related to the Charleton ball.

James let out a soft whistle and I looked up. "Found the list."

I stood and went around the other side of the table to peer over his shoulder. There were perhaps two hundred names.

No doubt the people who weren't listed would be mortified, their absence a sign that they were several rungs down society's ladder.

Together we searched the small print, with me reading from the bottom and James from the top. Three inches down, James's forefinger tapped, and there it was: *The Marquess and Marchioness Hargrave*.

"Oh." I let out a breath.

He grinned. "There."

I returned to my chair and sank into it.

His eyes were sparkling in the lamplight with satisfaction and something like relief. Relief for me, I realized. "A ball gives us options," he said. "It's much easier to slip in the house, with so much coming in."

"Food and wine," I said, recalling the delivery at the Wiltses' house.

"Not to mention musicians, furniture, flowers, tables, chairs, servants hired especially for the night. The servants' entrance will be wide open, and no one will be suspicious of a new face."

"But James, it's in less than a fortnight."

He shrugged. "At least we know."

"I don't suppose I can go in the front door," I said, my mind ticking through possibilities. "Even with proper clothes."

"Perhaps you could," he allowed, though dubiously. "You'd give your name to the footman to announce you, but the guest list will be large enough no one will know everyone, not even Lady Charleton herself."

"I'd be better going in as a hired servant. As a maid, I could circulate, bringing food or drink up to the dining room."

He hesitated. "How adept are you at removing a necklace from a woman's neck without her noticing?"

I shrugged. "I can practice. But could I go in as a servant, do you think? I've only ever acted the part for a dodge, and I don't know how I'd go about being hired."

"Emma does," he said. "She was in service before Ma died."

"She was?"

"Sarah can probably help you, too."

I hesitated. "I'd rather not involve her."

"All right." He stood and brought our cups to the sink

with its single tap at the bottom of a pipe. "You can look in the 'Situations Vacant' columns in the papers. But there's also servants' registries where you can enroll. Mrs. Massey's and Mrs. Hunt's are the two best. But give me a day or two to get a forged character for you, saying you've worked elsewhere, somewhere away from London they can't readily check. Then you can see about being hired by the company that's catering the event."

I found myself staring at his broad back, bent over the sink. *How does he know such things?*

He returned to the table. "Seems you have a good option to present Maggie," he said as he shuffled the newspapers back into an orderly pile. "Less complicated than Yale locks and safes, to be sure."

I stepped around the table to face him. With his shirt open at the neck, I could see the broad *V* of his collarbone, the pulse in the notch, the shadow of whiskers darkening his jaw.

I came near enough to feel the heat of him.

"Kit." There was a note of warning in his voice, but I ignored it and reached for him. His hands came to my wrists, stopping my hands before they could settle around his neck. His eyes were dark and fixed on mine, though his voice was hoarse. "God knows I want this." He gave a small shake of his head. "But not for helping you."

It wasn't just for helping me tonight, or for all the ways he'd looked out for me, or even the way he looked as if merely the sight of me on his threshold pleased him so. How could I explain it? A feeling stirred up under my heart, tipping it over like a wheelbarrow spilling sideways. It was for the way he threw back his head when he laughed at a story, the way he told me the truth about being afraid in prison like it wasn't shameful, and the way, after years of me taking care of Sarah, he made me feel like I wasn't the only one in the world who looked out for people more than they knew. I admired how he'd carved out lawful work for himself, and I liked the shape of his hands, the bulk of his shoulders, the way he could wink at me so quick no one else saw it—

But all that came out of me was, "It's not," in a choked voice.

Perhaps he saw some of the rest of it in my face, for his expression changed, and he let go of my hands to run his rough fingers into my hair, holding me apart, just looking. I had kissed men for badgering but never for wanting to, and it seemed he knew it, for his mouth brushed mine tentatively at first. The lightest kiss, but it tumbled joy onto my heart wide and high as the wake of a steamship. He drew back and I could look at him. I touched my fingers to his cheek and ran my thumb over his mouth, and he caught my hand, pressing the soft part of my palm to his lips. Then his mouth was hungry on mine, and as he kissed me, heat ran from the crown of my head down to my feet, razoring like lightning over my skin.

When at last we drew back from each other, I looked for some light of humor in his eyes. A glint of triumph or a spark of glee that he'd won me over.

Instead, there was a tenderness and wonder that turned my bones to water.

"Why now?" he muttered. "I've wanted to be with you for years."

"But you never told me," I protested. "You never said a word! You kept it secret as a load on a die."

He gave that sideways tilt of his head that meant I had a point. "You think I was going to hand my heart over to you just so you could stomp on it? Benny was sweet on you forever, and he got nowhere. When Caleb tried to kiss you, you smacked him so hard you bloodied his nose. You'd have nothing to do with the lot of us. Then again, we were all young and stupid."

"You're old and wise now?" I teased.

The skin around his eyes crinkled, and he drew my fingers to his mouth to kiss them. It reminded me of the gloves. "Do you know, I've never had something *bought* from a department store before you gave me those gloves."

"Oh, I stole them," he said, his face deadpan.

"You did not," I said, swatting him as he laughed. "You see the way you joke!"

His smile faded, and he looked at me questioningly. "Do you mind it?"

"No," I admitted. "I like it."

"All right then."

He bent and kissed me again until I pulled away to ask, "Why do you? Make a joke? Emma does the same when she's upset."

His expression turned thoughtful. "I suppose it began after Father died. Ma was . . . just so sad."

I remembered Emma had said her mother's heart was broken.

"We both tried to make her laugh," he said. "No one wants to see their mum cry like that, like she couldn't stop."

"I never saw mine cry," I said.

"Never?" he asked.

I shook my head. "She'd snap and scold, but she didn't cry."

"I've never seen you cry," he said.

"I guess I don't much see the use of it." I rested a hand on his chest, feeling the warmth of his skin through the linen of the shirt. "Sarah cries sometimes."

He put his warm hand over mine. "Are you worried about this dodge?"

A half laugh escaped me. "I always worry. If I stop worrying, that's when the bad things happen. So long as I'm watching and worrying, they don't."

"You know it's not so. People are out there causing all sorts of trouble your worrying won't stop." He tipped my chin up so our gazes met. "Are you considering getting out? Of having this be the last time?" His tone was even, but the look in his eyes told me my answer mattered.

"Sarah wants me to." The words stuck in my throat like a clump of dry bread. "And I would, but I don't have enough to stop."

"What's enough?" His voice was practical. "A hundred? Two hundred?"

"I don't know." I was trying to be honest. "It's been years since my mother died, leaving us with nothing, and I still have dreams that I'm running from door to door, hammering to get in because I need food for Sarah, and none of the doors open."

He studied me. "But that's not the truth now, is it?"

"No," I admitted. "I've enough put by to take care of us, if something happens, if Sarah gets sick or I can't work for a while."

He opened his mouth as if to correct me but closed it again, as if he thought better of it. "Well, for the next two weeks, until this dodge is done, let me worry for you, if it must be done."

"Will you worry over Sarah for me, too?" I asked wryly. "She *despises* when I do it, but she likes you, so she'd probably take it with better grace."

He laughed and bent to kiss me again, his mouth warm and tender and full of longing, like he had years to make up for.

We might have remained there for hours, but I drew back shakily. "I should go."

"Yeah?" he whispered, his forehead touching mine.

"Yeah," I echoed. "It's getting late. I need to tell Maggie I've figured out how I'll get that bloody necklace for her."

Chapter 18

James had offered to take me home, but I wanted time between the north bank and the south, time to think and feel before I had to keep my happiness off my face. I wasn't ready to share it.

Nothing could keep my heart in its proper place.

He put me in a cab back to Elephant and Castle. I found myself smiling.

Upon entering the inn, I approached Pat to ask where I might find Maggie only to find she'd left for Birmingham on the early train, back the day after next.

Deflated, I spent the next day with the uneasy, restless feeling of urgently wanting to act but being stalled.

On Monday morning, I went to the inn to ask for Maggie again, but still she hadn't arrived. I went for a walk, occupying myself as I could, and returned early in the afternoon. This time Pat's eyes flicked toward the stairs.

I found Maggie in the goods room with Silas Pike, going over ledgers. Remembering that Amelia told me Silas had been Maggie's lover before being Amelia's fence, I backed out and said I'd wait. Nearly an hour later, when he left, I entered.

She stood behind the desk, her fingertips on the edge. "Well?"

"I want to propose a different dodge," I said. "I've found a way to get your necklace. Safer and easier than taking it from the jeweler's."

"Oh?"

"I went to the shop, twice—in different costumes—and considered every angle. But Maggie, there's a clerk and the son of the jeweler present, mirrors everywhere, a safe behind a locked door, and locks on every cabinet, the back door, and the alley, not to mention a high gate. The entire family lives upstairs, so there's no way of coming in over the roof from above, as they'd hear the noise."

Her eyebrows rose. "The entire family lives upstairs?"

"Yes, including a son who returned from Crimea with terrible injuries. He's bedridden. Besides, the Fairleigh murders mean the constables at the end of every street are more vigilant. So I truly don't think it's possible to take the necklace off the premises, even at night, without being caught." I dropped my hands onto the top rail of the chair. "But there's a ball in a few weeks. That's why the marquess is having it cleaned and repaired at the jeweler's. I can retrieve it at the party."

To my surprise, there was no light of approval or even curiosity in her eyes.

"Sit down," she said and as I drew out the chair, she took a bottle of whiskey from the cupboard, pouring some into a glass. The smoky tang of it made me miss Amelia. Maggie put the bottle away without offering me any, not that I'd have taken it. There was something unpleasant coming, and I'd need my wits about me. She sat behind the desk across from me, but at an angle, her right forearm on the desk, her warped fingers around the glass with its amber liquid, her eyes on it as she said, "I want to tell you the story of the day I was caught. Would you like to hear it?"

Cold spiked down my spine. Was she finally going to tell me about the role my mother played? "Yes."

She tapped the glass soundlessly with her thumb. "I was once a girl much like you." Her eyes met mine. "You might not think so now, but I was very pretty. Twenty years in the blazing sun of Swan River ruined my looks, but I once had thick dark hair and a complexion as fair as yours."

I recalled the photograph. "I'm sure," I replied. That much was honest.

"Your mother was my jenny that day." She paused and gave an appraising look. "So you knew that."

I nodded.

"I don't blame her, you know," she said. "I never blamed her."

I wasn't sure whether to believe it.

"We were at Simonson's," she said.

She'd been caught at Simonson's?

My heart gave a thud, and I had the uncanny feeling of having trod in Maggie's footsteps—and Ma's.

Maggie shook her head, as if she'd followed my thought. "Remember, 'twas back when the shop was still in Northampton Square."

"Of course," I said.

"They didn't have the locks and safes and mirrors back then, but I was caught all the same."

"By a constable?"

The skin around her eyes tightened. "No. By the son, the bloody ratbag." She raised the glass and sipped, holding the whiskey in her mouth before she swallowed. "He took me to the back room and said if I gave up the jewels and let him fondle me a bit, he'd let me go. He wouldn't even call a constable, provided I was willing."

My spine pressed against the wooden slats of the chair, dreading what came next.

"I'm not a fool, and I'm no fish." Her fingertips went to her lips, rubbing from one side to the other and back, as if wiping away a kiss. "I knew he'd want more than fondling, but I'd *never* been taken so. He covered my mouth and shoved me up against the safe, so I could hardly breathe. I fought back, biting his hand and clawing his face, but he was too strong for me. I still remember the cold metal on my back. The knob jabbing into my spine." Her voice thickened. "And he laughed and kept saying in my ear how nice and soft and warm my pocket was. He was so bloody strong. The arms on him. The weight of him. He was twice my size." Her eyes flicked up to me, held. "When he finished and finally called for the police, it was a blessing."

With a chill, I began to understand. This dodge had never been about the Hargrave necklace. It had only ever been about the jeweler. The man who had been brutally vicious to Maggie was no doubt the same who had been mundanely cruel to the clerk. "I've seen him," I said hollowly.

"He told the constable he'd caught me thieving, and I'd fought back. Made himself the victim, pointing to his face and showing the teeth marks on his hand, with the constable grinning the entire time. The pig passed him some coins—he didn't even trouble to hide it—and I was thrown into a cell in Newgate, with nary a bed, moldy bread to eat, and only a metal pot for pissing. The next day, they walked me into the Old Bailey." She paused. "Have you ever been inside?"

"No."

"It's bigger than you'd think, with a balcony up above crammed full of people watching, dozens of benches on the floor, the jury under the windows, and a witness box, perched up in the middle so everybody can see. Just before me was a thief who'd killed an innkeeper's wife, and I think it put the judge in a mood to come down all the harder on me." She sniffed and gave a small shake of her head. "Simonson climbed up into the witness box and gave evidence, most of which was the scratches on his face, and I swear he'd scratched himself twice over to make it look worse. Then the constable got up and said his bit. The judge didn't even call me." Her eyes narrowed. "You mightn't understand, but it was a lesson for me. To realize that a villain can make himself out a victim by turning facts around."

"It wasn't fair," I said.

"No," she said. "So twenty years later, when I finally made it home, I bought some fine clothes and visited his new shop." An audible exhale flared her nostrils. "He didn't even recognize me. Can you believe the like?" Her mouth pinched in bitter wonder. "Tried to sell me some pearl earrings."

"This scheme of yours will hurt him back," I said.

"Not near enough." Her eyes flashed. "He should *hang*, but he's rich, so he won't. But this will do. He'll suffer longer."

I couldn't say I blamed her for wanting revenge.

"You're sure it was him?" I asked. "It's been years."

"I knew him straightaway. He's portlier now. The skin under his chin is wobbly, though he tries to hide it with a beard." Her voice was thin, precise as a blade. "And yes, it's been years. But God knows, Swan River taught me patience." Her green eyes held mine. "Call it revenge if you like, but before we die, we must all balance the scales if we want to die in peace. The reason I didn't die in Swan River was because God left me alive to do it. Do you understand?"

The set of her jaw reminded me of men who doubled their bet when they were behind. Maggie had dragged this revenge around with her for so long, it had a heft of its own, a weight, a value. Perhaps she couldn't set it down now, not without feeling a fool.

I made one last attempt to convince her. "Maggie, I understand you wanting revenge. I would, too. I'd want to slit his throat and let him rot in some back alley. But . . . *I'm* the one who would be taking the risk, along with whoever you sent with me."

"Are you frightened?" Her voice was edged with disdain.

"I'm not a coward, but I'm not a fool, either. Chances are, we'd be caught. The family lives upstairs. What if they hear? What if they come down? What if they have pistols?"

"My men'll keep you safe."

Men? Two? Or more?

"Then why can't you do this yourself?"

"This." She lifted her bad hand. "It's a hindrance, as is my eyesight, which isn't as keen as it once was."

I drew a breath. "Maggie, I can't get you the revenge you want. Not like this."

"Not even for two hundred pounds?" she asked. "What if I make it three?"

When I didn't reply, her face tightened with anger before she smoothed it back out to show only disappointment. "Why don't you think on it and come see me tomorrow? You've done most of the work already, looking into Hatton Garden." She raised the glass to her mouth and sipped. "I'll have something for you, whatever you decide."

"There's no need to pay—"

"No. I don't ask people to work for nothing. It's only fair."

"All right." I knew my answer, but I would give it to her tomorrow, if she preferred.

As I reached the door, I heard her voice behind me: "Have you talked to Amelia lately?"

Stifling a pang, I turned back. "No. Not since she left."

She smiled briefly. "Tomorrow, then."

I nodded and shut the door behind me, heading down the staircase with a feeling of relief.

My escape from Maggie's plan had been easier than I expected—indeed, so easy that it left me unsettled—and her story raised questions about the past that I knew only Amelia could answer. My chest ached with wanting to talk to her.

But who might know where she had gone? The only person I could think of was Emma.

A storm had rolled in while I'd been with Maggie, and it had begun to rain, one of those London rainstorms that slashed at windows and made the edges of the streets run with water. In the pub room, I plucked an abandoned, bent-spoked umbrella from the stand beside the door, took a lit lamp from the sill, and crossed the wide expanse of cobblestones in front of the inn. Usually at this time of day it was filled with carriages, costermonger carts, children, dogs. The downpour had emptied it and hid the façades of the buildings opposite, the only sign of them the light from the windows.

I headed to Emma's shop and knocked at the door. There was no answer, and I banged on the door again, louder. Emma emerged from the kitchen, peering through the shop toward the window.

"Emma, it's Kit," I called through the glass, tilting back the umbrella so she could see my face.

She hurried forward and unlocked the door. The bell tinkled as she pulled it open. "Good lord, Kit, it's pouring!"

I stepped inside, closing the door behind me. I didn't attempt to fold the umbrella as I wasn't sure I'd be able to open it again.

Her eyes searched mine. "What's the matter? Is it James?"

"I need to speak to Amelia."

Her jaw slacked, and she began to shake her head.

"It's important, Emma."

Emma wrapped one arm across her waist, crooking the other to put her hand in a loose fist over her mouth.

I was putting her in a terrible spot, I knew.

"Kit, she doesn't want anyone to know where she is. Including Maggie."

"She'd be the last person I'd tell," I said. "Please, Emma, trust me." A pleading note crept into my voice. "James does."

She lowered her hand to cross both arms over her chest. "Near Farringdon Market, in Shoe Lane, number thirteen."

Shoe Lane was between Old Bailey and Hatton Garden.

"The upper story," Emma added, her voice subdued. "And don't be followed."

"I won't."

As I reached for the doorknob, she added, "Just remember, Kit. She did the best she could for you all. She had no choice."

I turned back, perplexed. "I'm not angry with her, Emma."

She grimaced. "You look it."

"Well, I'm not," I said. "I'm just—worried."

"Go on, then. No—wait." She stepped to the corner. "Take my umbrella. You'll get soaked with that stupid thing."

I thanked her, put it up, and headed across the cobbles toward the railway station, where I could hire a cab.

Around the corner came a dark, broad-shouldered figure. Instinctively, I halted. With those shoulders, the man could be James, but the walk was wrong. The inn's door opened, and as he stepped inside, I saw his face.

Billy.

My heart gave a thud.

My first thought was, did his return make it less likely that he'd seen Sarah in Mayfair? Perhaps he felt safe, believing he hadn't been seen.

Or had he been drawn back by something so important he was willing to risk being caught? Was he one of the men Maggie was bringing in for her dodge? But why would Billy feel such loyalty toward her? She was nearly a decade older than he, so I doubted he was a lover. He couldn't be her brother—there was no obvious resemblance—

Then, like two pieces of fabric stitched together, the image in Fanny's photograph and Billy's face came together in my mind. Take the boy, add twenty years, longer hair, a beard and mustaches, and burlier shoulders—it was Billy.

That's Maggie's cousin, Fanny had said. *She took him in*.

Good lord, I thought, putting my hand to my chest to steady the sudden stutter of my breath. No wonder he'd come back.

But if Billy was involved in this dodge, it was because Maggie needed a bludger. She had been dismissive of the constables, but they wouldn't be silenced for good with money. Bribes could always be trumped with bigger bribes or threats.

If there had been any question in my mind, Billy's appearance resolved it. Tomorrow morning, I'd refuse whatever cut Maggie offered and say no in a way she knew I meant it.

At the railway station, I found a cab and sank into it, shivering. It drove through St. George's Circus and headed toward Blackfriars Bridge.

Had it been only two days since I'd ridden in a cab along this very route in the opposite direction, exultant over the plan to take the necklace at Charleton's ball? Yet again, I'd let myself stop worrying, blithely thinking I'd solved a problem when I didn't even know what the problem was.

When would I learn?

Chapter 19

The rain thinned as the cab headed north.

Emma's warning had only heightened my unease. What had Emma meant when she said that Amelia had done the best she could for us but had had no choice? Did Amelia have any idea Maggie was bent on revenge against the jeweler? I tried to squelch my sense of urgency, but it sparked like a blade scraping flint, making me want to seize the reins from the driver and whip up the horses myself.

Hurry, damn it, I breathed.

At last, we crossed Fleet Street and arrived in Shoe Lane, with its terraced shops, topped by three stories of rooms and crowned by triangular rooftops. I dismounted and paid the driver. The pavements ran down both sides of the cobbled road, with lamps at intervals, though it was barely tea-time and they weren't lit. Just south of St. Andrew's churchyard stood number thirteen. The bottom floor was occupied by a linen draper; I climbed the stairs beside the door to the top floor. There was no answer to my knocks, which left me nothing to do but wait until Amelia returned. A cold draft tumbled from somewhere above—a leaky rafter or a broken window. I leaned the sodden umbrella into the corner, plunked myself down on the landing outside her door, set my back against the wall, tucked my legs up, and wrapped my cloak close.

Over the staircase was a small arched window, set slightly askew, like an afterthought. It allowed a dim light for navigating the steps; there were no wall sconces. The clock chimed four, then the quarter hour, the half, three quarters. Still Amelia did not return.

At last, a door creaked open below and a few steps advanced. Light from a lamp drifted up the stairwell. Then the steps halted. Then began again, but this time descending. The outer door opened, and I leapt to my feet. "Wait," I called down the stairwell. "It's Kit."

The door shut again, and the boots resumed their journey up the stairs until they reached the landing at the turn. My hands rested on the banister, and Amelia peered up, a lamp in one hand, a pistol in the other.

"How did you know I was here?" I asked.

"The thread across the stair was broke." She eyed me for a moment before she continued up the steps. "Emma told you where I was?"

"I made her. It's important."

Her mouth pursed and she shrugged, as if she'd known this day would come. "Let's have a cup of tea. I'm bloody cold."

She turned the pistol's handle toward me. "Take this." I palmed the cold metal, and she withdrew a chain from around her neck and used the dangling key to open the door. We entered, and she lit a lamp. "It's dark in here. Light the others, yeah?" I set the pistol down on a table and lit two more lamps, taking care not to let them smoke. She busied herself at the stove, and I looked about. It was a large rectangular room, with its ceiling slanted on one side for the roofline and small windows. The kitchen contained the usual single brass tap and sink, a tarnished black stove, and shelving. In the living area were two doors, one likely to her bedroom and the other to a cupboard. The frayed upholstered chairs with the yellowed antimacassars, the ugly carpet, even the dents in the copper kettle she was using to boil water told me she'd rented these rooms furnished. I recognized nothing but her satchel in the corner. She could leave here on a moment's notice.

I waited until we were both settled into chairs. The delicate cup was blisteringly hot between my palms, but I was so bone cold, I welcomed it.

Amelia balanced the cup and saucer in her lap and waited.

"I need to ask you about Maggie," I began.

She sipped her tea. "What's she done?"

"Nothing much yet—aside from pushing Nell and Mary out of the ring." I raised a hand. "Nell is on her way to her sister's in Lambeth, and I've saved Mary's place in my room for the time being."

Her lips tightened, but she didn't reply.

I sipped the tea. It was too hot, but I swallowed it anyway, welcoming the burn down my insides. "Maggie wants me for a special dodge in Hatton Garden."

Amelia's cup stopped on the way to her lips. "What?" Her voice was razor sharp. "You haven't agreed, have you?"

"No, and I won't do it, especially since she's brought Billy into it."

She made a hard sound in the back of her throat, for she knew what he was. "God, no."

"I just don't know what to make of Maggie," I said. "The very first time I saw her was in the taproom one afternoon, even before you told me you were handing over the ring."

My tea was down to the leaves, and I set the cup and saucer aside. "She gave me the strangest look. But later, she said I resembled my mother, so I think she'd already guessed who I was. From the start, she's paid me special attention. Asking me about Sarah, flattering me, saying what a wonderful thief I am, even confiding in me about Swan River. But the whole time, I feel like she's trying to get round me."

"Why would she do that? To get you for this special dodge?"

"I don't know." My voice cracked. "I'm afraid it's for revenge. She said she doesn't blame my mother for being caught that day, but what if my mother tagged Maggie and Maggie found out? Is this revenge on my mother, through me?"

Amelia looked bewildered. "Why would you think your mother tagged her?"

"Because she was her jenny! James told me there was some bad blood between Maggie and her jenny over a man they both liked."

Amelia set her cup and saucer on the table with a muted clink. "You've got the wrong end of the stick here, Kit. First off, I don't remember bad blood between your mother and Maggie, over a man or not. And back then, we changed jennies all the time because Patty believed that having the same two girls going into a shop would make them easier to identify, as a pair, yeah?"

I sank back into my chair, feeling a mixture of relief and dismay that I'd put pieces of information together wrongly.

Amelia shook her head. "Annie didn't tag Maggie."

"Perhaps not." I wasn't wholly convinced.

She set her elbows on the carved wooden arms of the chair

and clasped her hands at her waist. "How do you know that Mary wouldn't tag *you*?"

"Because I know her. She's loyal."

"And so was Annie," she said firmly. "Maggie made sure your ma got away! Why would your mother betray her?"

"Because she didn't care about anyone but herself."

Amelia's spine stiffened. "You think some terrible things about your mother."

"Because she *was* terrible," I retorted. "Drinking herself to stupidity and letting men in the house with me and Sarah on the other side of the sheet—"

"And why do you think she did all that? Happy people don't act so." Amelia's eyes sparked with something like resentment. "It might be hard for you to understand, being only twenty, but grief and tragedy can change a decent person down to their *bones*, Kit."

I bristled. "You think I haven't felt grief? I've—"

She leaned forward in her chair, her voice rising over mine. "When your father left—when he betrayed her—it *broke* her. Do you understand? She *loved* him, and she thought he loved her. Then, a month after Sarah's born, he up and runs off with that woman, Violet. So, aye, your ma might have been drinking and neglecting you girls, but that was years later. Back in the day, Annie was good-hearted and clever and loyal to the ring, the way we all were."

"Then how did the police find out about the hotel theft?"

Amelia's eyebrows rose, questioning.

"Fanny's mother told her that Maggie's sentence was doubled because the police linked her to a hotel theft. Now, it could've been just the police pinning it on her, but—what if my ma told the police about it?"

Amelia's expression stilled. "Your ma didn't do that."

"How do you know?"

"Because she didn't know," she said, her voice thin. "Good lord. Oh, good lord." Amelia wrapped both arms around her belly. Then, with a moan, she stood and began to pace in a semicircle behind the chair like a dog at the far reach of its tether.

"Amelia," I said.

She turned. "*Rose* was Maggie's jenny at the hotel."

"Rose?" I echoed. "Mary's mother?"

Amelia's face had gone white, and I understood. A chill ran over me.

"So the bad blood over a man was . . . between Maggie and Rose," I said, my voice faint.

"Over Tim Lowry," she said. "Damn that man."

"What did he do?"

"Oh, nothing other than be stupid and selfish," she replied, her eyes darkening at the memory. "He strung Rose along, and she liked him, but then he started chasing Maggie, who knew he was only chasing her because she'd refused him. She had her eye on a bloke she'd met at the theater where she'd been an actress."

"What did he look like? Tim Lowry?"

"Tall, fair, handsome, wore a mustache."

"A small one, like this." I drew it above my lip.

"Yes," she said, surprised.

"He was in a picture Fanny showed me," I said. The pieces were falling into place, properly this time. "So you think Rose tagged Maggie somehow? She wasn't there."

"She could've sent a note to the jeweler. She could have known where Maggie was going that day."

"And then she told the police about the hotel theft to have Maggie sent away for longer," I guessed.

She bit her lip. "It's possible. Terrible, but possible."

"And somehow Maggie learned that Rose had betrayed her. But when? Before she left?"

"Police would've had to present evidence at trial, yeah? Likely a written statement about the hotel theft."

"All this over a man's attentions," I said in disbelief.

"It might've been more than that." Amelia's eyes darted about, the way they did when she calculated figures. "If Rose was already carrying his child, she'd want a father for her bairn."

Carrying a child? But Mary has no siblings.

"Mary?" I asked. "She's Tim Lowry's daughter, not her father's—I mean, not Charles's?"

"It's likely, near as I can figure. Rose took up with Charles soon after, but she said Mary was born early. No one questioned it, she was such a little thing. I remember holding her." She shook her head. "I don't know why I didn't see it before. Mary looks a good bit like Lowry, the fair hair, the high forehead, the roundness of her chin."

I sank back in the chair. I might have misread everything, from Maggie's penetrating look that very first night. It might not have been for me alone. After all, her expression had hardened *after* she'd seen Mary, who had been standing beside me.

I drew a breath. "Rose was murdered in March."

Amelia followed my thought, for she shook her head. "Maggie wasn't here yet. She came to see me in June and said her boat had docked in Liverpool three weeks before." Her expression changed. "Although that could be a lie."

"I think it was," I said, "and I think Maggie killed Rose."

"You've no proof of that," Amelia said. "I'm not saying it's impossible, but—"

"Maggie said that God kept her alive in Swan River so she could have revenge. That balancing the scales was the most important thing." My mind was leaping from point to point. "That first day when I saw her in the taproom, I *knew* I'd seen her somewhere before. I remembered her face, and nearest I can recall it was in a shop, months before."

"*When*, Kit?" Her voice was tight.

I closed my eyes and pressed my palms to the side of my head, trying to remember.

Where was it? A West End shop? But even as I thought it, I rejected the idea. The West End shops tended to be large and brightly lit, and the place in my memory had been smaller and dimmer.

Where the devil was it?

Someplace small, someplace smelling of fabrics, woolens, the faint smell of glue used in hat making.

Then it came to me.

Emma had run short on some threads and buttons for a coat she was making for Mrs. Prentice. A red coat, with a thick collar.

I opened my eyes. "Mr. Thorpe's shop, back in February or early March at the latest. There was snow on the shoulders of her coat. I was buying notions for Emma."

Amelia rested a hand on the back of the chair. "February or March," she said softly. "My God."

"Do you think Maggie killed Rose herself?" I asked. "Or had it done? By Billy?"

Amelia considered a moment before answering. "Two stabs of the knife under the ribs toward the heart? I'd say that's the way a woman like her kills, if she's bent on revenge."

I shuddered, imagining the scene.

"You need to be bloody careful with her," Amelia said soberly. "Will she let you say no to her dodge?"

My heart gave a sickening thump. Knowing Maggie was capable of murder with her own hands changed everything. "I said no tonight, but she told me she wants me to think on it and come back tomorrow. She . . . she seems fixed on it."

"Oh, Kit." Her eyes were dark with sympathy. "What did she offer you?"

"Three hundred pounds," I said. "Enough money to leave. She's all but said she'd want me to."

"Three hundred! What the devil are you nicking?"

"An heirloom necklace from Simonson's," I began and relayed everything about Roger Simonson, the Hargrave necklace, the store, the constables, the mirrors, the locks, the safe, the alleys, and the family living upstairs.

"You're right," Amelia said, her voice hollow. "It sounds near impossible."

"James and I figured out a way to get the necklace without going into the jeweler's shop—because the marchioness is wearing it at a ball in just over a week. We could take it from her there. But Maggie wants it taken from the jeweler, to disgrace him. To ruin him."

"I can see it," Amelia said, coming around to the chair to sit again. She put her elbows on her knees, her fingertips on her mouth for a long moment before she sat back with a sigh. "Well, she's had months to plan this, and she's clever enough to pull it off. God knows, she uses every tool she has."

There was a dark note in her voice that drew me up.

"How did she get you to hand over the ring?" I asked. "I know you said it was hers by rights, from her mother . . . but

Emma told me—and these were her exact words—that you did the best you could for all of us, but you had no choice. What did she mean?"

Amelia took a moment to answer. "The first time she asked for the ring, I told her I'd think about it." She tapped the first two fingers of her left hand on the chair arm, soundlessly. "When she came back the following week, I refused. I told her that I cared about all of you, and I didn't want anything to change. Plus, I'd built it into something beyond what her mother had done. Patty was clever, but there were only eight or nine thieves then, including herself, and no rhyme or reason to where we went or when. I reminded her that mostly, they'd only work when they were sober, which wasn't often."

"So what string did she pull to convince you?"

She lowered her chin and looked up at me as if I was being willfully obtuse. "Come now, Kit. What would do it?"

"She threatened *us*," I said slowly, thinking not only of Josie's arrest, mere days after Maggie appeared at Elephant and Castle, but of the brown-suited man who had nearly caught Mary and me. "There was a man at Pickford's, the day before Josie was arrested."

She blinked. "*What?*"

"I didn't tell you because nothing happened," I said hurriedly. "I didn't want you to think Mary should've seen him and keep her from working."

"Oh." Amelia pressed a hand over her face with a groan. "God, I wish I'd known. I thought Maggie was bluffing about having you all tagged. That takes time to arrange—finding people you can trust to alert the shops. I didn't think she could organize it in a matter of days."

"You didn't know she'd been here months," I reminded

her. "Or even longer. February was just the first time *I* saw her. And didn't you say that Silas Pike had been her lover? All she had to do was connect with him, and her network would start coming back to her."

Regret deepened the lines around her mouth. "If I'd known about you and Mary, I'd have believed it sooner."

"I know," I said. "I should have told you."

The silence was broken only by the fizz of coals in the stove.

"She threatened to burn you all, until I gave in," she said. "I told her I'd halt every bloody dodge if she kept on, and that she was being stupid—that she was cutting off her nose to spite her face. Training thieves takes time." She raised a shoulder and dropped it. "I told her I could hold out for months, given what the ring has saved and set aside." She paused. "That sent her into a rage."

"Because she wanted to pull this dodge at the jeweler's," I said. "She didn't want to wait months."

"Aye. So she pulled out her ace."

"What?"

Her eyes met mine. "Adam."

It took me a moment.

Adam was her brother, a mostly harmless ne'er-do-well drifter and drunk. Amelia paid his rent and hired a woman to keep house for him.

"Your brother?" I asked. "She knew him?"

Amelia's tongue darted out, licked her lips, and vanished as her mouth tightened. "When he was nineteen, he killed someone and was never caught. It wasn't outright murder—he was fighting back to protect himself—but still. Maggie knew."

"How?"

"Another Castle man was there when it happened. He was eventually sent to Australia himself. He found Maggie there and told her what he saw. She could tell the Yard." Her expression was resigned. "She has a witness."

"Who did Adam kill? Is it someone who matters, after all this time?"

"It was a Yard man who'd been arresting him," she said. "They'll care."

"Oh," I breathed. Yes, they would, even all these years later.

"He'd hang for it," she concluded. "If she tells them—and if they can find him."

I shook my head. "I can't believe this."

Her smile was thin. "No honor among thieves."

"But there *is*," I replied. "None of us would do this to each other." The bleak look on her face made something in my chest twist. "Where is Adam now?"

She glanced at one of the two closed doors.

My hands tightened on the chair arms. "He's here?"

"He's out at the moment, but aye, he's staying here." An unhappy look came over her face. "We already had to move once because Maggie came close to finding him last week in a gambling den in Bethnal Green. He only escaped because a friend of mine risked his own neck and went in after him."

No wonder Amelia took precautions like the thread on the stair.

"Couldn't you send him away? Somewhere safe?" I asked.

"Where?" She spread her hands, a jerking movement. "Where would be safe, unless I'm nearby? I left for four weeks once, and he nearly drank himself to death." Her voice fell.

"He's a drunkard and he's trouble, but he's my only family, yeah?"

"I know," I said.

I'd do the same thing for Sarah.

Sarah.

The thought slammed into me, screeching my heart to a stop, like a freight train avoiding a crash. I swear it did. Because I knew what Maggie's next move was—she might have already done it—

I bolted out of the chair, snatching up my coat and shoving my arms into the sleeves. I was at the door before Amelia asked, "Kit—what the hell—"

I spun back. "Sarah!" A single word, a cry that scraped my throat hoarse.

Amelia's face froze in horror—I whirled and went clattering, flying, half leaping and stumbling down the stairs—onto the street—into the spittle of rain—I'd left Emma's umbrella behind, and there wasn't a cab in sight.

I pelted west toward Mayfair.

I pounded on the servants' door, paused to listen, and beat it again. At last, through the crack at the bottom of the door the darkness changed, a bobbing light approached. I waited, gasping, bent over, my hands on my knees.

"Who is it?" came a woman's voice.

"It's Kit. Sarah's sister."

The lock clicked, the bar scraped, and the door opened. The housekeeper stood, arms akimbo. "This is a *decent* house. You've no right to—"

"Is she here?"

"No. She quit this afternoon."

I shook my head, my voice ragged and breathless. "She didn't quit. She's been kidnapped."

The housekeeper drew herself up, her eyes darting up the stairs behind me, to the street above, in the direction of the Fairleigh house. That crime had brought the possibility close, and she stepped back. "Come in out of the wet."

I shuddered in the sudden warmth, and she shut the door behind me.

"You're Mrs. Rice," I said, my voice shaking. "She told me about you. How you said her cleaning was impeccable. She was so proud of the compliment."

Her face softened and then took on a troubled look. "I thought it was odd she left her satchel behind. But she left for the market with two pounds and didn't come back."

"Two pounds." The laugh came out shrill. "She wouldn't have left for five times that. Where's her satchel?"

By this point, a young, dark-haired maid had come down the hallway in a wrapper, peering at me curiously.

"Fetch Sarah's things, Betty," the housekeeper said, not unkindly.

"Yes, mum. I have it right here." She vanished back up the stairs, a white hand on the railing, quick steps on the wooden stairs.

"Why would someone kidnap Sarah?" she asked me. "She's just a girl."

"To hurt *me*," I said.

Her eyes widened with bewilderment. "Why would someone hurt you?"

Betty reappeared on the stairs and hurried toward us with the satchel.

"You were her friend," I said. "Did *you* think she had quit?"

Betty bit her lip and looked sideways at the housekeeper. "No."

Mrs. Rice's face was pinched. "You did say so," she murmured to Betty before turning back to me. "Perhaps I should have called the police. But we've had maids disappear before."

"Sarah's different," I said.

"She was," Mrs. Rice admitted. "Shall I send for the police now?"

"It's too late. They won't find her. Besides, they won't lift a finger for a scullery maid who's been dismissed." I set the satchel on the bench and opened it. Clothes. Her photograph of our ma. The yellowback novel I'd given her last time she was home. I closed it back up. All of Sarah's life, all remnants of her, in this small, dilapidated bag. It cut my heart to pieces.

"I'm sorry," Mrs. Rice said awkwardly.

I left without another word and started for Elephant and Castle.

Chapter 20

In front of St. George's, I shoved my way onto an overcrowded omnibus, then leapt off at the Lambeth railway station and dashed to the inn, rushing straight up to the goods room, where Maggie and Billy each held a glass of whiskey. Maggie sat behind the desk, Billy perched on the windowsill, one heavy boot on the floor, the other swinging idly.

As if they were waiting for me.

Fear dug its fangs into my heart as I set down Sarah's satchel. "Where is she?"

Billy snickered and turned to Maggie. "You were right. It brought her round, even faster than you expected."

Maggie's smile was almost gentle. "She's not far."

"Is she alive?"

"What use would she be to me dead?" Maggie returned. She reached into a pocket and withdrew a silver chain, passing it over to me. Unthinking, I reached for it. From the chain dangled Sarah's locket, the one I'd given her. "She told me you'd recognize it."

"How did you find her?" My voice rasped.

"You told me she was a maid in Mayfair, so I had you followed, of course." Maggie smoothed back an unruly dark lock near her temple. "I've understood you from the first,

Kit. I saw your affection for Mary and your sister. Why do you think I told Mary I was cutting her from the ring? I knew you'd bargain to keep her here. After that, it was just reeling you in. When money wasn't enough to make you willing, you left me no choice. I *had* to use your sister."

I tucked the locket into the secret pocket in my bodice. "I want proof she's alive *now*."

"And you'll do what I ask?"

"If she's alive," I spat back. "You have me for your bloody dodge. But so help me God, if you harm her, I will make sure you hang, even if I hang alongside you." I sat on the opposite side of the desk and put out my hand. "Give me paper and a pen."

She took a piece of paper from the drawer and gestured to the inkwell with the pen in the brass tray that had stood on the desk—Amelia's desk—for as long as I'd been thieving. "Very well. Billy can take it."

I bent and wrote: *Sarah, I'm doing what Maggie asks, and she'll let you go. Reply to me on this page*. I hesitated. When she saw Billy, would she assume this had something to do with her seeing him in Mayfair? Would she try to reassure him that she'd keep quiet? She wasn't a fool or a child, but she'd be terrified. I couldn't take the chance she'd be thinking carefully. I added, *Say nothing*, and underlined it for good measure.

"Give this to her," I said, sticking the pen back in its place. "Have her write back. I know her handwriting."

Maggie took it from me, read the message critically, and handed it to Billy along with a stub of pencil. "Do as she says."

He pocketed it and ambled out.

In my mind, I followed him down the stairs, out the door, along an alley, into some dank boardinghouse, and into a cellar, where he shoved open a door, setting Sarah's nerves on fire with fright until he handed her my note. It filled me with a pain so complete I couldn't think.

Until my eyes returned to Maggie. Her expression of cool patience, even tolerance, told me she had no feeling for Sarah or me at all. This was only revenge, pure and practical and well planned.

And I had better start thinking practically as well.

I jerked my head toward the closed door. "So he's part of the dodge?"

"Yes."

"Then you're going to tell me everything," I said. "Who else is in, when and how."

She raised an eyebrow. "I'll tell you *your* part of it."

"No. You tell me *every bloody step*," I retorted. "So I can go over it in my head." She opened her mouth to protest, and my voice rose. "Damn it! I don't trust you and I certainly don't trust *Billy*. He's a lout with a temper, and you will *want* me to know the whole plan because if something goes wrong, he's not going to keep a clear head! He'll fly off the handle and kill more people than he needs to." Her expression altered. "You've given me no choice, so I'm doing what you ask." I spread my hands. "But I'm *not* bloody following your men in blind, like a stray dog on a leash. For God's sake, you wouldn't, either! Billy's reckless, and I don't even know what other devil you're throwing me in with. If we get caught, I want a plan to get us out."

A flicker of acknowledgment crossed her face. "All right."

I drew a long breath. "Now, why do you need *me* so badly?

Your cracksman can retrieve the necklace. And don't tell me it's because you don't want to end up with worthless paste. I can teach anyone to tell the difference, if you give me a day. So could you."

"I'm not nicking the necklace," she said.

Had she changed her plan? I sat back in amazement, for I'd have sworn she'd have scrupulously planned every detail. "Then what the devil are you nicking?"

"Much less," she said evenly. "Three stones out of it."

"What? Why not take the necklace? It's easier and nets you more. Simonson'll look careless and lose custom, and there's less risk to all of us."

"Because stealing the necklace would make him look like a victim of a crime. People will sympathize and say, 'Oh, it's so terrible, London is full of thieves.'" Her eyes were flinty. "Replace them with paste and people will say he's crooked. An unscrupulous jeweler. A fraud. A thief. A *villain*."

If he was caught substituting paste for real gems, no one would ever trust him again. His business would be ruined, he'd be jailed, and the villain and the victim would have changed places yet again.

This wasn't a change of plans; this had been her scheme all along.

Maggie took out the picture of the necklace, unfolded it, and laid it on the desk between us. "How long will it take you to switch out three stones?"

I studied the picture for a moment, buying myself time. "Any in particular?"

"No."

"These would be easiest," I said, pointing. "Medium sized diamonds, round cut. It looks like they're anchored by four or six prongs. Impossible to tell if it's gold or something else—silver or platinum. There might be adhesive, but I've a solvent for that." I set down the page. "Depending on the setting, changing out three stones would take forty or fifty minutes, I think, unless there's something odd."

"And if you have time to practice?"

"Quicker than that." I studied her, considering the next logical step. "How would the replacement be discovered? Surely you don't expect the marquess to detect the difference between real and paste, with the stones still in their settings, and only a few of the dozens replaced." Even I needed to remove stones to examine them properly with a loupe.

"The marquess shall learn that the jeweler has been known to replace real stones with paste, and he'll have it examined."

"So the second jeweler will find the three false ones."

"The story will break in the newspapers, and their reputation will be ruined." She took a sip of her whiskey. "It's simple, you see. That's why it will work. You've only to do your part. You can trust my men to manage the rest."

Men. That confirmed there would be at least one other besides Billy.

"And how will we get in?"

Maggie withdrew a second piece of paper from her pocket. It was her hand-drawn map of Hatton Garden, with the alleys now marked with *X*s. She pointed to one of them. "Through here."

"But there's a constable stationed at the entrance."

"Stop worrying about the constables," she said shortly. "There's only one who will be in your way, and the world could do with less of them anyway."

In our way and then dead. Because Billy couldn't just knock the man unconscious or tie him up. There was the risk of him regaining consciousness faster than the time it took us to get in, open the safe, exchange the jewels, and get out.

"So Billy will kill him," I said, "and drag the body out of sight. But what if another constable comes around and wonders where he's gone?"

"Billy will put on the uniform."

I gave a bark of a laugh at the absurdity of it. "While he's doing that, who's getting me into the shop and the safe?"

She refolded the picture of the necklace and the map of Hatton Garden, tucking them away. "We'll have a hook ladder, so the two of you can climb the gate and jump down into the alley. The jeweler's door is three down. As you said, there are two Yale locks, which my smith can pick."

"Who is it?"

"He's not from here," she replied. "But don't worry. He keeps a cool head and is the quickest I know. He'll get you into the office, which you'll examine, so you can leave it exactly as it was. He'll open the safe, give you the necklace, and after you change out three stones, he'll put the necklace back. It's an hour's work."

"Closer to ninety minutes," I said. "And I need a good supply of paste. The stones need to match. The right color and size, the same cut and brilliance."

She sniffed, touching her nose delicately with a lawn handkerchief. "Seamus has collected a variety—good ones, cut like the ones in the necklace."

So she'd roped Mr. Ardle into this, too.

The thought flicked into my mind that he'd had me doing more stone replacement and repair the past few weeks.

"There's variation in the stones," Maggie said, "so you'll be able to find three that are close enough. You can practice at his shop. You have plenty of time."

"Hardly," I snapped. "The ball is on Wednesday. That's only nine days. What if the necklace is being picked up tomorrow? Or has been picked up already?"

"The necklace will be picked up Monday morning."

"You have someone inside the jeweler?" I asked. "Why not have them do—"

"Not inside the jeweler," she replied.

So, someone inside the house. A maid or footman, bribed, no doubt, to divulge when the necklace was being retrieved. She'd crafted this dodge down to the smallest threads.

"So we must go before Monday," I said. "Less than a week. It's not much time to practice."

"You have clever hands."

Like yours were, once.

"And what if Simonson wants to take one last look at the necklace before it's picked up?" I asked.

"Simonson is away for a week beginning Thursday."

"Why?"

"Does it matter?"

I merely looked.

Her eyes rolled toward the ceiling in annoyance. "He'll be visiting his mistress in the country."

So you've hired someone for that, too, I thought. "You've anticipated everything."

"I've had years," she said softly.

I considered the dodge from her side, imagining her waiting here for us to return with the gems.

"And after I've finished my part," I said, "what's to prevent

Billy or your cracksman from killing me and throwing me into the river, to keep me from telling anyone what I've done? Why would they keep me alive?"

"There's no reason to kill you." She turned over the palm of her injured hand. "If you've done as I ask, you can hardly betray me without incriminating yourself."

But if I'm alive, I might let something slip—or I might hold what I know over your head, I thought. *No, you won't be able to live with that threat, so you'll have to kill me—and likely Sarah, too, unless we're beyond your reach.*

The truth struck me like a blow to the chin. If I managed to do this dodge—the minute I had Sarah safe—we would have to flee Elephant and Castle, perhaps even London. I stood and went to the window to hide the trajectory of my thoughts. The door to Mr. Ardle's shop swung open and shut as a customer left.

I turned and leaned against the broad sill, settling my hands on it. "Does Mr. Ardle know what you're doing with the paste?"

"Of course."

"You're holding out hope to him, aren't you? He thinks you'll love him for it. Because he loves you."

"He's *foolish* over me," she corrected me, a bitter little smile twisting her mouth. "Love is just another long con that hasn't ended yet."

A dark belief, but no doubt hard-earned and fixed.

"When's the dodge?" I asked.

She pursed her mouth. "You'll go Sunday night."

Six days. There wasn't enough time to rehearse her plan, much less make a different one.

I stepped forward until I could rest my fingers on the top

rail of the chair. My thumb found a crack in the wood. "And you swear that if I bring you the three diamonds, you'll give me Sarah, safe and sound."

She shook her head. "No. I need the story to break and see Simonson arrested."

My fingers tightened around the rail. "That could take weeks!" I shot back. "Once I hand over the gems, you'll have got everything you can out of *me*. I can't choose how quickly a story will appear or when Scotland Yard—"

"It won't be weeks," she interrupted. "The marquess will be advised to consult a second jeweler immediately."

The thought of Sarah in some basement, trapped, tied up, terrified for yet more days—it billowed fear inside my chest, and I clawed it back down. *She needs me*, I reminded myself. *I must keep my wits.*

Even in the direst moments, there was something to be gained.

"The gems and the story, then," I said stubbornly. "Not the arrest."

She scowled and made an irritable motion with her left hand. "The gems and the story for Sarah."

"The minute the story breaks, whenever it is, you let her go."

"I said I would."

"Swear it in a way I'll believe you."

Her eyes narrowed. "I swear it on my son's grave."

The words chilled me.

So she'd had a child in Swan River. She'd left his grave to return here. For this.

"All right," I said. "But I'm staying here until Billy gets back with that letter."

She was impatient at all these concessions, but she nearly had me, which was what she wanted most. "Fine."

She sat in silence while I tallied our takes.

The scales were balanced. We both had something the other one wanted more than anything—she wanted revenge, and I wanted Sarah.

But I considered—could I tip the scales in my favor? Could I take this moment to learn something that might matter later?

I went to the window, peered out, and saw no sign of Billy returning. There were only three stray dogs, heavily furred at the shoulder and furtive as thieves.

I reclaimed my position behind the chair. "Does Billy know you killed Rose Pratt?"

It was a stab, but it found its mark, for her breath paused, then resumed.

"You've no proof I did that," she said.

"Well, *I* don't, but the police have an eyewitness," I said. "He can identify you, once you're found. So if anything happens to me, there will be a letter that will land at Scotland Yard giving your name and a photograph."

She looked incredulous. "You've no photograph of me!"

"My ma did," I replied, passing the lie as well as I knew how. "I've no idea where she got it, but there's four of you. You're sitting next to Fanny's mum, June. Billy was in it, too, standing behind you, looking to be about thirteen, and there was a man. Tim Lowry. It was taken when you were an actress."

This shot told, too. Her lips parted.

"And if Sarah isn't returned to me alive, I will tell the police that I nicked the three gems at your demand, and the jeweler wasn't to blame," I said. "So your revenge will fail."

"You can't do that," she said dismissively. "You'll hang."

My two hands hard around the top of the chair, I leaned in.

"When will you understand I don't *care*? Love is *not* just a long con for me. For God's sake, you're *counting* on that!"

"I've no doubt you love her! But not as much as your own neck."

"I would risk mine to save hers."

Her jaw came out, jutting stubbornly. "This is a stupid conversation. I've no reason to harm Sarah or you. Why would I? Annie was decent to me. You're a tool for this, nothing more."

A tool that knows what you've done, I thought.

"Fine." I crossed my arms. "Then tell me. On the day we thieved together, why didn't you tell me my mother was your jenny?"

"Because it was clear you didn't trust me, and I didn't want you to make anything of it."

"When did you learn Rose informed on you to the police?"

"At the trial," she said. "As soon as they mentioned the hotel by name."

"You didn't expect it, did you? That Rose would do such a thing."

Maggie rubbed her thumb over a nick in the desk's surface, back and forth, like she was sanding it smooth. "We were friends, rather like you and Mary Pratt," she said, her voice brittle. "We slept in the same bed. We sat together at night, mending our pockets or our hems, drank together in the taproom, played cards, flirted with young men so they'd buy us pints. There used to be a man named Winkie John with only one eye who played the fiddle some nights, and we'd dance. We looked out for each other. No man could get the better of either of us, if the other was around." She laid her palm over the nicked wood. "Then along came Tim Lowry. He was shiftless and useless as every other Castle man, and he wouldn't let me alone. But he was handsome, and she wanted him." She shrugged, and I could guess the rest.

The door swung open, and Billy reappeared. He handed the note to Maggie, who read it and passed it to me.

I'm alive, Kit. Please be careful.

It was Sarah's tidy writing, familiar as my own hand. I looked up to find Maggie's eyes narrowed.

I folded the page and tucked it into my pocket. "All right, Maggie. You've got me. Now what?"

"Tomorrow, you'll go to Seamus's shop to start preparing your tools and stones," she answered. "I'll see you on Sunday morning, here." She laid both hands flat on the desk and pushed herself to standing. "Needless to say, you tell no one about any of this."

"I'm not a fool."

I turned away, left the room, and started down the stairs, cold running over me, scalp to arms.

I made it halfway down before I had to stop, my courage falling away. I set my spine against the wall, for my legs would no longer hold me.

Two deep breaths. *Steady, Kit*, I told myself.

I drew one more deep breath and kept on.

My fear for Sarah made me clumsy, tripped me down the final steps. Numbly, I made my way through the taproom, opened the front door, rounded a corner, and took refuge in a dark alley that ran beside the inn. A cat slithered around a dustbin with a mouse screeching and writhing in its mouth. I closed my eyes, pressing my spine into bricks this time, imagining Sarah, caught and terrified. Likely bound to a chair or bed and gagged so she couldn't cry out. But alive. And at least she knew that I knew and was doing what I could. She wasn't alone anymore.

I opened my eyes and scanned the open area in front of the inn, seeing as if for the first time the hundreds of rooms and attics and basements within half an hour's walk of the Elephant and Castle. Finding her would be impossible.

What could I do but go along with Maggie's dodge?

What frightened me wasn't simply being caught with the gems. If the dodge went as planned, I'd be embroiled in the murder of a policeman. I'd hang for certain if I was caught. And Sarah would never forgive herself for being taken.

As panic rolled over me, my head began to buzz. I bent over, settling my hands on my knees.

I couldn't give into it. I must be on my mettle.

There was always a way out.

When I was eleven, my mum locked me in a cupboard. She had her reasons.

For nearly a year, I'd been sent out to sew for Mrs. Beck, bringing home three shillings a week, which I deposited in a tin cup on the shelf. Ma had said it was needed for rent, and I felt a child's pride in helping to provide for us—until I returned home one night to find the tin cup empty, with every shilling spent on gin that turned Ma into a witch with hard brown eyes and a bitter tongue. I wasn't soft the way Sarah was. I had a temper, and I sassed her, which made her furious, and she pinched my shoulder and shoved me into the cupboard, turning the key in the lock. I beat my fists against the door and screamed. Then she snatched up Sarah—sobbing and crying for me—and left, slamming the door behind her.

In some respects, it was the kindest thing Ma could have

done, for the moment I was alone, I halted the fruitless banging of my fists, sat down, and began to think.

I reached into my pocket and found my sewing kit. The scissors were too big and the needles, even three together, were too small to turn the key she'd left in the lock.

I searched the clothes pockets, the tattered boxes, the shelf. Nothing of use.

The air was so thick with the smell of wool and rot and mouse droppings that I began to gasp.

I pressed my nose along the floor, near the crack at the bottom of the door, drawing deep breaths. The knowledge that I wouldn't smother to death slowed my heart and let me think again. As I swept my fingers along the sides and the back of the cupboard, something pointed pricked my thumb. I put it in my mouth and tasted blood. This time, I crept my fingers slowly forward until they encountered a metal shard. A bit farther along, they found a few inches of thick wire. Using the two pieces together, I manipulated the key. I groaned in frustration at my failures. I bent the wire into different shapes, squinting in the bit of light that wasn't anywhere near bright enough to see by.

To this day, I don't know what caused me to close my eyes. But the moment I did, my fingers moved more surely. My mother may have foisted darkness upon me, but this was a darkness I chose. I pleated the wire twice more. Patiently, I inserted it with the piece of metal, feeling the resistance of the key.

There was a catch, like a needle caught on a fiber, a scrape, and the key twitched. The second time, it twitched again. The third time, it turned, and I escaped, hours earlier than Ma would have returned.

I learned important lessons that day. To breathe. To slow myself rather than hurry. To manage the conditions of my trap. To take stock of my resources. To fashion a tool.

Where was the shard of metal and the piece of wire I needed now?

I drew a deep breath.

I knew where to find one of them.

I arrived at my room to find it empty. With all that had happened, it felt as though it should be midnight at least, but it was just striking nine. Still, Mary's absence put a lump of fear into my throat, especially when I noted her coat tossed on the bed. It was nighttime and cold outside—why would Mary have gone out without her coat? Had Maggie abducted Mary as well?

But why? She knew Sarah would be enough to compel me.

Had Mary fled? Believed she was in danger?

I yanked open the drawer where Mary kept her things and saw her undergarments, neatly folded, and the framed picture of her mother that she never would have left without.

Behind me, the key turned in the lock.

Mary stared in surprise at me, the open drawer, my hand inside it. "Kit? What are you doing?"

She wore a coat I'd never seen.

Relief made my voice hoarse. "Oh, thank God. Where did you get that coat?"

Bewildered, she replied, "I borrowed it from Bea. Why?"

I shut the drawer with a whine of wood against wood, peered out into the hallway and closed the door. Then I rolled a towel and stuffed it along the crack at the bottom.

"I need to talk to you," I muttered and began without even letting Mary unbutton her borrowed coat.

Perched on the side of her bed facing me, Mary had listened silently as I told her everything Maggie had done, from tagging us at Pickford's to Sarah's kidnapping and Maggie's dodge. She was already wide-eyed, and I hadn't even said a word yet about her mother's murder or Tim Lowry.

"Mary?" I reached for her arm. "Are you . . . all right?"

"I'm not falling into a faint, if that's what you mean, but bloody hell, Kit." She shivered, as if she was cold to the bone. "It's wickedness, pure wickedness, taking Sarah." Her eyes drifted toward the window, caught on her dresser, and returned to me. "Why were you going through my things?"

"I just wanted to see if they were still here. I was afraid she'd taken you, too."

"Oh, Kit." Mary's brow knitted, and she took my hand in hers. "What are you going to do? You can't do the dodge the way it's laid out. Not with Billy. He's—"

"I know." I laid my other hand on top of hers. "But there's something else, Mary."

"Go on." Her eyes were steady.

"This part is about you." I drew a breath. "When Maggie was caught in the jewelry store, her sentence was doubled to fourteen because one of her jennies ratted her out about another theft. A snooze, in a hotel."

She looked puzzled. "Your mother?"

I shook my head. "She was the jenny the day Maggie was caught. But *your* mother was Maggie's jenny at the hotel."

Her eyes widened, and her lips parted. "You think my mother . . ."

"There was a man named Tim Lowry, who your mother fancied, but he fancied Maggie, at least for a while. And . . ."

"My mum turned copper's nark over a man?" Mary's expression was horrified.

"And over you," I said softly. "Possibly. If Tim Lowry was your father, she'd have wanted him for *you*."

She dragged her hand from between mine. "Are you sure?" Her voice was ragged.

"Not *sure*, but Amelia says you were born early, and you look like him more than your da. Fair hair and blue eyes."

Mary's face was pale to the lips but resolute. "Tell me the rest."

I made my voice as gentle as I could. "Maggie came back from Australia for revenge, Mary. For two revenges. Your mother and the jeweler."

Her chest rose and fell with an uneven gasp. "But Maggie would have had to be here *months* ago to . . ."

"She'd arrived by early March." I touched her arm. "Given what she's put in place, I suspect she's been here even longer."

"Jesus, Kit." Her hands went to the soft area below her ribs.

"I know," I said again. "I'm sorry."

She stared unseeing at the bare wall opposite for a moment, her chest rising and falling. At last, she looked at me. "And now she has Sarah, and you have to do this thing to get her back."

"Yes."

"What do you need?" she asked simply.

The sheer generosity of it cracked my heart clear across.

"I don't know," I said, my voice wobbling. "I need a plan, and . . . I don't have one yet. Can you come with me? To James's?"

"Of course. Anything." Mary rose from the bed. "But if I'm to help you, we should make a sign of us parting ways. We don't want Maggie thinking you have any allies here. I'll put out that I found you poking through my drawers."

I never admired her more than at that moment. Despite everything I'd told her, she was still shrewd and quick, for my sake. But why was I surprised? She'd been my jenny dozens of times, and she'd never lost her head when I needed her.

"Where will you go?" I asked. "Maggie won't let you stay in any of the others' rooms."

"There's a room to let at Mrs. Watson's, next to the bakery. I'd be leaving soon anyway." She eyed me. "You won't be staying in the ring after this, either."

"No."

I watched Mary as she tugged the second drawer out of its track and slid her hand along the back, removing a knife with a leather sheath. She put it in the pocket of Bea's coat.

"I'll meet you on Blackfriars," I said. "You go first."

As she left I pulled out a drawer of my own, slid my hand underneath, and withdrew my own knife, concealing it in my pocket. I retrieved both of my money pouches and followed Mary a few minutes later, catching her on the bridge. She took my hand and together we went to find the two other people I could trust.

Chapter 21

As much as Amelia liked Mary, she wouldn't want her to know where she and Adam were staying, so I gave Mary James's address and went to fetch Amelia. I needed all of them, together.

Gas lamps cast my shadow over the cobblestones, broke it apart, and put it back together as I made my way to Shoe Lane.

Amelia answered my knock immediately and pulled me into a hard embrace. "Thank God you're all right. I've been imagining the worst."

"It is the worst," I said. "Maggie took Sarah to make me do her dodge."

"Oh." Amelia stepped back, the fingers of her right hand coming to her mouth. "God, Kit. I'm sorry."

"I can't do it the way Maggie wants," I said. "I need your help. Can you come with me to James's? Mary is already there."

Amelia handed me a lit lantern and plucked her coat from its hook without a word. The fog was thick, turning the gas lamps into yellow blurs, smaller in the distance. As we walked, I told her about Maggie's plan, concluding, "I know too much. Likely she'll kill me once she has the gems, so I can't rat her out."

"Or take over the ring," Amelia said. "You're the only choice, if enough of you wanted to break away. Although even she needs to give some thought to how many bodies she wants to rack up."

"She could frame me instead." I stepped over a pile of sodden newspaper. "Hide one of the diamonds in my room and tip off the police. Have an eyewitness say I killed the constable. She'd get her revenge, two of the diamonds, *and* me hanged into silence. But my best guess is she'll have Billy kill me afterwards. Not least because once Sarah is safe, she has no guarantee I won't go for revenge myself."

Amelia nodded soberly. "She lives by revenge. She wouldn't be able to imagine you don't."

"Even if Sarah and I left Southwark."

"You'd need to leave London, Kit. I told you she found Adam. Even if she's caught—even if she's in jail, she has reach."

An ache hard as a pebble formed in the back of my throat. The thought of leaving Amelia and Mary—and James—

"But first, you need to take this dodge in hand," she said. "Get her what she wants, but do it safer, yeah?"

I swallowed down the ache. "I know. I just need to think on how."

We paused at a corner, and church bells doled the half hour, muted by fog, as we crossed the cobbled road.

"Maggie was shrewd, choosing you."

"Because I'm a capable thief or because I work at Ardle's shop?" I asked.

"Because you have a sister you love that she could use," Amelia replied. "I daresay she caught on to that early."

I felt a pang of self-loathing at my stupidity. "Because I mentioned Sarah the day we met, in the goods room."

"Don't take yourself to task," Amelia said. "She'd have found out soon enough because she was looking." Her voice grew harsh. "She's like a bloody magpie, gathering up bits of information."

"At least I'm sure Sarah's alive." *For now*, I added silently, though I immediately squelched the thought.

"Do you have a good map of Hatton Garden—I mean one that shows alleys, passageways, and such?" Amelia asked.

"No."

"I can get one. But I need about half an hour." I opened my mouth. "Don't argue, Kit. It'll save us time in the end. Then we'll go to James's. When did you last eat?"

"I'm not hungry."

"Don't be stupid," she retorted. "You'll be no good to us if you can't think. We need you to have your wits about you."

It was almost a relief to hear her scold me.

She took me to a pub, sat me down, ordered a bowl of stew and some ale and said, "I'll be back in half an hour, likely less. Don't leave without me. I don't know where James lives."

I nodded. "All right."

A family entered the pub and took seats at a table nearby. It was late, and my guess was they'd just arrived by train from somewhere and wanted supper before bed. Or perhaps they were waiting for someone to come. It was a mother, a father, a boy of about thirteen, and a daughter a few years younger, talking and joking together. The serving maid brought four bowls of beef stew and a loaf of bread. The father ate ravenously, and I guessed he was a dockworker, from the size of his shoulders, bulky as an ox's, and the roughness of his hands. When the mother finished her stew, she began knitting by the table's lamplight.

The boy, with his brown hair flopping over his forehead in spears, was explaining something earnestly to his father. The girl lined up beads along the crack between the wood slats of the table, chattering to her mother, who paused in her knitting to look and admire.

Into my mind slipped a fragile trace of a memory, of me sitting beside my mother at our table. I'd been allowed to play with the buttons from her button box while she sewed. I placed the shining bits of shell into squares, grouping similar ones together. My mother was embroidering an apron with blue thread, and I must have asked her why, for I remember her words, in a voice that was mild, even indulgent: *Well, there's no harm in making it pretty.*

Yes, there *had* been moments when Ma showed me her better nature. It was Ma, after all, who had shown me how to sew with patience.

Why did I resist those memories?

Even as I wondered, the answer came: Because they showed me what might have been. I'd had it for a time, and I was keenly aware of the loss.

A sudden thickness formed in my throat and I choked it down with another bite of stew.

I've no use for people who feel sorry for themselves. But I couldn't help wondering, what would Sarah's and my lives have been like if my father had been like that man, if he'd never broken my mother's heart? Or if my mother had always been like this one? What if there had been more kindness, more affection, more loyalty, more family feeling?

Then again, wouldn't I have been different? I wouldn't value those traits nearly so much if they'd been handed to me, regular each day as bread. Why would I?

But I'd done my best to give them to Sarah, as often as I could.

The thought of her in some dark hole, ill-fed and cold, made me push the stew away. I sent up a small silent prayer that she wouldn't give up hope. Perhaps this was the silver lining of our parents' failures. They had cemented Sarah and me together in a way that wouldn't have happened otherwise.

I gulped the ale, feeling the cold of it down into my belly.

True to her word, Amelia reappeared in twenty-three minutes by the mantel clock, her gloved hands empty. I gave her a questioning look, and she tapped her pocket.

Together we made our way to James's lodging house.

Mary had already told James enough that even before we reached the doorway, James had flung it open, and he stepped forward to pull me fiercely close. I clung to him for a moment, relieved that his feelings ran as deep as mine. He drew back and I saw the disbelief and anger hardening his face. "Is she bloody mad?" The skin around his eyes tightened, and he shook his head. "Kit, love."

Over his shoulder, I saw Mary with surprise on her face, and I flushed and pulled back.

"I'm no 'love,'" I said shortly. "I was a *fool*, not to guess Maggie would use Sarah to force my hand."

James stepped away from the threshold so Amelia and I could enter and shut the door behind us. When we had shrugged out of our coats, he said, "Start at the beginning."

And so I did. With three pairs of eyes on me, I told the whole thing—beginning with Maggie asking me to assess Hatton Garden, the reason for marking this jeweler, and the dodge she'd drawn up, omitting only the fact that Tim Lowry might have been Mary's father. There was no reason to share that here.

I concluded, "I made Maggie swear to give me Sarah when I brought her the three gems and the story broke in the papers—and I think she'll keep that promise, even if I don't use her dodge. My thought is, I need to get what she wants, without killing anybody, before Sunday."

"Spike her gun," Amelia said.

I nodded. "But I've no idea how."

"That's what delayed us." Amelia unfolded the map and placed it on James's wooden plank table. "I had to fetch this."

James brought two lamps, resting them near the corners, and stood beside me. Opposite, Mary and Amelia bent over the map with us.

"I don't know how you could get into Simonson's off the street," Mary said. "Cathy told me there was another theft in the Garden two nights ago. They're keeping it out of the papers, but there'll be even more constables now."

"And you can't go in at the roof. I looked last night," James said. "Too steep, and it's slate. It'll be slippery if there's any rain or mist at all."

My eyes flicked sideways to him in surprise.

He gave me a look. "You honestly believe I've been thinking of anything else since you told me?"

"Besides, the family lives above. They'd hear for certain." I gazed at the map. "What about tunnels or passages from St. Etheldreda's or other buildings?"

"But that would still require going into buildings off the street," James said. "I think I have something better."

"What?" I asked.

"This is the Fleet, coming down at a diagonal from King's

Cross." His finger traced the river, slowly so we could follow, running from Euston Station southeast along Gray's Inn Road to Blackfriars Bridge.

"But that's too far west of Hatton Garden," I said. "By at least a quarter of a mile."

"There's a comb of tunnels off the river." He sketched them in. "Five that go east here, above Holborn. When I was smuggling, we used them to bring goods from the Thames, especially barrels, because we could boat them or float them instead of carrying them on our backs. There are passages all underneath that part of the city, from back when tea and opium were smuggled in, with trapdoors in the floors or the alley behind. There were at least a dozen shops that took in shipments, accepted their cut, loaded the goods into carts out the back, and pushed it inland."

I stared. "Simonson's?"

His eyes glinted. "Aye. At one time, that building had a trapdoor we used. But the jewelers split the building, and I don't know which side the trapdoor falls on."

"Simonson's moved from Clerkenwell only two years ago," Amelia said.

"Likely Willingham's moved in around the same time, once the building was partitioned," James said. "Did you see any sign of a trapdoor in either jeweler?"

"The floors were wooden planks, covered by a carpet in Simonson's," I said slowly, picturing them. "But I noticed something odd."

James's look was expectant.

"The inside walls of the two jewelers might have a gap of a few feet between them."

"Cor," James said. "I didn't notice. How did you figure that?"

"The windows." I turned to Amelia. "Do you have a pencil?" Amelia handed me one and I took out the paper with my note and Sarah's reply, flipping it to the blank side. I drew the building, with the doors and the plate glass windows. "When you're inside the shop, the edge of the window meets the counter, which is perhaps two feet deep and three feet from the wall. But from the outside, it's at least fourteen feet—around five paces, perhaps even six, between the two windows."

"That leaves at least four feet," Mary said.

"So if there's a trapdoor, it could be between the two," James said. "And then there'll have to be a door into each shop—or at least one of them—for the trapdoor to be of any use. But you said you didn't see one in the plaster on the inside walls."

"It could be behind a mirror. Or what about inside the stairwell?" I asked, sketching the jeweler's shop in a bird's-eye view. "To the side of the steps here?"

"That would work," James agreed.

"We need to be sure the tunnel still reaches the building," Mary said.

I looked at James. "I can't swim."

"Nobody's swimming," he assured me. "I'll get a lighter from one of the boathouses, and we can row until we reach the side tunnels. Unless it's a full moon or there's been a heavy rain, water levels are shallow enough to wade most nights, and full moon was last week." He refolded Amelia's map. "After the ebb tide tomorrow, I can try."

"I can go with you," I said.

"No need," he replied. "It's easier if I do it myself."

"So that may get you to the jeweler," Mary said.

I looked across the table to Amelia and Mary. "Do you know a cracksman you can trust?"

Mary shook her head. "Only Castle men."

Amelia replied, "I know someone, and I think he'll do it. Especially if I explain why." She said it as if she expected me to accept this addition without question.

But I couldn't.

James sensed my reluctance and saved me from asking: "Who is he, Amelia? Is he anyone Maggie could reach?"

"No. We've been friends for years. I broke him out of prison."

James turned to me, to see what I thought.

It still wasn't enough to reassure me.

"Kit." Amelia's eyes held mine. "Do you remember I told you a friend of mine risked his own neck to save Adam last week?"

I nodded.

"That's this man."

If she trusted him with Adam's life, I could trust him, too.

"All right," I said. "How much will he ask?"

"I think he'd do it for sixty or seventy," she replied.

Sixty or seventy pounds. Nearly half my savings, but I was grateful it wasn't more.

I withdrew the two pouches of money and held them out to James. "Can you keep these here?"

"Aye." With a steady look, he set them, softly clinking, on the table. "I wish we could bloody double-cross Maggie, but we can't until Sarah's safe. Maggie must get what she wants *and* think she got away with it."

"Yes. Sarah must be safe before anything else," I said sharply.

"Of course," Amelia said.

"Your safety comes next," James said to me. "Think about Sarah if you're not here, how she'd feel if anything happened to you." He didn't say a word of how he'd feel, but I heard it in his voice. Amelia's eyes darting from James to me and back told me she heard it, too.

I swallowed. What would he say if he knew I was planning to leave London? The thought put a pinch near my heart, but I couldn't think of that now.

"Once we're safe, then what? For everyone's sake, Maggie needs to be put away, for good." I turned to James. "Can't we turn her over to the Yard?"

He looked dubious. "How can we, without telling your part in the dodge? No Yard man will let that go. They can't."

"Oh, the papers would love that," Amelia said drily. "The Yard covering up a jewelry heist—involving a titled peer no less. They'd feed off it for weeks."

The newspapers.

"Maggie needs to see the story in the papers before she'll let Sarah go," I said slowly. "Once that's done, she'll have what she wants and might lower her guard."

"We need to have the police find the diamonds on Maggie," Mary said.

"But she'll conceal them somewhere. We need to plant one, somewhere we can tell them to look," I said.

"I can do that," Mary said.

"That means stealing four stones instead of three, and when the story breaks, Maggie'll know something's wrong," James said.

"She won't know I've taken four, if the story breaks that it's three stones." I turned to James. "Would your newspaper friend help us, if we gave him a story?"

James's eyebrows rose. "Printing false information isn't going to get him back in the Yard's good graces."

"It isn't really false information," I said. "Three stones *will* have been stolen."

"Because three is less than four," Mary added. "He could just say 'a few.'"

James ran his hand into his hair. "I'd like to say he would, but I don't think so."

"Would he do it," I asked, "if I could also give him the names of two Castle men who were seen in Mayfair the night of the murders at Fairleigh House? And give him an eyewitness?"

Mary and Amelia both turned to stare. "God's sake, Kit. Truly?" Mary asked.

"Yes. Sarah was on her way home that night and saw them."

"Who?"

"Billy and Tommy."

Mary turned to James and saw by his face that he already knew, and her head swiveled back to me, her eyes full of worry. "Did they see *her*?"

"We don't think so," I said. "The light was dim, and she stayed out of their way with her bonnet pulled up."

"And I haven't heard her name mentioned," James said. "I've been listening."

"A double murder in Mayfair's a bigger story than a burglary," Amelia said. "And according to the papers, they have no leads yet." Amelia turned to James. "But do you trust this friend of yours? What's his name?"

"Fuller." James bit his lip, considering. "He treated me fairly, I'll say that much for him, and he cares about people getting what they deserve." He touched my arm. "With information about the Fairleigh murders as bait, you might not have to say much about the dodge."

I was already assembling what I might tell him.

By the end of the night, we had a plan. We'd talked through it three times, combing through the details, stitching bits and pieces into place, and while we knew we'd have to be ready to improvise, it could work.

With a bit of luck.

"You're in charge of that part," I told James as he helped me into my coat. "Finding the luck. I never find it on my own."

James replied, "I'll go into the tunnels tomorrow night. Unless it rains again, the water level should be low enough. Let's hope the trapdoor is where it needs to be."

"I'll take a bracelet to Simonson's for repairs, so I can see how they return it to me," I said.

Mary's part required perfect timing, but she didn't hesitate. "I'll manage it." Mary's voice was quiet but her expression was as determined as Maggie's had been. "She took my mother from me, Kit."

The hard brightness in her eyes, so unlike her usual warmth, made me shiver. *Maggie doesn't have the corner on revenge*, I thought.

Amelia said, "I'll speak to my friend about the locks and safe." Her gaze dropped to my hands. "You practice, so you're quick. You should aim for switching out four stones in thirty minutes."

I nodded in agreement.

But I had already decided that I would be taking a fifth one, for reasons of my own.

Chapter 22

At four o'clock in the morning, Elephant and Castle was dead silent except for the bells of Newington Church. The pubs and brothels were shuttered, the nightsoil men come and gone, the earliest costermongers still two hours from rolling across the cobbles.

I slid out of bed and stole along the streets, empty aside from the scurrying of rats, the bang of a broken shutter, the soft howl of the wind around the corners. I picked the lock of the back door of Elephant and Castle and slipped inside. In the darkness, I felt my way up the stairs to the costume room, lighting a candle only long enough to filch what I'd need for a disguise—the fair-haired wig, two moles, spectacles. Together with my feigned limp, these were traits quickly noticed, easily described, and utterly at odds with my true appearance. Still in darkness, I locked the door of the inn behind me and returned to my room, where I stashed my disguise, together with the stolen bracelet, in a satchel, concealed it under the floorboards, and lay down again, combing through all that was to come during the next four days, as the morning light crept across my ceiling. At last, it was time to go to Mr. Ardle's shop.

I arrived at the back door and knocked as usual. Mr. Ardle let me in with his eyes averted and an air of apology. So he knew enough about this dodge—and my role in it—to feel guilty.

And so he should, I thought. I gave him a bitter look and stalked past him into the workroom.

He'd prepared a collection of paste stones, and using my loupe, I separated them into two piles: those that could pass for diamonds and those that could not. Paste, made of lead glass, wasn't as hard as diamond, and some stones had scratches on the surface and chipped or rounded facet edges, as if they'd been nibbled. Once I'd found twenty stones that satisfied me with respect to cut and size and brilliance, I began practicing on a necklace, taking the stones out and putting them into settings with different sizes and numbers of prongs. Three hours later, I'd already become quicker—from seventeen minutes each down to eleven. I needed more practice, but at least I knew I could improve my speed.

Mr. Ardle came over and dropped a few more stones onto the black velvet, separate from the two piles I'd made. "Here are four more, if you need them."

I looked up to find his gaze on the stones, avoiding mine.

"Do you know what she's done? And what she intends?" I asked. "Why are you helping her?"

He raised his pale blue eyes to mine. "She did what she had to," he said simply. "And there's nothing I wouldn't do for her, if she asked."

Even involve himself in a dodge that might require murder?

I felt a wave of scorn until I thought of what I was willing to do for Sarah.

Who was I to cast stones at Mr. Ardle, paste or real?

By three o'clock, my neck ached from bending over the

bench and my eyes felt grainy. I showed Mr. Ardle which paste sparklers to set aside for use, then left the shop, returning briefly to my room to pick up my satchel. I walked to the railway station, losing myself in the crowd to evade a tail, donned my wealthy watch-buyer disguise in the ladies' washroom, and hired a hansom cab to Hatton Garden. At Simonson's, I adopted my limp and put the gold bracelet—with a newly broken clasp—into the hands of a clerk I didn't recognize. I requested that it be mended within two days, to which he nodded agreeably. Then I departed, limping on, with a few quick checks for a tail, until I found a quiet alley where I could remove the pieces of my disguise before I continued on to Fleet Street.

To do the most unlikely thing I could imagine.

I'd once have believed it would be a cold day in hell before I offered to tell a newspaperman anything—much less a newspaperman with ties to the Yard.

But here I was, walking of my own volition to a coffeehouse where Mr. Fuller should be waiting for James and me.

James met me two streets away with his hand out for mine, an old signal of ours that meant he saw no one following me. While we walked the remainder of the way, James told me that he'd go into the tunnels just before midnight. "Amelia has spoken with her friend—his name is Art—who can manage the locks and the safe."

"Will we meet him beforehand?" I asked.

James nodded. "Tomorrow night. Amelia will bring him to my rooms."

"She doesn't want him knowing where she lives?" I asked.

"I think it's more that she doesn't want *me* knowing where

she lives," he replied. "I don't mind—and I don't blame her. Besides, I have the feeling she won't be there long."

"Why?"

"Just a feeling." He squeezed my hand. "There's Croom's, up ahead."

My stomach tightened, for this was the part of the plan I felt least sure of. I'd never met this man Fuller; we'd be giving him very little and asking for a promise in return.

I drew James to a halt. "How much did you have to tell him?"

"Nothing, as we planned," James said. "In my message, I only said I wanted to speak to him about the Fairleigh murders and to meet me here. Given what he did for the information about the boathouse murders, I'm guessing he'll do just about anything for this, short of giving up his children."

"He has children?"

"Two, I believe. And a wife."

Illogically, the thought of Mr. Fuller having a family made me feel better. "All right."

"Stay out here. Let me be sure he's inside." He pulled open the door and vanished, while I dawdled before the shop window next door, surveying the writing papers, pens, and French postcards of scantily clad women in wholly improbable poses—the Society for the Suppression of Vice would be outraged—all the while keeping my eye on the door. When it opened and James nodded, I approached. He looked troubled.

My every nerve tightened. "What's the matter?"

"He looks like he's been ill," he said.

"Oh." I stepped inside and the smell of coffee and chocolate, bitter and smoky, filled my nose.

"Corner table, left," James murmured. "He hasn't seen me yet."

He led me toward Fuller, weaving between the well-worn rectangular wood tables, where men—and a few women of a sturdy sort—sat, engrossed in newspapers, conversations, or their cigars.

Mr. Fuller was partly turned away from us, so I first saw his right shoulder, his arm, his hand resting near a coffee cup, and a plate with two thick slabs of bread untouched. I had a peculiar feeling as I moved toward him. The round head, the reddish hair that flopped over his forehead, the beakish nose, and the pasty complexion: I recognized him from somewhere, and it only took a moment to remember. He'd been outside the Fairleigh house when I'd been talking to the Yard man. Had they been there together? Or had the Yard man been observing him?

My every nerve was pulled taut as James and I approached. As Mr. Fuller's brown eyes caught sight of James, he gave a look of recognition that had some pleasure in it, but upon seeing me, a resentful frown formed a single furrow, sharp as a knife cut, between his gingery brows. He'd guessed I knew how they met, and he didn't like it.

"It's been a fair while," Mr. Fuller said to James.

James nodded and drew out a chair that would put my back to the room, so anything I said would be imperceptible to others. James nudged a third chair to where he could keep an eye on the room for us both.

Mr. Fuller turned to me. "And who is this?"

"A friend," James said easily.

Mr. Fuller's lips pursed irritably. "Ah. Well, hello, friend." I nodded a greeting, and he turned back to James. "Are you still at the Custom House? Is it working out?"

"It is," James said.

Mr. Fuller relaxed visibly, and his gaze grew keen. "And do you really have information for me about the murders?"

"I do," I said shortly.

Mr. Fuller's hand raised in a gesture meant to placate me. "Where are my manners? Some coffee or chocolate for you?"

"Coffee," I said, and James nodded.

Mr. Fuller turned, caught the eye of the server, and pointed to his own cup, raising two fingers. At the table beside us a man flapped the *Telegraph* open and refolded it into a manageable rectangle.

I assumed that Mr. Fuller would lean forward, eager to have me relate what I knew about the murders. To my surprise, he sat back and studied me, so I did the same, absorbing details that told me a bit more: The suit was once a good one of fine wool, but was now worn, shiny at the elbows, and looked slightly too large for him, as if he'd lost a stone or two; the cuffs of his shirtsleeves were frayed, though the threads had been trimmed. His hands were squarish, and the second finger on his right hand bore a formless gray ink stain beside the top knuckle; the third finger had a narrow gold band, the sign of his aforementioned wife.

James leaned in. "Begging your pardon, Fuller, but you don't look yourself. Have you been ill?"

"Influenza," he said soberly. "My daughter nearly died of it last month."

I felt a poke of sympathy, and James said, "I'm sorry to hear it." The server brought our coffee, together with tin spoons not worth stealing and a silver plate sugar bowl, much dented.

Fuller's eyes flicked between us. "Before you tell me

anything, you should know that if you're trying to get information to the Yard, I don't have their ear. They don't trust me anymore."

James stilled, and his face registered dismay. "Is that because you helped me?"

Fuller's mouth tightened, as if he wished it were only that, but he shook his head. "No."

"Then why?" I asked.

The look he gave me was coolly assessing. "If you must know, I'll tell you, but I'd appreciate it if you don't spread it about."

"Of course."

Fuller drained his coffee cup, leaving some dark grounds stuck to his upper lip. He licked to remove them. He settled his palm on the table, tapping his thumb several times, then stilled it with an air of having decided where to begin, and looked up at me. "I once had the confidence of a Yard inspector. He's young and grew up outside of London, and frankly, he was a bit at sea when he arrived at the Yard. But he has an amiable manner that made me want to throw him an oar, so to speak, so I shared with him certain . . . insights about the underworld, gangs, docks, corruption in Whitehall, and so on. In return, he sometimes shared information with me. Naturally, if he asked me to hold a story back for a time because it would compromise his detecting, I would." His eyes dropped to his coffee cup, and his mouth twisted into a regretful line. "Six months ago, I was working on a story about counterfeiters here in London—it's a rampant problem—and I had discovered a coin man in a basement not far from here. I trusted someone I shouldn't have, and that evening, the story appeared, complete with the counterfeiter's address, in another paper. The counterfeiter was tipped off. He gathered his belongings, stole a hansom cab, killed the driver, and left London hours before my inspector was going to arrest him."

"So he doesn't trust you anymore," I said.

"No," Mr. Fuller replied. "Not that I blame him."

"And you want to get back in his good graces."

"No, I'm genuinely bloody sorry," he said shortly, his eyes blazing. "I'd make amends, if I could." He set a forearm on the table and leaned toward me, close enough that I could smell the coffee on his breath. "The duty of every decent newspaperman is to tell the truth and bring unknown stories to light, to improve our city, to make it safer, to uphold justice, to help those in need. We *do* make a difference."

That's true enough, I thought, recalling the Canterbury orphanage that had burned down and been rebuilt because of a sympathetic story in the paper.

"It's the whole reason I came today. If I can help solve the Fairleigh murders"—Mr. Fuller tapped his thumb in that restless tattoo—"it could save the Yard, which is of crucial importance for London."

"What do you mean, save the Yard?"

"A majority in Parliament has been trying to close the Yard for over a year, since that scandal with those four corrupt inspectors. Every failure wins more MPs to their side. They want to send the detectives back to the separate divisions—a decision that would hamper the entire enterprise! The detectives need to be in the same building, talking among themselves, because crimes in London don't stay confined to Mayfair or Bethnal Green or Whitechapel. Criminals cross those boundaries, which are wholly artificial, as any fool knows."

"This matters to you," I said, surprised by his ardent tone.

"It should matter to anyone who gives a damn about keeping our citizens safe," he said shortly.

He was prickly, but I rather liked him.

James reached over and squeezed my hand. His expression was encouraging. After a moment, I nodded.

"You did me a great kindness once," James said to Mr. Fuller. "It made all the difference. We have a favor to ask, but we also have information that could lead straight to arrests."

"In exchange for what I'm telling you, I will need something from you in return," I said, "and unfortunately, I can't tell you much."

A snort flared his nostrils. "You haven't told me anything yet."

"I'm about to," I retorted. "I have a younger sister who is fourteen. She recently took a position as a scullery maid in Mayfair, not a quarter mile from the Fairleigh house. On the night of the murders, she was walking back to Elephant and Castle to spend the night with me, when she recognized two men walking on the other side of the street—"

"Two?"

"Yes, two," I said firmly. "Castle men, dressed as gentlemen."

"So as to appear they belonged," Mr. Fuller said and sat back. "What are their names?"

I gave him a look.

He spread his hands. "I can't use any of this without confirmation, and neither can the Yard—"

"Because it's hearsay," I interrupted. "I know. But my sister can bear witness."

"Then why isn't she here?"

"Because she's been kidnapped." My hands knotted in my lap.

His jaw sagged with dismay. "By the Castle men?"

"No. By someone else, for a different reason. They're separate matters. The people who took my sister want me to do something for them, which I will. Once it's reported in the newspaper, they will let her go. Then, she can be your witness. She can come to the Yard, so you get the goodwill."

"I see." His expression softened. "How old did you say she was?"

"Fourteen."

He groaned. "Damn. Poor girl." He drew a long breath and blew it out in a huff. "So I write the story, your sister is released, and she gives me the names of the men she saw. But how do you know she'll talk to me? To the Yard?"

"She will, if she understands that you've helped me free her."

"I know her," James interjected. "She's a sensible girl, with courage. She'll do it."

I sent James a grateful look.

Mr. Fuller cocked an eyebrow. "Will it be true? The story I print?"

"What I tell you will be true," I said. "What you write is up to you."

He looked wary. "But I'll have only your word."

"And mine," James said. "I'll be there, too."

Mr. Fuller frowned and folded his hands over his waistcoat. "What *are* you doing? Can you tell me anything?"

"No," James said. "Not yet."

I held my breath, waiting.

At last, Mr. Fuller's face screwed up with regret, and his

eyes met mine. "I'm truly sorry about your sister. You should go to the Yard. They can help."

"No, they can't," I said between gritted teeth.

"Well, I can't print something I can't verify. Last year, a newspaperman was thrown in jail for six months over a false story. I can't risk my family going to the workhouse."

My hands tightened on the arms of the chair as I felt him slipping away.

But I'd seen pain on his face when I told him about Sarah being kidnapped. This was a man who cared. I made one last desperate attempt. "Please, Mr. Fuller," I said, my voice cracking. "She's my only family. She nearly died of whooping cough, and I can't lose her. She's all the things I'm not—kind and gentle and sweet. She makes people love her. What I'm doing could get me killed, but if I don't do it, they'll certainly . . . kill her."

Mr. Fuller looked at me for a long minute. Then he turned to James. "Is this true?"

James nodded.

Mr. Fuller's gaze roamed the coffeehouse while James and I waited in anxious silence.

"All right," Mr. Fuller said to James. "I'll do it. When will you get me this story I'm to write?"

I let go the breath I'd been holding, too relieved to speak.

"Within the next week," James said. "To be put in as soon as you can."

"Naturally."

Mr. Fuller placed a small pile of coins on the table. As our business seemed concluded, I began to rise, but he put out his hand to prevent me.

"Miss, wait," he said, and I sat down again. His voice

lowered. "I believe you've played fair with me, so I'll play fair with you. I know who you are."

James stiffened with alarm.

"Who I am?" I echoed.

"I don't know your name. But you're one of the women thieves from the ring out of Elephant and Castle."

I didn't acknowledge it or deny it, and I didn't even glance at James. But I could tell he was as shocked as I was.

"Why do you think so?" I asked.

"There's a sketch of you at the Yard. In it you have spectacles, but otherwise, there's a strong resemblance."

My heart thudded sickeningly, and heat razored down the veins of my arms.

"One of the Yard men has been investigating the ring—"

"What does he look like?" I interrupted.

"About my height, with a paunch—"

"Brown wavy hair, clean-shaven, perhaps just under forty years of age? Owns a brown suit?"

He sat back, his eyes keen. "Yes. His name's Maynard."

It was the man at Pickford's. My heart thudded again over my narrow escape with Mary. "Go on."

He opened his mouth as if to ask a question but thought better of it. "The Yard has had a few tips and sightings of the thieves"—*No small thanks to Maggie*, I thought—"but no success in apprehending them. First, only one man was assigned to the case, then two, then three—until the Fairleigh murders, when all available inspectors were reassigned to that. But they'll be back eventually because the thefts are a matter of concern for influential people, and there's an election coming."

"I know. Shopkeepers are leaning on the elected officials."

He scratched his head above his temple. "It's not only the shopkeepers. The Society for the Suppression of Vice is advocating for harsher prison sentences, several of the wealthier churches have taken up the cause, claiming thieves shred the moral fabric of the city, and *Reynolds* prints up handbills openly mocking the Yard men. Have you seen those?"

"Of course." I'd laughed at the illustrations of the Yard men with holey nets, haplessly chasing rats dressed in fine dresses and jewels.

"The police feel humiliated. It's firing their desire to shut the thieves down." He sniffed. "I would strongly advise you to leave off. The newspapers may depict Yard men as fools, but they've solved more cases than the papers report. They can't reveal their methods."

The room had become more crowded, and the server hovered.

I swallowed down the fear Mr. Fuller's warning had stirred, for this was a matter for another time. But he'd played fair with me, and I would with him. "I saw you the other night outside of Fairleigh House. There was a Yard man under one of the plane trees across the way, watching everyone. I don't know if it matters, but I'm sure he saw you there."

His face went quiet. "What did he look like?"

"A head taller than I am, fair-haired, brown eyes, about twenty-three years old, speaks well, like he had public schooling, and good shoes. Was this your inspector?"

His eyes sparked. "It sounds like Stiles. And yes, it matters that he's on this case." A pause. "Quid pro quo."

"I don't know what that means," I said.

"A fair trade," James said.

But Mr. Fuller's expression told me this had been more

than a fair exchange of favors. It was the start of a small piece of trust.

At last, we rose from the table. Before we'd even stepped away, the server had stacked our saucers, cups, and spoons and swept the coins into his pocket.

We walked out together, and on the pavement, I gave Mr. Fuller my hand, genuinely grateful that he'd promised to help. "Thank you."

His hand was steady, but his face was full of warning. "Be careful, miss."

Chapter 23

The following night, Wednesday, when I went to James's rooms, he greeted me at the door with the news that the tunnel was exactly what he'd hoped, so the only piece of the plan yet to be fixed was the locksmith, who was being brought by Amelia. Not ten minutes later, they arrived.

Amelia embraced me warmly and introduced her friend.

Art was a slender man of Far Eastern descent, about forty years of age, with shining black hair, unreadably dark eyes, and a raised scar under his jaw that suggested a blade had once been held just below his ear. It reassured me to know he'd had the skills to evade it.

I was keenly on edge, but he greeted me calmly in a tone that was soothing, even mellifluous. Did he have any nerves at all?

My gaze went to his hands. Long, delicate fingers.

"You're Kit," he said, the *T* stuck in the back of his throat, pure Cockney. "Wi' the wee sister 'oo's been taken."

"Yes."

"Amelia tol' me the plan, but let's go over i' again, all together."

Amelia's map was already open on the table, and James bent over, pointing to the wharf with a boathouse that was poorly secured as the place we would begin. "It's an old padlock, easy to pick." He glanced up at Art, who nodded. "We'll row along here, and into the Fleet. There's no foot access, and the water is fairly deep and fast."

"Remember, I can't swim," I said.

"I can swim like a fish," James said, for Art's benefit.

"So can I," Art said.

"The tunnel is the third one up," James said. "The water was chest height when I went last night, but so long as it doesn't rain, it'll be down far enough we can wade from where the side tunnel branches off. It's about two hundred yards to the metal ladder that leads up to the trapdoor we need." He tossed me a ball of red yarn. "This is the distance from where we'll park the boat, and I marked the ladder with an *X* on the third rung, in case the yarn breaks, because there are two others not far away. You don't want to climb the wrong one."

"It's a ladder?" Art asked doubtfully.

"Well, metal bars," James replied. "Old but anchored into the stone solid enough. The trapdoor is latched from the underside and easy to open. Push it up and turn to the right. You'll see a door. That's Simonson's."

"How big a door?" I asked.

"Smaller than average. About so," James said, his hands sketching a rectangle the width of his shoulders that reached from the ground to his chest.

"Locks?" Art asked.

"Just one. Standard. Obviously, I didn't attempt to open it."

Art nodded.

"You should stay outside," Amelia said to James. "So it's just the two of them."

"The door opens to the shop?" Art asked.

"With a door that size, no," I said. "The mirror was horizontal, not vertical. So I think it'll open in the stairwell that leads to the upper floor. From there, we'll enter the main room, and the office, which will likely also be locked."

Art scratched his chin. "Inside door's no trouble."

"And then there's the safe."

He gave a small smile. "Doan worry. I go' the tools."

"The most important thing is we must leave no trace," I said. "If they suspect anything, they'll examine the necklace one more time before they return it to the marquess."

"That's obvious, innit?" Art replied.

We were all silent for a moment, studying the map with James's pencil marks, committing it to memory.

"I'll have the boat turned around for when you return," James said. "The tide will be running out, so it's an easier row back to the boathouse. The entire thing should take no more than four hours."

Art's mouth twitched skeptically. "You 'spect this to go as planned?"

"No," Amelia said, and James shook his head.

Of course not, I thought.

I itched to carry out our plan that very night, but Simonson didn't leave London until the following day. Besides, James had assured us the waters would be most favorable late Friday night, barring a storm.

Friday morning, I woke to rain against my window, and my heart turned over.

Feeling almost feverish with worry, that afternoon I did the only thing I could to further our plan. I donned my disguise and retrieved the bracelet from Simonson's. Although I had given it to them in a small black pouch, it was returned to me in a box with a ribbon and a red wax seal, with a large scrolling *S* for Simonson's. I drew a breath of relief; wax and a ribbon would be easy to remove and reattach.

By the time I emerged from the shop, the rain had stopped. From Hatton Garden, I went to James's rooms, hoping against hope the additional rain hadn't thwarted the dodge for the night. James's expression as he opened the door told me it had. "The water's going to be too high, Kit. It'll have to be tomorrow."

The thought of waiting yet another day before being able to release Sarah was nearly unbearable. "But the rain's stopped! Can't we at least *try*?"

"There's no point," he insisted. "The water level will still be dangerous, and we can't get hurt."

I strode back and forth in his room, my boots hard on the boards. I fidgeted and fumed until James pulled out a deck of cards and gestured to the seat across the table. "Come on, let's play."

"Cards?" I burst out. "Are you mad?"

He spread his hands, half the deck in each. The cut revealed the six of clubs. A terrible card to have in *vingt-et-un*. I pushed away the thought of it being an omen.

"You can't stew and fret like this, Kit. The plan's solid, and there's nothing to be done tonight. Spinning your nerves into a tangle isn't going to help. You need to sleep and be ready for tomorrow."

He was right, of course. I'd have said the same thing to him if our positions were reversed and Emma was the one being held. Still, I was nearly drowning in worry and impatience.

"What if we can't do it tomorrow, either?" I asked, but

answered before he could: "I know. It means I go through with Maggie's plan, including a constable's murder. And Maggie will make sure I hang for some part of it, to save the trouble and risk of killing me herself."

James stilled. "You still think she wants you dead?"

"How can she not?" I asked. "With what I know? I could hold it over her head forever. She won't let that happen."

James closed the deck and set down the cards. "I won't let Maggie hurt you, or Sarah." He came around the table and cupped my face in his hands, his face sober. "I swear to you, Kit. We will get you out of this whole and alive. And Sarah, too." His eyes fixed on mine, his words came fast. "Maggie's damned clever, and she's plotted it well, but she's not cleverer than all of us together. Remember, Maggie thinks you're going along with it. I'm not saying she'll let her guard down. But she's not looking for you to spike her dodge. Sarah's alive, and we'll do this tomorrow night. Stay the course, love." He rested his forehead against mine before drawing back. "All right?"

"I'm afraid," I said, my voice breaking. Tears burned, and I blinked them back. "What if I fail?"

"Ah." His face softened, and he pulled me against his chest, pressing his lips to the crown of my head while my fists clenched the back of his shirt. "You've never failed her, Kit. You kept her alive and safe for years after your mum died, against odds no better than these. Remember that."

Not wanting to tip Maggie to anything out of the ordinary, I planned to remain around Elephant and Castle for all of Saturday. Feigning a quarrel, Mary had left our room on Thursday, so I had it to myself, which was for the best, as I struggled to sleep.

In the early morning, I looked over my choice of black trousers, dark woolen sweater, and coat, and placed them back under my mattress. Then I practiced at Mr. Ardle's shop for several hours, slipping the necessary tools into my pocket, and took an early supper at the Elephant and Castle, keeping an anxious eye on the darkening sky. There were clouds, but no rain.

At nine o'clock, I turned out the light in my room; at ten, I donned my borrowed clothes, picked up my tools, and slipped out of my room. By a circuitous route, I made my way across the river, and at half past eleven, I arrived at James's rooms. Though my dark brown hair was tightly pinned, he gave me a black cap to cover it.

Amelia was there, as was Art. He picked up an unlikely looking sack that clinked as he angled the rope strap over his shoulder and across his chest. I handed him my bound parcel of tools to put inside.

Amelia pulled me close, muttering in my ear, "I'm sorry."

I drew back. "Don't, Amelia. She did this, not you. And we'd never have this plan without your map and Art."

"Come to me afterward." She looked me hard in the eyes. "Keep your wits about you, and you'll be all right."

At midnight, James, Art, and I departed.

The Thames was a few hours into an ebb tide, with its lowest point three hours away. James was timing our arrival at the tunnels for two o'clock, coming out at four. We didn't want to be fighting the Thames more than we had to.

Above, the clouds had peeled back to the margins, leaving the moon a yellow yolk above the rooftops. We stole west along Upper Thames Road, with its long shallow puddles, the air holding the musty smell of damp stone and earth from the previous rains. Past Queenhithe Dock, we cut down an alley to Maidstone Wharf, where a wooden boathouse stood. An old padlock linked two ends of a chain around the doors; Art had it undone in under a minute, and I let out my breath. I trusted Amelia's judgment, but still, Art's ease at this first obstacle reassured me.

The inside smelled of rotting wood and trapped sewage. Together we lifted the small boat off the pegs, flipped it, and dropped it into the water carefully so it didn't slap or overturn. Art climbed in and folded himself into a small shape, drawing his knees to his chin. I followed, and James gave me the oars to hold until he pushed us away from the piling. Despite the late hour, half a dozen boats and ships were within sight. The Thames was never empty.

James took the oars back, dropped them into the metal oarlocks, and settled in with his back to me, rowing us away from shore and through the inky water toward our landmark, Blackfriars Bridge, the gaps between the carved posts of the guardrail showing like Belgian lace in the moonlight.

Under the bridge we went, James's steady stroke bringing us near the opening where the Fleet poured into the Thames. The bells of a nearby church chimed two, the sound a doleful echo. Art lit the lantern, keeping it dim, as the boat slid toward the dark semicircle of the tunnel above the water. Though it was unnecessary, I instinctively ducked going inside. The Fleet was still deep and moving quickly, with fits and starts, so it was hard work rowing upstream, and James had sweat on his brow by the time we reached the third tunnel, the one that led to Simonson's.

"I'm turning," he warned us. I tightened my grip on the

thwart, and an agile maneuvering of oars pivoted the boat into a smaller waterway. Immediately the rushing noise subsided, and the boat's hull scraped against the side of the tunnel. "Go on, get out," James said. "It should be a foot deep at most."

The boat rocked as Art and I shifted our weight. I clambered out first, awkwardly, the cold water reaching just below my knee, and Art climbed out after me. But as James stepped out, a sudden rush of water from the main river flung the boat into the wall—with James's leg caught between the two. He managed to avoid dropping the lamp, which would have cast us all into utter darkness, but his shoulder met the stone with a thunk.

"*Merde*," burst from him in a hoarse whisper.

I seized the lamp from his hand as Art sprang forward to help James get out from behind the boat. James hopped, and it was clear he could put no weight on the leg.

James let out a soft groan and lifted his foot into the boat to roll his trousers. Even before he reached the place where the boat had struck him, I could see the blood. The metal gunwale had cut the skin, a three-inch gash straight across.

"Keep i' up. The water's fe'id and full o' poisons," Art said as he reached into his bag. He withdrew a narrow roll of silk fabric and wrapped James's leg half a dozen times, so deftly I wondered if he was a surgeon on top of everything else. "Likely the bone's cracked," Art said. "This'll stanch the bleedin', but we should get ou' of here."

"No," James barked. "I'll stay here with the boat. You go. You know everything you need."

"James," I said.

He was shaking his head at me. "I'd agree with you if we had another night, but we don't."

I swallowed down my aching regret as I watched Art bending his head to bite a small rip in the cloth's end, then tearing it lengthwise, so he could wrap the split bandage opposite ways and tie a knot. "Sit down and stay still, wi' your leg up," Art said.

"What's the mark?" I asked James. "The one you made on the ladder?"

"I scraped an *X* on the third rung."

"I hate this," I said. "Leaving you."

"Don't," he said. "I'm fine. Just don't dawdle." He managed a smile. "Good luck. Don't forget the string. Tie it there." He pointed to a jagged bit of metal sticking out of the curved wall.

Art started down the tunnel, holding the lamp. I turned around to see James one last time, and he was watching. The light was dim, and only then did I realize we would be leaving him alone in utter darkness.

I touched my fingertips to my mouth and extended them toward him, a kiss. He lifted his chin in reply. Then I turned and followed Art, pausing to take the yarn from my coat pocket. I tied the end where James indicated, knotting it three times to make sure it was secure, and began to unwind it. We would need it to guide us to the proper ladder, for we were only twenty steps along, fighting the mild current, and I already saw a set of metal bars ahead of us to the right. God only knew how many there were along this stretch.

The lantern light cast our shadows, huge and misshapen, on the curved walls of rough-hewn stone. About a hundred yards on, a rope ladder, the metal bars shining in the light of the lamp, dangled from above instead of being attached to the wall. Art glanced at the ball of yarn in my hand, and I shook my head. "Not yet."

We went on, and I felt the ball shrink ever faster until it was only a string a few inches long. I stretched it taut and walked on, and as my fingers reached the very end, we saw a set of half a dozen metal rods unevenly spaced in the wall leading up. I handed Art the end of the string and stepped toward the bars. They looked none too sturdy, but I reached up and dangled from one. While it wobbled, it held my weight. I set a foot on the bottom rung, reaching upward. "Raise the light," I said. I wanted to see if I could find James's scratch—and there it was, an *X* on the side. "Found the mark. Let go the string." We didn't need it anymore, and it would sink and drift down current. On the slim chance smugglers came through here in the next hour, I wanted no sign of which ladder we'd climbed.

Behind me, Art climbed one-handed, holding the lantern, and by its light I could see the latch. It was rusty from disuse, but James had told me to expect that, and the door wasn't heavy; I'd be able to manage it. From my pocket, I removed a pair of James's pliers, heavier than those I used for jewelry, and eased the metal bar from the hook. Gently, I pushed up, half an inch, feeling resistance from the hinges. Art handed up the jar of grease, and I slathered some to prevent a squawk of metal against metal, waiting a moment before pushing the door up all the way.

I climbed out, turning to take the lantern from Art. A quick look around confirmed James's description: the space was less than three feet wide, windowless, with walls of plaster and wooden beams above. Art stepped out and laid the trapdoor back in place, and we turned to the right, to a narrow door. I held the lamp while Art withdrew his set of picks from his pocket.

Cold air struck my wet ankles and feet.

Art went to work. "Do you need more light?" I asked, my voice low. I could turn up the lamp, but I wanted to save our oil for the trip back.

"No. I do i' by touch," he said.

His eyes were closed.

It recalled the moment in the cupboard when I'd closed my own.

The lock snicked. "There," he said. He'd opened it in under two minutes.

My clenched shoulders eased with relief. James's injury had set us back, certainly, but the luck I'd asked him to find was with us.

Art swung open the door and stepped back. He had an odd look on his face.

I raised the lantern so I could see why.

It was a bloody brick wall.

Chapter 24

Art turned to look at me, a question in his dark eyes.

I drew a breath.

Damn everything.

But there was no way James could have known what was behind the door. I put my hands to the bricks to be sure it wasn't a façade, a trick of the eye, a painting, but the wall was solid. I shut my eyes to think.

I stepped back to survey the wall for another opening, a sign of a crawl space or an entrance to an attic.

Nothing.

"We have to go back down, take one of the earlier ladders up," I said quietly. "James said one of them led to a trapdoor in the alley."

"He said there are constables, and we'll be seen through the gates." For the first time I heard a sharpness in Art's voice. "I doan kill people."

"Neither do I," I shot back. "We'll need a diversion. Just let me *think*."

I put the map of this building in my head and walked around it to the alley, which connected to Ely Place—

A church bell rang behind me, followed by another immediately to my right.

The map pivoted in my head. "This is the wrong wall," I said.

"But the door's supposed to be to the right, innit?" Art asked.

"I know." I pointed. "But that way's north. Those bells were St. Etheldreda's, which is behind us, and St. Peter's, in Saffron Hill to the east."

He drew back dubiously. "I'm sure James knows his directions—"

"And I know Hatton Garden, and I'm telling you, he must've got turned around," I retorted. I carried the lantern over to the other wall. Like the one opposite, it was rough plaster. I ran my right hand along at eye level, searching for a crack. Nothing.

I dropped my hand lower and ran it back.

My fingertips dropped into a divot. "Here."

He stepped forward.

"Hold the lamp," I said. Art took it from me, and I brushed away dust. There was no door handle, but a small square not much larger than one revealed itself to my fingertips. It was a hinged door, smaller than a Judas window, and I took out my knife, slid it into one side, and pulled it open, revealing a door handle, locked. And now I could see the outline of a small, squat door, half the size of a normal one, the plasterwork done so perfectly it was barely visible. With no hinges on this side, the door would open inward.

Art went to work with his picks, and the knob turned. Cautiously, he pushed the door open and peered in. I laid a hand on his arm, so he'd let me go first, and I swung the lantern over the threshold. As I'd guessed, we were underneath the staircase that led to the upper floors. The stairs were supported by vertical wooden beams set approximately every two feet apart, easy enough for us to slip through.

Out of the corner of my eye I saw a glint of something shiny. I lowered the lantern toward it and found two small bells suspended from a thread, ready to be set off. I gave Art a warning look, and he nodded. I stepped inside first, and he followed into the area beneath the stairs.

I bent to slip off my boots and my wet socks, and Art did the same. We ran the bare soles of our feet along the dry part of our trousers above the knees, to be sure we wouldn't leave prints if the floor was dusty. We eased between the vertical beams to the door. Slowly, Art rotated the knob, and we slipped into the main room. The air was still; it smelled of the musty wool carpet and the linseed oil used to polish the cabinets. I pointed Art toward the door of the office, and he bent to examine the lock, withdrew his picks, and let us in with the faintest snick.

By the light of the lamp, we saw the safe, a shiny imposing black block with a silver circle on the front.

We could leave no trace of our work, so once more I put out a hand to halt Art, giving me a moment to study the room—the position of the chair, the carpet, and the drawer of the desk, left half an inch out.

When I dropped my arm, Art removed his coat. I took it from him, placing it against the bottom of the door, where the light from the lantern might sliver through, alerting a passing constable who might peer through the front window.

Art stepped toward the safe and paused to appraise it, his hands running over the front, top, and sides. From his sack, he withdrew my leather wrap of tools and handed it to me. Next, he set a small, peculiarly shaped box on top of the safe, crouched beside the dial, put his right ear to the metal, and closed his eyes.

There are minutes that last hours, and these were some of them.

I knew better than to urge him to hurry; I'd only delay him by saying a word. But as I watched, I thought of how so much that was precious to me depended upon this stranger's hands.

His eyes opened and met mine, the handle of the safe pivoted, and the door swung out.

Art stepped aside, and we examined the contents of the six shelves without touching a thing. Art pointed to what looked like the necklace lying on a black velvet tray and raised a questioning eyebrow. Did I want to see it, just in case? I shook my head; only the copy would be left loose on a tray. I pointed, and Art removed the largest rectangular box. None of the others would hold a necklace of this size laid flat. Like the box for my repaired bracelet, this one had been closed with a ribbon and a crimson wax seal stamped with the jeweler's *S*.

I carried the box to the jeweler's desk and put down the lamp at the corner.

From my pouch of tools, I chose a knife that could remove the seal without breaking it. My loupe. Two sets of pliers. The small sack of paste stones. The tiny bottle of adhesive.

I picked up the knife and said over my shoulder to Art, "Move away, please. I can't concentrate with someone watching."

Silently, he stepped toward the door, and I turned my back to him.

I began the delicate work of removing the wax seal from the ribbon. It peeled off with little difficulty, allowing me to breathe again.

I set aside the box's lid. One look through my loupe told me this was the marquess's heirloom.

I studied the way the necklace was attached to the velvet backing: two straight pins at the top, piercing the links beside the stones four away from the clasp, the clasp flat, the tiny emerald above. At the bottom, one pin through the hoop connecting the ruby pendant to the chain. I undid the pins and lifted the necklace away from the velvet. It was heavier than I expected, and I set it on the table.

Given the stakes, I should have been shaking. My breath was shallow, my stomach twisting. But my hands didn't fail me. They were steady.

In the corner stood a clock whose insistent ticks felt like a mocking reminder. What I would've done to silence it, but of course that was impossible. And as I settled to work, the sound vanished.

I began on the first of the jewels. It was delicate work, for the prongs were thicker than the ones I'd practiced on, sturdy talons around the gems, one at each of the four corners. But they bent like any other, and by undoing three of the four prongs, I could ease the gem out and replace it with the fake. I'd brought over twenty stones, and I found matches to slip in without difficulty. The third stone, however, had some sort of adhesive holding it in. Shoddy work by a jeweler. I bent the prongs back into place and moved on to the next stone.

The hours of practice told, for my hands managed the tools almost without my conscious direction.

"Kit." Art's whisper, barely more than a breath, came as I finished the fourth substitution.

I looked up. He had one finger raised. Pointing upward.

I held my breath to listen, and I heard it. Footsteps. Heavy ones, crossing the floor upstairs.

My heart skipped.

I prayed it was just someone using the privy.

"That's the last, innit?" he asked.

"Almost done," I whispered back.

Four wasn't enough. I *must* get the fifth stone. Sarah and I needed it to start a life somewhere else. I wasn't leaving without it. My hands were my faithful partners, and the fifth stone slipped in even quicker than the first four.

The footsteps above continued. Then came a cough, phlegmy.

"Done," I whispered.

It felt like hours, but the clock told me thirty-seven minutes.

I allowed myself to sit back and draw a breath, letting it out in a ragged exhale, before I picked up the necklace and placed it on the velvet.

One of the three pins was missing.

My heart skipped again.

The footsteps were more distant—were they heading toward the stairs?

We'd been almost perfectly silent. He couldn't have heard anything. Or would some instinct bring him down here?

I turned to Art, panic growing inside my chest. "I'm missing a pin," I whispered shakily. The necklace wouldn't remain in place without all three. The moment it was picked up, it would slide noisily around the box.

Together we scoured the top of the desk and the rug below. The hinges of the box, the edges, the velvet folds. Growing frantic, I began to consider looking around the workshop for another pin when Art whispered, "Your sleeve."

I bent my elbow to look. There it was.

I sucked in my breath and released it, plucked the pin, and fastened all three in place, matching them to the previously made holes in the velvet. I closed the box, replaced the seal, and handed the box to Art.

He placed it on the proper shelf, closed the safe door, spun the knob twice, then carefully set it. "I' was on three," he murmured.

I hadn't thought to check it when we arrived, for I hadn't considered that might be a sign of an intrusion, like a thread with bells.

One last painstaking survey of the room: chair returned to its position, drawer ajar, nothing left on the table, no footprints. I handed my tools to Art, and he put them in his sack. He took up his coat and we slipped out the door as silently as we'd come, replacing our boots outside the secret entrance.

My hands were shaking, and I let them, for a moment.

As we reached the trapdoor, Art opened it and went down first. Before I climbed down, I placed my hands on my pocket, feeling the small drawstring pouch with the stones.

Three diamonds for Maggie.

One to plant.

And one for me.

Chapter 25

We climbed down the metal ladder and stepped back into the water, which felt even colder to my feet and ankles. My teeth chattered audibly as we made our way toward the boat. The red string had vanished, lost underwater.

From up ahead, we heard the intermittent echoing bleat of voices.

Art immediately doused the lantern, and I froze.

Instead of the complete darkness I expected, there was a dim light glimmering in the black water ahead. Was it light from the Thames? Or from someone else in the tunnel?

I prayed no one had found James. He could hold his own in a fight, even against two, but not when he was injured.

"Close your eyes," Art whispered. "Use your hands."

I obeyed and instantly my other senses became more acute. The plunks and smacks of the waves against the walls, a creak from something up ahead. The sour, briny smell of rot and the river. With the water sliding up and down my shins with each step, my right hand felt along the stone, finding jagged edges, chips and divots. Art and I proceeded at a snail's pace, silently enough that I could hear the difference between the slaps of water against the bricks and the sloshing flow of the Fleet as we neared it.

At last, I opened my eyes to near-complete darkness.

Whoever was here had doused their light or moved away. Out of the corner of my eye, I sensed movement. It vanished as I turned toward it.

"James," I said softly.

"Shhh."

Then I heard it. The echoes of splashes and voices. I held my breath listening, hoping they were moving away, but after a moment I could hear them more clearly, and then well enough to distinguish a word. I inched my feet forward until I heard "Kit," not more than a few feet from me. I expected my shin to hit a gunwale but found nothing.

"Smugglers," Art whispered.

"They came downriver and went into the tunnel above this one," James muttered. "They're coming this way."

"Where's the boat?" I groped and found his arm.

"Near the Thames by now, I hope. Had to shove it off or they'd hear it and find us." He must have felt my fear, for he added, "You'll be fine, Kit. Art will help you."

"Can you swim wi' your leg?" Art asked.

"I'll manage."

The thought of his open wound in the vile water turned my stomach, but there was no help for it.

Art stepped forward. "Put your arm over my lef' shoulder, mate," he said, his voice low. "And Kit, take the other. It'll be over your head in the deep part."

"Get me to the middle," James said, "where I can swim. I just can't walk to get there."

I gripped the coat over Art's right shoulder, and he stepped out into the Fleet.

I anticipated the river water moving faster than in the tunnel, but the sudden icy lurch of it against the middle of my back stopped my lungs. My hand slipped from Art's shoulder, and the water rushed over my head, dunking me. I came up gasping, Art's hand grasping my coat. My hands clutched his shoulder, tighter this time. Art braced himself, one foot forward, one back, and then he moved. Now that we were in the river, we could hear the voices more clearly. They sounded close, but they had doused their light, for all was darkness behind us. They could no more see us than we could see them, so long as we stayed silent.

But they were moving faster than we were. The voices grew louder. If I could have swum, we all could have moved faster, and in that moment, I vowed that if I ever got out of this, I would bloody learn to bloody swim. I cursed in my head, but stayed as still as I could so as not to throw Art off-balance.

The water swelled. It was at the middle of my back, and I could feel the strain in Art's shoulders as he tried to keep the three of us afloat. I knew what James was thinking as clearly as if he'd spoken. He wanted Art to get me to safety—and I wanted the same for him.

"I'm letting go. Ready?" James said, and Art braced again while James slid ahead of us with soft splashes. Art and I could move faster now. I held myself as still as possible, and the water grew colder and faster. I fought down my panic as it reached my neck.

"'Old your breath," Art said, and I felt him lose his footing. But I could see the Thames, with the moonlight on it, not twenty feet ahead.

"Hey!" came a shout behind us.

The light coming from the end of the tunnel had thrown us into silhouette. I turned and saw our shadows as vague enormous shapes—heads and shoulders—moving on the wall.

"Stop!" came the voice again. "Or we'll shoot!"

"Kick!" Art shouted at me. Silence was pointless now. The report of a gunshot snapped, then echoed through the tunnel.

We wouldn't make it.

"'Old your breath!" Art said again.

I gasped for what air I could and shut my eyes, letting him swim ahead, pulling me forward to the Thames. Below the water, we were invisible.

A second gunshot rang out, but it was muted by the water.

It's a different world below the surface, I thought. My eyes remained closed, and I felt Art's hand with a firm grasp on my coat, and we moved through the water in bursts driven by his strong kicks and my lesser ones.

Suddenly the water changed again, like the prow of a small boat pressing along the right side of my body. I clawed my way up to the surface, with Art's hand still clenching my coat.

We'd reached the Thames.

"Turn on your back! Suck breath into your belly," he shouted, and I heard the note of relief in his voice.

I did as he said, and to my surprise, the water stopped rushing at me or past me. It carried me, fast, and Art and I let it bear us east on the tide until we reached a dock where James lay flat, a long plank extended out over the water for us.

Art grasped it and hauled me forward until my hands reached it too. I was so cold I barely felt the wood against my palm, but I hung on for bloody life and James pulled us out of the flow and toward the pilings. I grasped the post and found cross bars and notches for my feet, pulling myself over the top, where I flopped down, panting, my cold cheek against the river-rotted plank.

Art clambered up after me and rolled onto his side, retching.

"Hullo, water rats," James said, a wry note in his voice. But a moment later, he cursed. "*Merde*. Stay down. They're looking for us."

A bull's-eye lantern appeared, arrowing light across the water. I bent my forehead to the planks, and through a crack between them, I saw glints on the wavelets below.

At last it was dark again, the boat gone, and I turned my face toward James. Blood trickled over his forehead.

"What happened to your head?"

"Hit it on the dock."

"How's your leg?" I asked.

"Fine," he said, but shortly. He was in pain.

"Y'need a doctor," Art said. "I know one no' far from here. But first." He withdrew a flask—was there anything he didn't have inside that bag?—and offered it to me. I took a swig, letting the spirit burn down my insides, and handed it to James, who drank and returned it to Art, who, meanwhile, had taken out something wrapped tightly in oilskin, tied closed with a length of twine.

He unwrapped a pistol and handed it to me. "You know how to shoot i'?"

The metal was ice-cold but dry, heavy against my palm. I nodded, checking the chamber the way Amelia had shown us. There was no bullet. I thought about what Art said about not killing people, and my heart sank. This gun was only for show.

"Bullet's in the second chamber," Art said as he stood. "First one's empty for safety."

Art took James's left arm over his shoulders, and I hooked myself under James's right. The difference in our heights made us a clumsy trio, but we shuffled up the pier and into Whitechapel. James made no jest of it, which told me how badly he was hurt. We stopped often, each time longer. When we reached an alley and Art pointed toward a door, I stepped behind, following them through damp muck underfoot that almost made me slip. "Is this the doctor?" I asked.

"He won' make it to the doctor," Art said. "I'll bring the doctor here. This is a friend. She gets to her shop early." He knocked quietly, three raps. Then three more.

"Who is it?" came a woman's voice.

"It's me."

The lock slid and the door opened to reveal one of the most beautiful girls I'd ever seen. Her golden hair fell in a long braid over her wrapper, and her bright eyes darted over us. "Come in then," she said and stepped aside, beckoning us through the open door.

Something about her gesture, the ready kindness of it, turned my heart over.

I gave her a grateful look as I entered.

A sturdy Irishwoman stood in the kitchen, pouring tea.

God only knows what she thought of us, drenched and stinking of the river, with James bleeding all over his face and ready to drop.

But she only said, "Why, Artie." Her eyes were wary, watchful, questioning, and it seemed she and Art understood each other.

"He needs a doctor," Art said. "Can I bring 'im here?"

The woman set the kettle down, caught up her apron, and dried her hands. "No names."

For everyone's protection.

"You're drenched," said the beautiful girl to me. "I've a dress you can borrow." She led me into a bedroom with two narrow beds and a squat black stove whose open door revealed coals, red and ashy. The door shut behind us and my limbs began to jerk like a street show marionette. In the sudden warmth, I couldn't manage them. She fetched a towel and threw it onto a chair nearby. "Jaysus, Mary, and Joseph," she murmured. "Let's get you out of these clothes."

I managed the buttons on the front of my coat, but the ones on my shirt were too small for my numb fingertips. I dropped my hands to my sides and let her unbutton me and peel the sopping, muddy shirt and the chemise off my skin, too cold and too tired to worry about modesty. She handed me a towel. I wiped my face, hands, and hair and then wrapped it around me.

"Sit," she said, and pulled off my boots and socks. My feet looked like a shorn sheep's skin, white and shriveled by the water. She tugged at my trousers, leaving the bottom half of me naked. She handed me a dressing gown, which I drew around me. Soft and warm. She studied my face. "That'll be a nasty bruise," she said.

I put my fingers to my cheek and could feel the swelling compared to the rest of my face. I ran my tongue over my teeth; they were still all in place. I must have struck my face on something. I didn't recall it.

Everything stank of the river, and to her credit, she didn't gag as she took up the clothes. "Sooner we get rid of these, the better. All the washing in the world won't take out that smell."

She began bundling them into a sack.

"Wait!" I cried. "I need the trousers."

It is a testament to how our bodies crave warmth and safety that I had forgotten the diamonds, however briefly.

A dubious look crossed her face, but she offered them, the waist pinched gingerly between thumb and forefinger. I undid the buttons that held the pocket closed and slid my hand inside. I had a moment of panic when I couldn't feel the pouch. The pocket had crumpled into a misshapen wad around it. But the sharp edges of the stones inside the cloth gave them away.

Father Thames hadn't nicked them.

I could feel her curiosity, but she tamed it, turning away to let me slip the drawstring pouch into the pocket of the dressing gown. It was an act of true generosity. I'm not sure I could have managed it myself.

She departed, and I remained in the chair. I thought she'd left me for good to the heat of that lovely stove, but she returned with a cup of hot tea, a blanket, and a dress that was slightly too large but warm and dry. There were no pockets at the seams, but I transferred the gems from the dressing gown into the bodice of the dress. The tea was hot and burned my insides. I gulped it anyway.

I began to drowse until I heard the outer door open, and a man's voice sounded. The doctor? He called out, "Art, my boy," in an accent as Cockney as Art's own.

His father? Or just someone he knew?

But God help me, I was so bone-tired that my curiosity wasn't enough to rouse me out of the chair.

After the icy coldness of the river, the warmth drove me hard to sleep.

I woke an hour or so later, my neck stiff. I turned my head, and the movement brought my nose near my hair.

I gagged.

Stiffly, I shifted the blanket off of me, pushed myself out of the chair, crossed the room, and opened the door. Every muscle hurt. Through the window above the sink, I saw the sky was just starting to lighten. Art and James were gone; the doctor—had I imagined him? No, I remembered his voice. The ashes were cold on the hearth, the kitchen orderly, with no sign of Art's bag or the pistol I'd set on the table. The beautiful girl and her mother were no doubt still in bed.

One of yesterday's newspapers lay on the table. The *Falcon*. I scrounged for a bit of pencil in a drawer and scribbled along the top. "Thank you." And after a moment, "Bless you."

No names. There were three dark cloaks by the door, and I hoped they wouldn't mind me borrowing. As I lifted one from its hook, a woman's voice came from behind me.

"I thought I heard you awake."

I turned. It wasn't the beautiful girl, but her mother. Short but sturdy, with shrewd blue eyes.

She finished tying the sash around her wrapper. "You slept some, then?"

I nodded. "I've never slept so soundly."

"Well, that's a sorry thing. Tells me you need a new bed," she said.

A soft chuckle escaped me.

"Is James all right?" I asked.

The look she gave reminded me there were to be no names, but it was followed by an understanding smile.

"Ach." She grimaced. "'Twas an ugly cut, but he were washed and bandaged up proper and taken to hospital."

My heart plummeted. I'd never known anyone to come out of a hospital alive. "Where?"

"Denmark Street, right here in the Chapel. Visiting hours begin at one. He'll be in one of the men's wards."

"Did he say James would be all right?" My voice cracked. "He was in the river for a long time."

She saw how desperately I wanted reassurance. Her face was kind, but she wasn't going to lie. "He's a fine doctor, and he'll do everything he can. Your man's in good hands."

Good hands, I thought. Not dangerous ones that dragged him into a mess he didn't make.

I swallowed. "I must go."

She spread her hands. "O' course. Take the cloak with you. Bring it back as you can."

Yet another true kindness from people whose names I didn't even know. "Thank you," I said.

I slipped out the door and into the murk of the morning street. Disoriented, I peered around. The dawning sun was to the east, so the river would be to the south. I walked toward it until I could see the bridges.

Southwark Bridge, dead ahead, told me where I was. I started west toward Amelia's, my shadow stretching long ahead of me.

Chapter 26

It was only a mile walk, but I was so shaky by the time I arrived at Amelia's door that I had to pause at the second-story landing. Amelia's door opened, and she looked out. "Kit?" She hurried down the steps to put her arm around my waist and help me up the final steps. Her usual aplomb was gone.

"What on earth happened?" she asked. "I expected you back hours ago! Are James and Art all right?"

"They're alive," I said.

She blew out a sigh. "Sit here." She poured a glass of whiskey and thrust it into my hand. "Drink this. Good lord, you're white as a sheet and your hands are like ice. I'll put on water for tea."

I bolted the whiskey and let the burn sink into my belly as I sat shivering in a chair by the warm stove.

"The diamonds?" she asked.

I nodded. "But James is in hospital."

Her look of relief gave way to dismay. Her shoulders drooped over the kettle, the cups, the saucers, the spoons. I watched her in silence, suddenly, desperately wanting to do nothing, to plan nothing, to decide nothing. I struck a bargain with the world.

Only for as long as it takes to make tea, I thought. *Surely you can grant me this much.*

I closed my eyes, letting myself think nothing until she finished pouring.

The kettle clinked, hollow copper on sturdy cast iron.

She stood before me with a cup of steaming tea and a hunk of bread slathered with butter. "Here, eat this. What happened?"

I was ravenous, my insides hollowed out by the hours in the cold water and fear.

Between bites, I told her everything from the moment we reached the tunnels until I woke up in the chair at the strangers' house, concluding, "I never met the doctor. I only heard him. He spoke with a Cockney accent. He said, 'Ah, Art my boy.'"

"It's likely Art's father."

I stared. "His father?"

"His mother was Chinese," she said. "His father was a doctor on a merchant ship. He met her in one of the port cities and brought her back here. She died not long after Art was born."

"We could never have done this without him," I said soberly. "He swam me out of that tunnel, Amelia. I'd have drowned. Who is he?"

"An old friend. Dependable as the day is long. Like James." She gave me a searching look. "You love that boy, don't you?"

I nodded unhappily. "I haven't told him I'm leaving."

"No, I can see that," she said. "Some might say it's heartless, but it's for the best until he's cured." She twitched at her skirt. "I'm not the praying sort, but . . . he's young and strong, he has that on his side."

"I hope so."

"And you have the diamonds, so you'll have Sarah soon. You'll see Maggie this morning?"

I wrapped my palms around the cup. "I need to see Mr. Fuller first. Maggie won't release Sarah until the story breaks. I hope he'll talk to me without James." I drank the last of the tea. "Can I borrow your pistol?"

She raised an eyebrow. "To convince Fuller?"

"Not him," I said. "Maggie. In case I need to remind her of our bargain. She'll be furious I did this on my own."

My hair, bundled into one of Amelia's nets, still stank of the river, but at least I appeared respectable in one of her dresses and her coat, which fit me better. With her pistol in my pocket, I made my way to the newspaper offices, putting my prepared letter for the marquess into the post for delivery before noon.

It was still early when I pushed open the door with THE MIRROR in metal letters above, and the desk near the entrance was unoccupied. From behind the wall came the steady thump of the press. I climbed the rickety steps to the first story. Half a dozen men sat at canted tables, with wooden boxes holding bits of lead type in the upper cases and lower cases, their fingers quick, setting the letters in rows.

The noise of the press was louder here, and I had to speak up to have one of them notice me.

"Where's Mr. Fuller?" I asked, half shouting.

The young man nearest to the door turned, and his mouth fell open. "Ach, miss!" His eyes goggled at me, and I repeated my question. "How'd you get in?"

"The door was open," I said.

He pointed. "Up those stairs, down the hallway."

I climbed again, a narrower set of stairs with no banister. I reached a windowed hallway with long, dusty floorboards and half a dozen doors. The first one on the right was open, and I found a young woman of about twenty-five seated at a desk, a lamp on either side, her pen dashing across foolscap.

The press was still audible, but up here I didn't have to shout to make myself heard. "Begging your pardon," I said. "I'm looking for Mr. Fuller."

She paused her pen, settling her elbow on the desk. Her eyes were bright, inquisitive, mischievous, even. She studied the bruise that had darkened and ran diagonally along my cheek. "You look like you could tell a story."

"I have one," I admitted. "But it's for him."

She shrugged good-naturedly and pointed the top of her pen to the right. "Three doors down."

I continued on and paused at the threshold. Mr. Fuller was bent over a cluster of written pages, a pen in his right hand, making notes in the margins. His gingery hair was thinning in an uneven patch at his crown, and the sight unexpectedly made my heart soften. He was a man, after all, not merely a journalist.

"Mr. Fuller," I said.

He started and looked up, blinking through silver-rimmed spectacles, which his left hand promptly removed.

"Where's James?"

I stepped inside and closed the door. "He's in hospital. There was an accident."

"So you're here to deliver the story instead." He scowled his disapproval, and I didn't blame him. He trusted James; he barely knew me.

I'd spent the walk here trying to decide how I would unfold the story for him.

Over the years, I had seen how different newspapers portrayed crimes, how they presented facts in ways that left varying impressions, cast the police as heroes or fools, danced around questions of blame, even left perpetrators unnamed, and yet still told a tale worth reading.

Like dodges, they gave people a story they could readily believe.

I knew that Mr. Fuller wanted to write the story. His promise to James and me aside, I believed he wanted to help Sarah; he longed to help the Yard; he wished to see justice done and the brutal murderers caught.

The story of stolen jewels was good newspaper fodder; the sticking point would be naming the Simonsons.

Still, Mr. Fuller was clever, and I believed he could manage it.

But would he want to?

Instinctively, I felt a call to right an injustice was my strongest card. Simonson had behaved vilely—criminally, and he had escaped punishment. I'd draw Simonson as a villain and hope it was enough that Mr. Fuller would want to find a way to implicate him.

But first, the proof.

I slid my hand into my pocket. At Amelia's, I'd separated the diamonds, folding two inside a handkerchief; three were still in the pouch.

Inside my pocket, I loosened the drawstring, took the diamonds into my palm, then set them gently on the scribbled page before Mr. Fuller.

He drew back as if they were a vial of poison. "Are those real?"

"They are." I removed Amelia's coat, folding it over the back of the wooden chair, sat facing him across the desk, and said, slowly and carefully, "These three diamonds, from an important family heirloom, have been replaced with counterfeit gems on the premises of Simonson's Jewelers in Hatton Garden."

His expression was wary. "What heirloom?"

"The Hargrave necklace," I replied. "Lady Hargrave is to wear it at Lord Charleton's ball this week."

He picked up one of the stones, replacing his spectacles and bringing it close to peer at it.

"Each of those is approximately one carat weight, clear and well cut, valued at over two hundred pounds. A thief could disguise them by having them cut down. The owner might never know of the substitution, until it was too late to recover them."

He set the stone down. "Can you put those away, please?"

I replaced them in their pouch. "You promised us you would print the story we gave you," I reminded him.

"I *will*, so long as I don't have to commit a crime to do it." He sniffed. "I have not forgotten your young sister. The thought of a kidnapped child harrows my bones. But to accuse a jeweler of fraud—to destroy his livelihood when he was no true party to it—"

"You simply write that it occurred in his shop, where it was being cleaned and repaired. That is the truth."

"I need to know why."

I'd expected he would.

"What do you know of a woman named Maggie Wirth?" I asked.

His eyes narrowed. "Nothing."

"Patty Wirth?"

His face cleared. "The Southwark thief. Of course."

"Maggie is her daughter, and twenty years ago, she was

caught thieving by a jeweler," I began. I unfolded the story, piece by piece, describing the day of the theft, giving every detail I could remember about Simonson's attack on Maggie.

Horror dawned in his eyes. "He outraged her?" It came out in a voice scraped raw, barely above a whisper.

It didn't take a clairvoyant to understand this cut close to the bone for him. I shouldn't have been surprised. Women in London were assaulted every day. It wasn't unlikely he knew one.

He pushed back his chair with a slow scrape, crossing the creaking floorboards to stand at the window, his back to me. His fingertips rested against the sill, his thumb beating his usual tattoo. He stood there for so long that at last I spoke his name.

"He should have been hanged," he said thickly.

"Wealthy men don't hang in this city," I said. "Not for assaults on women. You know that. And the law will do nothing to him, twenty years later, not on behalf of a convicted felon."

He returned to stand behind his chair, resting his hands on the top rail. "Go on, finish."

I described the injustices of Maggie's trial and dwelt on the suffering she experienced in Swan River. Despite what Maggie had done—was still doing—to Sarah, I had the peculiar, surprising sense of my sympathies shifting toward her.

I'm not immune to dodges I work on myself, I thought. But I could see it working on Mr. Fuller too. The lines around his mouth deepened with pain. "Thus, we have two monsters, one begotten by the other. God, there's no end to it."

He said this more to himself than to me, and I held my tongue.

"So Maggie returned to London, wanting revenge," he said heavily.

"When Maggie discovered that Simonson's was cleaning the famous necklace, she saw her opportunity. She knows people who can pick locks and crack large combination safes."

"And she pulled you into it by kidnapping your sister."

I nodded.

"But how will the fraud be discovered?"

"A letter, sent to the marquess, alerting him."

His fingertips pinched the chair rail. "And it'll ruin Simonson, when it's made public. The marquess's word will be above question, which she's counting on, no doubt."

"The difficulty is that Maggie's scheme required violence—the murder of a constable."

His face paled.

"Maggie planned it for tonight." I spoke slowly, wanting to be sure I was understood. "It was done last night instead, with no one harmed."

Understanding dawned in his eyes. "So you headed her off. Does Maggie know?"

"I'll see her after I leave you."

"Ah."

"The marquess will receive a letter this morning warning him to retrieve the necklace and have the gems checked for authenticity. It's already in the post." I patted my pocket where the diamonds were. "I'll deliver the diamonds to Maggie, you print your story about the necklace, naming Simonson's." I swallowed down my fear that he would refuse. "And my sister will be released. You'll have your witness, the Fairleigh murderers will be found, and the Yard will have solved an important case."

"Is there any chance the diamonds can make their way back to the necklace?"

I hesitated. "I think so. Maggie would likely hold on to them for a while, until the fuss dies down, before she has them cut."

He sat, picked up his pen, and drew a fresh page toward him. "Simonson deserves worse than he'll get with this."

My relief made my breath catch, and I couldn't reply.

He dipped the tip in the well, shedding the excess in three taps. He stared off into space a moment and then looked at me. "Can you keep silent for twenty minutes?"

I nodded and turned up a palm as a sign for him to go ahead.

He began to write—the black nub of his pen moving across the page, scratching line after line. I watched, marveling at his steadiness and haste, until I recalled that he'd no doubt had great practice in composing his stories quickly, much as I'd practiced changing out gems.

He reached the bottom of the page and began a second without pause. A dip of the pen, scratch, scratch, scratch, another dip. All the while I sat in silence, though I itched to seize the first page and read it. When he reached the end of the second page, he set them side by side and reread them, crossing out a word, amending a line. Finally, he spun them toward me. "See if it's the truth."

I brought them closer to my side of the desk and began to read:

FRAUD AT HATTON GARDEN

Who among us but a thief can tell a diamond from its false sister, paste?

No one, of course. This is what unscrupulous jewelers depend upon when defrauding a naïve customer who has entrusted them with precious keepsakes and heirlooms.

This newspaper has witnessed definitive and undeniable

proof that three diamonds from an important family heirloom have been replaced with counterfeit gems at Simonson's Jewelers in Hatton Garden.

The public should take note, for this is no small theft. The diamonds, each approximately one carat in weight, are estimated to be valued at over two hundred pounds. It is likely that in an effort to disguise them, they will immediately be cut into smaller stones, diminishing their overall value but making them easy to sell in the open market. They are likely gone forever—and were it not for the truth brought to this paper by a knowledgeable informant, the owner might never know.

The necklace, an heirloom worth well over two thousand pounds, was taken into custody by the jeweler for cleaning and repair, in preparation for its appearance at Lord Charleton's Grand Ball next week. This ball has long been considered one of the most important events of the London Season, where two of Queen Victoria's children shall be present.

It is the responsibility of the jeweler to safeguard all valuables from theft—whether it be a tradesman's modest watch or a duchess's tiara. Simonson's makes a grand show of this: There are locks on each door, front and back, and a large black bulwark of a safe with a combination lock and impregnable hinges. It is nigh impossible that even the canniest, most practiced thief could enter unobserved and obtain access. Indeed, the obvious conclusion is that this theft must have been enacted with the knowledge and willful collaboration of, if not by, the jeweler himself.

Ever since the discovery of the mines at Kimberley in the southernmost regions of Africa, diamonds have been considered rare and precious stones, surpassing rubies, sapphires, emeralds, and pearls in value. However, by virtue of their luster and transparency, diamonds are easier to counterfeit than other stones.

The newspaper has received no comment from Simonson's Jewelers.

I looked up in admiration at the cleverness and opaqueness of his sentences. Nowhere did it state outright that Simonson had perpetrated the fraud. "Strictly speaking, it's true," I said cautiously.

"Have you anything to add?" Mr. Fuller asked.

"You might want to say, 'several diamonds,'" I said. "And two locks on the front and back doors, of the Yale variety, as well as the usual devices to prevent thievery, including mirrors and camlocks on the cases."

His eyebrows rose, but he added those words. "Anything else?"

"No."

He set it aside. "The story will be typeset this afternoon and will run in the morning."

I rose. "We'll go to the Yard as soon as my sister is free. We'll try to be there by eleven o'clock tomorrow."

"Begging your pardon." Mr. Fuller's eyes were narrowed. "I don't mean to frighten you, but do you think Maggie will keep her word and let your sister go?"

My stomach plummeted, and I took reassurance from the thought I'd clung to for days now. "I don't know what she'd gain by not."

"True," he conceded.

"She has my sister," I said. "What choice did I have but to try?"

From the newspaper offices, I crossed Southwark Bridge and walked to the Elephant and Castle, for what might be the last time. I climbed the stairs to the goods room and pushed open the door. Five women stood there, women I didn't recognize—Maggie was replacing us quickly, it seemed—and the room went silent as they stared at me. Yes, I had an ugly bruise on my face, but I doubted that was why.

"I need to talk to Maggie," I said.

"Go on, girls," she said, and they filed out, passing me with curious looks.

I closed the door and reached into my pocket for the cloth pouch. I spilled the three diamonds into my palm and showed her.

She stared for a moment, then her gaze flashed up to me. Her expression was furious, and her voice was a lash. "That was supposed to be tonight. You were *not* supposed to do this yourself!"

"Doing it my way, I didn't have to kill anyone." I placed the gems on the desk before her. "But it's done, exactly as you would have wanted. The gems taken and the necklace put back in its box. It was already sealed with ribbon and wax, so as you said, it's not likely it'll be inspected again before it reaches the marquess. I left everything exactly as it was, down to the number that was at the top of the combination lock of the safe when we arrived—which was three."

She withdrew a jeweler's loupe from her pocket and rolled the diamonds toward her with the fingers of her good hand, taking them up one by one and peering at them. She set them down and nodded. "Now we need only wait for the story. I'll send a letter. It may take a few days."

"No, it won't," I said. "I put a letter to the marquess in the post this morning. He'll retrieve the necklace when the shop opens, I imagine. Give him a day to find a jeweler to verify it. He'll report it to the Yard, and the story should run by tomorrow. You'll have the diamonds and the revenge, and I get my sister—immediately. You swore to me on your child's grave, Maggie. The minute the story runs, you give me Sarah." My hand clenched Amelia's pistol, though I didn't remove it. "And if you don't, I go to the Yard and tell them everything. Don't think I won't."

Her eyes flashed to my pocket and back to my face. She saw I meant it, and there would be no easy disposal of me in the meantime. She shrugged. "Why would I keep her? You'll have her back as soon as the story runs."

I started for the door.

"Where are you going?" The tone of her voice turned me back to her. She seemed truly curious, as if now that the end was in sight, and I was no longer her tool, we might return to our former footing. I sensed that she had other questions too—not the least of which was how I'd accomplished the dodge.

"It's not your concern," I replied, my voice flat with indifference. "Not anymore. I'll see you tomorrow."

It was only half past twelve, with visiting hours another thirty minutes away, but at the hospital in Denmark Street, a surprisingly kind nurse saw me fidgeting on the bench and motioned me over. I asked to see James.

"I suppose you'll say he's your brother?" she asked drily.

Clearly, she expected a lie, but I was tired of lying. Tired of double-dealing, of ferreting out other people's thoughts and motives so I might counter them. Whether she let me in early or not, I'd tell the truth.

"No," I said simply. "But I love him. He got his leg cut up and broken helping me."

Her expression softened. "Ah, get on with you, then," she said, pointing to the flight of steps. "Second story, through the door on the left."

The unexpected kindness put a lump in my throat. I croaked a thank-you and headed upstairs.

It was a long ward, and I found James halfway down one of the whitewashed walls in a narrow metal bed, with a pocket watch–sized white plaster on his head and a much larger one enveloping the lower part of his leg. His eyes were shut, his cheeks pale under the beginning of dark whiskers, and guilt thickened in my chest at the thought of what he'd done for me, at what might be a terrible cost. All this for someone who would likely be leaving him.

The thought clenched cruelly at my heart.

I couldn't let him see it. I forced a few measured breaths and composed my face before I put my hand to his shoulder. His eyes fluttered open. His pupils were shining black buttons. Laudanum, no doubt, for the pain.

"Kitten," he slurred.

Was it a warning?

I leaned in to kiss his forehead. It was cool to the touch—no fever, not yet, thank God—and the pool of hope in my heart grew. "There's no one here watching us, is there?" I murmured.

"Only you." His eyes closed again, and his hand groped for mine. "Why?"

"You called me 'Kitten.'"

His eyelids flickered open again, enough that I could see the smile tucked into the corners.

"I like to call you that in my head. My name for you and no one else's."

Something between a laugh and a sob bubbled up. "That laudanum's addled you something fierce," I said, trying to keep my tone light, and was rewarded when one side of his mouth turned up. I poured a cup of water for him and helped him drink, then pulled a chair close. "What do the doctors say?"

The drink roused him. He put out his hand again and drew my fingers to his mouth before he replied. "It's a fracture and a bad cut but it'll mend. I can come home in a few days, with crutches. You can wait on me. Hand and foot."

I managed the laugh he wanted. "But what about the filth in the water?"

"No infection yet. When I got here, they soaked my leg in some carbolic solution that hurt like the devil."

I swallowed, hoping the pain meant the medicine was strong enough to work its magic against the river's poison.

"Tell me what happened," he said.

"How much do you remember?"

He was silent a moment, thinking, and his voice wasn't much above a whisper. "The tunnel. You and Art behind me. A gunshot. A doctor, but I don't know where I was. I was half out of my mind with pain. Were you there?"

"In a different room, but yes."

He looked at me, his worry piercing the laudanum fog. "Good lord, Kit, how bad was I? I wasn't talking, was I?"

"You didn't say a word," I assured him, and his face eased. "And I'll tell you everything."

So I did, including what happened when I saw Maggie and that Mr. Fuller's story would appear in the morning paper. "Then I'll have Sarah back. Maggie said she had no reason to keep her," I concluded, wanting to give him that assurance.

He nodded and his eyes closed. Exhaustion deepened the lines around his mouth and his fingers folded over my hand, which lay on his chest. I felt his breath, rising and falling like a tide. He could have died last night. We both could have.

And the dodge wasn't over yet.

Suddenly overcome by feeling, I bent my forehead to his chest, a single jagged sob escaping, and his other hand came up to rest on my hair. "Oh, love," he murmured. "Oh, love." I turned my head to lay my cheek on his chest as sobs wracked me like some terrible sickness.

I couldn't remember the last time I'd cried, and it made me think of the day I'd found Sarah weeping over Little Nell's death in that book by Dickens. Her tears weren't just for Little Nell. I understood that now. They were for Ma's death too. For Da's leaving. For all the sadnesses she'd ever seen.

Perhaps all our sorrows are linked like this, a basted stitch of red thread, appearing and disappearing, on the right and wrong sides of the cloth. Losses and near losses, whether real or in novels—all part of the same strand, each new one sadder because of the previous ones. And it seemed to me that nearly losing James was one more stitch along that line of losses—only he wasn't gone. He was right here, solid under my cheek, his hand in my hair, murmuring to me in as tender a voice as I'd ever heard.

Yes, grief and tragedy could change people down to their bones.

But so could loyalty and love.

Chapter 27

The next morning, having slept at James's, Mary and I left early for Elephant and Castle. Mary went to her room to retrieve her things; I headed for the London and South Western Railway station near Elephant and Castle, where the papers always arrived first.

I had my coins ready and found a boy hawking the *Mirror*—"Scandal! Scandal! Yard on the case!"—thrust a shilling at him as he took a breath, and opened the paper to find the headline in two-inch letters, followed by the article Mr. Fuller had written.

"What's 'a matter?"

I looked up to find the newsboy staring and drew a full breath for what felt like the first time in days. "Nothing at all."

Tucking the paper inside my coat, I cut east on Westminster Bridge Road, with Bedlam on my right and the Asylum for the Blind on my left. Straight to the Elephant and Castle and up the stairs to the goods room. To my relief, Maggie was there. Perhaps I'd made it clear I'd stand for no tricks this morning.

I dropped the folded newspaper onto her desk. "Now give me Sarah," I said.

Her eyes lowered to the paper long enough to take in the headline, then they looked up, glinting as a serpent's. I could see her thoughts as clearly as if they'd been headlines: She was wondering how far she could push me.

"I told you, I will go to the police and tell them the whole story if you don't." My fist closed again around the handle of Amelia's pistol.

She didn't miss the movement, and her mouth twitched. "No need to threaten me. I'll do as I promised."

The smirk that curved her mouth told me she had intended to give me Sarah all along. She just wanted to see me twist with uncertainty for those few extra seconds. It was her revenge for me having done the dodge my way instead of hers. The hate that blazed over me made sweat prickle across my shoulders.

"Come with me," she said.

I kept my hand wrapped around the pistol inside my pocket and followed her down to the street, pulling the door of the inn shut. Maggie started west on St. George's Road toward Bedlam, and, behind her, I glanced down Temple Street, where Mary appeared at the door of Mrs. Jonas's bakery. She stood still, and our eyes met.

Hours spent thieving together had taught me to read her postures and her gestures, down to the very angle of her chin. It isn't often people can say it truthfully, but I knew her expressions better than I knew my own. The look she gave me carried even more weight than the moment called for—more than merely, *I promised I'd take care of this part of the dodge; I am ready; it will be done.* It was something else. I sensed an apology—but I couldn't pause to be sure.

Maggie led me past the synagogue, past Marshall Street and Garden Row, turning just before St. Jude's Church into Richmond Street, where she stopped before one of the many cheap lodging houses. She opened the door and gestured for me to precede her upstairs. "No," I said. I was not such a fool as to go upstairs in a strange house, even with a pistol. "Bring her down."

Maggie shrugged and went up. Several minutes later she returned, with my sister in front of her. If anything solidified my desire to see Maggie hang, it was the look on Sarah's face, the relief at seeing me in proportion to the fear she'd suffered for a whole week. Sarah's eyes filled with tears and she hurtled herself down the stairs at me, tumbling the last two steps, throwing her arms around my neck.

The church bell tolled the hour, telling me that Maggie and I had only been away from the goods room less than fifteen minutes.

But that was enough time for Mary to do what I needed, to place the fourth diamond in the secret cupboard behind the paneling, wrapped in a bit of dark cloth, so no incidental glint off its facets could betray our final step.

With Sarah clinging to me, we made our way back toward the main road. At the corner, I pulled her into my arms, one arm around her back, my hand in her hair, as she gasped jagged, hiccupping sobs into my shoulder. We stood that way for several minutes until she subsided into silence. Finally, I asked, "Did they hurt you?"

She pulled back, her eyes searching my face.

"Sarah," I said, gentling my voice, mindful of not looking angry like my mother. "Do you need a doctor?"

"No." She swallowed. "I'm fine, truly. I had a bed and they fed me." Her expression was full of dread. "But what did you have to do, Kit?"

"Nothing that can't be changed back," I said.

Relief filled her face, and she slumped against me. "I was so afraid they would make you kill someone."

"No." I kissed her forehead. "But I do need something from you." With my arm around her, I guided her toward St. Jude's church. There was a gap in a stone wall where a metal gate had rusted away, and I led her through it into the graveyard where our mother was buried. We sat on a stone bench, partially concealed behind a boxwood hedge, and Sarah's head dropped onto my shoulder. The leaves of the plane trees overhead rustled, the standing stones were tipped and the etching faded, the damp earth at our feet gave off a nutty, musty smell. The place held something like peace. Sarah gripped my left hand fiercely in both of hers, crushing my knuckles against each other, but I'd have let her break my hand if it helped her.

From here, Ma's grave wasn't visible. It was marked with a small stone, set flush with the ground, with only her name and the years of her birth and death. As we sat in the silence, feelings warred in my heart. There was my anger, longstanding, at how Ma had abandoned us for drink and for men. But there was a new feeling now, a sense of sorrow for her, a sense of kinship. Ma had been desperately unhappy, and perhaps afraid, too, not knowing how she would support herself and two girls after her husband left. I thought of what I'd always considered my mother's last, selfish lie, how she'd said on her deathbed that we would be fine. We hadn't been fine, not by a bloody mile, because she'd spent nearly every farthing we had. But perhaps it hadn't been merely a lie to free herself from blame; perhaps it had also been meant to encourage me. Perhaps she knew how hard I'd work to keep Sarah and me safe. And perhaps she'd seen enough of me to know what I was capable of.

Sarah lifted her head from my shoulder. "You said you need something from me. What is it?"

There wasn't a soul close enough to hear us; still, I kept my voice low. "Sarah, I made a deal with a newspaperman, who helped me set you free . . . in exchange for you doing something for him."

Her forehead wrinkled worriedly. "What could I do for a newspaperman?"

"I need you to tell him what you saw in Mayfair."

Her eyes widened in horror. "Kit! I can't be a copper's nark!"

"This is different." Slowly, I explained everything that had happened—from the moment Maggie approached me, suggesting a theft in Hatton Garden, to the newspaper story appearing that morning.

She had sagged against the bench's back by the time I finished. "Is James all right?"

"He's in hospital," I said. "But he says he will be."

The clock chimed again.

"I know how brave you are, Sarah," I said. "I'll be with you the whole time."

She nodded her acceptance, subdued. "Must we go now?"

"In a few minutes." I put my arm around her, drawing her close. Her head returned to my shoulder. "We can sit," I said, stroking her hair. "Catch your breath."

Naturally, the peace didn't last long.

Billy appeared beyond the church's stone wall, on the far side of St. George's Road. The thick bulk of him was still, only his head moving as he scanned the street.

Damn everything.

Of course, Maggie would send him after us the moment Sarah was free. She'd double-cross me, just as I'd double-crossed her.

I slid my hand into my pocket, feeling the reassuring weight of the pistol. Still, Billy would have a bigger firearm and more certain aim. And if by chance I shot and killed him? I couldn't. I'd rot in prison for the rest of my life.

We needed to be somewhere with more people.

Even as I thought it, Billy caught sight of us. He took one step into the road and drew back just as quickly to let a cab roll by.

I snatched at the precious few seconds of a head start.

"Sarah, we must go. Billy's just there, looking for us." I rose, and after one small terrified cry, Sarah leapt up, and we hurried behind the small church and around the side, my left hand pressed to the rough stone of the old wall. I peered around the corner.

The street was empty. But I heard footfalls on the church's flagstone path behind us.

Picking up our skirts, Sarah and I pelted down the street. I turned to cast a quick look behind us.

Knowing we'd seen him, Billy made no pretense about keeping secret. He hurried after us with long, purposeful strides. We'd never outrun him—there were no shops on this stretch—nowhere for us to take refuge.

Sarah turned and gasped. "Kit, he's coming! What should we do?"

Grabbing her hand in mine, I dodged into a grimy little alley, barely a snicket. "In here. It cuts through to London Road. Run, Sarah!" I pushed her ahead of me.

Past dustbins and over muck and dung, past broken crates and closed doors, we raced toward the busy street at the end, but Billy was gaining on us.

We flew around the corner toward St. George's Circus, the busiest place in this part of Southwark, known for every kind of crime.

"Kit!" Sarah pointed. "It's a constable."

We ran straight toward the man in uniform.

Yet another thing I never imagined doing.

The constable was young, and he started as Sarah threw herself at him, clutching his arm. "Please, sir, there's a man frightening us!"

"What?" He drew himself up and scanned the street, palming the side pocket of his trousers, where he kept his truncheon. "That one, there?"

Billy came to a quick halt. Sarah nodded and pointed—her little finger was as effective a weapon as a gun—and Billy melted back into the alley.

"Can you take us to the nearest police station?" I asked through gasps. "Please?"

"That'll be the Yard," he said. "Come with me, ladies," he added gallantly. He offered his elbow to Sarah, and she tucked her hand inside, as if she'd done it a dozen times. I wondered where she'd learnt that bit of manners. From someone at the Willitses' house perhaps.

"Thank you. We're ever so grateful. You may not hear it often enough," Sarah said earnestly, "but many of us girls are very glad you're patrolling the streets."

He halted and looked down at her, askance at first and suspicious that she was teasing him, but then genuinely pleased as her eyes remained on his. "You're right. We never hear that."

"Well, it's true, even if the papers don't print it."

I fell behind and let Sarah chatter to him the entire way to the Yard. She was clever, yes, but she was also sincere. I couldn't have done it as well. For my part, I was content to be silent and follow where they led.

Our constable took us through a heavy stone arch into a cobbled yard, where clumps of hay lay scattered about and the smell of horse piss was sharp in the air. Half a dozen boys lurked near the back entrance, fidgety as hungry cats. A plainclothesman appeared at the door, wagged a finger at one, and handed over a folded note and a coin. The coin slid into a pocket and the boy trotted across the yard and through the stone arch, and vanished into the street.

The door opened four more times as we crossed the cobbled yard, with people going in and out. You could tell the Yard men, in their plain clothes and tall top hats. Rumor was their brims were reinforced with enough cane to break someone's nose.

As we reached the entrance, our constable swung the door open with a flourish and gestured for us to enter.

Yet another thing I never imagined doing, walking into Scotland Yard of my own volition. This was indeed a fortnight for unlikely events.

The constable took us straight to a sergeant, whose wooden desk faced the door. There was a ledger before him of roughly the same shape and size as our thieving one, along with several morning newspapers. As he saw us, he picked up his pen and his eyebrows rose slightly. "What is it?"

"These ladies have something to report," the constable said.

"Very well." He nodded an abrupt dismissal to the constable, whose face fell. To console him, Sarah gave him a warm smile, and he touched his hat to her and left.

I said to the sergeant, "I've been told to ask for Mr. Stiles. Is he here, by chance?"

"He is, mum," the sergeant replied. His eyebrows crept higher. "What's this regarding?"

"The Fairleigh murders," Sarah said.

His bristly eyebrows rose another notch. "All right, then. I'll fetch him fer ye in a moment. Yes, sir?" Waving us toward a bench, he turned to a red-haired plainclothesman who was tapping his boot impatiently beside the desk.

From our wooden seat, Sarah and I watched the bustle of activity in the main room, with desks in three tightly packed rows, extending across the entire floor, some occupied by plainclothesmen, others by only stacks of papers. Apparently the men who belonged to those desks were out detecting clues. Dim sunlight fell in rays through dirty windows overhead, catching on motes of dust, and the air smelled of cheap tea. Several sergeants and inspectors glanced at us as they passed, and I found myself recalling that Mr. Fuller said my sketch was here at the Yard. I wondered if I might be recognized, but so far no one had given me more than a passing glance. And why would they? No one would expect a known thief to be sitting bold as brass on this bench hoping to speak with an inspector.

Having finished with the impatient plainclothesman, the sergeant made his way to one of the occupied desks at the far end of the room, where he spoke to a young man with fair hair, interrupting him in his writing. The inspector turned, and I peered at his profile. Yes, it was the Yard man I'd seen at the Fairleigh house. Mr. Stiles. He turned to look at us, then nodded, rose, and put on his coat—a gesture of politeness he needn't have made, as his shirtsleeves appeared quite crisp and fresh.

"You only have to tell them what you saw in Mayfair," I said to Sarah quietly.

"I know. Don't worry, Kit." Her triangle chin lifted and set.

"Oh, I won't," I said. "You're managing young men just fine this morning."

"Of course I can," she said. "I've been watching you for years."

I hid my smile.

Mr. Stiles came forward. He had no umbrella this time, and he'd had his dusty boots shined.

I stood and he met my gaze. "Why, you're—" he began.

"I didn't give you my proper name before," I interrupted. "It's Kit Jimeson."

"Ah." He looked at my sister and then back at me. "I understand you have information about the Fairleigh murders."

I gestured to Sarah. "This is my sister, Sarah, and she does. But we need to wait for Mr. Fuller before we tell you."

"Ed Fuller, the newspaperman?" A frown of mistrust creased his brow. "What has he to do with this?"

"A friend of ours vouched for him, and it was he who vouched for you. We wouldn't be here, telling you what we know, if it weren't for him."

The crease eased. "Very well. Is he coming shortly?"

"I asked him to meet us at eleven o'clock. But I'd like to speak to you alone first," I said.

"Kit," Sarah murmured in protest.

"Just for a moment," I said. "Anyone touches you, scream bloody murder."

She nodded.

The clock showed twenty minutes before eleven. Twenty minutes to gain a better sense of how far I might trust Mr. Fuller and Mr. Stiles both.

"Very well. Come with me." Mr. Stiles led me to an ugly, windowless whitewashed room, with one table and three chairs. It smelled of mold and fear. "Would you like tea?"

"Yes, please."

He returned with cups for us both and took the seat opposite, his brown eyes pleasant but shrewd. "When we met the other night, you told me you're a needlewoman. I believe you might be something else."

"I *am* a needlewoman," I said. "I was sent out at age ten. I've worked in a dressmaker's shop for years."

"In Elephant and Castle?" he asked.

"Yes," I said. "Although Sarah and I won't be there much longer."

Mr. Stiles sipped at his tea. "I'd like you to trust me. The last thing I want is any harm to come to either of you."

Why would he, after all? "I believe you," I said.

He set the cup in its saucer. "May I ask, who vouched for Mr. Fuller?"

"I'd rather not say," I said, and at his look of disappointment, I added, "but at my insistence, Mr. Fuller did tell me something of himself, and why he fell out with you. He said he made a mistake, and it ruined one of your investigations. Is that true?"

"It didn't just ruin the investigation," he said soberly. "Three people died because of it."

"He told me about the hansom cab driver."

"Yes, well, after the counterfeiter killed him and fled this part of London, he broke into a house and killed the two sisters who lived there because he needed a safe place to stay," Mr. Stiles said.

"I don't think he knows about the two women," I said. "But he feels rotten about the driver. Bringing us to you is his way of trying to make amends."

His expression softened. "Well, God knows, we all make mistakes." Despite my wariness of a Yard man, I felt my heart tip toward trust.

A knock at the door was followed by the appearance of the desk sergeant's face. His eyebrows were as high as they could go. He was having quite a morning.

"That jackanapes Mr. Fuller's here, sir, and he says you're wanting to see him!" He shook his head in disbelief. "I told him you wouldn't—"

"But I do, Jurgens. Thank you."

Jurgens blinked in bewilderment.

"And please send my sister in with him. She's sitting on the bench," I added.

No doubt Jurgens felt even more surprise at receiving a command from me, but the poor man's eyebrows couldn't go any higher up his forehead. The surprise settled in his nose instead, which scrunched up so high that dark nose hairs emerged. "Good lord," he muttered. Then, at Mr. Stiles's gentle cough, he said, "Yes'm," and vanished. A moment later, Mr. Fuller and Sarah entered the room together.

Mr. Stiles saw that Sarah was nervous, and after greeting Mr. Fuller, civilly but with restraint, he asked Sarah if she'd like some hot tea and drew out a chair for her, trying to set her at ease. She nodded and thanked him, and he left.

I pulled my chair closer to Sarah and took her hand.

With a glance at Mr. Fuller, she gently drew it away and clasped her hands in her own lap.

"I'm Mr. Fuller," he said, his voice subdued. "I heard about your ordeal. Are you all right?"

"I am," she said. "Thank you, Mr. Fuller."

I'd never been so proud of Sarah as I was at that moment. She held herself with dignity, waiting until Mr. Stiles returned with her tea. She thanked him and took a sip, then set the cup in the saucer with nary a jitter.

Mr. Fuller remained silent as Mr. Stiles settled in his chair.

"Now, Miss Jimeson," he began, his voice kind. "I understand you have something to tell me. I'm going to take notes so I don't make mistakes, and please take your time in answering. There's no hurry." He took out a piece of foolscap and a pen from a drawer in the table, then asked her name, her age, where she lived, and where she was employed—simple questions, which Sarah answered with growing confidence. At last, Sarah explained what she'd seen that night in Mayfair and where exactly she'd been when she saw Billy Winston and Tommy Finch.

"Did they see you?"

"No," she replied. "I knew they didn't belong there, so I turned my face away, hiding inside my bonnet and stepping away from the gas lamp."

His pen hesitated. "But you're certain about who it was?"

She nodded. "I am. I saw their faces, though they wore hats. Billy has round, burly shoulders, a heavy way of walking, and a deep, rumbly cough, which I heard that night. Tommy has always followed Billy, doing whatever he said, and he's thinner and has a limp from his right leg being a bit short, from when he broke it falling off a ladder years ago when climbing on Mrs. Wickford's roof. And most of all, I heard Tommy speak to him, in his high-pitched voice. It was those two, I'm certain of it."

These specifics seemed to assure Mr. Stiles.

"You've known them how long?" he asked.

"Since as far back as I can remember," she said. "I'm fourteen now. Nearest I can recall, I first knew their names when I was eight. I've seen them hundreds of times at Elephant and Castle."

"What do you know of their characters?" he asked. "These are serious charges, theft and murder. Do you truly believe them capable of it?"

She considered for a moment. "It's impossible to know what other people might do," she said at last. "But my first memory of Billy Winston is him beating a dog in an alley. I don't believe he has a heart."

I stared. Sarah had never told me that story.

"Good lord," Mr. Fuller muttered.

The door opened, and a stern-faced man asked, "Stiles, how much longer? We've that serious matter to attend to this morning."

I kept my face expressionless, but I had a feeling I knew what the serious matter was.

God bless the speedy London post.

"We're nearly finished," Mr. Stiles said pleasantly, and I found myself admiring him all the more for not being rattled by this other man's agitation.

Mr. Stiles thanked Sarah for her testimony and then turned to me. "Do you have anything else to add?" he asked.

Mr. Fuller cleared his throat, and I shot him a glance.

Mr. Stiles had set down his pen, and I couldn't help but smile inwardly. He had no idea just how much I would be adding.

"Billy Winston is Maggie Wirth O'Connell's cousin," I said. Mr. Stiles picked the pen up and noted that down. "Do you know who Maggie Wirth is?"

Mr. Stiles's mouth twitched. "Peggy Wirth's daughter. She recently became the head of a thieving ring in Elephant and Castle, or so I've heard."

Mr. Fuller stifled a chortle.

"Maggie raised Billy from the time he was little more than a child," I said, "and he took lessons at her knee. Those two are cut from the same cloth." Mr. Stiles's face sobered as he took my meaning. "Twenty years ago, Maggie was transported for thievery, with her sentence doubled to fourteen on the word of another thief named Rose Pratt."

That pulled Mr. Stiles up short. "Rose Pratt," he echoed as he drew out his pocketbook and flipped through some pages, pausing at one. "She was murdered at the London South Western railway station five months ago."

"Yes, she was," I said, letting the words sit heavily in the air.

I felt Sarah go motionless beside me, but I fixed my eyes on Mr. Stiles.

Understanding lit his face.

"Maggie's been back since March of this year," I said. "If not before."

As he jotted that down, I played my last card.

"Also, you'll find one of the diamonds taken from the Hargrave necklace in a secret compartment in the goods room, which is on the first story of the Elephant and Castle."

Mr. Fuller sucked in his breath; Mr. Stiles looked up, his pen frozen; Sarah whispered, "Kit."

"Astonishment all around," I observed.

Mr. Stiles sat back in his chair as if I'd shoved a hand against his chest, caving around the blow. "Well." He blinked several times. "Where exactly?"

"It's behind a panel on the wall to the right of the window," I replied. "There are bottles of liquor and wine and glasses in it. I suggest you send someone promptly."

He held his pen at the ready above the page. "Anything else?"

I looked at Sarah. Her face was full of questions for me, but she shook her head. "No," I answered for us both.

He scribbled a few more notes and stood. "Thank you, Miss Jimeson." He turned to Sarah. "And Miss Jimeson." We rose, and as we reached the door, Mr. Stiles said, "Fuller, stay a moment, would you?" His voice had warmed, and he shut the door, so the two of them occupied the room alone. I hoped for Mr. Fuller's sake that Sarah's story was enough to earn him back some trust. Mr. Stiles's trust seemed worth having.

Sarah and I walked down the short corridor to the entrance, Sarah murmuring, "Mr. Stiles was kind, but I'm glad that's over." We nodded goodbye to the desk sergeant, whose eyebrows had returned to somewhere close to their usual position, and stepped out into the cobbled yard and the weak sunshine. Three constables stood together by the single arch that led out to the street. I wondered if one of them would fetch us a cab. We couldn't be on foot. Billy might guess where we'd gone.

"What should we do now?" Sarah asked. "We can't go home, now that you told him enough to break the ring."

"It won't break the ring," I said. "I asked Mary to warn Bea. She'll be just the person to take it over, and she'll have moved them. But Billy will have told Maggie we went to the police."

"Oh, of course he will. Stupid of me." Sarah chewed her lip. "Where can we go?"

This would not be easy.

I drew a breath. "We need to leave London."

Her eyes widened and her jaw sagged, though she remained silent.

"You know how dangerous Maggie is, and I don't know how far her reach extends. She found Amelia's brother, all the way up in Bethnal Green. He got away," I added hastily at her look of alarm. "But he's left London for good."

"What about Amelia?"

I hesitated. "She's still here, but I think she plans to leave, too."

"Oh." Her shoulders fell. "But won't Maggie be caught? You gave the Yard what they need, didn't you?"

"Even if she's in prison, she'll have someone on the outside, whether it's Billy or someone else. We just don't know." I paused. "And if she's in prison, just think about the kind of revenge she'd want to take on me."

That was enough to put a sudden, stark terror into her eyes. But a moment later, she stiffened and tried to look as if she wasn't afraid. It wrung my heart. I didn't want her to have to act braver than she was anymore.

She swallowed. "When do we have to go?"

"This afternoon," I said gently. "We'll be all right. I have ready cash. My bags are at Amelia's."

"But you always said we didn't have enough saved," she protested.

"I took a fifth diamond," I said.

"Oh," she gasped. She wrapped her arms around herself, her fingers clutching at her sleeves. "But, Kit," she said, her voice catching. "We're leaving everyone we know. Amelia and Mary . . . and James."

"I know."

The door slammed and Mr. Fuller emerged, striding toward us with a satisfied air.

"All right?" I asked.

He nodded, but his attention was caught by Sarah, who—bless her—had not yet mastered the art of concealing her feelings. "What's the matter? You look upset, and you did beautifully."

"I'm glad it's over, that's all," she managed.

He frowned dubiously. I took Sarah's arm, and the three of us started across the cobbles toward the giant archway.

A constable rushed past us, legs churning, arms pumping, huffing with urgency.

Mr. Fuller spun to watch him. "He's from Lambeth. I wonder what the devil's happened now."

Chapter 28

It could have been anything, of course. A railway disaster at the station. An accident with a costermonger, or a carriage. A murder that had nothing to do with us.

But an undertow of worry sucked away my relief over Sarah being safe and her story told.

"We'll wait here," I said to Mr. Fuller. He nodded and started toward the door, the ends of his coat flapping like bat wings.

Sarah stared at me. "What's happened?"

"I don't know. Let's wait," I said quietly. Mr. Fuller reentered the division, shutting the door behind him.

Sarah took my elbow firmly, turning me toward her. Her eyes locked on mine. "Kit, answer me. What's happened? What haven't you told me?"

I couldn't reply, for all I could think of was the look on Mary's face as she spoke of Maggie having taken her mother from her—and the look on her face not three hours ago, as she came out of the bakery.

Oh, Mary, I thought, fear scalding my insides. *What have you done?*

I never would have believed it of my friend, but into my mind came Mr. Fuller's words about monsters. One begets another. *Dear God, has Maggie turned Mary into one, too?*

My heart ached, twisted, tightened inside my chest as we waited. Somewhere beyond the omnibuses rattling over the cobbles, the hiss of the wind cutting the corner, the muted chatter of steamers and the blaring horns of tugboats, there was the sound of a moan, perhaps, a last breath of air coming through teeth.

Sarah's hand on my arm tightened. "Kit, he's back."

Mr. Fuller strode toward us and stopped in front of me. "She's dead," he said grimly. "I hope you know what you're doing."

"*Who's* dead?" demanded Sarah.

"Maggie O'Connell. They just found her." His brown eyes blazed an accusation. "If you've mixed me up in this, so help me . . ."

Sarah gave a small cry, but I kept my gaze fixed on him.

"How could *I* have done it?" I retorted. "I've been here at the Yard for the last two hours! And before that, I was with Sarah. Last I saw Maggie, she was alive. And Sarah was with me when I saw her."

"It's true," Sarah added shakily. "She was alive. It was close on ten o'clock."

"It doesn't mean you didn't plan it!"

"I didn't!" I said through gritted teeth. "I swear to you!"

Mr. Fuller grunted and his manner eased. "Who did it, then? Who else had a motive?"

Beside me, Sarah drew in her breath.

To keep his eyes away from her, I replied. "I don't know. Perhaps someone resented her taking over the ring."

He gave a look of impatience. "You know but you won't say."

"I *don't* know," I repeated. It was the truth, and perhaps he saw it, for he threw up his hands and stalked back to the Yard entrance.

I turned away, praying Mary was already on one of the trains out of Lambeth.

"If Maggie's dead, does this mean we can stay?" Sarah whispered.

"I don't . . . I don't know, Sarah." Heartsick, I couldn't think. "Let's get away from here."

Now I understood Mary's final look. For her mother's sake, and perhaps for mine and for all the other thieves, she had killed Maggie, taken the diamond, and gone. I'd never see her again.

The look she'd given me hadn't been only an apology. It had also been goodbye.

Together Sarah and I headed to Amelia's. She would want to know that the Yard had been told and what Mary had done. We took an omnibus east, dismounted, and walked north, Sarah holding my hand the whole way. I pushed open the door from the street and remembered the first time I'd climbed these stairs, not noticing that I'd broken the thread across the step.

I knocked at the door, and it was opened—by Mary.

"You're still here?" I hissed, stepping inside and shutting the door. "You need to get out of London! Maggie's body has already been found. The constable arrived at the Yard when we were still there!"

"I didn't kill her, Kit," Mary said.

"You didn't?" Sarah asked breathlessly. "But . . ."

My eyes darted about the room—still furnished, as it had been let, but emptied of any sign of Amelia—no coats on the rack, no satchel in the corner. Mary's eyes filled with tears, and her lower lip trembled.

"Amelia," I said and dropped my hand from her arm.

"She made me swear not to tell you." Mary drew a long breath. "She felt responsible."

"She shouldn't have. It was Maggie who caused all the trouble."

"I know." Mary dashed her tears away and pulled a folded letter from her pocket. "She left this for you."

I opened it and found only this: *My dear Kit, change is not always bad. Take care of Mary and Sarah. I shall miss you. A.*

The sight of these last words, in a hand that was so familiar, broke me.

Sarah read over my shoulder. "At least she'll be able to join Adam, wherever he is."

Mary said to Sarah, "She left you a letter, too. It's in there." She pointed to the room Adam had occupied. Sarah went to fetch it, and I took Mary by the arm, pulling her over to the window where the street noise would hide our words.

"Did Amelia leave *you* a letter?" I asked.

Mary shook her head.

"Because she didn't need to," I said slowly. "You were in this with her, weren't you? How did she do it?"

Mary's gaze flicked to the room where Sarah had gone and back to me. "Two quick stabs under the ribs, same as Maggie did to my mum. Then she flipped her cloak and got on the train."

"Where?"

"She didn't tell me where she was go—"

"No, I mean, where did she do it?"

"In the railway station."

"In a crowd," I said. "And people didn't notice?"

Mary's blue eyes were steady. "There might have been a disturbance farther down the platform at roughly the same time."

"Kit, look what Amelia's done for us," Sarah said, coming toward us with an opened letter. She handed it to me, and I read aloud:

> *There is a shopfront on Dean Street off Fetter Lane, only a few streets from my rooms, that I think would be an excellent location for a sundry and stationer shop and tearoom, especially as a tearoom just closed nearby and people will be looking for a new one. Mary's bakery items will be just the thing. Contact Mr. Brownlee at Dean Street, number sixteen. He is expecting you.* Ádh mór ort. *A.*

I wondered how long Amelia had known she wouldn't be here. But she'd made sure Mary was. My heart tripped an uneven beat of grief and gratitude.

Mary reached her hand for mine. "Don't go," she said softly. "Don't leave London. The Yard will catch Billy—if he's even still here. He'd be a fool if he was, with the newspapers all carrying his picture and Tommy's."

Sarah's eyes were bright with hope and pleading.

I felt myself weaken. I couldn't say no to them both. "We'll stay for now," I said.

Two days later, I woke in James's bed with Sarah beside me. Mary remained at Amelia's, for the rent had been paid through the end of the month. James was still in hospital but improved enough that he was allowed to come home, and Sarah and I planned to fetch him in a cab. I slipped out from between the sheets.

"Kit! Where are you going?" Sarah sat bolt upright in bed, her eyes wide with alarm and accusation. As composed as she had been at the Yard, she was jittery in the aftermath. I imagined she would wake like that for a while.

"I want to get the papers," I said. "And I'll bring back something for breakfast. Don't worry. You're safe here. Lock the door behind me."

She shifted her legs around the edge of the bed. "No, I'll come with you."

I was about to refuse until I saw her face. "All right. Go on and dress. I want some fresh rolls while they're still hot—and some jam." We were less frugal these days, treating ourselves to delicacies.

Sarah donned a dress, I buttoned her up the back, and we walked out toward the bakery with Sarah's hand looped through my elbow. The streets were comfortingly busy, and I kept my eye out for anyone from Southwark but saw no one. It was a blessing to be unknown, and not for the first time, I longed to truly make a fresh start here.

"Scandal! Scandal!" bellowed a boy on the corner, waving the paper.

It seemed to be the catch-all word for any sort of news.

"You get the rolls," I said to Sarah. "I want to buy a paper."

She nodded obligingly and stepped inside the bakery. I approached the boy, gave him a coin, and took the *Mirror*, unfolding it to read the headline and scan the story—which occupied two-thirds of the front page—right there in the street.

SHOCKING SUCCESSES FOR THE YARD! FAIRLEIGH MURDERS SOLVED! CRIMINALS APPREHENDED!

A quick glance through the article confirmed that both Billy and Tommy had been caught, the trial was set for three weeks hence, and Sarah's name was nowhere to be found.

With a sigh of relief, I tucked the paper under my arm, and when Sarah reappeared with a brown-paper parcel, we returned to James's rooms, where we dove into the rolls, slathering them with butter and jam. When we'd eaten our fill and finished the pot of tea, I extracted the rooms-to-let listings from the paper and handed them to her, folded neatly. "I'd like you to take these and begin looking for a place nearby for us—you, Mary, and me. Can you do that?"

A moment's hesitation, then she asked, her face cautious. "Are we going to stay, for good?"

"I think we can," I said, brushing crumbs onto my plate.

Her face brightened, and she slathered one last roll with jam. As she finished it, she looked thoughtful. "It's silly, I know, but I found myself wondering what they think of me at the Willitses'."

I'd not given that much thought. "Mrs. Rice suspected you of running off with the two pounds she gave you for the market. I told them you hadn't."

Her brow furrowed. "I'd hate them thinking I'd do that."

"You aren't thinking of going back in service, are you?"

"Of course not," she assured me. "I'd much rather run a shop with you and Mary." She hummed as she began to read the to-let notices.

I hadn't yet broken it to Sarah that the thought of running

a shop didn't appeal to me in the least. A new idea was brewing in my head, but I didn't want to say anything yet.

Sarah and Mary found us rooms in Crane Court, not far from James's and the new shop. Sarah and I shared a room, and Mary took the second.

Sarah took to our new life gratefully, making our cups of tea in the morning, curling up with a novel in the comfortable chair for an hour, then going out with Mary to shop for shelves, tables, chairs, lamps, and such. For my part, I went out for long walks, gleaning a sense for my new surroundings and reflecting on the events of recent weeks, teasing apart the rough tangle of threads so I might wind them more properly around their spools. With Sarah safe and Maggie no longer a threat, my thoughts turned down odd and unexpected paths.

I would be twenty-one in a fortnight, the same age as Maggie when she'd been transported. Maggie's death had freed me from being frightened of her—and in the absence of fear, I found myself feeling a measure of pity for her. What might Maggie's life be had she been allowed to continue acting at the theater? Or if Tim Lowry had never come to Southwark? If Simonson hadn't been a fiend? If Rose hadn't turned on her? If she'd found a more benevolent man in Swan River? Some of what happened to Maggie was of her choosing, but a good deal of it wasn't. I felt no small resentment at a system so weighted on the side of wealthy men, who flaunted the rules. And what would have happened to me, if I'd had a jenny who betrayed me? There but for the grace of God went I.

With my pity for Maggie came pity for another person as well: my mother. Some nights when I lay awake with

Sarah beside me, I thought of her. Sarah looked more like my father than ever, and I probed at the possibility: If Sarah were, one day, to simply walk out, what would that do to me? It would unmoor my heart. I might hate and distrust the entire bloody world.

As grateful as I was to have Sarah back, I felt the loss of Amelia keenly. As I walked the pavements of my new neighborhood, more than once I could've sworn I saw her across the street or at the end of a lane. Of course, it wasn't her, just the shadows of her in another woman's figure, in her walk, in the way she turned her head, in the way her cape swung out as she turned a corner. I worried about her and wondered where she had flown. Were she still here, she would have insisted the decision to kill Maggie was hers and hers alone, but I knew I'd had a hand in it. Had I thought farther ahead, I might have wrested a promise from Amelia to let Scotland Yard find the diamond and put Maggie through the process of a trial and into prison. But as Mary reminded me, it was Amelia's choice, and she might have found some relief from her guilt, however unwarranted it was.

Between the money I obtained from pawning the fifth diamond, funds Mary and I had put by from thieving, and a modest sum contributed by Sarah, they were able to purchase the necessary cooking implements, chairs and tables, and the first supply of sundries without taking on credit. Sarah was in her element, dusting shelves and sorting books. When the shop opened after weeks of preparations, it was almost an immediate success, partly because the tea was always hot and not watered-down and the biscuits and cakes were homemade by Mary.

I was pleased for them. They fell into chairs at the end of

the first week, arms flopped over the sides, their legs sprawled toward the stove, exhausted but happy.

James had left the hospital on crutches and returned to the Custom House, where he was allowed temporarily to keep records at a desk, with his leg propped on a stool in front of him. He'd fully recovered, without even a limp to show, the only sign of his injury being a reddish scar a few inches long.

One afternoon when I was alone in our new rooms, the street bell rang downstairs. Our landlady answered it, and a few minutes later, a knock sounded at our door.

I opened it to find Mr. Stiles, and I welcomed him in. Stepping over the threshold, he removed his hat and looked around at the bright room appreciatively.

"How are you, Miss Jimeson?"

"You can call me Kit, you know," I said. "And I'm fine."

He set his hat on the table, removed his coat, and gestured toward a blue chintz-covered chair, one of a pair that Sarah had chosen. "May I?"

"You're too polite," I said. "Of course."

He waited to speak until I'd taken a seat in the other chair.

"I came to tell you that Billy and Tommy were tried and found guilty in the Fairleigh murders," he said. "The verdict was returned this morning."

"Thank you for telling me."

"I thought it would set your mind at ease, but that isn't the only reason I came," he replied. "May I ask, what do you plan to do with yourself?"

I chuckled. "Are you afraid I'll go back to thieving? Give you more trouble?"

"Well, I don't want that." His eyes were frank, and he gave a good-natured laugh. "I came across someone at a theater who is looking for help. Would you consider becoming a costumer?"

"A costumer?" I echoed.

"It's the person who creates the costumes for the actors." He paused. "It isn't just needlework. You design them, too. It's important to get them right."

"Here in London?"

He nodded. "At the Arthurian."

I hesitated. "To be honest, I am still considering what I'd like to do for work. But thank you for thinking of me."

His face fell. I understood that he wished to help, and I added, "Don't worry, Mr. Stiles. Whatever I do, it won't be thieving."

"Well," he said as he rose, reassumed his coat, and picked up his hat. "You can let me know if you'd like an introduction."

"Mr. Stiles," I said. "Are you happy as a policeman?"

That stopped him in his tracks. He gave a snort and a rueful chuckle. "Oh, I *wish* we could have you at the Yard. You'd be a better source than all the books of photographs. Not to mention you're cleverer than most of our constables." I opened my mouth to protest that I hadn't been hinting for a position. "Someday we may allow women to become detectives, but not yet."

"Of course not," I said. "Besides, I'd look dreadful in those hats you all wear."

He looked befuddled.

"I'm asking," I said, "because it seems to bring you satisfaction, and . . . well, I was wondering why you became one. You're clearly educated, and you seem as if you might have chosen banking or even the law." He didn't reply at first, and I added, "You needn't tell me, if you'd rather not."

"No, no, it's a reasonable question. I don't mind." Mr. Stiles redeposited his hat on the table nearby and lowered himself back into the chair, crossed his ankles, and interlaced his fingers at his waist. "I know there are lads at the Yard who are disgusted with London, sour about all the filth and detritus, the constant wave of crime, the many ways people injure each other day upon day. Burns calls it 'man's inhumanity to man' that 'makes countless thousands mourn.'"

"That sounds like poetry."

"It is." He rubbed his chin thoughtfully. "But I don't think man is innately inhumane. I believe crime and cruelty are caused by things such as hunger, exhaustion, illness, death of loved ones, loneliness, a feeling that no one cares."

He must have seen my puzzlement, for he smiled and drew a breath, with a look that suggested he was reminding himself to tell a story from the beginning rather than the conclusion. "I told you I grew up on a farm, in a small town outside London. And I told you about my sister Cathy."

"The one who's fourteen, like Sarah."

"Fifteen now," he amended. "Her birthday was Saturday last."

He seemed to expect something, so I murmured, "Ah, lovely."

"When she was eleven, she saw her best mate, Ellie, run over in the street by a cart that had rolled backward on a small hill. The wheel crushed the life out of her. And Cathy gave such a shriek that . . ." The memory halted him, and his face was bleak. "I was coming out of a shop across the way, so I couldn't see beyond the cart, and for one awful, awful moment I thought it was Cathy under the wheel."

I knew exactly how he felt.

"I ran to where I could see her, standing with both hands over her mouth as if she was trying to stop her shriek, but it just kept coming out of her, on and on. Then she dashed toward Ellie. Within seconds, the entire town came forward and gathered around, trying to help—the doctor, the apothecary, her parents, her friends. Nothing could be done. Ellie died in her mother's arms, with Cathy holding her hand."

The scene arose vividly before my eyes. "It's terrible," I managed.

"It was," he said. "But afterward, there was such kindness." His brown eyes were bright. "For Ellie's family and for Cathy. Even for the carter, who was nearly out of his mind with guilt. 'I didn't see her,' he said over and over, tears running down his cheeks. The poor man was nearly broken by it. Ellie's family could have blamed him out of anger, but they didn't because the truth of it was, he'd done nothing wrong. Mr. Banks had seen the whole thing. Ellie had tripped and fallen at the very moment when the cart rolled backward, hardly a single turn of the wheel. It was just an accident." He rubbed at his temple. "We all took care of each other out of loyalty and decency. Oh, we always had small feuds. Arguments over who should be elected magistrate or where the new school should be built. But in that moment, our loyalty was stronger than our squabbles." He gave a rueful smile. "I'm waxing philosophical, aren't I?"

"I asked," I reminded him.

He tapped his fingertips on the chair arms. "I'd done my schooling in London, and I thought I'd like to try to help people here take care of each other. That sounds very grandiose of me. One man trying to change a bit of London."

"Not at all," I said.

He looked almost wistful. "I do believe a tragedy can remind us of our better natures. The loyalty and compassion we owe each other. Our duty to make the world a better place for everyone. The importance of finding the truth, not just blaming the easy mark. I could do a small bit of that, for whoever stood in front of me. We all can do that, policeman or no."

I'd rarely been to church, only for funerals, but his words resonated like a solid chord from the organ at the end of the final hymn, perhaps because I'd been feeling something like this myself in recent weeks. I knew what loyalty looked like—not just my own to others, but that of Mary, Amelia, Sarah, and James to me. I'd seen kindness from strangers. I knew the importance of truth telling. I'd seen Mr. Stiles and Mr. Fuller trying to create some fairness in this corner of the world.

My fingers pleated my skirt absently. "Mr. Fuller said something like that, about how newspapers could make the city a better place, bring justice and help to people who need it."

"How did you convince him to write that article for you?" he asked.

"I told him all that Maggie had suffered, beginning with Simonson brutally assaulting her in the back room when she was caught."

His entire expression changed, and he looked sickened. "Well, that would do it."

"Why do you say so?"

"It's a particular cause of his," he said. "Did he not tell you?"

"No."

"Two or three years ago, Fuller wrote a series of articles about women who had been outraged in London. He interviewed nearly fifty of them, and the articles stirred up enough public sentiment that they led to the creation of the Society for the Protection of Women, which has worked tirelessly to advocate for laws requiring mandatory fines and punishment for offenders. They work out of one of the churches in Covent Garden."

"He didn't tell me." I had observed Mr. Fuller's distress when I told him about Maggie. "Did he know someone personally?"

"He never said so," Mr. Stiles replied slowly. "But I would guess perhaps he did, given the way he pursued it. You might read the articles sometime. They're very moving."

Or perhaps taking down fifty stories, all of them terrible, had profoundly affected him.

"Well." Mr. Stiles stood with a smile. "Let me know if you think more of the costumer position."

I thanked him again, and he plucked his hat from the table a second time. He looked at me sideways. "It seems that five diamonds were stolen from the necklace, not just one. I don't suppose you know what happened to the others?"

I shook my head. "If I were Maggie, I'd have hidden them all separately."

He pursed his mouth. "And I don't suppose you know who killed her."

He'd been truthful with me, and I felt sorry I couldn't be more truthful with him. "I didn't witness it."

"It wasn't ten steps from where Rose Pratt was stabbed—and in exactly the same manner." He turned his hat in his hands. "Seems someone had a sense for poetic justice."

"I don't know anyone but you who's much for poetry," I said.

"She didn't have many friends that we could find."

That made me think of Mr. Ardle for the first time in weeks, and my heart sank, knowing the grief he'd surely feel at her death.

"The Yard has pretty well washed their hands of the case," he said. "There are no clues to speak of, and she was a dangerous woman."

"She was an angry one," I said. "And not wholly without cause."

"Most of us come by our anger honestly." He settled his hat on his head. "Goodbye, Kit."

"Goodbye."

The door closed behind him.

A costumer, I thought. It was kind of Mr. Stiles to ask me. It was certainly suited to my talents. But with other things he'd said, Mr. Stiles had unwittingly given me encouragement in a wholly different direction.

Chapter 29

I'd shared sleep since I could recall.

For years, I'd had Sarah in the same bed and my mother close by, snoring thickly. Sarah slept the way she lived, more quietly than I, though often I'd wake to find some part of her touching me—a hand on my shoulder blade, a foot on my shin. After Ma died, Sarah and I shared a bed in the lodging house, and later, after Sarah left to work in Mayfair, I slept alone in my bed, but still in a room with Mary, whose whistling snores sometimes worked their way into my dreams.

But I'd never woken up to a man until now, for I'd taken to spending one or two nights each week with James.

It was a Sunday morning, and neither of us had a reason to rise early. James's face was soft in sleep, his dark hair tumbled, his lips parted.

My own mouth felt hot and tender from last night's kissing. I shifted my limbs cautiously, remembering James's hands on them and feeling a pleasant heat run over me at the memory of it.

I might have stayed there just to watch his face, but practicalities intruded.

I slipped out of bed and found the chamber pot. Using it is one of the few things I cannot do stealthily, and when I crept back, I found him watching me, his eyes still sleepy and a grin on his face.

"You weren't thinking of sneaking off, were you?" he asked.

"No," I retorted, climbing back in under the quilt. "Not without my morning tea, which you're going to make for me, seeing as it's bloody cold in this room."

He drew the quilt up over both of us, rolling so his body covered mine. "It's not so cold," he said. "I'll make your tea later."

We'd loved and dozed until we could no longer ignore the sun blazing through the window. His hand rested on the sheet, and the light was enough I could see a scar on his thumb that I'd never noticed.

"Seems you have scars all over you, on every limb," I said, kissing it. "Where did you get this one?"

"Ach," he shrugged. "Wrapped a rope wrong way around a cleat a few years back. Wasn't paying attention."

"Hmm," I said.

He began coiling a lock of my hair around his finger, like a bandage covering the scar.

"Mr. Stiles came by a few days ago," I said.

"Oh?"

"He said he could find me a position as a costumer at a theater. It was kind of him, but I don't want to sew for my living."

"I can see that."

"And Sarah and Mary are happy as clams in the shop, but I can't imagine standing at a counter all day, talking to strangers, fetching tea and helping them with purchases."

"It's going well, isn't it?"

"They've already installed a second oven for Mary." I drew a breath. "From what Sarah says, their tearoom is crammed from opening to closing."

James nuzzled into the warm spot between my bare shoulder and my neck.

"But I've been thinking," I said, pushing him away so I could sit up. "Do you think the *Mirror* might take me on?"

James propped himself on an elbow, palming his temple. "The newspaper?"

"Mr. Fuller owes me a favor, don't you think?" I asked. "And there's a woman working there. I spoke to her. She's not much older than I am. She has an office right near him, and she was writing."

Understanding lit his eyes. "You mean to write stories for them."

"Well, I don't mean to be hawking them on the street."

He laughed. "I didn't think so. Scandal, scandal."

I rolled my eyes. "Sometimes the truth is scandal enough, and there are plenty of things I could write about that they might be able to use." I studied James's face, and to my relief he wasn't laughing. "It would be a new game for me, but I think I could reuse some of the cards I picked up during my last one."

"Would seem so."

"Mr. Fuller could steer me in the proper direction."

"I'd think he'd be glad to have you." He took my hand in his own and raised it to his mouth to kiss my bare fingers, one by one, in a way that shredded my breath to nothing. "Clever girl."

James walked me to the offices of the *Mirror*, left me at the front door, and went to a pub nearby to wait.

I entered through the heavy wooden door. Recent rain had

swelled it, so it stuck in the frame, but I pushed harder and it gave way.

I took it as a good omen.

At the desk sat a young man scribbling on a page in front of him.

"What's the name of the young woman who works here?" I asked.

"Miss Mitford," he replied without looking at me.

"Is she in?"

"Dunno."

Clearly, he didn't think much of her. And nothing of me. Well, that was no matter. Most men wouldn't admire Miss Mitford for what she was doing or welcome another woman newspaper writer.

However, I wasn't disheartened. This wouldn't be the first time I'd made my way into a place I didn't belong and left with what I wanted.

"Can I go up?" I asked.

He shrugged. "Please yourself."

I walked up to the first story, where the typesetting room was noisy with chatter and the click of metal type into lines. I poked my head in to watch for a moment, liking the very smell of the metal and ink and the busyness of it all. As I watched, the press started belowstairs, beating a steady thump. It gave me the odd fancy that I had placed my fingers on the very heart of London, the pulse of life in every borough, the tide of the Thames, the turn of the railway wheels. Motion, all of it—people everywhere, waking to their cold rooms or to the sound of curtains being drawn by servants, selling fruit from their carts or buying it to feed their children, offloading barrels from a French ship or sipping tea brought from India. Most of us simply wishing to keep ourselves and those we loved safe and warm and well-fed, wanting to find our place, to feel we belonged, to believe that when we spoke, it mattered.

I took the stairs and followed the hallway. When I reached Miss Mitford's door, it was open. Her head was bent over a pamphlet, the toe of her boot jiggling under the desk as she read.

I knocked on the doorjamb, and she looked up in surprise. Then her face transformed with a smile. "Ah, the girl with a story."

"Kit Jimeson," I said. "And you're Miss Mitford."

The chair scraped as she stood and stuck out her hand cordially across the desk for me to shake. "Frances."

"I was wondering what you're writing about."

She turned the pamphlet upside down on the desk, tenting it to hold her place, and pointed to the chair by the wall, which I pulled toward her desk so I could sit.

The wooden chair creaked as she resumed her seat. "At the moment, I'm writing an article that concerns meat that is improperly butchered and prepared, leading to disease. Mostly I report on social problems."

"Women write those stories?"

"Of course. Why not?" she asked. "Have you not heard of Eliza Meteyard? Frances Power Cobbe? Mary Howitt? They all write for the papers. There's an entire cadre of us and more each year."

"I don't know the word 'ca-dray,'" I admitted, grinning. "It sounds vaguely improper, like a ring of thieves."

She laughed. "Rather, though I suppose we like to think of ourselves as doing good rather than harm."

"I didn't realize women did this, until I saw you here."

"Well, we women can often get stories the men can't," she said frankly. "We're not so intimidating, so people talk to us. But it isn't for the faint of heart." Her expression sobered. "I've been threatened twice by managers at the slaughterhouses for what I've written so far."

"I can imagine."

She studied me. "Are you looking for a position?"

"Yes," I said simply.

"You can read and write, I assume?"

I bristled a bit. "Of course."

"No offense meant," she said, amused. "Which papers do you read?"

"The *Dover Chronicle*, the Kent *Advertiser*, the *Canterbury Journal*, the *Daily News*, the *Standard*, the *Times*, *Reynolds's*, the *Falcon*—"

Her eyebrows rose. "So many? Why?"

"I'm from Elephant and Castle," I said, thinking of the six roads converging, not to mention the railway bringing people and news from all over England. "All the papers come there."

Her eyes narrowed, then sparkled, as she put this bit of information together with my allusion to the ring of thieves. "Ah." Her mouth crooked in a funny smile as she sat back and folded her arms across her chest. "Tell me a bit more about yourself."

I told her a quarter of an hour's worth of truth, with her startling at parts and chuckling at others. At the end, she smiled in satisfaction and rose from her desk. "You certainly have the knack of telling a story. And I assume Mr. Fuller would vouch for your character?"

I wondered about that, but I nodded as if I was certain.

She marched around her desk. "Come, shall we go and see the editor, Mr. Murdaugh? I believe he shall be intrigued."

Author's Note

Most of my novels sprang to life because of a moment of surprise—a moment when some aspect of Victorian history pulled me up short, drew me in, and felt large enough to carry a book: a terrifying railway disaster involving Charles Dickens, the thrilling world of the dozens of London music halls, a tragic fire in Mayfair that burned millions of dollars of paintings and furniture, and the worst steamship disaster the Thames had ever seen.

This time was no different. In 2021, my daughter spent her fall semester at Oxford, and I flew over to spend the fortnight afterward. We rented a tiny apartment in London and did our usual favorite things—taking long walks, visiting museums and tea shops, prowling around fancy shops and bookstores. One stormy afternoon, with our umbrellas imperiled, we dodged into the Great Scotland Yard Hotel. To my delight, I discovered a lobby full of glass cases containing Yard memorabilia, from mug shots to truncheons. Then, we headed for the bar, which had the curious name The Forty Elephants. With the Victorian theme of the hotel, I assumed the "forty elephants" had something to do with the nineteenth-century British imperial project in India or Africa. We entered, and I immediately noticed that just below the ceiling hung at least a dozen black-and-white photos of women, striking and bejeweled.

Who on earth were these intriguing women? Fortunately for us, there was a QR code on the table that provided some history.

The Forty Elephants were women from Elephant and Castle, an area south of the Thames in Southwark, and home to a notorious (and infamous) inn by the same name. Dating from 1765 (although some claim it existed as early as 1754), the old coaching inn was situated at the nexus of six (or seven, depending on how you count) major roads, some of which had been there since the Roman times. By the early 1800s, the roads brought in travelers from Dover, Canterbury, and various parts of London. If legend is true, wealthy stagecoach travelers were put in a comfortable chair by the fire, dosed to sleep with wine, and robbed of everything down to their shoes overnight.

The gang that eventually became known as the Forty Elephants came into being in the 1870s with the rise of department stores. The heyday of the Forty Elephants was between the two world wars, and they were still active through the 1940s, although Scotland Yard made many attempts to shut them down. The earliest leader of the gang was probably Mary Carr, born in 1862. She became loosely involved with the male thieving gang from Elephant and Castle in the 1870s, eventually working her way into the leadership position, with the nickname "Queen of the Forty Thieves," until she was tried, convicted, and imprisoned in 1905. From 1915, the gang was led by Alice Diamond; the thieves were beautiful, well-dressed and well-coiffed, capable of violence, and talented at disguise. (For more information, read the historical account *Alice Diamond and the Forty Elephants*, by Brian McDonald. The book *The Forty Elephants* by Erin Bledsoe provides a well-researched fictional version of the gang, set in the 1920s.)

I have given my gang members all manner of tricks, some of which are fictional and others not. The Forty Elephants did conceal stolen goods in muffs, their hair, the mesh lining of coats, and special pockets. They did use disguises, and they employed dodges involving all kinds of distractions. While none of the women in my book are real, I did lean on the legends surrounding many women thieves who lived prior to the 1870s, including Mary Frith (1584–1659), alias Moll (or Mal) Cutpurse, a notorious English pickpocket and fence famous for cross-dressing, who was immortalized as the heroine of *The Madde Pranckes of Mery Moll of the Bankside*; Mary Moders (1642–73), a bigamist and con artist who bilked a dozen wealthy older men of their fortunes; and Mary Young (1700–41), a pickpocket and cutpurse known as "Jenny Diver," who eventually became the leader of a thieving ring and was hanged at Tyburn before a crowd of two hundred thousand. Other notable thieving legends—not named Mary—include the Irish pirate Anne Bonny, the partner and lover of the notorious English pirate captain Calico Jack Rackham, operating in the Caribbean in the early eighteenth century. Another famous thief from this period is Sofia Ivanovna Blyuvshtein, known as "Son'ka the Golden Hand," a Russian thief and con artist who specialized in stealing jewelry, often with the assistance of her trained pet monkey, who would swallow stones. And of course there was Marm Mandelbaum, "the queen of thieves," who fenced over ten million dollars of stolen goods in post–Civil War New York.

Here are some other bits and pieces of true history.

Hangings were public until 1867. The last public hanging was Michael Barrett's, for setting off a bomb in Clerkenwell, London. One of the most notable public hangings of the Victorian era was that of François Courvoisier, who murdered his employer, Lord William Russell, and was hanged in July 1840 at the scaffold outside Newgate Prison (not far from Hatton Garden); both Charles Dickens and William Makepeace Thackeray wrote harrowing accounts of the day, which I've drawn upon for Kit's memory of the hanging she watches with her father.

Hatton Garden, located in the Holborn district of the borough of Camden, is still home to hundreds of jewelers and artisans, as well as to the charming St. Etheldreda Church. In the 1500s, it was the residence of the Bishops of Ely, with a palace and gardens. During the 1570s, Sir Christopher Hatton, a favorite of Queen Elizabeth, developed Hatton House on the property, which remained in his family until the 1780s, when his descendant George Finch-Hatton sold sections of it. Jewelers migrated into the area, and after the Kimberley mines were discovered in Africa and developed beginning in the 1870s, the diamond trade became firmly planted there, with the arrival of De Beers. Some of the greatest jewelry heists of the past few centuries happened here, not to mention the heist in *A Fish Called Wanda*.

The River Fleet runs underground in London, roughly from below what is now Euston railway station southeast until it reaches the Thames near Blackfriars Bridge. The parish of Holborn, which it cuts through, takes its name from "old bourne," with "bourne" meaning brook or small river. The Croom's coffeehouse, 16 Fleet Street, where Kit and

James meet Mr. Fuller, is also real and was a gathering place for newspaper writers.

The Society for the Suppression of Vice and the Encouragement of Religion and Virtue was founded in 1802 and played a significant role in opposing the vices of pornography and prostitution in nineteenth-century Britain. It was broadly concerned with suppressing not only profane publications but also confidence games, thefts, fortune-telling, cruelty to animals (although not children), the racier acts in London's hundreds of music halls, and nearly everything published and sold in London's notorious Holywell Street. The group dwindled due to lack of funds and ceased its work in 1880, although it was revived five years later as the National Vigilance Association.

There was a small but highly effective and prolific group of women journalists by the 1870s. These include Eliza (Elizabeth) Meteyard, a pioneer in investigative journalism; Frances Power Cobbe; Harriet Ward; Harriet Martineau; Mary Howitt; and Margaret Oliphant, among others. Many were novelists and social activists as well. There were hundreds of newspapers in England during the 1870s, after the stamp tax had been revoked and as literacy rates were rising. However, the current daily tabloid, the *Mirror*, was begun in 1903. Ed Fuller's daily paper, the *Mirror* of 1879, is fictional.

As the relationship between Yard inspector Gordon Stiles and Ed Fuller suggests, the Victorian police had a fraught relationship with the newspapers, hovering between cooperation and competition. It led Sir Howard Vincent, director and reformer of Scotland Yard beginning in 1878, to write—at length—on this topic in his new procedure manual in 1879:

> **Police must not on any account give any information whatever to gentlemen connected with the press relative to matters within police knowledge, or relative to the duties to be performed or orders received, or communicate in any manner, either directly or indirectly, with editors, or reporters of newspapers, on any matter connected with the public service, without express and special authority . . . The slightest deviation from this rule may completely frustrate the ends of justice.**

And, as I depict in this novel, *Reynolds's* was consistently critical of the police, presenting them as either corrupt or fools. For example, from 1880: "Scotland Yard persists in holding out every inducement to police to trump up charges in order to obtain the rewards that are given to those who procure the most convictions."

Finally, a word about some aspects of the Victorian world. The ground floor is what Americans would call the first floor; the British first floor is the American second, and so on. Regarding monetary values: When Art is paid sixty or seventy British pounds in 1879, that is roughly the equivalent of nine to eleven thousand US dollars in today's money. Currency valuation is not an exact science, but one website I've found helpful is this historical currency converter: https://www.historicalstatistics.org/Currencyconverter.html

For those interested in Victorian history, I want to share a few of the resources I consulted; all errors are my own. These include Haia Shpayer-Makov's brilliant *The Ascent of the Detective: Police Sleuths in Victorian and Edwardian England*; Gilda O'Neill's *The Good Old Days: Crime, Murder and Mayhem in Victorian London*; Henry Mayhew's *London Labour and the London Poor*; Babette Smith's *A Cargo of Women*, about women convicts in the penal colonies; C. Willett Cunnington and Phillis Cunnington's *Handbook of English Costume in the Nineteenth Century*; Sarah Wise's *The Blackest Streets*; and Peter Ackroyd's comprehensive *Thames: The Biography*, which also includes information on the River Fleet.

If it takes a village to raise a child, I think it takes two villages to produce a book. I have been undeservedly lucky to find people who have provided unflagging support in my writing journey for nearly twenty years. First thanks go to Josh Getzler, who, back in 2014, took a chance on a novel about a railway crash in 1874 London. Jillian Schelzi and the entire team at HG literary have been extraordinary partners. Enormous thanks to Juliet Grames. I'd been muddling over this idea of women thieves for over a year, and when I described the premise to Juliet, her eyes lit up, in a way that every writer longs to see. She said, "I want to read that book." So I wrote it. It simply would not be in the world without her enthusiasm and encouragement. Special thanks also to other lovely people at Soho, including Elizabeth Wakou for the cover illustration, Julie McCarroll for her exquisite copyediting, and Rachel Kowal for her guidance and patience with my old maps.

Thanks to my beta readers—my daughter, Julia, who always reads my jumbled first stabs; and to those who read early drafts of this book, especially Kate Fink Cheeseman, Mariah Fredericks, Anne Morgan, Cindy L. Spear, and Tina Miles. A special thanks also to Edwin Hill and Rob Osler, who have offered tremendously valuable career advice as well as lovely friendships over the years.

One of the unsung rewards of being an author is meeting

people from all over the world who love books the way I do. My gratitude overflows toward all those who responded warmly to the publication of my previous books, including bookstores, book clubs, professional organizations, and libraries. Thanks to Barbara Peters of the Poisoned Pen in Scottsdale, for hosting every one of my book launches since *A Dangerous Duet* in 2018; to Phillip Payne and KT Tierney at Anticus Gallery in Scottsdale for their lovely, steady support of me, my teaching, and my books; and to Phyllis Taylor of Barnes and Noble. My gratitude goes out to all the book clubs and group leaders who have graciously organized and hosted author events for me, especially Debbie Arn, Patty Bruno, Jules Catania, Peggy Chamberlain, Donna Cleinman, Lisa Daliere, Bill Finley (of the Tucson Festival of Books), Ann Florance, Karen Greenberg, Amanda Goosen, and Mb Thomas. Thanks to all the bloggers and book champions, including Dayna Linton, Melissa Makarewicz, Dru Ann Love, and Kris Zgorski (of Bolo Books). Special gratitude goes to the Arizona Commission of the Arts, who supplied me with a grant for my work, and to Sisters in Crime, which has been the foundation of my literary community for many years.

Thank you to my friends, too numerous to name here, who have encouraged me when I was ready to throw in the towel or simply fretting. A heartfelt thanks to my mother, Dorothy Lootens, to my sisters Kristin Griffin and Jennifer Lootens, to my niece, Amanda Lootens, and to my mother-in-law, Nancy Odden, for their constant interest and support. Deepest gratitude to my husband, George, and my two children, Julia and Kyle. You are always the tide beneath my boat.

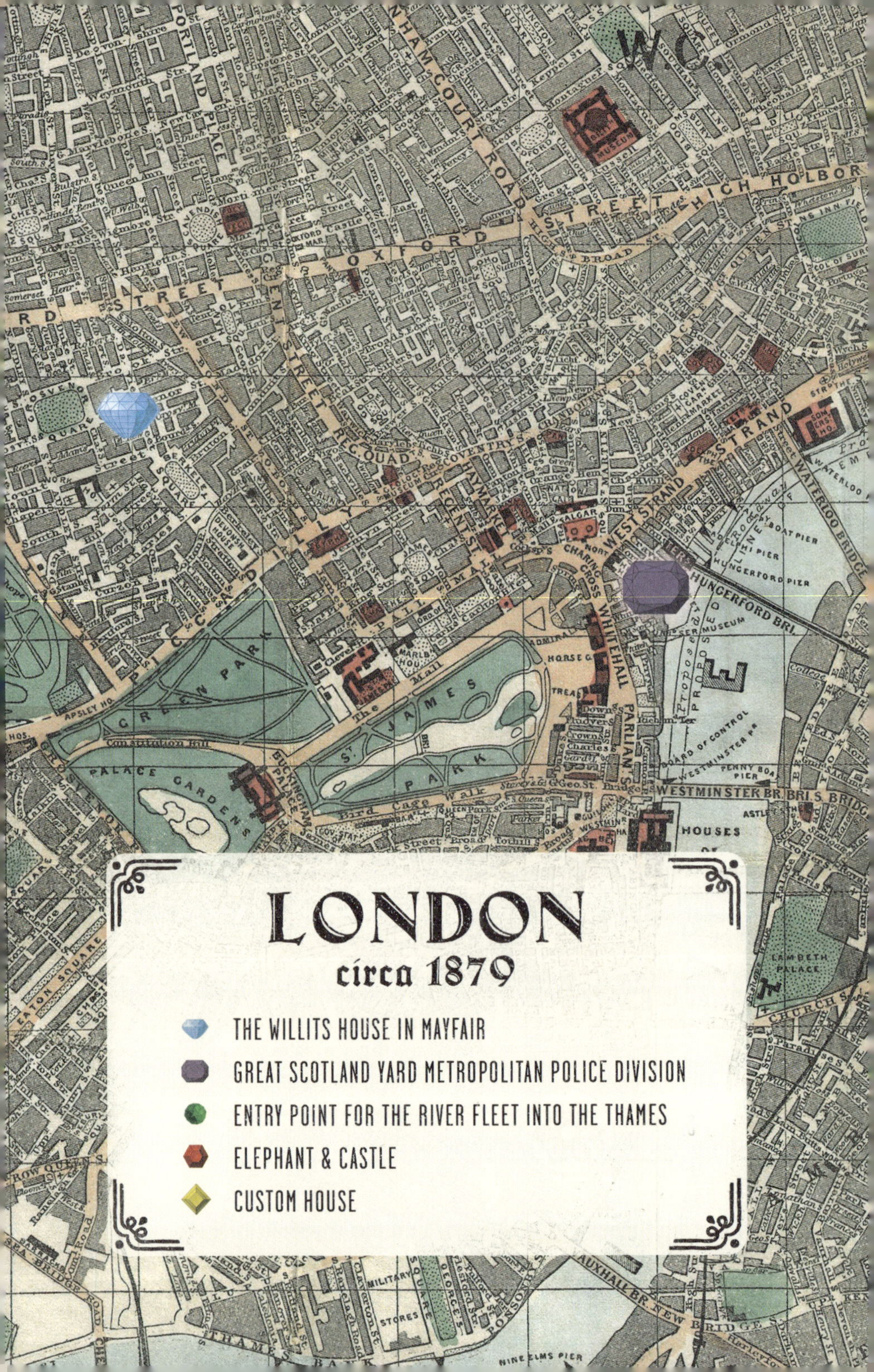
LONDON
circa 1879
THE WILLITS HOUSE IN MAYFAIR
GREAT SCOTLAND YARD METROPOLITAN POLICE DIVISION
ENTRY POINT FOR THE RIVER FLEET INTO THE THAMES
ELEPHANT & CASTLE
CUSTOM HOUSE